DIS

They each threw the dice: a five. A six.

A one. A two.

'You lose,' he said. 'Your body is entirely mine, for the entirety of one hour. This is what you do first. Climb on top of this table. Open your legs very wide and rub your cunt upon the glass above my cock. I shall watch you do this and masturbate. When I come, I will direct my semen up against the underside of the table. Instantly, you will get under the table and lick the underside clean. If a single drop falls to the floor, you will be punished. Do you understand?'

'I am dreaming,' she said.

'You know you are not dreaming. Do you understand?'

'Yes.'

'Do it. Now.'

DISCIPLINED SKIN

Wendy Swanscombe

This book is a work of fiction.
In real life, make sure you practise safe sex.

First published in 2000 by
Nexus
Thames Wharf Studios
Rainville Road
London W6 9HA

www.nexus-books.co.uk

Typeset by TW Typesetting, Plymouth, Devon

Printed and bound by
Cox & Wyman Ltd, Reading, Berks

ISBN 0 352 33541 6

Author's Notes

Nymphalis antiopa
A regular migrant with a powerful flight, it occurs through-
out Europe, although its appearance in Britain is rare. The
adults feed on tree sap and bask in sun with wings
outspread. *WS*: 60–65 mm; *Flight*: June–Sept; *Gen*: 1; *FP*:
Willow (*Salix*); *D*: Europe.

The Mitchell Beazley Pocket Guide to Butterflies (2000),
Paul Whalley.

One day Father Sebastian came to take us to *Ana o Keke*,
the special bleaching place of the *neru* virgins. *Neru* was the
name given to specially chosen maidens who in old days
were confined in a deep cave to become as pale and white
as possible for special religious festivals. For a long, long
time they might see neither the light of day nor other
people . . .

Aku-Aku (1958), Thor Heyerdahl.

His theory is speculative, suggesting that when people
migrated to northern Europe they were faced with the
problem of keeping up a body temperature that was used
to a warmer climate. A mutation that increased the
efficiency of the nervous system and upped the level of
norepinephrine (one of the major neurotransmitters) would
also have raised their body temperature and offered a
survival advantage. Unfortunately, it would also have left
them with a more reactive nervous system and a more

timorous temperament. Where does the pigment come in? High levels of norepinephrine can inhibit the production of melanin in the iris and can increase the level of circulating glucosteroids that can inhibit melanin production as well. So blond hair and blue eyes and shyness may be a common biological package. This may explain the purity and innocence of the standard image of the blonde. Whether it explains the appeal of blondes to men, we can only speculate.

Survival of the Prettiest: The Science of Beauty (1999),
Nancy Etcoff.

– Allons, mademoiselle, dit le gardien, faites-nous voir, je vous prie, si le reste de vos charmes répond à ceux que la nature place avec tant de profusion sur vos traits.

Et comme cette belle fille se troublait, comme elle rougissait sans comprehendre ce qu'on voulait lui dire, le brutal Antonin la saisit par le bras, et avec des juremens affreux:

– Ne comprenez-vous donc pas, petite pécore, que ce qu'on veut vous dire est de vous mettre à l'instant toute nue . . .

Les infortunes de la vertu (1787),
Donatien-Alphonse-François de Sade.

Author's note: Certain erotic and sexual words used in *Disciplined Skin* will be found defined in a glossary at the back of the book.

At the author's request, certain characters in the text have been emboldened.

One

Sunlight. A thin golden bar of it had found its way somehow through the heavy curtains and lay in a small, elliptical pool on the carpet. Anna stared at it, wondering whether Madame Oursor had deliberately arranged for this to happen, so that she could observe what they did. Gwen was still talking about their medical history in her soft, slightly lisping voice. Madame Oursor spoke and Anna took her eyes away from the pool of sunlight and looked at her.

'And this is very rare?'

She was sitting tall and slim behind her desk, dressed in dark, eastern-looking robes, her eyes concealed behind slim oval sunglasses, the white fingers of one hand playing with a couple of polished crystals (clear red and translucent black) on the desk, her thin lips closed and slightly pursed as she waited for Gwen's reply.

'Very rare. Unique, our doctors tell us.'

'Unique,' said Madame Oursor, seeming to ponder the word. Her sunglasses suddenly flashed as she looked away, towards the curtains and the golden bar of sunlight.

'Ah, *mesdemoiselles*, I am sorry – quick, would one of you draw them tighter?'

As Anna got to her feet she caught a glimpse of herself rearing up distorted in the lenses of the sunglasses before she turned aside and ran for the window and the curtains. She tugged at the cord beside them, but the wrong way, and for a moment they began to open fully, letting a sudden flood of sunlight into the room. Beth screamed behind her, bird-like, and Anna thought, just for a moment, as she corrected her mistake and the curtains slid back again, fully closed, that Madame Oursor had gasped a little, as though excited by the scream. But when she turned back to the room, the interviewer seemed not to have moved. Gwen and Beth were staring towards her and the window, both flushed, Beth looking frightened too, but smiling now the danger was over.

Anna walked back to her chair and sat down again, noticing that the slim white fingers across the desk had stopped playing with the crystals. Now they moved, and the soft clinking that had accompanied the interview till then began again.

'I truly apologise, *mesdemoiselles*. The curtains should have been double-checked. But you were in no serious danger, I hope?'

Beth replied for them this time, in *her* soft, slightly lisping voice. Strangers could not tell the voices of the three sisters apart, but to Anna Gwen's voice and Beth's voice were like honey from roses and honey from lilies: both sweet, so very sweet, but so very different.

'No, not really. But we *are* rather neurotic about the sun, I'm afraid.'

'You are afraid of the sun?'

'Well, yes, that too. From when we were children.'

'Ah, yes, children. Please tell me more about your childhood. Herr Bärengelt is anxious to know a lot about all of your lives. He hopes you will be working for him for a long time, that you will develop a very close relationship, and so you and he must have topics of conversation. So please, more about your childhood.'

Gwen began speaking again and Anna found her attention wandering. She had heard almost everything so many times before, as the three of them had sailed across the flood of media attention that followed their appearance on the Jerome Sprockett Show. For six delirious months they had travelled from chat-show to chat-show, living permanently in hotels, flying complimentary first-class all over the world, followed by an aggressive pack of reporters and photographers employed by papers and magazines whose hunger for the smallest details of their lives was seemingly insatiable. A dozen or more magazines devoted to them had appeared for the general market; more specialist magazines had quickly followed for their teen and sub-teen, gay and lesbian fans, or chronicling their clothing, their hairstyles, their taste in music and films; and 'Camberwell Sisters' websites and newsgroups had multiplied on the Internet like wildflowers springing up to colonise a bare, blackened patch of forest after a fire. Gwen had spent hours exploring the sites, as excited by this manifestation of their fame as she was by all the others, but Anna, disgusted and frightened by the lurid sexual fantasies she had come across on one early newsgroup, had soon begged her sister not to discuss them or even mention them any more.

Now all that was over: their fame had gone as quickly as it had come. Only on the Internet were there still traces of what had been, with one or two newsgroups still active and a few dozen obsessive male and female fans running websites in their honour. Anna was relieved, glad that their lives and bodies were no longer part of the fantasies of so many millions, but she knew Gwen still visited the sites and newsgroups, and suspected that she even masturbated to the fantasies still being exchanged on alt.sex.camberwell-sisters.

She shifted in her seat at the thought. Beth was speaking now, telling their interviewer of their lives as teenagers. The sunglasses were turned on Beth, but Anna had the impression that the eyes behind the dark lenses were closed, as though the woman were just listening to the words, not watching the face as well. Just listening to the words. The fingers had stopped moving the crystals; now, they stirred again, and the crystals chimed together as Madame Oursor asked:

'And were you not lonely?'

'No,' said Gwen.

Beth echoed her: 'No. Not at all.'

3

'But surely . . .? Three young girls – beautiful young girls, if I may say – unable to go out, to participate in the normal activities of teenagers?'

Beth laughed a little.

'No, truly Madame Oursor, we were not lonely. This will sound a little clichéd, but it is true – we had each other.'

She smiled at each of her sisters in turn, head turned one way, then the other. Anna smiled back.

'Ah, I see,' said Madame Oursor. 'You had each other.'

She picked up her silver pencil and made another note on the pad next to the crystals. Anna had tried to read these notes, but they were in a strange shorthand that she did not recognise. She watched the slim hand lay the pencil down and return to the crystals, stirring them together, chiming them as the thin lips opened and Beth was asked another question. A sudden image entered her head, of that slim hand between the slim thighs that were surely concealed beneath the robes, stirring and chiming the folds of a slim . . . cunt. Slim cunt.

She shivered at the thought, feeling a trickle of heat begin in the base of her belly, and then almost began to blush as she realised the dark lenses were turned on her now, and the thin lips (a little thicker now, maybe, than when the interview had begun?) were opening to speak to her.

'But you, *ma petite*, we have heard so very little from you so far. Have you nothing to add to what your sisters have told me?'

Anna swallowed.

'I . . . I suppose I'm the quiet one of the family, madame.'

'*La timide*? The, uh, mouse?'

Beth laughed.

'Sometimes, madame,' she said. 'But she shows her claws sometimes too. Though not as often as Gwen and me.'

The hand picked up the silver pencil again.

'Ah, so you all have claws. Even Anna, sometimes. Herr Bärengelt will be very pleased to hear that. He loves especially young women of spirit.'

She seemed about to say something more, but stopped, and laughed.

4

'Yes, especially young women of spirit. Beauty and spirit, that is what he seeks to surround himself with. I envy him your company.'

'But will you not be accompanying us, madame?'

'Ah, so you can speak for yourself, *ma petite*! No, alas, I will not. I am Herr Bärengelt's agent in this country and there is always much work for me to do on his behalf. But I shall see you all again at Christmas, perhaps. Do you look forward to it . . . Anna?'

It was the first time she had addressed any of them by first name. Anna felt the trickle of heat in her belly widen and quicken. She knew the folds of her cunt were opening, and she had the sudden conviction that across from her, underneath the table, so were the folds of Madame Oursor's. The folds of Madame Oursor's cunt. The two of them were smiling at each other beneath the table, cunt opening unto cunt.

'I . . . yes, Madame Oursor. I look forward to it. I look forward to it a lot.'

And for the first time those thin lips curved into a smile, and Anna knew that now the eyes were opened wide behind the oval black lenses, fixed on her face and answering smile. Then the smile faded. Madame Oursor looked away, picked up the pencil, made a final note.

'Good, good. Then, *mesdemoiselles*, I congratulate you. Herr Bärengelt has made a very wise choice: I am certain you shall make him excellent secretaries.'

'Then?' Gwen said.

'But yes, Gwen –' Anna felt her heart twist suddenly with jealousy '– you have the job. Or should I say, jobs? Why else should I ask your sister if she looked forward to seeing me again at Christmas? As I have said, Herr Bärengelt loves to surround himself with beauty and spirit. What kind of agent should I be if I did not conform with his wishes? If I turned away such prime specimens of beauty and spirit as the three of you before me?'

'Prime specimens, madame?' Gwen said, and Anna suppressed a shiver at the way her voice had become softer, quieter.

5

'Yes. Prime specimens.'

'You speak of us as though we were butterflies for a collection, madame.'

'Ready to be put into boxes,' Beth said.

Madame Oursor seemed not to have heard what Beth had said. The black lenses of her glasses were pointing at Gwen. The thin lips pursed, almost smiling.

'And you, I think, Mme Gwen, you I think are the most spirited of all. Herr Bärengelt will be especially anxious to meet you.'

'Am I the primest specimen, then, madame?' said Gwen.

'That will be for Herr Bärengelt to decide, Mme Gwen. But look! I am keeping you all too long! The interview is over, you have been successful, so please, go and celebrate! I will confirm your appointments in writing, and we will meet again to discuss what you must take with you, what you must wear, what flights and trains you must take. But that is for then; for now, celebration.'

Beth said, 'Won't you come with us to celebrate, Madame Oursor?'

The black lenses swung again.

'But perhaps I was wrong. Perhaps you, Mme Beth, are the most spirited. Oh, but I envy Herr Bärengelt the pleasures of comparing each of you against the others –'

'Like butterflies?' Gwen said.

'In boxes?' Beth said.

Mme Oursor laughed.

'Like butterflies in boxes, like beautiful young women. But you will not, I am afraid, be able to repay him the compliment, for Herr Bärengelt, I promise you, will be like no one you have ever met before. Nor will you ever meet anyone like him again. You will not be able to compare him to anyone or anything. But this reminds me: you have not yet asked me the question I was expecting of you.'

'About what, Madame Oursor?' Anna said.

'About whom, *ma petite* Anna. About Herr Bärengelt. Are you not anxious to learn a little more of him?'

Gwen said, 'Of course – there are hundreds of things we would like to ask.'

6

'Thousands,' said Beth.

'But there is one that I think comes first,' said Madame Oursor. 'As yet, you know only half his name.'

'Then what is the rest, madame?' Gwen said.

'The rest, Mme Gwen,' said Madame Oursor, standing up and moving around the table, 'the rest is Abraham. Herr Abraham Bärengelt. That is your new employer's full name.'

Two

'Anna, wake up!'

Groaning, blinking, slack-limbed, Anna awoke. Gwen and Beth were bending over her, one at each side of her hotel bed. She tried to sit up but one of Gwen's hands pushed her down by her right shoulder and one of Beth's by her left.

'What is it?' she asked. 'What's wrong?'

'Nothing,' said Gwen.

'Nothing that we know about yet, that is,' said Beth.

'What do you mean?'

Gwen and Beth looked at each other. A hidden signal passed between them. Beth smiled and licked her lips. Gwen said, 'Anna, darling, were you dreaming? Just now, when we woke you?'

Anna tried to sit up again.

'No, dear,' said Gwen, 'Stay still. And answer the question please.'

'I don't understand what you mean.'

Beth said, 'It's simple enough, Anna. What we want to know is: were you dreaming?'

'Just now,' Gwen said. 'When we woke you?'

'No, of course not. Why would I be dreaming? I'm very tired –'

'Anna dear, are you sure?'

'Absolutely sure?' said Beth.

'Yes, I'm absolutely sure. What a stupid question. And what busi –'

'What business is it of ours?' Beth said. 'What business is it of your loving sisters? Of course it's our business. And it's also our business –' She glanced across at Gwen.

'It's also our business, Anna dear,' said Gwen, 'to punish you when you do wrong. When you lie to us, for example. To us, your loving, elder sisters.'

'I haven't lied to you! Why would I lie to you?'

'Keep still, Anna dear. Don't get so excited. It's no good, you know, because we *know* you've lied to us. You *were* dreaming. Weren't you? Come on, admit it. Oh, dear, Beth, it looks like she's going to be stubborn. Come on, let's have her up.'

Beth ran quickly round the bed to join Gwen and Anna squealed as they set to work on her, pulling her blankets down, seizing her flailing limbs, and hoisting her up and out. She struggled, still squealing, as they stood her up between them.

'Now,' said Beth, 'were you dreaming?'

'What if I was?'

'So you were?' said Gwen.

'No. Yes. Maybe. What does it matter?'

'What were you dreaming about?' said Beth.

'None of your business.'

A slap rang out. Gwen's hand had swung neatly on to the right cheek of Anna's silk pyjama'd buttocks.

Gwen said, 'It's *all* of our business. What were you dreaming about?'

'None of your business.'

She jerked, trying to avoid Gwen's hand, but it was Beth's this time that swung, catching her neatly on the left cheek of her silk-pyjama'd buttocks.

Beth said, 'Were you dreaming about Madame Oursor?'

'What if I was?'

A double crack this time, Gwen's and Beth's hands landing almost simultaneously.

Gwen said, 'So you were. What were you dreaming about?'

No answer. Crack.

'Shall we tell you? Shall we *show* you?' said Beth.

No answer. A double-crack.

Gwen said, 'OK, we'll show you then. Take your top off. Take it off! Now! No, don't you dare – ow!'

Sucking at her bitten hand, Gwen pushed Anna on to the bed.

'Hold the little bitch down while I get her top off. Get round to the other side of the bed and we'll hold her across it. Put a pillow over her face if she doesn't shut up.'

She didn't shut up and her shrieks and squeals were suddenly muffled and cut off as Beth picked up a pillow and held it down over her face. Silk tore as Gwen wrenched and tugged at her younger sister's pyjama top.

'Anna, if you shut up, Beth will take the pillow away. Will you shut up? Nod your head if you will. Is she nodding, Beth?'

'Yes.'

'Then take the pillow away and hold her down by her arms. I'll kneel on her feet on this side. Good. That's right. Good. Now, Anna, darling, stop struggling if you know what's good for you.'

She dropped the torn pyjama top to one side as Anna was held down across the bed, her torso and breasts stripped bare, her head shaking from side to side so that tears flew in silver sparklets left and right. Panting, Gwen knelt on Anna's feet, settled her weight into them, and said, 'Now what do we have here?'

She reached forwards and brushed Anna's nipples, allowing the rise and fall of Anna's chest to drag them back and forth across the tips of her fingernails.

'What's your diagnosis, Beth?'

Beth chuckled.

'They're swollen, Gwen. Badly swollen. What a naughty little girl she must have been being in her dream. A right little slut.'

'I think you're right. But let her answer for herself. Anna, Beth just said you must have been being a right little slut in your dream. Were you?'

'No. I wasn't. I wasn't dreaming about anything. I wasn't dreaming about Madame Oursor.'

'No?' said Gwen. 'Then why could we hear you calling out her name? Ah, that's quietened you, hasn't it? You *were* dreaming about Madame Oursor, and we know what you were dreaming about *doing* with Madame Oursor. Beth was right, you are a little slut. At least, that's how it seems, but are we being too ready to condemn? What do you think, Beth?'

'No. Look at her nipples. Swollen. Tumescent. Turgid. She's been dreaming about humping that French bitch, no doubt about it. And she's got to be punished for it. Now.'

'Well, perhaps. It's a delightful prospect, but shouldn't we look for some more evidence? For some definite *proof* of her crime?'

'No. I say, punish her now.'

'And I say, first proof, then punishment. So let's go a little deeper into the question. Or shall we say, a little lower?'

Squealing, Anna tried to throw her off by kicking her legs, but it was no good: she could barely move. Beth chuckled again as Gwen reached up and slowly began to pull Anna's pyjama bottoms down. Her belly-button rose into view above the descending hemline, then the twin peaks of her pelvic bones, then – 'No knickers,' Beth hissed – a tuft of pale gold pubic hair, then an inch, two inches, three, four, five of a pair of smooth, pearly thighs, the muscles in them still working as Anna struggled to break free.

'As you say, Beth. No knickers. And do you smell anything?'

'Yes. I smell proof that she's been a slut.'

'But the proof of the pudding,' said Gwen, reaching forward between her sister's thighs, 'is in the eating.'

Her forefinger snaked into the pubic tuft, slipped lower, began to delve and rummage. Anna squeaked and moaned.

'Is she wet?' asked Beth.

'Wet? It's like a swamp down there. And yes, let me see . . . mmm . . . yes, it's slut-juice, all right. Fresh slut-juice. Proof positive that our little sister has been making a beast of herself in the privacy of her own bed. Or, should I say, in the privacy of her own head? With that awful French-woman.'

'That bitch of a Frenchwoman. So can we punish her now?'

'Certainly. We have our proof, so we may also have our fun. But we have to make sure *she* doesn't enjoy it as well. See if you can get that swelling in her nipples down.'

'How?'

'Let's think. Try squeezing them.'

Beth laughed, gasping a little as she transferred her hold on Anna's arms into one hand and reached forwards to squeeze the swollen, grape-purple nipples sitting atop the white breasts in front of her.

'They're very hard,' she said, the tip of her tongue circling her mouth as she squeezed and tweaked first the left, then the right.

'Squeeze them,' said Gwen. 'Squeeze them hard.'

'I'm trying to –' there was a squeak from Anna '– but they won't go down.'

'Harder. Squeeze them harder. And scratch them with your fingernails. We can't punish little Anna while she's in a state of sexual arousal from her filthy dream. Otherwise she might become one of those awful perverts I once heard about. What are they called?'

'Masochists.'

Another squeak from Anna as Beth set to work with her fingernails.

'Yes,' Gwen said. 'Masochists. Those awful perverts who like being hurt.'

'I think we're too late. Look – they're more swollen than ever.'

'Yes. Urgh. It's disgusting, isn't it? And she's obviously enjoying it down here, too. She'll be leaking on to the bed in a moment. And we can't have that, can we? Filthy slut-juice all over these nice clean sheets. But what shall we do?'

'Lick it up.'

'Lick it up? Her slut-juice? Yuck.'

'It's better than her leaking all over the bed. What would the maid think in the morning? She might think it was one of us.'

'She might not see it.'

'She will. Or she'll smell it.'

'Oh, dear, maybe you're right. Well, I think I'd better do it, then. It will taste horrid, but we can't have the maid thinking it was one of us.'

She began to lever Anna's thighs apart.

'Perhaps,' she added, her voice becoming a little hollower as put her face between them, 'perhaps if I hold my breath . . .'

She started to lick, slurping a little. Tremors ran through Anna's body, making her breasts quiver, the nipples atop them almost blurring into invisibility as they swung through tiny arcs left and right, right and left. Anna was biting her lip, rocking her head from side to side. Her tears had dried and light was reflected from them in two broad silvery streaks down either cheek. Beth watched closely as the black head of Gwen bobbed between her sister's thighs, her own pink tongue occasionally circling her lips.

Gwen lifted her head, gasping.

'Was it very nasty?' Beth said.

'Yes. Very. What horrid slut-juice she's got. If you were a slut, I bet yours wouldn't taste like this.'

'Thank you. I don't think yours would either, if you were a slut.'

'Thank you. But I still think there's a little bit left.'

She put her head forward again, licked and slurped. Tremors reoccupied Anna's body, her tits shuddering, nipples swinging. Her mouth came open and she started to moan.

Beth leaned forward, whispering urgently: 'Gwen! Gwen!'

The slurping stopped. Gwen lifted her head again.

'What?'

'Look – she's enjoying it. If I hadn't called you, I think she would have *come*. Isn't that disgusting? She was *enjoying* you licking up her slut-juice and she would have *come*. And you her own sister, too.'

'Well, I always suspected she was like this. One of those horrid leslie-thingies.'

14

'Lesbians.'

'Yes. Lesbians.'

'And a masochist.'

'A lesbian masochist, yes.'

'An *incestuous* lesbian masochist. Disgusting.'

'Disgusting.'

'So don't you think it's time to punish her?'

'Well, yes, I'm afraid I do. It's no good trying to lick up her slut-juice anyway. I was *almost* getting used to the taste, but she's making more all the time.'

'The slut.'

'She's a slut, all right. So we'll just have to punish her and risk her leaking on to the bed. We can always leave a note for the maid saying it wasn't us.'

'Let's make *her* write it. And sign it.'

'Good idea. Roll her over then. We'll make her write a note and sign it. "I, Anna Camberwell, leaked slut-juice all over this bed last night" – oops-a-daisy – "because" –'

' "Because," ' said Beth. ' "Because I am an incestuous lesbian masochist and I enjoyed being punished by my two sisters for having a filthy dream about a Frenchwoman." '

Anna was face-down on the bed now, held down firmly. Gwen stroked her buttocks.

' "Signed," ' she said. ' "Signed Anna Camberwell, incestuous lesbian masochist." How lovely and smooth they are.'

' "Incestuous lesbian masochist *slut*." '

'OK then. "Signed Anna Camberwell, incestuous lesbian masochist slut." And soft. Beautifully smooth and soft.'

'All the better for punishing her on.'

'Yes, all the better. Say when.'

'Now.'

Crack. A red palm-print stood out on the white satin of Anna's naked left cheek.

'Now.'

Crack. A red palm print stood out on the white satin of Anna's naked right cheek.

'Twice this time. Very quickly. Now.'

15

Crack-crack.

'Now rub them. Stroke them. Very gently. It will make it worse next time . . . Wait a few more seconds . . . Now.'

Crack.

'Now.'

Crack.

'Stroke them again. Are they getting hot?'

'Yes. They were lovely and cool before, but now they've started to get hot.'

'And is she making more slut-juice?'

'Let's see . . . yes, lots more. But . . . mmm . . . it still tastes horrid. What next?'

'Stick your finger up her bottom.'

'But what if it isn't clean?'

'Then we'll punish her some more.'

'OK . . . No, she won't let me in.'

'Hit her.'

Crack.

'Still no good.'

'Hit her some more.'

Crack. Crack. Crack.

Panting a little, Gwen said, 'Still no good.'

'She's a *disobedient*, incestuous, lesbian masochist slut. Put some of her slut-juice on your finger and try again.'

'OK . . . she's open enough down there. And, oh dear, she *has* leaked on to the bed. Now, let's see . . . yes, that's worked. My finger's right up her bottom now. But she's still very tight.'

'Slap her again with your other hand and see what happens.'

Crack.

'Oh! That was funny!'

'What happened?'

'When I slapped her, I could feel her bottom tighten even more.'

'Her arsehole. Sluts have arseholes.'

'Yes. Her arsehole. Just think, Beth. It must be wonderful to be a man and have your cock up a tight, hot, little arsehole like this when it tightens like –' crack '– *this*. And like –' crack '– *this*.'

'Do you think she has?'

'Has what?'

Crack.

'Has had a man's cock up her arsehole?'

'No. She's a lesbian, remember. She wouldn't like that.'

'She might like it –' crack '– if it was a *dildo*. If it was Madame Oursor with a dildo. Perhaps that was what she was dreaming about. Madame Oursor –' crack '– putting a big dildo up her little arsehole.'

'Her *tight* little arsehole.'

'Her tight –' crack '– *hot* little arsehole. Oh, I can hardly get my finger out. Did you hear that? It made a popping noise. Like a cork coming out of a bottle.'

'A champagne cork. Was her arsehole clean?'

'Let's see. It looks OK. And it smells OK. But the proof of the pudding is mmm in the eating. Yes, it was clean.'

'Lucky for her.'

'Yes, lucky for her. It's almost as though she *knew* we were going to do this to her. Almost as if we *told* her we were going to do this to her.'

'Almost. But we didn't, did we? Because if we had done, that would make us incestuous lesbian *sadists*.'

'Incestuous, lesbian, sadist *sluts*.'

'Just like her.'

'Almost just like her. Did she come?'

'Twice, the little slut.'

'The little incestuous, lesbian, masochist slut,' Anna's voice said sleepily. 'And it was three times.'

Three

FREQUENTLY ASKED QUESTIONS

Who are the Camberwell sisters?
The Camberwell sisters are three hyper-clenchy British *muchachitas* called Anna, Beth and Gwen.

What's so special about them?
Apart from being so hyper-clenchy, you mean? They suffer from a very rare genetic condition called Lissestreicher's Syndrome that means they can never go out in the sunlight – not ever. They can't even be in a room with a window that lets sunlight thru. This means they have the whitest skin you have ever seen.

What happens if they get touched by the sun?
Their skin-cells would mutate and they'd get something called ichthyosis, which is kind of like where your skin turns into fish-scales, only a lot worse. Probably they'd end up dying now they're grown-up. One of them (Beth) got caught by the sun like that when they were young and they were really frightened by it.

But what do they do if they can never go out in the sun?
Mostly they just go out at night, but if they have to go out during the day they dress in special foil-lined clothing, with masks and gloves, and stay indoors as much as possible.

Apart from their white skin, what do they look like?
Gwen (the oldest) is 5'5", brown eyes, black hair; Beth (in the middle) is 5'8", green eyes, red hair; Anna (the youngest) is 5'3", blue eyes, blonde hair.

Who's your favourite?
It's really hard to say but I suppose it's Anna. But I like them all LOTS.

How did they get famous?
Like most other rab fans I know, I first saw them on the Jerome Sprockett Show in Fall last year. I was completely blown away, believe me. That was where it all started and I have worn out way too many tapes of that particular show to mention since then.

Where do they live?
Everywhere, at the moment. They've been to the States seven times this year now, and I'm counting the hours to their next visit. Their home address in England is a BIG secret, but if you want to snail-mail them, just address your letter 'Anna, Beth and Gwen, Planet Earth' and it will get there.

What about e-mail?
Their official fan-club is at http://www.camberwellsisters.com and you can e-mail them there like this:

anna@camberwellsisters.com

beth@camberwellsisters.com

gwen@camberwellsisters.com

Gwen replies to fans quite a lot, Beth replies sometimes too, but Anna never does. I've never got a reply from Gwen or Beth though – and it's not for want of trying, believe me.

Return to Index

Jenny Murphy: With me this morning are the three Camberwell sisters, Anna, Beth, and Gwen, fresh from a triumphant chatshow tour of the United States and now rumoured to be considering a move into the pop world. So, Gwen, am I in the presence of the next Femme-37?

Gwen: (laughs) If you'd heard our singing voices, Jenni, you wouldn't ask. We respect Femme-37 for what they've achieved, but we don't think we're ready to challenge them just yet.

Murphy: So that isn't a definite no?

Gwen: It's a definite maybe.

Beth: And we always preferred the Spice Girls. Or Anna did, anyway.

Murphy: (laughs) So 'Girl Power' *is* something you've been inspired by?

Gwen: Well, Beth and I have been but Anna hasn't, funnily enough.

Murphy: Anna?

Anna: Uh, well, yes, I did like the Spice Girls.

Gwen: She liked Baby Spice. Cute, quiet blonde, and that's our Anna.

Murphy: Whereas you would have liked Scary Spice?

Gwen: Yes. Black-haired and butch. I can identify with that.

Murphy: What about you, Beth?

Beth: Oh, Sporty Spice, I guess. Sweaty and glowing. Just the way I like them.

Murphy: But – and you'll recognise this as a delicate way of raising the accusations that have been thrown at you – what did you think of the so-called 'manufactured' image of the Spice Girls? The girl for every male taste, with a 'girl power' slogan invented by a man?

Gwen: Feminist listeners may remember the same accusations being thrown at Charlie's Angels. They were before our time, first time round, but we are fans and we have to say, well, yes. Absolutely. Charlie's Angels were manufactured and overtly male-controlled, the Spice Girls were manufactured and covertly male-controlled, and we obviously take things on to the next level. We're neither manufactured nor male-controlled.

Murphy: So the rumours of a mysterious Svengali who's overseen your astonishing rise to fame and popularity are just that, rumours?

Beth: If there is a mysterious Svengali behind us, he is taking mysteriousness to ridiculous lengths, because we don't know who he is.

Gwen: We don't even know that he is a he. Maybe he's a she. But to be honest, it really is all total crap. You'll have heard this a thousand times before, but the British media will love the successful for just so long, and then they have to attack, try to bring them down. Bite the hand that feeds, because successful people sell newspapers.

Beth: The Australians call it the tall poppy syndrome. If a poppy is taller than the rest, it's likely to get its head knocked off. I suppose it's a natural reaction, in some ways.

Murphy: But a hurtful one?

Beth: Not hurtful. Boring. Girls just wanna have fun, y'know?

Murphy: And is that what you see yourselves as: girls who just want to have fun?

Gwen: Definitely. We didn't ask to be famous, but now that we are – and for as long as it lasts – we are going to make the most of it.

Murphy: So you don't anticipate that it will last?

Gwen: It won't last. We know that. We're flavour of the month, just maybe flavour of the year. But it *will* end. Definitely. But hopefully by then we will have established ourselves in the things that really matter to us and that, well, that really matter.

Murphy: Work for charity?

Gwen: Work for women's health. We're in a position where we know every moment of every day how important health is. We have it, but we're on a knife-edge. We could fall off any moment. Just a stray sunbeam and really, that could be it.

Murphy: So you don't mind me mentioning to listeners the precautions we've had to take at the studio today?

Beth: No. Not at all. We're used to them, Jenni. By now all this comes almost as naturally as breathing.

Murphy: And do you intend to concentrate on – consults notes – Lissestreicher's Syndrome in the work you do for women's health? Because it is, if I've understood it right, a female-only condition?

Gwen: Yes, but it's more than that. It's a Camberwell-only condition. We're unique in having this particular syndrome, with its strength and so on, but there are other conditions related to it. But they're all rare too and we've decided to concentrate on things that aren't rare. Mainstream women's health. Problems that still aren't getting the attention they deserve, particularly in the Third World. There's that old Chinese slogan: women hold up half the sky. At least. But we'd like to help them do it without one hand being tied behind their backs.

Transcript of interview on *Girls' Half Hour*, BBC Radio Four, 17 September 2003.

23

WHITE IN BLACK

The three Camberwell sisters, Gwen, Beth, and Anna left the United Kingdom on Tuesday to take up secretarial appointments with the billionaire German businessman Abraham Bärengelt at his secluded Schloss in the Black Forest.

The Daily Telegraph, 21 July 2000.

Four

Anna opened her eyes. Closed them. Tight. Opened them. She had died and gone to heaven. But she was in a bed and heaven was a painting on the ceiling. A copy of Michelangelo's painting on the ceiling of the Sistine Chapel. God stretched forth His hand . . . to Eve. A slender, apprehensive Eve. And that was a whip in God's left hand, its tassels studded with nodes of hardened leather.

She looked away from the ceiling, around the room she was in, only her eyes moving at first in her motionless face, her head propped against a huge pillow. Her vision was still clearing, but she thought it was the largest room she had ever been in. Her bed was dwarfed by it, and her bed was huge. Eighteenth-century furniture: tables, dressers, but no chairs, with *art nouveau* lamps glowing amid *art nouveau* sculpture. The light of the lamps didn't – couldn't – fill the room completely, and there were shadows everywhere. Acres of carpet, purple with green and red and gold *fleurs-de-lys*. A piano – no, a harpsichord – in one distant corner. No chairs. Heavy black curtains, fully closed. Tapestries on the walls. She vaguely recognised some of the images, but they were pastiches too. Every sexual position and practice she had ever imagined, and some she hadn't.

She slowly turned her head from side to side. Tested her limbs. For a moment she thought she was paralysed, but it was only the weight of the bedclothes on her naked body. She lifted her arms up and free and struggled to sit up.

Away from the pillow, the air felt suddenly and strangely cool on her head and she lifted a hand to it. Sharp/smooth stubble met her fingertips, then a crescent-shaped scar, five or six centimetres long, edged by stitches. She opened her mouth, tested her jaw and tongue. She hummed, then said, 'What the hell?'

Nothing answered her. She pushed the bedclothes down, lifted her legs free, and knelt on the bed. She massaged her neck for a few moments, rubbed her arms and legs, then crawled to the edge of the bed. She felt a little dizzy. When she reached the edge of the bed she stared down at the carpet. A gold *fleur-de-lys* sat directly below her. The pile of the carpet was very thick. She sat on the edge of the bed and put her bare feet down on to the carpet. Into the carpet. Soft and warm.

She got off the bed and stood up. For a moment she thought she was going to fall over, back on to the bed. How long had she been lying there asleep? She looked for the nearest piece of furniture, a long dresser with a series of arched mirrors, and began to walk towards it. Her feet sank into the carpet as though she were walking in a kind of sensual, fibrous mud. She was dizzy when she reached the dresser and she leaned on it, drawing three deep breaths.

Then she looked in one of the mirrors. The scar was a vivid angry red, a bloody crescent of waxing moon hanging against the golden field of her stubble. She grimaced at the dismay in her face. Her hair would grow back. The scar would be invisible. Something caught her eye at the far end of the dresser. A slim grey book, one corner of it hanging over the edge, over the *fleurs-de-lys* in the carpet. Supporting herself with one hand on the dresser, she walked to it and picked it up.

The cover was soft and smooth, some kind of velvet, with the title stamped rather than printed into it. She ran her fingers over the letters and words, hardly able to read them. EROI – no, EROTIC WO – no, VOCAP, no, VOCABULARY. EROTIC VOCABULARY. And beneath this, smaller and in italic, almost impossible to read: *To be learned*. She opened the book and frowned, straining to read one of the entries, which were printed in paler grey on pale grey.

twengle: tr. vb. to squeeze and pluck a nipple between the second joints of the index and middle fingers, as though playing a musical instrument.

She frowned. This was crazy. She put the book down and pushed herself away from the dresser. Her legs were stronger now and she walked around the room from table to dresser to dresser to table to dresser, stopping to examine the sculpture that rested on them. No chairs. Nothing at all to sit on. The *art nouveau* was all erotic, some heterosexual, some lesbian, the bulbs of the lamps set into breasts or cockheads, between thighs or buttocks. In one of the lamps, depicting a slim ivory girl fellating a giant onyx negro, some kind of rotating mechanism inside the fellatrix's head made light flicker around her mouth and chin like threads of semen.

She left the table and walked across to another. The sculpture atop this was a *soixante-neuf sapphique* performed by jade Oriental twins. She thought they were Oriental from the straightness of their hair: she couldn't see their faces, but the sculptor had depicted every other detail of their bodies down to the way the fingers of each sank into the firm flesh of the other's buttocks as she clutched them down on her hidden, working mouth and tongue. Anna ran a finger tip over one twin, then the other, watching the way light played off her fingernail as her fingertip rose and fell over their curves and grooves. The jade was cool and very smooth.

She sighed and looked for a door. Something moved in one of the mirrors and her heart was thumping industrially in her chest before she realised what it was. Who it was. Beth. Naked, head shaved, walking across the room behind her. She spun, but the room was empty. She turned back to the mirror but Beth had gone from it. But reappeared in a second mirror, disappeared from it, reappeared in a third. But was not in the room.

Anna sank to the floor and crouched, holding her head in both hands, fingertips gently resting on the outlines of the scar. She closed her eyes and listened. Nothing. She opened her eyes and stood slowly. She looked around the room and saw a curtained doorway on the far side. She walked towards it, trying to hold down her panic. A clock began to chime thinly somewhere in the room, joined after a moment by three, four, seven, eight others whose notes seemed to mingle in a distorted fugue, a pastiche, she thought, of Bach or Handel. And she thought the clocks were striking thirteen.

She reached the doorway and tugged the curtains back. They were heavy black velvet and ran against her body as she pushed through them like the pelts of giant bears or panthers. There was an open door on the far side, flooded with cold, clear light. She stepped through it, the bare soles of her feet suddenly shocked with the broad kiss of cold marble.

She was on a landing at the top of a wide set of stairs that twisted down in a dozen or more flights around an open stairwell. The floor of the landing and treads of the stairs were white marble-veined and smudged with yellow and purple, green and orange, like the skin of white buttocks bruised by beatings over two or three days. The stair-rods and bannisters and railing were black marble, veined with white and a thin, glittering silver; and bronze thorns and teeth were set atop the stair-railing at irregular intervals. The air was no colder here than in the room she had just left, but the light and marble made it seem so and she shivered suddenly at the thought of sliding down the bannisters in a spray of blood and shredded thighmeat.

Her nipples had hardened. She walked to the railing, rested a hand on it beside a bronze thorn, and looked down into the stairwell. Fifty or so metres below, another *fleur-de-lys* stared back at her. Blood-red this time, a mosaic in a broad pool of black marble where heraldic gold fish disported. She turned away and started to walk down the stairs, setting her hand to and lifting it from the railing between the thorns and teeth. The soles of her feet grew accustomed to the cold of the marble in a dozen or so steps and took pleasure in its smoothness almost as they had taken pleasure in the deep pile of the *fleur-de-lys*'d carpet in the bedroom. Her bedroom?

There were thirteen steps in each flight of the stairs, thirteen flights and landings to the bottom, with another black-curtained alcove on each landing. Anna counted treads, flights, and landings, her hand lifting from and falling to the stair-railing. The air grew warmer as she descended and her nipples softened. There were hairs around them again, glints of blonde against the puckered pink of the areolae. She remembered plucking them on the last day before they had left for Germany. How long had she been lying in the bed? Had she wakened and eaten and drunk and gone to sleep again there for days? She must have done, but she couldn't remember. She thought of the scar. She had injured her head recently. Fairly recently. Less than a month ago, but perhaps more than a fortnight.

She reached the bottom of the stairs and felt a new quality in the floor she stepped on to, the marble and stone of many mosaics, all, save for the *fleur-de-lys* she had seen from thirteen flights of stairs above, following the by-now familiar theme of sexual practice and perversion, square and triangular chips of a hundred different marbles and minerals mimicking expertly the textures of flesh and fluids, tits, cocks, backsides. But there was a new emphasis here on S&M: flagellation, bondage, breath-control, all inflicted by men on women. By a single man on many women. By a single goatman. He was tall, black-haired, with a flowing black beard but a shaved, smooth, nut-brown torso. His tireless arms swung a hundred whips, tightened a hundred knots, lifted and adjusted a hundred sets of female buttocks. His phallic horn was huge, his legs those of a goat – shaggily furred, shining-hoofed – and he had horns on his head. *Io Pan.*

She had been walking across the mosaics to a black-curtained doorway: now she reached it and stepped through, lifting the curtains apart left and right with her forearms. She stopped abruptly, swaying back as though someone had tried to hit her in the face. The room that faced her seemed infinitely huge and she felt that she had stepped on to the threshold of a senile universe into which she might at any moment be sucked and torn apart by the gravity of invisible dead suns.

For the room was so black. The walls and floor – for a few moments she could see no other details – were utter, ultra-velvet black. The word seemed to hammer at her. Black. Black. Black. Slowly details began to emerge from it. Eighteenth-century furniture: ebony tables, dressers, with jet *art nouveau* lamps glowing amongst jet *art nouveau* sculpture. No chairs. It was like the room above in which she had woken, but with all colour sucked out of it. Black, utterly black. She stepped forwards on to rich, deep, black carpet, and stood still, realising that she was being watched before she realised who it was that was watching her.

Across the room from her was a man sitting motionless in a black throne. He was wearing a bodysuit of black leather or plastic, his head and face hidden completely beneath a black helmet in which there seemed to be no eyeholes. Half-automatically she began to walk towards him. There was a strange distortion of the air in front of him, but it was not until she was only a few metres away that she realised it was a wide glass table.

There was nowhere to sit on her side of it. She reached it and stopped, touching her hands lightly to its smooth, cold surface. As she did so the man stirred – there were horns on his eyeless helmet, she saw – and began to fumble at the groin of his bodysuit. Through the table-top she watched him lift his cock out and roll back the foreskin. Something glittered on the cockhead.

She said, 'What is that?'

'The lens of a camera.'

His voice came at her from many directions from hidden speakers; it was electronically treated, rumbling tigerishly with infra-bass harmonics that she savoured a moment before replying.

'A camera? In the head of your cock?'

'In the head of my cock. I have a screen inside this helmet. It is fed images from cameras hidden in various places in this room, and also from the fibre-optic camera in the head of my cock.'

'Was it painful? To have it fitted?'

'Exceedingly. But more than worth it for the sight of you walking across this black room of mine. Your skin almost burned my brain with its purity and whiteness. It almost burns my brain now. I see you from several angles simultaneously.'

She was silent for a moment.

'I am dreaming,' she said.

'You will see.'

'Who are you?'

'I think you already know. And I think you already know that this is no dream.'

'Perhaps. Can I sit down?'

'No. From now on, you never sit down. You kneel or lie, never sit.'

'Where am I?'

'Again, I think you already know that.'

'You are Herr Bärengelt. And this is your castle in the Black Forest.'

'*Ja. Es ist mein Schloß im Schwarzwald.*'

'Where are my sisters?'

The horns on the helmet swung left and right.

'No. If you want to ask any more questions, you must play me at a game.'

'At what game?'

'At this – or this.'

· He gestured at the table. Now she saw that there were objects sitting atop it, made of transparent glass too, almost seeming to float on the air. A chessboard, on the left, and four large dice, on the right. She looked at the chessboard. The knights were girls clasping slim thighs around the bulk of giant cocks, curved forwards and dribbling in the throes of ejaculation; pawns erect pricks with Prince Alberts; rooks gaping cunts with sharp crystalline teeth; bishops martyred saints (Sebastian, Lucy, Lawrence, Agatha); one king and queen (she didn't understand) a man and woman in eighteenth-century

31

French clothing, the other a man and woman in 1960s clothing.

'Not chess,' she said. 'I am no good at chess.'

'Then dice.'

'OK, dice.'

'Pick them up. You will choose one and I another. Then you roll them both. Thirteen throws. If you win, I will answer any question you have. If I win, then you shall give your body over to me to do with as exactly I choose for exactly one hour.'

'What will you do?'

'I will give you your orders when you lose.'

'But what if I win today and tomorrow and the day after?'

'It is unlikely that you will win on any day.'

'Are the dice fair?'

'Yes. They will all roll truly.'

'But you have some advantage?'

'Yes, of course. I have the advantage of choosing after you have chosen. So choose.'

She picked up one of the dice. The spots were marked with indentations, hard to see, but read easily by her stroking fingertip. Read easily, but strangely: she turned the die over several times, staring, stroking. Some of the faces had four spots, some had none. She counted. Four faces had four spots, two had none.

She picked up another. It was easy to learn the numbers on this one: all faces had three spots.

She picked up another. Three, no, four faces had six spots, two faces had two.

She picked up the last. Four faces had five spots, two faces had one.

She looked up at Bärengelt.

'Fair?' she said.

He nodded.

'Yes. They are perfectly fair. There would be no satisfaction in possessing you if I cheated.'

'So I choose, and then you choose?'

'Yes.'

32

'Not the other way around?'

'No.'

She picked up one of the dice.

'I choose this one.'

He put out a hand and air-tapped one of the others.

'Then I choose this one,' he said.

'And if I change my mind?'

'Change your mind. Change it as often as you like.'

'Then I change to the one you just chose. Or do I? No, I choose this one.'

He looked at the dice and air-tapped one of the three she had not chosen.

'OK?' he said.

She shrugged, nodded, saying 'Do I roll them?'

'Roll them. First yours, then mine. Yours, then mine. Thirteen times each. And I will beat you.'

She rolled hers. A five.

She rolled his. A six.

A one. A six.

A one. A two.

A five. A two.

A one. A two.

A five. A two.

A five. A two.

A five. A six.

A five. A two.

A one. A two.

A five. A two.

A five. A six.

A one. A two.

'You lose,' he said. 'Your body is entirely mine, for the entirety of one hour. This is what you do first. Climb on top of this table. Open your legs very wide and rub your cunt upon the glass above my cock. With the eye in my cock I shall watch you do this and masturbate. When I come, I will direct my semen up against the underside of the table. Instantly, you will get under the table and lick the underside clean. If a single drop falls to the floor, you will be punished. Do you understand?'

'I am dreaming,' she said.

'You know you are not dreaming. Do you understand?'

'Yes.'

'Do it. Now.'

She put one knee on the table and slid forward on to it, lifting the other leg up with her, kneeling on the glass, opening her thighs towards him as she pushed the centre of herself down at the table-top. His grunt of pleasure struck at her ears from the speakers, loud enough to start threads of bass feedback that ran and multiplied, humming like giant bees. She put her head back, closing her eyes and seeing the black, glistening facets of bees' eyes against the golden hexagons of honeycomb as she began to work her cunt at the surface of the table, grunting a little herself at the effort of holding herself down against the resistance in the tendons of her thighs.

The glass was smooth and cool against her heat; soon, just smooth. Slowly the tendons in her thighs relaxed and her cunt flattened fully to the surface of the table, full of a honey-thick itch that the smoothness could not scratch or ease. She was beginning to leak, smearing the glass with her juice.

He grunted again, thickening the bee-rumble of feedback, and she put her head forwards and opened her eyes, bucking now at the table-top, her thighs fully opened, cunt purple-pink and oozing, the folds of her labia held apart by the pressure with which she pressed herself to the glass. Beneath the wide and thickening smear of her juice she could see through the table-top that he was masturbating below her, his black hand cycling on the white rod of his cock, the eye of the fibre-optic camera winking at her as the foreskin rode over it and back. *What could he see?* she wondered, fitting the question into her mind almost painfully through rising orgasm. But the glass was too smooth. Too smooth. The itch in her cunt was not satisfied by it. The rhythm of her thrusts had quickened and she knew her inner thighs were going to ache for a long time, taxing her over hours for moments of pleasure, but the mad notion had come into her head that if she drove her flesh hard enough at the glass she might grind out roughness in it, something to spark the full orgasm that was too slow to come.

But his voices were groaning something in German and, looking forwards again, gasping, she saw the head of his cock begin to spurt whitely, splattering against the underside of the table in a moist explosion of orgasm. She pushed herself backwards, swinging her cunt free of the table-top, one hand darting into it free of her conscious will, strumming frantically at the engorged folds of its lips and the erect nub of her clitoris as she slid off the table on to the floor and crawled quickly underneath to the patch of semen clinging to the underside.

She was too late. Even as she lifted her face to it, mouth open and tongue emerging to lick the glass clean, drops struck her chin and cheeks and she knew some of it must have reached the floor. She started to come as she licked at it, the glass cool and tasteless on her tongue beneath the saltiness of his semen, hand still busy at her cunt and clitoris, and she groaned in mingled pleasure and despair, still licking futilely at the glass.

'That is enough,' his voices rumbled. They were calm again, but anger had started to crack through them. She thought it was simulated. He was trying to become angry. Working himself into it, as though this were a game.

'Bitch, that is enough. Out from under there. Stand and face me.'

Which it was. With her body as the toy. She crawled from under the table and stood up, rubbing at her face and chin with the back of a hand. Her inner thighs were aching, stinging with the strain she had put on the tendons, and her orgasm had been savagely unsatisfying, sexual tension lingering unresolved in patches at her nipples, in her armpits, the hollows of her elbows and knees.

He had returned his cock to the bodysuit.

'Bitch, you failed. What were you commanded?'

'To frig myself on the table-top while you watched and masturbated yourself beneath me. To lick your come clean off the underside of the table before any of it dripped to the carpet.'

35

'But it dripped, didn't it?'

'Yes.'

'You failed.'

'Yes.'

'So you must be punished.'

'I am dreaming.'

Relentlessly his voices came at her again from the dozen or more hidden speakers.

'No, you are not dreaming. You failed, so you must be punished.'

'Yes.'

'Yes, *master*. Say it.'

'Yes, master.'

'Louder.'

'Yes, master.'

'Louder.'

'Yes, master!'

'Bitch,' his voices muttered. He stood up from the throne. 'Get over there.'

She walked where he was pointing, not seeing the black apparatus clearly until she was almost upon it: a piece of surreal furniture with no easily apparent purpose, stooped over by the huge sculpture of a flower in black iron, its petals tightly closed. She turned back towards him as he followed her from the table, light gleaming off the tips of his horns.

'What is it?' she asked.

'A whipping-horse. Climb on to it.'

He had moved but his voices had not. She climbed on to the thing, uncertain of how to position herself.

'Face-down!'

She swung herself over and straddled the thing.

'There are stirrups for your feet, here and here.'

He tapped left and right with a long black cane that she had not noticed him pick up. She pushed her feet into the stirrups, wincing as her thighs opened again, then biting her lip as he tightened a strap savagely on her left ankle, then on her right. Something stung momentarily at her left buttock, as though he had flicked at her with the cane, catching her just with its tip.

36

'Bitch,' his voices rumbled. 'Did you fail just before?'

'Yes, master.'

'So you deserve – put your hands here – to be punished?'

'Yes, master. I deserve to be punished.'

'How?'

'I think with the cane, master.'

'No. You must say: "As you please, master". How will you be punished?'

'As you please, master.'

'And how is that?'

'With the cane –' she gasped as a strap bit into her left wrist, her right '– master.'

'I could not hear you clearly. How do I please that you be punished?'

'With the cane, master.'

'Good. Now, lift your head.'

The cane tapped the back of her head and she bent her neck backwards. Something swung down over her face, covering her eyes, blinding her, smelling of cool plastic and leather. There was a click and the thing tightened suddenly on her face and scalp and ears. His voices came to her again, muffled through the thing – the helmet, she realised it must be.

'What can you see?'

Her mouth was free. She licked her lips.

'I can see . . . nothing, master.'

'And now?'

She gasped and jerked, for she was suddenly standing far above and behind herself, staring through a distorting lens down on a white doll strapped to a tiny whipping-horse beside which a black doll stood and waited. There was a screen on the inside of the helmet, fed from a lens among the petals of the iron flower behind the whipping-horse. The black doll that was Bärengelt waved to her and patted the buttocks of the white doll that was her. She felt his touch – the cool leather of a glove – and saw it from what seemed to be many metres away, a fissure of dissociation opening in her head.

'Comfortable?' his voices rumbled at her, muffled and thickened by the helmet.

'No, master.'

'Good.'

He threw another strap across her-body/the-doll's-body just above her/its buttocks and tightened it hard, then a second and third. She was held helpless, unable to move, watching her pinioned doll-self as he circled the apparatus to which she/it was strapped, muttering to himself in his dozen bass voices as he tested the straps.

'Comfortable now?'

'No, master.'

On the helmet screen he crouched suddenly. There was a tremor in the whipping-horse and it moved beneath her, lifting her, spreading and tugging at her feet so that her buttocks tightened and rose, presenting themselves to the air and the ever-present threat of the cane. He was adjusting something at her head now.

'Watch,' he said.

She looked and the camera in the flower began to zoom in on her doll-self, which swelled and rose on the screen, filling it, overflowing it, then locked on the twin mounds of her buttocks, magnified to slightly above life-size. Something tightened and rode in her throat at their whiteness and shape.

'Are they not beautiful?' his voices rumbled at her.

'Yes, master.'

'And does this –' the black line of the cane bisected the screen, dropping to lie flat against the satin swell of both cheeks '– not frighten you?'

She swallowed.

'Yes, master. It frightens me.'

'Good. I am glad to hear it. OK, I am now turning off the screen inside your helmet. What can you see?'

The screen winked off and she stared into blackness.

'Nothing, master,' she said.

'And can you move?'

'No, master.'

'And are you comfortable?'

'No, master.'

'Good. Now, bitch, listen. I am going to give you one stroke with this cane. One very, very hard stroke. It will hurt exceedingly. Hurt more than anything else you have ever experienced before, I hope. I *know*. But the stroke and the pain of it must be completely unexpected. And yet it cannot be. Do you understand?'

'No, master.'

'Listen. Can you hear this?'

A metronome close to her left ear began to tick on a second-and-half rhythm.

'Yes, master.'

'Can you count its beats?'

'Yes, master.'

'Then count them.'

She swallowed, licked her lips, and said, 'One . . . two . . . three . . . f –'

'Good. That is enough.'

The metronome stopped.

'So, you will count them. You will count thirteen beats. On one of those beats, I will cane you unexpectedly. Very, very hard. Exceedingly painfully. But also unexpectedly. Do you understand?'

'No, master.'

'Then pay attention carefully. On one of the thirteen beats that you count I will cane you unexpectedly. But how can I cane you unexpectedly? Suppose at the twelfth beat you have not been caned. Then you know that on the thirteenth beat I will cane you. The stroke will not be unexpected. Therefore I cannot delay the stroke to the twelfth beat. Is that not so?'

'Yes, master.'

'Nor, by the same reasoning, can I delay it to the *eleventh* beat, for you would know then that I must cane you on the *twelfth* beat, and the stroke will not be unexpected. Do you understand?'

'Yes, master.'

'Do you understand how I cannot cane you at all?'

'I – no, master.'

'Listen again, you stupid bitch. The stroke of the cane must be unexpected. I must make it on one of the thirteen beats of the metronome. I cannot make it on the twelfth stroke, nor the eleventh. But if I cannot make it on the eleventh, nor can I make it on the tenth, or the ninth, or the eighth, or the seventh, or any beat after the first. Therefore I must cane you on the first stroke – and if I *must* cane you then, it will not be unexpected. So I cannot cane you at all. Do you understand?'

'Yes, master.'

'So, bitch, count.'

The metronome began to tick at her left ear.

'One ... two ... three ... f –'

She shrieked.

Five

The bath was huge, a cuntish oval metres long and wide
with a floor of white and walls of purple marble, and might
have taken half an hour to fill from ordinary taps. But the
taps here, like everything else in the Schloss, were extra-
ordinary: supporting a wide entablature of white marble,
thirteen silver caryatids knelt on the rim of the bath, the
thighs of each splayed, her head thrown back in Dionysiac
ecstasy as the fingers of one slim hand folded apart the
gilded lips of her cunt to reveal her own deep cunt-oval.
Gilded lips? Not gilded: using the tip of a nailfile from an
overstocked cosmetics cupboard behind a wall-tapestry,
she had scratched at one and had gouged out a sliver of
what she thought might be almost pure gold.

By then hot scented water was flooding between the
cunt-lips of all the bacchantes into the bath, for she had
turned one of the master controls that sat, hooded like
clitorises, at one end of the bath. The sliver of gold sat on
her palm, insubstantial, heavy. She closed her hand on it,
then threw it across the bath into the gathering steam,
wincing as the movement reawoke the strains of her session
on the whipping-horse, thirteen floors below. The water was
already ankle-deep, rising quickly. She had discovered the
bathroom in her room soon after she had crawled and
hobbled back up the stairs. The cane-stroke was still burning
across her arse like the track of the lick of a poisonous
tongue, and in one of the mirrors it had glowed huge, broad,
but faded to a delicate pink from its former scarlet.

She had wept over it, crouched on one of the dressing tables with her arse to the mirror, watching over her shoulder as her white hands stroked and soothed at it, dipping into her arse-cleft and swinging apart over the stroke incused into her abused arse. Watching her hands in the mirror had made it seem as though they were the hands of someone else, but the pain had continued to sting and burn at her until she stood up and limped around the room, looking for the bathroom Bärengelt had hinted she would find there.

The bastard. She remembered his shout of triumph at her shriek of pain and the way the screen inside her helmet had exploded at her with the image of the stroke already burning angrily red across her white skin. He had produced a magnifying glass and bent over her, tugging distractedly at his re-exposed cock as he traced the outlines of the stroke he had smashed into her buttocks.

'*Wunderschön!*' his voices had rumbled. 'This is marvellous! The colours! Their delicacy! I feel almost as a master artist applying the first stroke of paint to a virgin canvas. And yet it is a canvas that shall paint itself! You, my sweet bitchling, will have a bruise whose evolution I shall trace day by day. And shall film! How I should love to touch and lick it, but I must not disturb it. This, however, I can do.'

And she had watched on the screen as he positioned himself atop the whipping-horse, feet on running-boards that she realised must have been placed there specially, and adjusted his cock above her arse to masturbate slowly until with hoarse grunts of pleasure he had spilled himself on to her. Even now she remembered the way the hot stickiness of his semen had felt, reported through the searing pain of the cane-stroke as it spread and flowed, oozing between the cleft of her buttocks, tingling across her anus and down her perineum until she felt its kiss on her fourchette and the lower juncture of her labia.

Then he climbed off and left the screen and, she thought, the room (the soft active hiss of the speakers died and she seemed to hear a door close somewhere). Still splayed, strapped to the whipping-horse, she could only curse and ache and watch her abused buttocks on the helmet screen, the glowing brand of the cane-stroke glistening with his trickling semen. She did not know how long she had waited for his return, but her whole body ached and if she had not had the evidence of the screen she might almost have begun to believe that her buttocks had been set on fire, the pain of the cane-stroke slowly melting, finally igniting their fat, with tongues of transparent purple and gold flame licking along the stroke of the cane.

Then the loudspeakers had rumbled awake and he was back again.

'Comfortable?' his voices asked her.

'No,' she muttered, almost weeping.

'Good.'

The helmet screen snapped off and inside the black shell of darkness she suddenly felt the leather fingers of his gloves at her cunt, stroking and teasing. She groaned as her body responded, muscles tightening in her thighs and back and buttocks, reawakening the sharp aches that time had softened and blunted. Pleasure and pain ran together simultaneously in her body. As the lips of her cunt unfolded and began to ooze she heard a soft buzzing and he was slowly inserting a vibrator into her, slowly withdrawing it, probing at her cunt-lips with it, rubbing it in slow circles around – but, cruelly, not on – her clitoris, reinserting it in her cunt, rewithdrawing it. He pleasured her, tortured her like this as he released her, unstrapping her ankles and wrists one by one while the vibrator buzzed gently half-inserted into her.

'You're free,' his voices rumbled.

The vibrator was withdrawn and not returned. Its soft buzzing stung at her: he had brought her to the verge of orgasm but denied it to her. She wept atop the whipping-horse, hating him for the torture, yet wanting it to continue.

'You're free. Time to be clean. Before the hour is up.'

He must have moved the vibrator near the microphone that captured his voice, for the loudspeakers were suddenly rumbling with a bass echo of it, a deep buzzing that mocked at her as she struggled to move off the whipping-horse. She was cramped, strained, half-full of denied orgasm, weeping, swearing. When she had climbed off she could not stand and sprawled on the floor, still wearing the helmet. The buzzing of the vibrator died on the loud-speakers and a door closed softly somewhere again. She managed to loosen and remove the helmet, but the effort made her head buzz and she lay on the floor, staring up at the black ceiling. A movement caught her eye even as she fumbled a hand down to her cunt and began to rub out the orgasm seething half-formed in her body: a glittering between the now opened petals of the black iron flower: the lens of the camera that had watched her, that had shifted to watch her now as she masturbated herself towards orgasm.

Orgasm came, brief and unsatisfying, and she rolled over, struggled on to her hands and knees and began to crawl from the room. By the time she reached the door, her muscles still aching but loosened by the exercise, she was able to get to her feet and hobble outside, the cane-stroke beginning to burn again as it met the air lying cool and still above the marble, above the mosaics of the giant-cocked Pan and his female victims. She had hated herself as her nipples and cunt responded to the images, hardening, widening, and she knew that she had been corrupted by a single session with him. She was a slave now who needed a master.

Climbing the stairs had brought her to tears four times, and once, too weary to continue, she had sprawled on a landing and masturbated herself to orgasm again. The aches and strains in her body seemed like a field of ash and cinders over which she strewed the petals of roses and violets shredded by her moving hand at the lips of her cunt, and their bruised scents drifted tantalisingly on the fringes of air so that she felt a deep breath would bring them to her. Then she rose to her feet and struggled on, for the room above and the bath whose presence he had hinted at in the black room. Or the Black Room – already it had taken on a special status, and she knew she would be counting the hours till she could return, play dice again with him, lose again, be abused again. Eyes and cunt leaking, his semen dried in thin, flaking sheets on her burning arse, she had struggled upwards.

Now, stretched out in the bath, she reviewed the session, reviewed her review of it, and her review of her review, frigging herself to orgasm after orgasm under the warm, scented water, mind and body still achingly ripe with the sensations and memories of the day. When the water grew tepid she crawled – almost swam – back to the master controls and swung the tap marked DRAIN. Water began to slide from the bath, sucking at her legs and feet, and she half-expected to see it drawing out golden strands of the hair she no longer had. Sighing, she swung the tap marked FILL and the caryatid-cunts began to gush steaming water. Sleepily, musingly, she began to frig herself towards her seventeenth or eighteenth orgasm of the day, absorbing the sensations of the contrary currents of the incoming and outgoing water into the sensations of her moving hand, imagining herself floating in the scented piss of thirteen living women, silver-fleshed . . .

Then she screamed with fright. There were fish in the water with her, pouring into the bath on the water from the gilded cunts, sparks of vivid colour flung outwards on the steaming curves of water, dashing and turning through the water around her, touching her skin with brief smooth kisses. Her bladder and bowels let go and she screamed again as the fish swarmed to the offerings, snatching crumbs of dissolving faeces from the water, turning through the piss-yellowed water, a few of the boldest beginning to swim forwards to nibble at the skin around her cunt and arsehole. She heard footsteps on the marble at the far side of the bath. Bootsteps.

'Harmless,' said a voice. Voices. Rumbling from all sides of the room. Her heart pounding, her mouth still open with shock, she looked across the bath and saw the thirteen caryatids in silver had been joined by a fourteenth. A fourteenth in black leather. Made indistinct by the steam rising from the surface of the water he was kneeling on the rim, cock out, slowly masturbating.

'Your shock was delightful,' his voices rumbled. 'Let them eat. Let them bite at you. Open your legs and encourage them forwards on to your cunt. Piss again if you –' his voices grew indistinct and, though she did not catch sight of its five or six leaping arcs, she heard his semen splashing into the water.

He stood up, folding away his cock.

'They like your piss. If you can, piss again. Shit again if you can, for they like that even more. Taste it yourself and see.'

Still speechless, she shifted in the water, flapping a submerged hand at the fish clustering between her legs. The boldest had been joined by the bolder, and her cunt and inner thighs were tingling with the contact of their mouths. There was a little shit left floating in the water, but even as she tried to take hold of some of it fish were rushing in and snapping it from her. He had started to walk around the bath; now, as a slim, discoid black-and-white fish snapped a remaining fragment from her probing fingers, his voices said.

'*Pterophyllum scalare.*'

Six or seven strides further on, as another fragment of her shit disappeared into the mouth of a narrow-bodied fish tinted in reds and purples, his voices said:

'*Bedotia geayi.*'

He had moved; his voices had not. Another six or seven or eight strides, another snapped-up fragment of shit:

'*Cheirodon axelrodi.*'

Then, with a gasped intake of breath:

'Your arsehole, you silly bitch. Try your arsehole.'

He had completed a circuit of the bath and begun another. She shifted again in the water, trying to overcome her distaste at the busy mouths between her legs and the threads of pleasure they were starting to sew into her, and swung her buttocks up to allow a finger access to her anus. She pushed at it, felt inside it. It was rich with shit. She hooked out a fragment – fish flashed at her fingertip even in the second it took to lift it free of the water – and examined it.

It was not shit. She sniffed cautiously. It was not shit. It was – she sniffed again – chocolate.

'Taste it, you silly bitch.'

Cautiously, reluctantly, she tasted it. It was chocolate.

'How . . .?'

'Shut up. Watch.'

He had reached the far side of the bath again. He stopped, indistinct again through the steam. He moved, reaching for the head of one of the caryatids, grasped, gripped, tugged – and she screamed again as the head came away in a fountain of crimson fluid that splattered against the underside of the entablature and sprayed in all directions.

He grunted, or said something she did not catch. The crimson fluid was pouring down the black leather of his bodysuit; rivulets of it were already streaming over the rim of the bath and a pink mist was spreading through the water.

He grunted or spoke again and tossed the head into the bath. It splashed loudly and she heard the faint clang as it hit the bottom a moment later. He was striding back towards her side of the bath.

'How do you feel?' his voices said.

'F –' she started to reply; and then the first tendrils of paralysis appeared in her toes and feet. She tried to push herself backwards, away from the spreading pink stain in the water, which had not reached her yet (not visibly reached her, she thought) but it was too late. Her feet and calves responded sluggishly, as though she were wearing lead shoes, lead boots, then seemed paralysed altogether, drained of the same power that was now draining from her thighs, her buttocks and back.

'It's a neurotoxin,' his voices said. He had stopped behind another caryatid, reaching from behind to grasp a breast in each hand, gripping, tugging, tearing them away in twin fountains of crimson fluid that this time poured directly into the bath. She could no longer move her legs. What was the phrase? Paralysed from the waist down.

'A harmless neurotoxin. Harmless, but very effective. In another thirty seconds or so you will be unable to move at all.'

He tossed the silver breasts into the bath, *splash* . . . *splash* . . . and *clang* . . . *clang* . . . She was trying to pull herself backwards with her arms and hands, but she had to put her arms deep into the water to do so and her fingers were turning to pasta, strength draining from her hands and forearms, her upper arms and shoulders suddenly having to make much more effort, making her gasp. The paralysis in her body was as high as her breasts now; outriders of it were tickling her throat and armpits.

'You would drown, if I were not here.'

The strength left her arms fully and she fell backwards, unable to hold herself up any longer. The water closed over her head, deep and pink. She lay on the bottom of the bath, unable to close her eyes, waiting for the last patches of strength in her neck and face to shrink to nothing as she watched the swaying plane of the surface and the fish that criss-crossed the darkening pink water beneath it, snapping at silver bubbles that rose from somewhere near her. No, not from near her: from *her*. It was her breath, bleeding out of her. The surface was cut and splashed by two shapes moving down towards her. Gloved hands. His hands. She felt him grip her head, her chin, and her eyes told her that she was moving, being lifted, dragged to the side, breaking the surface.

The loudspeakers rumbled at her from all around the room.

'As I said, you would drown if I were not here. But do not worry, it will begin to wear off soon. Relax, enjoy it. At least, accept it.'

His hands were under her shoulders now, pulling her towards the side of the bath. Her neck could not support the weight of her head, which lolled, swinging slightly as he moved her. Under her slackened eyelids she could see only the red water and the fish. She felt marble against her back and felt him lifting her arms, swinging them apart, attaching her hands to something on the walls of the bath.

'It will begin to wear off in your upper body soon. It is a contact poison, *Liebling*. Here, this will help.'

There was a second's delay and then the red water was splattered by droplets of liquid. He was pissing on her. The sudden warmth of it in her skin seemed to feed something below her skin: strength was returning to her arms and torso, neck and head, deepening the absence, the paralysis in her legs and buttocks. It was as though she had been chopped in half and had not yet fallen in half. She could open her eyes now and move her head a little. She looked left and right to where her arms were stretched wide to wrist restraints.

'Here,' his voices rumbled at her. 'The helmet again. You will be in time to watch the last drops of my piss dripping off your nipples. See?'

And the helmet descended over her head, the screen opening inside it to show her herself as captured by a lens on the far side of the bath. Her white skin stood out clear and detailed against the purple marble of the bath-wall, glistening with the yellow sheen of his piss, of which, as he had said, drops were still gathering at her nipples to fall into the paralysing water. Behind and above her he was standing, folding his cock away into his bodysuit. He gestured to the camera with one hand as though in salute, then stooped and picked up something. It was the black cane again. At the sight of it the memory of the single stroke in the Black Room rose into her mind, reawakening the pain in her buttocks, which burned oddly beneath the water, rising in her body as the paralysis had done, brushing at the lips of her cunt, stiffening her nipples.

She licked her lips, tasting his piss on them. He was bending forwards, holding the cane to the water, through the water, nudging her left foot to the left, her right foot to the right. He was opening her legs: on the helmet screen she could see them glimmer through the red water, her white skin darkened by it to pink.

'I will switch the helmet to infra-red now. You will be able to see very clearly what they do to you.'

The scene in the helmet flickered, returned with full clarity, and she could see into the water as though into a shifting pool of multiple molten crystal. Her legs were opened wide and flickered with auras of red and yellow that darkened and concentrated on the splayed oval of her cunt. The fish (glittering greens and blues) turned and crossed the water near her, some still venturing hopefully between the 'V' of her legs, piss-thirsty, shit-hungry.

'Now watch.'

He had left his position behind her and walked to the taps. He bent, spun at one of them, then another. The fountaining crimson from the decapitated, demammified caryatids sank away to rivulets, rills, threads, then died completely.

'What do you feel?'

She licked her lips again.

'Nothing,' she said.

'In the water, you silly bitch. What do you feel?'

'Noth –' she started to say, then stopped. The water, just perceptibly, was beginning to cool. The change was visible on the screen inside the helmet too: the reds and yellows of the shifting pool of molten crystal were darkening towards purple, orange, blue.

'The water is getting cold,' she said.

'Yes. Now watch, and feel.'

The fish had suddenly become nervous, turning and crossing the water more quickly. The temperature was dropping faster and an anticipatory shiver ran through her upper body, strangely cut off at her waist. The first fish butted against her cunt. She gasped.

'Knock, knock,' his voices said, and laughed (she felt the shudder of it in the marble of the bath). 'Little bitch, little bitch, let me come in.'

The first fish had returned, struggling against the lips of her cunt, suddenly joined by two, three, four others.

'It's now the warmest place in the bath, you see, and they want to be near it. Ideally, inside it. So let them in, little bitch.'

She gasped again, half with disgust, half with pleasure. There were ten or fifteen or twenty fish now fighting for space at her inner thighs and cunt, their bodies smooth and slippery against her submerged skin, which the paralysis seemed to have sensitised, as though a layer of it had been flayed, peeled back. She gasped again. Their fins were pricking at her (an absurd image rose into her mind of her naked body bound, legs apart, to a Lilliputian beach with a half-hundred miniature tattooists busy between her thighs) and the largest and most energetic were now trying to fight their way into her cunt.

The water was cold now. On the screen she could see the fish fighting at her cunt, a storm of green and blue bolts rising and rising at the ramparts of a fortress on fire: her cunt, a burning flower, rich red and purple and yellow. And now – her gasp was half a groan – one was inside, a sharp/smooth parasite simultaneously painful and pleasurable to its host. Her cunt had responded to the touch of scales and fins against its folds, had opened itself to them, and they were pressing forwards to occupy it.

She groaned again, and tears blurred the scene inside the helmet.

'They're raping you,' he said. 'Tiny fish, raping you for warmth. Let them rape you. Let them all in. All of them. All in.'

How many were inside her now she could not tell. She felt packed, ballooned with them, the scrape of their fins reported on every nerve inside her cunt, and there was the mass still outside struggling to join them, biting at her now in their desire to escape the cooling – cold – water. Biting at her clitoris. Which she knew was erect. Like a sentinel thorn on the glowing flower of her cunt. Bitten at, by the raping fish. The absurdity of incoherence. In the cold – freezing – water. She began to scream, and come, and scream, and come, feeling her cunt clench on the fish that packed it, squeezing them, crushing them.

He switched off the infra-red and on the screen inside her helmet the pool darkened again, veiling her opened legs and cunt. She could see the small bodies of fish floating on the water. The water was bitingly cold, sucking at her submerged skin, numbing her flesh, drawing warmth out of her as though she were cut open and warmth were blood.

He was unfastening the wrist-restraints, taking hold of her arms, pulling her up and out of the bath, twisting her body over as though to examine all of it.

'Look!' his voices said.

She was looking, seeing on the screen how her body had been bisected by the freezing water: her submerged legs, calves, thighs, buttocks were pale blue; her emerged arms, back, belly, breasts still pure white. Even the brand of the cane-stroke across her arse had changed colour: a dull purple now; and her nipples were dark red in the pink circles of her areolae. She watched herself from metres away on the screen and simultaneously felt his touch on her as he lifted her and laid her face forwards on one of the black marble benches that ringed the room.

He was stooping over her arse, running his fingers delicately along the cane-stroke, then parting her frozen buttock-cheeks and testing the seals of her anus with a fingertip. His voices muttered something in French and he reached down underneath the bench for something. The lubricant felt smooth and warm, stroked slowly in and around her anal whorl, and slowly began to burn at her, as though her anus had become a large, newly minted golden coin, still glowing from the mould. Now he was taking out his cock, anointing it with the same stuff. She was shivering, but as he put the head of his cock to her anus she tensed, moaned a little in protest, tried to push herself up on her arms.

'Quiet, *Liebling*.'

He started to push; she groaned.

'Silence! Submit to me!'

He withdrew a little, put a hand to each cheek of her arse, pulled them wide, repositioned the head of his cock '– Open for your master –' and pushed slowly, irresistibly. She screamed. He was sliding into her like a tongue of fire, splitting her, tearing her, she was sure, but even as she thought it the pain was beginning to fade, swallowed in a rising, delicious warmth spreading from his cock into her bowels, moving deeper as he lowered himself deeper into her.

He paused, lowered himself a little more, and then slowly began to thrust at her, his cock rising and falling within her, sheathed in that delicious warmth for which her whole lower body craved. Her cunt, packed, bruised with dead fish, was loosening, liquefying, and she could feel the fish begin to slide out of it. His breath was sighing on the speakers, in, out, and he began to gasp to the rhythm of his thrusts, spearing into her, pumping the heat deeper inside her. Something splatted on the floor – managing to concentrate on the screen for a moment she saw it was a fish, fallen from her cunt, glittering dead and vivid on the marble floor – and the muscles of her belly and thighs were beginning to tighten with pleasure, his cock now a burning spear rising again and again into her vitals, setting her innards on fire. He rose out of her and fell, rose out of her and fell, rose out of her – and did not fall.

He had withdrawn from her. She groaned with frustration. He was lifting her, pulling her off the bench, kneeling her on the floor, sitting on the bench and pushing her mouth on to his cock. She took it in, sucking and licking at it greedily, her tongue passing over the hard stub of the lens of the fibre-optic camera in the cockhead, tasting the chocolate he had mined in her bowels as she reached a hand down between her legs to strum at her clitoris. But he grabbed at her hand, grabbed the other, forced her arms behind her back and pushed down on her, sealing her mouth harder over his cock.

'Suck me, you bitch. Don't worry about yourself.'

He was jerking at her, thrusting his cock deeper into her mouth, his voices beginning to grunt again, then swearing again in French as he came. Coughing, choking, she struggled to swallow his semen as it pulsed thickly and saltily into her. When he had finished he released her hands, withdrew his cock, stood up, pushed her away from him. As she sprawled on the floor, still coughing, a heavy boot descended on her buttocks, sinking cruelly into their softness, pinning her to the marble floor, holding her down as the helmet was unstrapped and pulled roughly off her head. The boot spurned her, lifted free of her, and began to thump against the floor in contra-rhythm with its twin, departing from her as, beneath the crystalline chiming of a hidden clock, his voices rumbled at her from their unchanged positions: 'The hour is up, so that is enough. I have left a gift for you in the bedroom.'

Six

The gift was a book. Plain white cover with the title in black. It was lying on one of the mirror-tables in her bedroom. She picked it up. Then put it down. The mirror-table was no mirror-table, for the mirror was no mirror. It was a screen. A screen catching an image projected – she turned, craning her neck – from a dark opening high in one wall. An image caught inside some cupola of the Schloss and bounced from mirror to mirror until it slipped into her room to lie against this not-mirror of this not-mirror-table. A pale image, leached of colour by its passage from the outside world. A garden. A pale image of a garden lying under bright sunshine (her skin tingled to look at it). A garden with an ornamental lake, long terraces, pornographic topiary sculpted from dark ever-greens, the white marble of pornographic classical sculp-tures (her pupils widened with recent experience, her anus tensing and wincing at one of them: a tableau of Pan buggering a nymph). He had meant her to see all this, or else why had he left the book here?

But after a minute or so she had seen all she wished to see, for the moment. She reached to pick up the book and then let her hand fall. In the garden something had moved. A dark figure on one of the most distant terraces. Hooded. With its back to her. Glancing back for a moment before descending an invisible set of steps and disappearing. Anna frowned. For a moment she had started to know who it was. A woman. A woman she had seen before. But who? Where? When?

She picked up the book again, half-expecting another movement from the garden. But nothing. She looked at the front cover of the book. It said: *222 Ways of Sodom*. She opened at random and blinked in surprise. It was not written in the Roman alphabet and yet she could understand it.

εχοππλ παπγγτ ϛϥⲝοϥ λλϛλιϕгτ οπϥгχτϥιϥ χπτγгγ.
ϛοτρνιοω нλτνιϕгε εϲогχϕλгϛοτωϛι μονοϕ ϕπιπθιнιрϥ
πγϥνγн γπωχϲπολι. τλοϕϥιρκγρ нγπϕκιχⲝθϥλⲝ λτλχθκιрг
ϕκγλχορκ λοτωχⲝτ μεггιϕγθϛ. εлхϕλϲθ χλιτργγг
λλрϕϕγμχⲝ θοⲝοπнωκιθ ωϛενλ ιλθ τχοωгκ. ϕομωγϕ
ϛμιϕϛοτεθϥ ωλγωλннιθπλ χοθχτκιϕг τχπχκι βοπϥχⲝ.
ωϛιπορλγнοⲝοτ ϕϛενгγττ гοχθϕμε χϛιω ονχνιπϕοϲε
ϛϕγθнορϛοπн нτοχⲝθнχн θγχεμγр λχροогг οϕϛολμ
ϲιнрεωωι γτωрπιωκγθнιрϥ гλετθγрκ εκογθτχωκο ⲝχπϥχⲝ
ⲝλγϲιι ωγϥγρн ⲝγгγϕολγϕ λεргϕ χοτιϥιιϕχπκιπϥ θτγϕϕοπн.
ιλεχκγτωμιⲝοχλ οнπχϕεωχγθοθн τⲝοωλκωκγ νοτχοϥ
γⲝοϲγϛг. χθνλλμγθϛερн нχнϕορκωϛινχϥ λλχϲγιτ οππτοнι.
ωκγτοωε χκχλν рκ λнгτοωλ ϥμγγнπγⲝοн βγχϛμιτϕ
гεθγμχιϲ χϲκιργг ϕπομνω. τλγωλοορ гγрⲝοτϕγг γθωλ
εгοχгλλιπ нχⲝτιωλг ϥμγλгорнϥγро рεϕωι. ιγλγϕϥγτ
επγωλοτχγνορ ϲχωγπϕοϥο. χωλθγω εθγⲝϲεγωοωι
νοωωνγ τιнϛιεг ⲝγϕⲝλοнκ нχϲπλτοεωχϕ. ωκιτϲο τεμελιϥ
βοχλгοεϲ ϥγλϕοτϕγнχιн οⲝιрϕχϕ γωγτω ιωωλιτ μχнωγг
εϲιρϥ μγχοϲιнγπ. χκιρεωωγ ϥλποϕχρ χγλγϕ μθογω.
ϕγοτϕϲεθгχⲝр ϛιτλκγγλτ гϕχργϛϛ ϛγϲλλγр λрχγλοτ
τκιλχπϛϕχϕω гϲοθ γрωχϕϛι ϲοωϕο. ιτωϛινοнω ωπιθθιг
нγⲝριрϥ нγϥλог κγτⲝπεϥϥοτιπϥ ϥγχονω μοωϛχ.
λλεωετπγ ϕθιон λγрϕϕλμ ωγνεⲝοπг ωλοθχϛεπϥι
χρωβγϕϥκ. ωλγωεπχϕκγϕ χλχοπϥ θεϕ
χϕτϲνεϕϛχθκιрг ϥκχτρορκ οϛιγрωϕχλο ⲝоргхⲝ ικεοθ
νλгλϛοϛλγτ χτχονγ. ελεωβοχϥκϕκο μχρλονολοϲ
γгнοθгγϲϥγϕ рχπλιτϕϛτιγ χρωγнγ. τκγτιωνχν
ϥϛγποϕογβ ετϛιχοϥλεπϕ. ωκχτωγπογ рοϕ
гλπιτλϲπιοϲτι εϕϛοнϛοτ κοϕⲝιχτχ νοθϲοθκοχ κιτϥερχ.
οϕнχⲝοω ελειροϥιειπϥ ιχⲝϛνοϥλ οϕβγχϥκωϛιχ επππλⲝϕελε
ϕλχινλ χⲝκοτ. ιγχⲝϲгγϕ ϛιτχλτχϥ οϛοπϥϛλπ λϛϲεωωο
οθωγ λιτλεπχιπϥ νιωωλϲⲝεχγ βοωκοω. τϛογϥγιω ногι

ωβοφχοη χγφκϥγφϛεφφοπϥϛχττγϲ. ιγχϩтнιт κοτφaмιθ
κιϲϛγοϥ εϛοοπωϥχλι ϥοϥιγϛφκο πγϲεοнγλιϥεθнπχнϥ
κοϥπγнтεϲιтχ. ϩοχϥλοπн ϛοϲτθοεϥοϥκεργ θχϩοχϩιт
λιϥгεθω ϩχϩϛχλο νοταγγγλιϥ λμχaнεπгθγιϥ χωγρι
γϛωλγθατχοτγωγλ χϛγπκτ ιχϩωι οϩοττιιρ. нγτργφο
ϛιττγπϛ χκγβγποπφ κοχφγπϛ ετχaωοϥ ϥαφϛο
πιτφεϲϩιωχγθ. φκοτωχιφωοπκ χϩнεφϲ. aγεεнλ
φϛιγρτϩγχϥκ θγθορφοϲγπιοθϥωκγ ραοτι aнωλοθaωaϲ
τφετφορϛχϲ нγτε ωογχργ πιλοω ϛγφπχφο λγϲϛaχωορϛ
χθωλι τγϥο aϛφϛοπχϲχϩнολιϲοθн ϛοπμχθ ωγωκιϲεφφγ.
οχφθμεοφχθ γϩγφφκο χγπϥχϩορн ωκγωτϥιθγρн.
εγaγτгοφ κιφϩελμ ωχϛιφгιωο ργωγθϛ οωωκιτπαφφ
λχρφϲaμaϛ ϛοϲϩγχγμργ λπεнгγϲχγχ. χλγθaχaϲεωϛ
φϛγχθωϩχϩϥλ θϲγθοϲμι. ωϛγρεφφγ φϲнοφκοτιρϥ гλετθφ
aϩιφχκο χϩθгχϩοнεγπ ϥaϩιϲγρκγφ гaнϲμιχοπιραχ.

She dropped the book, turned away from the not-mirror-
table, doubling up, and began to vomit, feeling even through
the pain in her belly and throat the stabbing pain in her anus
as the sphincter tightened with each spasm of disgust driving
the contents of her belly up and out. With the first bolus she
could taste his semen, mixed with honey (how? she was
asking herself even as she continued to vomit), pouring,
dripping from her mouth to form a small pool on the carpet.

Now she could smell his semen too, and the honey. It
seemed to be all she had in her stomach. She had started
to cry, and a few tears splashed into the pool before she
turned away from it and stumbled towards the bed. She
needed oblivion (the scene in the book was repeating in her
head, and she feared her reaction this time might be,
however infinitesimally, different) and sleep was the fastest,
the cleanest, the surest way to oblivion. Her next-to-last
thought, as she slipped aching, her arse and arsehole still
burning from the cane-stroke and buggery, down the dark
slope to sleep, was of the mysterious honey in her stomach.
Her last thought, almost at the foot of the slope, almost
absorbed into oblivion, was of the mysterious chocolate in
her arse.

* * *

She opened her eyes again, widened them, looking up at the painted ceiling. A smile of cruel satisfaction had appeared on the lips of God, and the apprehension on the face of the slender Eve had been replaced by pain and tears. He had whipped her: streaks of noded red had appeared on the satin hemisphere of an arse-cheek and she was reaching back to grip at her burning flesh, soothe it. How had the painting been changed? A ceiling panel slid away, replaced by another? Had Bärengelt – the pains and aches in her body, half-submerged during sleep, re-emerged fully at the thought of him – been watching her as she slept? And how long had she slept?

She sat up, looking towards the not-mirror-table and the screen. But it was dark: the garden was not there. She gasped. Something had moved on the floor beside the not-mirror-table: wide wings, opened, closed. There were huge tropical butterflies – velvet or metallic yellow, white, red, green, purple – clustering at the pool of her honey/semen vomit, sipping at it through the thick black threads of unreeled proboscises. Another of them slowly opened and closed its wings.

She pushed the bedclothes off, crawled to the edge of the bed, climbed to the floor, groaning a little with pain. She stood straight and peered over her shoulders at her arse, trying to see the cane-stroke across it. She couldn't, but her fingers told her – she winced – that it was at the first tender, swollen stage of bruising. She tightened her anus experimentally and winced again: a shaft of pain had speared upwards inside her, retracing the route of his lubricated cock.

She looked back towards the butterflies: they did not seem to have noticed her at all. She took a step towards them and was halfway through another when, unpeeling left and right around the pool, they took lazily to the air. But not because of her, she felt: at some hidden signal. Bärengelt was watching her from somewhere in the room.

She examined the cane-stroke in a mirror: it had darkened, turning purple, almost black at the edges. She picked up a hand-mirror from one of the tables and squatted to examine her cunt. The lips were tender, minutely cut and bruised by the crowding fish, and the walls of her vagina (spreading her legs, she folded back her cunt-lips) were streaked and patterned with ideograms of abuse: she remembered the care with which she had had to hook dead fish from herself after Bärengelt had left her sprawled on the bathroom floor. Her anger at him was growing and, as she stood up and replaced the hand-mirror, she gestured obscenely at the air, hoping he was still watching her on the screen inside the helmet she knew he was wearing as he sat waiting for her now in the Black Room thirteen floors below.

The gesture froze in the air, her hand suddenly beginning to tremble in time with the thumping of her heart. Beth was walking across the room in one of the mirrors again. No, not Beth: Gwen. Naked, head shaven. In the room, but not in the room. She seemed to be walking towards the door of the bathroom, disappeared from the mirror, reappeared in another, disappeared, reappeared, yes, walking towards the bathroom. Anna realised that she had been holding her breath and released it. Gwen disappeared from the final mirror. Anna walked after her (though Gwen had never been there – only on the mirrors) and lifted aside the curtains of the bathroom door. No one was there.

She stepped back into her bedroom and went from mirror to mirror, examining them, running her fingertips and fingernails across them, even tapping them. She found nothing and saw no one in the mirrors again. She crossed the room quickly, trying not to look towards the door of the bathroom, and walked out on to the stairs. She descended them quickly, half-running, reached the bottom, crossed the mosaic, planting her feet with conscious rebellion on the face and body of the abusing Pan, and entered the Black Room. Across the room, he sat awaiting her in his black throne behind the glass table. The speakers coughed as though they had just been switched on and his voices rumbled at her.

'Good morning.'

She shrugged as she walked across the carpet to stand at the table.

'Is it morning?'

'If I say it is. Did you sleep well?'

For a moment she wondered whether to mention what she had seen: Gwen, in the mirror. No.

'How did you expect me to sleep? My arse hurts. My cunt hurts. Because of you. And my stomach, when I think of that . . . book. It was vile.'

'Good. Good. I am glad to hear you are in pain. But do not speak of the book in that way, as though you have discarded it. It was vile, and it *is* vile. You will read it again. You will read it again today.'

'No. Never. I feel sick to be near you, knowing that you wrote it.'

'I did not write it.'

'Who did?'

'I will answer no questions, not till you have beaten me at dice. So choose a die and roll.'

She thought of picking up all four dice waiting on the table and throwing them into his face – only he had no face, only the blank, black, eyeless mask of the helmet. She turned the dice over slowly with a fingertip, reacquainting herself with their faces. On the first: faces with four spots, and faces with none. On the second: all faces with three spots. On the third: faces with six spots, and faces with two. On the fourth and last: faces with five spots, and faces with one. She chose die four: five spots and one. He air-tapped die three: six spots, and two.

She rolled hers. A five.

She rolled his. A six.

A one. A two.

A five. A two.

A five. A six.

A one. A two.

A one. A six.

A one. A two.

A five. A two.

A one. A six.

A five. A two.

A five. A two.

A one. A two.

A five. A two.

'I win,' his voices rumbled. 'Your body is entirely mine for the entirety of an hour. Over to the whipping-horse.'

She clenched her fists momentarily, thinking of refusing, throwing an accusation of cheating at him. He stood up.

'Disobedience, little Anna, will be punished most severely. And I should so hate to cane you across that exquisite young bruise, which is developing so well. To the whipping-horse. Now!'

She turned away from the table and walked across the black carpet to the whipping-horse.

'Sit astride it.'

She climbed on to it and lay forwards, slipping her feet and hands into the stirrups and waiting for him to tighten the straps.

'There will be no need for that. I do not intend to cane you again – if you behave. Merely to examine this exquisite abused arse of yours at close quarters. Watch.'

The helmet was slipped over her head again, and the screen sprang open with a close-up of her buttocks and upper thighs, videoed from the camera in the iron flower.

'See how it is beginning to develop?'

The tip of the cane came into shot and delicately traced the furrow of the stroke it had delivered the previous day. She shivered.

'The technical term is extravasation, I believe,' his voices rumbled. 'A transient ecchymosis. Beneath unbroken skin blood seeps from damaged tissue and a number of complex chemical and physiological changes begins to take place. *Vulgatim*, it is a "bruise". For the lumpen majority of mankind the term is adequate, but for you it is very sadly inadequate. For you, I have coined the word *skinflower*. I have sown the broad seed of a skinflower into the field of your arse and will now watch it grow and bloom. Against a skin such as yours, its development shall be an unsurpassed spectacle. I have decided against a permanent record of it: the video recording I am making shall be destroyed unviewed. Instead, I must try to store up an unfading memory of it by daily inspections. Watch.'

The scene on the helmet screen swung back and up a little and she could see that he was releasing his cock. He stepped on to the whipping-horse, lowered himself over her naked buttocks.

'An unfading memory: visual and tactile –' she jerked as he began to stroke the head of his cock against the bruise '– even olfactory. Gustatory.'

He stepped off the whipping-horse and the screen inside the helmet suddenly snapped off. There was a click behind her and when his voices rumbled at her again there was a different quality to them. He had taken his helmet off, retaining the microphone that caught his words and transmitted them to the rumbling, concealed speakers. She heard him sniffing.

'Your skin smells delicious. I am sure it always has, but surely it has been seasoned and spiced by this skinflower. I can smell the collected blood. Can I taste it?'

This time she gasped, for cold lips were pressing to her arse, and a tongue had begun to lick left and right along the groove of the cane-stroke. And what was that faint, bristling harshness above and below the probing lips? A beard?

'You taste exquisite too. I should love to eat your arse. How firm, yet how soft it is!'

Gloved hands began to cup and knead the cheeks of her buttocks.

'*Quel cul!* What an arse! The Greeks had a term for it, you know: καλλιπυγη. *Callipygé. Schönarschige.* She-beautifully-arsed. One might devote a lifetime to study of this arse and do no more than scratch the surface. And how delicious to scratch the surface of this exquisite arse! To draw a splinter of sharpened diamond across its delicate curves and see tiny beads of infinitely more precious ruby well up. And how even more delicious to put one's mouth to those rubies and lick them up! Savour them on one's tongue!'

He snorted, the gloved hands squeezing harder for a second, and then the lips and tongue were back again, working left and right in the groove of the cane-stroke, then up the cleft of her arse, then down dropping low enough for his tongue to work against her anus (her sphincter tightened, and the shaft of fire spurted again inside her bowels).

Then his lips and tongue were withdrawn and the screen inside her helmet snapped back on. She watched him climbing back on to the whipping-horse, tugging at the head of his cock, grunting to himself. She jerked again, moaning a little as he laid the head of his cock back to the bruise, rubbing it slowly left and right over the skin moistened and lubricated by his saliva.

'*Wunderbar*,' he muttered. '*Es ist sehr gut. Wunderbar.*'

He shifted his cock, now beginning to slide it up and down the broad cleft of her buttocks, pressing it against the hot, saliva-sticky coin of her anus, sliding it higher again, sliding it left and right in the groove of the cane-stroke. He began to speak, his words punctuated by gasps and grunts of pleasure and excitement (on the screen his black, leather-encased body jerked and rose, concealing and revealing the white plain and hemispheres of her back and buttocks as he guided the head of his cock over her arse).

'What further proof – of God's existence – could be – required than this – this – arse? It is designed – to give pleasure, inside – and out. This cleft was – designed for my cock – I swear it. See how – they fit each – other so perfectly! Oh, *Callipygé*, what – I would give – to bugger thee – again, *now* – but by restraint I shall – double my pleasure – in the final reckon–ing and this is – more than – sufficient for – now. There! there! Canst thou feel me flood over thee?'

She could: his warm semen was spurting over her buttocks, provokingly gentle against the re-awakened ache of the re-abused bruise. He stepped off the whipping-horse, folding away his cock, casually saluting the camera in the iron flower.

'*Danke*, *Liebling*. But now, on your feet again – my second hour of control has many minutes yet to run.'

The helmet screen snapped off again and she got carefully off the whipping-horse, feeling the trickling semen on her buttocks change direction and speed as she stood up again. She reached a hand to wipe at it, smear it flat so it would not flow, and gasped in pain. A gloved hand had closed tight on her shoulder.

'No, Annaleinchen. It is a token of my dominion over you. It must be left to its own devices. While we make a short journey. To the greenhouse. To warm air and . . . *und die Schmetterlinge.*'

The trickling semen had reached the crease below her buttocks, some of it flowing inwards around the curves of her upper thighs to find, ticklingly, the delicate skin of her inner thighs. She was marched by him across the room, blind in the blinded helmet, her feet falling as silently as his boots into the deep carpet; and then the air was suddenly colder on her skin as her feet fell on to cold marble again. They had left the Black Room. The trickling semen had reached her knees now, finding the sensitive popliteal hollow behind each, and was beginning to run in separate threads down her calves, on to her ankles and feet. The humiliation of it against her skin was strong, and yet somewhere in her a wanton submission was rejoicing in it, proud to wear and endure this fluid symbol of being broken to his will.

They climbed a stair (the treads cold marble, colder marble, cold marble, colder marble), and then her nostrils caught a warm humid scent of vegetation coming from ahead of her. Tendrils of warm air brushed against her skin. She cleared her throat.

'The greenhouse?'

The gloved hand tightened on her shoulder again as though in momentary surprise. Then speakers woke high above her, fastened, she supposed, to the walls of the corridor down which they were marching.

'*Ja. Das Gewächhaus. Und die Schmetterlinge.*'

She was enfolded completely by the warm air now, the cold marble growing cool, warm, under her feet, and then he had pushed her ahead of him through a doorway (a fine, warm spray of water passed over half of her body, diluting some of the trickle of semen so that it flowed faster over her skin) and she could smell and sense the full presence of a greenhouse.

'*Das Gewächhaus*,' a fresh set of speakers rumbled from a wide, tall space ahead of her. 'The greenhouse. Forwards!'

He pushed her forward into a warm, humid, whispering space that she could sense opening to each side of her and rising high above her. She walked forwards on warm marble, sprays of warm water passing over her again at regular intervals, until his semen had been mostly washed from her. After fifty, sixty, seventy strides, he turned her, pushed her backwards and down, and she gasped as cold metal touched her skin.

'Keep still,' his voices rumbled. Metal snicked and clanked, closing coldly over her wrists and ankles, nudging against and settling to the skin of her knees and elbows, buttocks, thighs, back. The screen inside her helmet snapped on again, and there she was, videoed from somewhere above the door through which he had pushed her, a white Christ/ina crucified against a framework of glittering steel, an offering on the altar of a cathedral of vegetative greens and fallen fragments of rainbow: the greenhouse was huge, six or seven or eight times head-height, the central spine of its arched roof studded with glowing lights beneath which the air sparkled with the fine jets of automatic sprinklers, its sides crowded with orchids in full, vivid bloom against huge, hexagonal panes of mirrored glass that each held an image of the place, stretching its dimensions to phantasmagoria.

Bärengelt was testing the metal framework in which she was held. His cock was out and erect and she could smell the musk of his recent ejaculation through the scent of humus and orchids and, warmed by the air now, the leather of his bodysuit. He stepped back, stood to one side, tugged at a lever. The framework tightened on her like a powerful but toothless jaw, lifting her wholly helpless from the ground; opening and adjusting her legs so that her cunt was presented naked and exposed to the air; pressing at and arching her back so that her breasts swelled, swung, lifted, white and cherry-nippled.

'Your nipples,' his voices rumbled, 'point upwards at an angle of 34°22'. How do they feel?'

The index and middle finger of his right hand, encased in warm, smooth leather, closed over her right nipple as though over the stub of a cigarette or cigar, and he began to squeeze and twist and tug at it, hard and cruel, but slowly, very slowly, as though he was trying to wring each drop of sensation out of the singing nerves of her tit. His left hand swung up and began to brush gently at her left nipple, the gentleness of his fingers here heightening the pain in her right nipple, the sensations of the caressing and the twisting mixing inside her, both nipples stiffening, the lips and chamber of her exposed cunt beginning to swell and ooze, pain and pleasure increasing the flow of sweat that the heat of the greenhouse had already begun to draw from her skin.

'Do you like this?' his voices rumbled.

'No . . .' she said, gasping as he twisted momentarily harder at her right nipple. 'It hurts.'

'Some of it hurts. But the part that is bitter strengthens the part that is sweet, and the part that is sweet strengthens the part that is bitter, like black against white, like white against black. Like salt on your tongue with honey.'

He swung himself across her and, still torturing one nipple, caressing the other, began to rub his erect prick against her thighs and stomach. She felt the heat glowing in its unpeeled head, gliding up and down against her sweat-slickened skin. His torturing fingers left her right nipple (the pain glowed on, fed by the gentle touch of the fingers of his left hand at her left nipple). The movements of his cockhead against her skin changed, became directed, purposeful, and she knew his right hand had gripped his cock, was rubbing it against her skin, rotating the head to smear it fully with her sweat. She felt the hard stud of the lens of the fibre-optic camera again and imagined what it was showing him as his cockhead slid to and fro over her white skin.

Then he pulled his cock away from her and began to gasp, a tremor of movement reaching her through the fingers of his left hand: he was masturbating himself, his cockhead lubricated with her sweat. She expected him to come on her, spraying his semen up her belly, over her breasts, and flinched when his gasps deepened to a groan, shuddering out from the speakers, and she knew he had come. But there was no spray of semen against her belly and as he released her left nipple and stepped away from her, his black body swinging to unshield her white one, she saw on the helmet-screen that his gloved right hand was clenched over the head of his cock: he had caught his semen inside it.

'Salt on your tongue, with honey,' his voices rumbled. 'Taste this.'

He moved back to her, lifting his right hand, opening it so that semen began to drip from it, falling towards the floor (a few drops caught her skin). He smeared the hand over her mouth.

'Lick,' his voices rumbled. 'Hold it on your tongue.'

Her stomach opened and dropped. Her nostrils were already full of the musk of his semen, rising from her smeared lips. She opened her mouth and slowly passed her tongue over her lower lip, harvesting what he had sown there.

'Hold it on your tongue. Taste this.'

He was pushing the fingers of his left hand at her mouth now, and a different scent expanded in her nostrils. Honey. She licked at his fingers, full of honey.

'Salt on your tongue, with honey,' his voices rumbled, and his hands, laden with honey, laden with semen, were pressed against her mouth, rubbing and smearing.

'Lick them.'

She licked, tasting harmonics of leather beneath the fundamentals of semen and honey.

'Is it good?'

She nodded, still licking, working her tongue down and between his leather-encased fingers, the stitching of the glove rough under her tongue, cutting slightly into her. His hands suddenly jerked away from her, and her surprise hung for a second and then was smashed as they returned to her, lower, harsher, clasped together into a double fist that he drove into the pit of her stomach with, from all along the walls of the greenhouse, arriving overlaid with split-second delays that she had not noticed before, his triumphant cries of 'Bbbiiitttchchch!'

She threw up down herself, choking and gagging in the metal framework, flooded with tears at the pain of the blow, the pain of his treachery, his cruelty. He was laughing as she vomited and choked and wept, and his hands returned to her, closing on the vomit oozing down between her breasts, beginning to smear it wider over her body, working it into her breasts and nipples, into the sweat-glossy hollows of her shaved armpits, scraping it together to press a handful against her cunt, smear it over the lips and inside the chamber.

He stepped back from her and through a haze of tears she saw her body white against the metal framework, light glistening from the smeared vomit, brighter than the glistening of her sweat and the trickles of her cunt-juice.

'It is time,' his voices announced. '*Die Schmetterlinge!*'

He gripped and heaved at another lever on the framework. Some of the hexagonal mirror-panes in the walls of the greenhouse slid aside, and clouds of colour, silk kites, artificial birds, no, living butterflies, tropical butterflies, giant ones and dwarf ones, metallic and pastel, green, gold, red, orange, blue, purple, white, yellow, were pouring into the cathedral space of the greenhouse air, breaking apart and diffusing up/down/left/right like dye poured into clear water, flapping along the orchid-lined walls, bright mobile flowers sampling bright immobile flowers, their moving colours and shapes thrown back by the hexagonal mirror-panes, but soon scenting the semen/honey/sweat/cunt-juice/ vomit with which her white body was smeared and stained and beginning to move down and towards, gliding and flapping up the diffusion gradient of her scents.

The first landed on her right breast, wings wide and metallic green against her white skin on the helmet-screen, its feet like six velvet needles, and began to dab its tongue – another velvet needle – at her glistening nipple and areolae. She groaned: the shuttling delicacy with which it drank was sharpening the ache of the abuse the nipple had endured. Another butterfly, tigerishly striped in gold and blue, joined it drinking at the nipple; another, metallic blue, landed on her left breast; there was a cloud of them sampling the scented air at her cunt, the insubstantial zephyrs of their wingbeats tickling at her inner thighs. One landed, each foot reported separately by her sensitised skin, jumped a little into the air again, and was dipping its proboscis into the smeared and oozing lips and oval of her cunt; another landed; a third, and fourth, and fifth, and one of those at her breasts took to the air in a neat hop that ended it head-down on her *mons Veneris*, where it began to drink and shuffle downwards towards the liquid richness that had enticed it away.

On the screen her body was almost veiled now by shifting screens of the butterflies, emptying from the wider air on to the most strongly scented space around her body, landing on her in twos and threes and dozens, reclothing her with their shifting wings. The sensations of their tiny feet against her skin, the tiny threading pulses of their proboscises, were multiplying second by second, and on the screen her body was covered now in a living, shifting cloth, broad coloured wings opening and closing windows through which her white skin was discovered and covered, the larger butterflies treading on the smaller, all thirsty for the sweet and briny fluids with which she was coated, with her nipples and cunt, more thickly coated, attracting greater numbers, as though she was wearing a *peignoire* of butterflies over a bikini of butterflies.

Again there was the paradox of watching herself at metres' distance and feeling or smelling what she watched no more than a skin's-breadth or inhalation away: the rainbow cloth of butterflies treading and flapping on the helmet-screen; their feet and probing tongues on her skin; the tickling acrid or creamy, musky or sweet dust of their moving wings wafted to her nostrils. The dislocation yawned inside her mind, a mental cunt gaping for penetration, sharpening to the pleasure sewn into her by the butterfly tongues busy on her nipples and the lips of her cunt, on her unsheathed clitoris (a fragile tongue was working like fever on the *glans*), so that her cunt oozed thickly, adding a marine musk of arousal to the tickling dust rising from the butterflies' wings.

'Arse,' his voices rumbled. 'Your arse. Open it.'

On the helmet-screen she watched him tug at another lever, and from somewhere in the framework behind her a blunt point of cold metal rose to press against her anus.

'Little pig, little pig,' his voices rumbled. On the helmet-screen she watched him jerk at the lever so that the nub left her anus and rose again to it, left it and rose to it, left it and rose to it. She relaxed her sphincter and gasped as the metal pushed slowly into and inside her, a bar, a rod of cold metal that rose inside her bowels like a never-softening cock, almost searing her with cold, stretching and filling her almost to the point at which she feared she would be split open by it. There was a dark pleasure in the penetration and she realised she had gasped aloud as her sphincter was pushed open and the rod began to rise into her.

'Auto-pilot, now,' his voices rumbled.

A faint throbbing began in the framework to which she was strapped and the rod fell away, then rose again, fell away and rose again, raping into her, relenting, raping into her, relenting, and began, startlingly, to swell and shrink in size so that the sphincter of her anus stretched and relaxed, stretched and relaxed. Orgasm had been incipient in her body before, being stitched together by the busy tongues of butterflies, but the buggering metal was too much for her: it had thrust into her fewer than a dozen times before she was crying out with pleasure, her anus clenching on the thrusting phallus-rod, the bruised walls of the chamber of her cunt clenching on each other, sparking pain that heightened the pleasure, the butterfly tongues finding the bruises on the lips of her cunt, delicately reawakening the aches of the abuse she had suffered in the giant bath, Celtic curlicues, arabesques on the rocketing eruption of orgasm.

And when orgasm was gone the phallus-rod was still rocking and thrusting into her bowels, the butterfly tongues still busy against her skin, and she knew Bärengelt intended her to come again, and again, until the second hour of his dominion was up. She felt warm and thick fluid begin to spurt from the phallus-rod in simulated ejaculation, pooling in her lower bowels, slowly pumped deeper into her bowels by the movement of the rod, then drained from them as the rod hummed and began to suck her empty, still rising and falling. She groaned, unable to control the response of her flesh to this new assault on her senses, and fresh butterflies were deserting her tongued-clean nipples and breasts for her streaming armpits and the still-flowing well of her cunt: threads of cunt-juice had leaked down her thighs almost as far as her knees, and the butterflies seemed almost drunken on her, their wingbeats coming in wild and irregular bursts, sending warm breezes up her body, across the newly deserted skin of her breasts and sternum, exciting the clusters of butterflies at her right and left armpits, tongues probing busily into her sweat.

She groaned and began to come again, her anus clenching again on the thrusting phallus-rod, her empty cunt aching to clench on the same thrusting hardness. The rod began to ejaculate into her again, the thick fluid hotter, denser, pooling under gravity, pistoned up into her. She realised she was working to thrust her buttocks against it in contra-rhythm, to enhance the stretching, hollow, alien sensation of this giant metal invader of the chamber that lay beyond her arsehole.

Dazedly she became aware that Bärengelt had stepped in front of her, that his voices were rumbling at her, telling her to come again. She tried to answer, breath drawn moistly in and out of her mouth on the uncontrollable gasping with which she responded to the buggering rod, but she couldn't.

'Come again, you bitch,' his voices rumbled (the framework trembled with the bass). His black-gloved right hand rose again to her right nipple, gripped it, twisted, tugged, harsh and cruel, as his left hand cradled her left breast, squeezed it gently, rocked it from side to side, stroked the skin in a loose, inward spiral that ended with gentle tweaking of her left nipple.

'Come again, bitch! Again! Now!'

The fingers of his right hand tugged at her right nipple as though it were rubber, the skin of her breast rising beneath it, then released it, allowing it to snap back against her. The hand dropped towards her cunt and grabbed suddenly at the butterflies clustering there: on the screen they exploded on to the air with fright, and she heard those his hand had caught crumple and splinter in his grip like tough paper and delicate wood. He began to stuff the handful of murdered butterflies inside her, sliding them between the lips of her cunt, poking them deeper into her. The thought of this beauty destroyed struck at her like a blow, underlaid with the pleasure the stuffing hand was bringing her, its fingers welcome inside her streaming emptiness, the wings and bodies of the butterflies scraping the walls of her cunt-chamber with a soothing irritation.

And she began to come again, cunt tightening on the remains of the murdered butterflies, anus clenching again on the working phallus-rod of the automatic sodomiser. The rod began to spurt again into her, the fluid almost a sludge now, almost at scalding heat, and then, without draining her, sank away and left her body with a muddy belch. The fluid began to leak from her gaping anus, stinging the back of her thighs with heat.

Then his gloved right hand, sticky with her juice, dusted and sprinkled with the remains of the butterflies, was at her lips again, and his voices were rumbling at her.

'Lick it clean.'

Seven

Back upstairs she did not dare take a bath for many minutes, fearful that the second hour – she did not know when it had begun – was not yet over and that he would appear as he had done the previous day, to force some new horror on her. Up her.

So, shivering with fear and tiredness, smeared with honey and semen, coated with wing-dust and wing-fragments from the butterflies, aching fiercely at cunt and arse and right tit, she had waited while the clocks in her bedroom chimed away enough time, and more than enough time; and she then walked into the bathroom and ran the taps. The dead fish that had covered the floor on the previous day were gone and the bath gleamed as though new-made, all its encircling caryatids intact, unstained. She bathed for nearly an hour, half-lolling, half-swimming through shoals of foam – she had discovered a well-stocked cupboard of scents and gels behind one of the tapestries that hung around the walls – then climbed out, dried herself on another of the tapestries (sapphic nymphs in an olive-grove), and came into her bedroom intending to go straight to bed.

The book had stopped her. She remembered that she had dropped it the previous day when she had begun to vomit, but there it was again on the mirror-table that was no mirror-table. She walked to the table and placed her hand slowly, reluctantly, on the book, looking into the not-mirror in the hope of seeing something that would kill

the worm of curiosity in her head. But the screen was dark.
She opened the book.

ΧΚΟΔΚΥΠΥΤΟ ΟѠФΟΜΙΠΥΧΥΤ ѠΥФSΥΥΗΗΟ ΧΓѠSΙΤΥΔS.
ΙΔΔΓΔΥΧѠΙ ΙΡΟΠΙϤФΤΟϤ ΒΙΠΗΤФSΓΥΓΟΥѠΥC ФΧΚΥC
ФΖΥѠΔΔΧΘΚѠSΙ ѠΟΖΥΠ. ΕΑΧΔΕФΔSΓ ΚΙCΜΙSФ ΟΙФΗΥФΤΧ
ΙΗΗΧCΥΡΚΧΚΙΖΙΙΧΔΙ ẍΜΑΧΓѠѠФΥΙΘΤϤΥΧΘ SΙФФSΔΔΜΓΙϤ ΙΡΓΔΧΟΤ
SΟФΧΔΧΖΟ ФΠΔΔѠΜΥΠ. ΙΧΔϤΔΧΥΓΗ SΟФФΟΗΚΧΥΙC
ΧΔΙΡΥCΗΟФ ΔΥФCΧSΚΤΗ ΔΙΗϤΔΧΖ. ΕΥΧΔΔΧ ѠΚCΥΧΚΔΧФ
ΙѠФΚΙ ΙΗẍΔΒ ΧΔΟϤΠΕΓΥΤϤФΟΟΝΥΠS ΕФΥѠ ΓΔФѠФSΙ ΔΧΘΙ.
ΙΠ ΕΧΕΜΟѠSΥ ѠѠΕΠΘΥSS ΙФФΚΥ ΤSΔΧΠΗΙΤ.
ΕCФΟΙΝ ϤΝΧΔϤΧФ CΧΠΤΥΡΚ ΔΔФΧΗΔΥФ ΓΕΤΧ ΟΘΔΔΚΔ ѠΔẍΙ
SΟѠФΟΡSΟ ΗΤΥΕΘΗ ΗΔΤѠΕ ΥΤSΟSΧΙ ΠΟѠФΥΤ ϤΥΝΧΖ
ΒΥѠΚΙSΕΟΘФ ΔΕΧΔΜΟΟФ ФΘΠΟФΧΙCΧΘΚ ѠΔΕΠΗ. ФΚΙФ
ΙΤΙΝΠΙΧCΧϤΕΜ ΤΧΙΧΔΔΧФΔSS SΟΤΜΟΓФ ΙCΘ ΟΧΖΚΥ ΥΜΔΔΧ
ѠΧΟΡФΚΙ ФSΧΔΗΗΟC. ΙΥΧΥΤΓΟC SΥCẍΟΘΧ ΓΧΤΖΙCΗΟΘΗ ФΜΟΗΥ
ΕΥΧΤϤΜΥΔϤΠΕẍΤΟΔΕФΥϤ ϤΧΓΜΔCSΥΤ ΟCѠΙΔΕΧ ΙΧΖΜΘΔΒ
ѠSΙΜΠ ΗΙΧΘΧ ΧΘΟΓΙΧ ΤΟΔΥΡΓΤSΤΥΠ ΜΔФѠΧS ΔΝΧΥΓ ѠΥΟSΧΟΤ
ΙSΥΧΚΠΧΤΟΔΔФ ѠΚФΧΤѠΤ ΕΔΕΘΧΝΠ ΔΔФΟΡϤ ΔCϤΥΤΧΔΥ
ΚΧΟΤΓΤ ѠΧΜΥФ ΚΙФΗΔ. ФSΙΤѠΟΘΓΤ ΤΧΟΙΧΠS ΧΠѠSΙ ΟϤΚΥΟΡΓ
ΙΔΧФΥΠΓ ΔΟФΥΧΙΤ ΧΥѠΚΟ ΧΟΚΥCΥΔФ ΜΟΔΝΧΘѠΚΥ ΕΤФΟ.

She closed her eyes and read the sensations in her body.
Her stomach had tightened, was rolling, and there was a
harsh, sour taste in her mouth. But. But her nipples. And.
And her cunt. Yesterday the book had disgusted her. She
had thrown up. Today the book had disgusted her again.
But it had excited her too. And she could not tell whether
the disgust or the excitement were stronger.

She opened her eyes and turned back several pages to
read again.

ΔΜΔΔΓѠѠΕCΧѠ ѠΥΥΧΔΙ ΕФΥΕΡϤ ΕΥΧCΤΔΧѠѠΠΥΘΚ ΔΔϤΝΕΡϤ
ΓФΧCΓΥΖΘ ΔΡΧΥФSΥ ΧΡΥΘΤΕΤΟΠ. ФSΙѠSΥΕSSΧ ѠSΙΧΕΤΥ
ΓΟΠΥΝΧΤΔΧΡS ΚΟФΟCѠΥ ΠΙΔΥФѠΚΟ ѠΙΠФΕѠΧΔΠΤ
ΟΖΥΘẍΥΧФΥCΕΡΓ ΒΔΥΡ ΔΔΔϤΥΠΟ ΟΧΤФΥ ΔΕФΓΕΠϤ
ΝΔΘSΜΕΤΧΖΡΗ ѠΚΕѠ ΔΥΔΓΥΥΠ ΒΟΟΝ ΧΚΥΠ ΥΧФΔѠΟC.
ΕΥΔΖΥΧΚϤФΕΧ ΧΥѠΚΕΟΔΜ ФΠΧΤΡΙΘϤCΔΡ ΚΙΤΘΧΡS.
ΤSΟѠΙΙΘΤΧΔ SΙѠΙ ΓΕΧΠѠΟΗ ΔΔΧΖΔΟΡ ΔΔΧФΧΟФѠ

74

ΘΤΧϥΧΡΗϕΣΥ ΣΙϹΥΡΚ ΤΕΟΠΥΓ ΚΙϹΟΤΤΥΚΥΝΙΒΥΧΚ ΙΧλΤΓΥΡΗΥϕ
ШΚΟΣϕλΕΡШ. λΝΥλΓ ϕΟΠΥΠ ΕΘϥΧϕ ΕΤΥΟΝΜ λλΒΧΠΗ
ΣΤλΘλΥϹΟΤΚΧΜΥ λΧШΥϹΧΘΗ λΥλϕΗΥΠΗΙϕШ. ΙΥλΖΟΡΙ
ϕΚΙΘ λΡΧΚΥΤΧΤΟΠ. ΥΧ ΥΘϕΚΙϹλΤΟΘ λλΧΥϹΓΟΤΣΙϕ.
ϕΣΟΣΕΕΤΓϕ ΡΧΠΠ ΚΥΤΧΕΓΝΖΕϹΓШΕΠΗ ΣλΠϥΚΙϹ ΥШΥϹ
ШΚΥϹλϕΕΡ ΝΥΗШΕΡΟϕΧ. ΚΙΤΙϕШΥΣΥΜΥ ΥϕΗΤΧϹΡΧΠΗ ΥΠШΥΟΧ
λΧΖϕΣΟΤΡΧΖ ШϕΕΥΘΗ ШλΤλΧΖ. ϕΚΥΧλΠ ΧλΟϹΧΘ
ΕΧΕϹΙΡΙΙΧ. ΙΥΧΚλΠΓ ΥΧΠΥΥΗϥλΟΧΥϥ ϥΙΤϹΟΝ ΥΣϕΚΙ ϹΟШШΥΜ
ΟΘΣΤΧΠϕΥΣ λΥϹΗΙλΟ. ΤΣΟΤΧΟϕΧϕ ШΧϹΙΧΠΥΡΣ ΟΠΓΤλϥΓΟΘΠΕ
ΕΘΕΤΤΧΗ ΝΥΠΕΘΓ ϥΜΧΖΓ ΡΥϹШ ΗϕΧΝ ΣΥϹΤΟλΥΜΥ
ΓλΠΜΧΖΙϥ ΧΙΕΓΧΠΝΧϹΥΣ ΝΧΡΕΟΓ ШλΧШ. ΟШΝΟΡΗΤ ϕΣΧϥΜΠΕ
λΡШλΙΡΧϹΙΠ.

Her right hand moved down to her cunt. She told herself
that she just wanted to feel how aroused she truly was, how
sticky the lips had become, how far they had opened, but
she knew she was lying to herself. The arousal in her cunt
and tits was thick, almost painful, nagging at her to be
crystallised and splintered in orgasm. Victimised, she
longed to victimise. In two days he had twisted, inverted,
perverted her. She wanted to torture others as he had
tortured her. Brutally. Pitilessly. Deliciously.

Her fingers started to brush the lips of her cunt as she
turned back and read the earlier passage in the book. The
pain of it. On another woman. As she imagined herself into
the place of the anti-hero of the action, the pleasure from
her moving fingers deepened, began to rise and fill her
whole body. She lifted her left hand from the page to
squeeze at her nipples, then almost stopped masturbating
as the page she had been holding down turned over. But
now there was another passage in front of her eyes: the
passage that she had read the previous day; that had made
her vomit; that today liquefied her guts with delight and
brought her to a mewing, gasping orgasm before she had
even read halfway through it for the second time.

She closed the book with her left hand – her right hand
was dripping – and walked over to the bed, yelm bubbling
from her cunt as the muscles in her stomach and thighs
relaxed. Suddenly she knew that he was watching her again

(had her subconscious caught the mechanism of a camera being switched on and beginning to hum?). And she wanted to please him. Her master. She climbed on to the bed and crawled to the centre of it. She sat in the lotus-position, cunt presented between her splayed thighs to the watching air, and began to lick the fingers of her right hand. When it was clean she dipped it to her cunt again and masturbated herself to another orgasm, slowly, carefully, staring with unfocused eyes ahead of herself, hoping he was watching and listening to the noise her fingers made as they moved on her cunt.

Orgasm this second time was almost painful – the tendons in her splayed thighs stood out sharply, casting thin shadows on her white skin – and the cunt-juice on her fingers and hand had an added flavour, something delicate, elusive, that she chased with her tongue over the skin of her hand and seemed closest to catching on the webbing between her fingers, as though it had concentrated there. She began masturbating for the third time, gathering a fresh handful of juice with which to please her watching master, but she would not remember whether or when she had orgasmed for the third time, only that sleep overcame her sometime before or after or while.

She awoke as she had done the previous day, the previous days, suddenly, on her back, opening her eyes to the pastiche on the ceiling where, again, there was a change: the smile on God's lips was wider and new whip-strokes had appeared on the arse of Eve, fresh red strokes crossing the darkening, empurpling strokes of the previous day. There was a change inside her too: for the first time that she could remember in the Schloss, she was hungry: her stomach grumbled softly as she climbed out of bed and left the room to descend the stairs to the Black Room and Bärengelt.

She descended quickly, almost running, wanting to see him again, hating herself for wanting to see him again. She crossed the mosaics, feeling her cunt and nipples respond to the images there with a double pleasure: the pleasure of the one desiring to hurt and the one desiring to be hurt. On

76

the first day she had been X, a variable waiting to be filled; yesterday $X = M$; today $X = S + M$. She held apart the curtains of the doorway and stepped through them. Even on the threshold, looking into the room, she saw at once that there was something else on the glass table today: laid out on the table-top between the dice and the chessboard were a bottle and a row of what she saw as she got nearer were (her stomach arpeggioed and her mouth filled with saliva) chocolate bars. Mars bars. Seven of them. And the bottle was champagne. She reached the table and stood at it, resting one hand lightly on the glass.

'I am hungry,' she told the blank mask of his helmet.

'Good,' his voices rumbled at her. 'Good. Choose and roll.'

She chose the die with four spots and none. He airtapped the die with five spots and one.

She rolled hers. A four.

She rolled his. A five.

A four. A five.

A four. A five.

A four. A one.

A zero. A one.

A four. A one.

A zero. A five.

A four. A one.

A four. A five.

A four. A one.

A zero. A five.

A four. A five.

Bärengelt reached out a hand – the glove was gleaming, cleaned or replaced from the previous day – and picked up one of the Mars bars.

'Do you want this?' his voices rumbled.

A thread of saliva had escaped from her mouth before she could lick it back. It dripped from her chin on to her left breast. She wiped at her chin, sucking the rest of the saliva in her mouth back and swallowing.

'Yes,' she said.

'Good. You shall have it.'

He tore the wrapper away from the top of the bar. The smell of chocolate was instantly in her nostrils. Her stomach arpeggioed again, disassembling complex discords.

'Yes, you shall have it. I shall feed it to you myself. Get on top of the table. Kneel on it and turn yourself round so that I have access to your arse.'

She climbed on top of the table, the glass smooth and cool beneath her knees and hands again, and swung to present her arse to him.

'Hold the cheeks apart. I want to see your arsehole. Point it upwards.'

She reached behind herself and pulled the cheeks of her arse apart, tilting her body to aim her anus at the ceiling and the camera she knew was watching there.

'*Wunderbar!* That is one of most beautiful sights in nature: a virgin female arsehole. Tenge. And you are swiffed! So delicately and beautifully swiffed.'

She felt him slip a gloved finger into the dell of her arsehole, stroke and tug gently at her blonde anal hairs.

'Your arsehole is like the cavity of a jewel case made from the pink leather of a foetal gazelle and trimmed with gold silk. So beautiful. Fabergé could not have created anything to match it.'

She felt him brush and tug at her anal hairs again, then heard him sigh strangely on the speakers as his hand left her arsehole. The wrapper of the Mars bar tore again. There was a rustle as he dropped it to the floor. Then something hard was pressing against her arsehole. For a moment she thought it was metal again, another metal rod conjured by him to fuck her with, but in the next moment she realised it was the Mars bar. She *was* going to have it – he was going to feed it to her. Up her arse.

'Relax your sphincter,' his voices rumbled. The blunt end of the bar had already begun to soften against the heat of her anus. She relaxed her sphincter and he slowly pushed the bar inside her. It slid in smoothly, smearingly, already beginning to melt. The leather of his gloved finger rasped against her sphincter as he pushed the bar in fully.

He withdrew the finger. Her stomach had become hollower, grumbling in protest at this hysteron-proteron, and she was swallowing saliva every few seconds. Another wrapper tore, there was another rustle as he dropped it to the floor, and she felt another bar pressed to her anus, which was heavy with chocolate now, as though she shat herself and been unable to wipe.

'Relax.'

The second bar slid inside her, its passage lubricated by the chocolate smeared by the first around her sphincter and the walls of her rectal chamber. Her bowels had already started to feel full, as though she had eaten heavily a few hours before: the sensation was odd, paradoxical, strengthening her hunger and sharpening the smell of chocolate in her nostrils. The leather of his gloved finger rasped against her sphincter again as he pushed the second bar fully inside her. He began to pull the finger out, then pushed it in again, pulled it out, pushed it in, rubbing at the delicate ring of her sphincter.

'Do you like that?'

Without waiting for an answer his other hand came up between her legs and felt along and between the lips of her cunt.

'You like it,' his voices answered for her. She felt dizzy with hunger and the pleasure of his moving hands, the smooth leather of his gloves rough against the soft flesh of her sphincter and cunt. He withdrew his finger from her sphincter but his other hand continued to tickle and stroke at her cunt, the leather of the glove moistening with her juice. Then he withdrew that hand too. Another wrapper tore, there was another rustle, and a third bar was pressed against her anus.

'Relax.'

He slid it fully into her, held the gloved finger inside her for a moment, and then withdrew it, knowing that she wanted him to work at her sphincter with it again. His other hand came back up and brushed the folds of her cunt tantalisingly, not pressing hard enough to give her real pleasure. She began to ooze even harder, excited again by his cruelty. His voices rumbled at her.

'Do you need to shit?'

Her head drooped.

'Yes,' she murmured.

'Louder. Do you need to shit?'

'Yes.'

'Then shit into my mouth. Shit chocolate into my mouth. Feed me what I have fed you.'

She heard straps being undone and knew he was taking off his helmet. Her head was humming with pleasure and hunger. He put his hand to her cunt again, lifting the middle finger between its lips and pulling back against the lower wall of her chamber.

'Push backwards,' his voices said (their tone had changed as it had done on the first day). She pushed backwards, and felt a mouth being pressed to her anus. A tongue licked clockwise, counter-clockwise. The mouth withdrew.

'This time, open your sphincter and shit into my mouth. Shit it all into my mouth.'

The mouth was replaced. Her bowels were full of thick melted chocolate: all she had to do was open her sphincter and it would begin to pour out: but for a second, two, three, she was unable to will it, not wanting to release the richness inside her body. The tongue probed at her anus, trying to push between the sphincter, and she knew he would punish her if she disobeyed him any longer. She tried to relax, to release her sphincter, but it stayed closed for a moment longer, then surprised her as it opened, the mass of chocolate inside her bowels shifting at once, flowing downwards, squirting out through her anus into his waiting mouth. His gloved middle finger had emerged from the chamber of her cunt and shifted higher, settling on the nub of her clitoris, working at it with a juice-lubricated fingertip.

Head humming, stomach rumbling, nipples stiff and aching, cunt oozing, she shat liquid chocolate into his mouth and waited for orgasm from his moving fingertip. He had pushed his tongue forwards against the flow of chocolate and was moving it between her sphincter, adding more pleasure to her body, mixing another amalgam of pleasure-and-pain inside her: the pleasure of his moving fingertip and tongue, the pain of hunger and the unsoothed ache of her nipples. Orgasm was filling her, rising from her cunt into her stomach and breasts and armpits, down her thighs into her calves and feet and toes, congesting the skin of her face and lips and ears and thickening the pulse of blood in her ears.

Orgasm came and she gasped it out, almost fainting from its strength, feeling the chamber of her cunt clamp and her anus tighten against his moving tongue and lips. Her bowels were almost empty now: the chocolate had almost squirted from them in the final second before she came. She crouched on all fours on the table, gasping, uncaring that saliva provoked by the scent of chocolate was streaming from her mouth, stretching in long threads to a gathering pool on the table-top, a transparency on a transparency.

His tongue left her anus.

'Good,' his voices rumbled. '*Das hat gut geschmeckt.* Soon I will be ready for more, but for now there is a little cleaning up to do. Relax yourself.'

His tongue returned to her anus, working busily clockwise and counter-clockwise for the traces of chocolate clinging to the rim of her anus, probing through and beyond her sphincter to the smears of chocolate left along the walls of her rectum. She strained to hold her sphincter open, to pump her bowels completely empty for him. His tongue and mouth left her anus again. Straps rattled and clicked. He was putting his helmet back on.

'Good. Now, roll over. Look up at the ceiling. Close your eyes.'

She rolled over, looked up at the ceiling, closed her eyes. There was a few seconds' pause – she heard him stand and move around the table – and then the familiar weight of the video-helmet was settling over her head again. The screen was black: she stared into it, wondering when he would switch it on for her, what she would see today.

'Open your legs.'

She swung her legs apart. His voices muttered on the speakers and she jerked at a sudden bang. He had opened the bottle of champagne. There was a soft sound as the cork hit the carpet a few metres away.

'Now,' his voices announced, 'I am going to catheterise you. Keep still.'

His gloved hands were suddenly on her cunt, probing and lifting. Something was pressed to the hole of her urethra.

'Are you ready? If so, nod your head.'

She nodded, and screamed as the something slid inside her: what was he doing to her? Only the fear of some as-yet-unparalleled punishment kept her on the table, kept her legs apart, kept her from throwing herself backwards.

The thing had stopped sliding inside her and his voices were rumbling at her. She struggled to overcome her panic and decipher the words.

'For fuck's sake, what is wrong?'

Whimpering, she said, 'What are you doing to me?'

'Why? Did it hurt?'

She considered, recalling the sensation as the thing had begun to slide into her, testing the flesh around it now as it paused inside her.

'No. No, not really. But what is it?'

'I told you. A catheter. I said I was going to catheterise you.'

'I . . . I don't know what that means.'

'Then why for Christ's sake did you say you were ready?'

'I was ready . . . but I didn't know what for.'

The speakers snorted.

'You silly fucking bitch. A catheter is a tube passed up the urethra and into the bladder to drain or introduce fluid. You know what your urethra is, don't you? It's your piss-tube. I am sticking a catheter up your piss-tube so I can pour champagne into you. So you can piss it back out again, on to me. Do you understand now?'

'Yes.'

'Good. Then relax and let me finish.'

She tried to unclench her muscles, relax as the catheter began its slow movement inside her again. She could feel its passage up her urethra, like the gentle scratching of a tiny soft fingernail, and the sudden little jump as the tip of it reached her bladder.

'Good. It is in. Now, are you ready for the champagne?'

'Yes.'

'Sure?'

'Yes.'

She felt a sudden prickling on the surface of her inner thighs – bubbles of champagne bursting against her – and her bladder was suddenly, perversely, beginning to fill. The prickling ceased against her thighs and the screen inside her helmet flashed on. For a moment she was disorientated, unable to decipher what she was seeing and where she was seeing it from. It was herself: her own body, very close up: the white, gleaming planes and curves of her flesh: pink-nippled breasts, stomach, arms, thighs as background: the pink, blonde-capped folds of her cunt, with a black tube sticking from it, as foreground. She was seeing herself as he saw her, from the eye of some hidden camera in his helmet. A black-gloved hand came into shot, gripping the black tube and gently pulling it from her. It left the shot.

'Are you ready to piss?'

She examined the sensations in her body. Her bladder was full, painfully full, and a new sensation was leaking out from it into her flesh. The fluid there was cold: the champagne had been chilled.

'Yes,' she said, a momentary shiver running through her (on the screen she watched her breasts judder, the pink nipples swinging through tiny arcs).

'Good. Then stick this –' the hand returned carrying the champagne bottle and set it on the table between her thighs '– up yourself and ride on it. When I am ready, you will piss on me. Piss at me.'

She had to pause before reaching for the bottle: seeing herself as he saw her was disorientating and when she reached out her hand flailed a moment, unsure of left and right, before closing on the neck of the bottle and pulling it towards her.

She drew her legs in, knelt, squatted, adjusting the neck and mouth of the bottle, rubbing it up the length of her cunt to judge its weight and solidity before opening her legs fully and slowly lowering herself on to it. She watched it sink between the lips of her cunt and felt it: the glass was cold and hard and traces of foil left around the mouth and on the neck tickled at her electrically.

'How does it feel?'

'Cold,' she told him. 'The glass is cold. And hard.'

'Good. Ride it.'

She had finished lowering herself on to the bottle; now she paused, and then began to rise and fall on it, feeling slivers of metallic pain from the traces of foil rising through the sensation of the cold glass against the walls of her cunt, the pain rising through the strange, auto-voyeuristic pleasure of watching the bulk of the neck swallowed and disgorged by her cunt as she rose and fell, riding the bottle as he had ordered her to. She longed to rise fully off it, to work the mouth higher to her cunt, sliding the smooth rim, moistened with her juice, over the nub of her clitoris, but she feared to anger him.

'That is good,' his voices rumbled. 'Very good. But deeper. Faster.'

She was raising and lowering her body from her thighs and knees now; as he spoke she anticipated him, lengthening and quickening the rhythm with which she pushed her cunt down on and over the neck of the bottle and brought it free with a thickening *sklup*, her juices beginning to flow as the pleasure of riding the bottle swelled inside her, mingling with the sensation of her bladder, her painfully full bladder. The screen inside the helmet shuddered and swung, and she was dizzy for a moment, disorientated, almost falling to one side, before she realised he was taking off his helmet, laying it on the table before him so that the watching lens captured her embottled cunt from below. His head was bare: if she grabbed for the helmet she could turn it towards his face, perhaps catch a glimpse of him before he brought his hands up.

But he would be very angry and the thought of what he might do to her for the mere attempt tightened and chilled her stomach and throat, adding a new edge to the pleasure of performing for him – and for herself.

As though he had read her thoughts his voices rumbled:

'What are you? Describe yourself.'

'I ... I am a voyeur of myself. An, uh ... an auto-voyeur.'

'Voyeuse. Auto-voyeuse. So piss on me, auto-voyeuse.'

She almost had to push her will down into her cunt and thighs and wrest back control from the pleasure filling them, and for a moment she thought that her bladder was too full to open; that it would fill and swell for agonising hours until it burst inside her; but there, before her own body had reported it to her, the screen told her that she was pissing, a shaft of clear, sparkling fluid: the champagne, arcing on to the air after retracing its journey up her urethra. Where it struck him she would not have known, but the speakers were suddenly full of the sound of his gulping, his gasping words of praise for her: he was drinking it, catching it in his mouth and drinking it, chilled champagne pissed from her warm body.

Eight

She had wondered, hearing the news, why she had not been torn in two by it, and then torn in two again, and again, and again, like a thin sheet of paper in strong hands. She was wondering it now. Why did she feel no grief? Was she numbed? Had she refused to believe it somewhere inside? To believe that her sisters were dead. Both of them. With Bärengelt's chauffeur. In the same car-crash as she, the sole survivor, had received her head-injury.

In the Black Room, after the chocolate-shitting, the champagne-pissing were over, she had challenged Bärengelt to answer her questions. The three games had been played and she had done all he asked of her. Now it was time for him to do what she asked of him. And, turning off the screen inside her helmet so that she looked into blackness, he had said that he would.

'Am I in the Black Forest?' she had asked, still sitting atop the table, naked, her cunt and thighs aching from the energy and speed with which she had fucked herself with the neck of the champagne bottle.

'Yes,' his voices rumbled. 'In the Black Room of my black Schloss in the Black Forest.'

'And how long have I been here?'

'A little over a month. Five weeks. Today is the thirty-seventh day of your stay here.'

'Then have I been unconscious?'

'Yes. You were in a coma. And a semi-coma. Occasional periods of consciousness. You suffered a head injury.'

'Where are my sisters?'

'Yes, your sisters. They were travelling in the same car. You were being driven to meet me by my chauffeur. They, like him, were in the same car-crash. They, like him, were injured.'

'How badly?'

'Badly. Very badly. He was killed.'

'And my sisters?'

'Yes, they too. They too were killed. Instantly. They suffered no pain. I promise you of it.'

'My sisters are dead?'

'Yes. Your sisters are dead.'

'Gwen? Beth? Gwen is dead? And Beth?'

'Gwen is dead. Beth is dead. Both are dead. Your sisters are dead.'

She had suddenly choked with laughter. It wrenched at her stomach and chest, tore at her so that for a moment she thought she would vomit. Then it had gone. She found that she had pulled her legs up and together, and was squatted on the table with her arms wrapped around her knees, glad now that the helmet-screen was empty black.

'A minute ago,' she said, 'I was fucking myself with a champagne bottle, waiting for you to tell me to piss on you – piss *at* you.'

'Yes. That is what you were doing.'

'And you knew all the time that my sisters were dead.'

'Yes. I knew. Both your sisters.'

'I will never give myself to you again. I want to leave here at once.'

'You may leave here at any time you choose. In any direction.'

'Where am I?'

'You know that. In the Black Forest.'

'Where in the Black Forest?'

'A long way from anywhere.'

'How far?'

'A long way. It would take you many hours to get to the nearest town. Even as the crow flies.'

'Which direction?'

88

'That I will not tell you. I give you freedom to go whenever you choose and in whatever direction you choose. Beyond that I offer nothing.'

'If I do not know which way to driv –'

'Not drive. Walk. Remember: beyond the freedom to leave when and whither you choose, I offer you nothing. Nothing.'

'I walk? Where are my clothes?'

'I offer you nothing. I will give you nothing.'

'Then the freedom you give me is to leave here naked and walk without knowing where I am going?'

'Yes.'

'It is no freedom.'

'It is great freedom. The freedom to choose.'

'Stay here, with you, and live, or leave, and die?'

'Why should you die?'

'If I do not know where I am going I could walk for more than a day.'

'It is possible.'

'Then the sun will rise on me. And I will die.'

'You may be able to hide. There is deep shade in the forest. A thick carpet of pine-needles with which you may cover yourself. There may be clouds.'

'And will you let me have food and water?'

'Nothing. Beyond freedom I offer you nothing.'

'Then you offer me the freedom to die. To leave here naked, without food or water, and walk without knowing where I am going, without knowing where I am.'

'You are in the Black Forest.'

'On the planet Earth.'

'Yes.'

'You offer me the freedom to die.'

'You will not die.'

'Are you sure of that?'

'Who can be sure of anything? Perhaps if you stay –'

'What?'

'Perhaps if you stay something else will happen. Who can say? Who knows what tomorrow will be? *If* tomorrow will be?'

'Bollocks. My sisters are dead and you're talking bollocks.'

'I offer you the freedom to leave me, leave my Schloss.'

'The freedom to die.'

'No: the freedom to leave.'

'Leave and let die?'

'I do not understand you.'

'I want to take my helmet off.'

'When I have left the room.'

'Then leave the room. Leave it now. I no longer want to see or hear or speak to you again. I no longer want to be fucked by you. I no longer want to be raped by you.'

'I have never raped you.'

'You have raped me for three days. My sisters are dead.'

'Your sisters are dead. My chauffeur is dead. I am alive. You are alive.'

'Leave me. I want you to leave me. Now.'

He had not answered her and after a time she realised he had left the room. She had loosened the straps of the helmet and pulled it off, the air feeling suddenly cold on her sweat-moistened skin. The champagne bottle had been sitting on the table beside her, its neck smeared with her cunt-juice. She had picked it up and thrown it away. It had hit the carpet softly, bounced, rolled. Again she wondered who cleaned the rooms, who had cleaned the bathroom after he had raped her with the fish.

She climbed off the table and walked to the door. She stopped, looking back behind her. The glass table had disappeared as it always did at a distance, swallowed by the air, and for a moment she thought the champagne bottle had disappeared too, but there it was, lying where she had thrown it. Would it be gone the next time she came into the room? But she would not come into the room again.

She walked through the door, across the mosaics (gesturing once, obscenely, at the abusing Pan – the raping Pan), and began to climb the stairs. Her mind was exploring the thought of her sisters' death like a tongue exploring a tooth. Was there a hole in the tooth, an opening to the raw pulp of the nerve? Would grief suddenly flood her, as though the tip of the tongue had slid across and into the hole, touched the waiting nerve?

She was surprised to find herself almost on the floor of her room: she had climbed without noticing that she climbed. From below, more felt in the soles of her feet against the cold marble than heard, came a fragmentary rumble of Bärengelt's voice – voices – on the speakers. In the Black Room. He was back there again, and speaking. Was he directing a servant, one of the invisible army who serviced and cleaned the Schloss? She did not care; she did not ever want to see him again; she would go to bed and lie awake wondering when the news of her sisters' deaths would acquire meaning and whether, when it did, she would choose to leave the Schloss – to leave, and let herself die. To kill herself. Be the one that joined the two so that they could become three again.

She climbed the last tread of the stairs and walked to the doorway of her room. Softer than before, barely felt in the soles of her feet, almost unheard, Bärengelt's voices rumbled again in the Black Room, and her cunt stirred a little. Only a little. She walked into her room. A solitary clock was striking the quarter hour – several (she had never been able to tell which) were keeping strange times – threading strange bird-like notes into the silence. She walked to her bed, and paused. On the table beside it, which had been empty ever since she remembered waking in the Schloss for the first time (though she must have wakened before then: Bärengelt had told her (her cunt stirred again. A little. Only a little)) there was a magazine. A shiny magazine. Very new. She picked it up. It was called *Zoof*.

She opened it. A second later her mouth opened, a small wet mouth echoing the open mouth of the magazine, the open mouths and mouths of the colour picture that shone up at her. Her stomach lurched. Perhaps he was already watching her again from the lens – lenses – hidden somewhere in the room. She started to throw the magazine away, throw it across the room the way she had thrown the champagne bottle, but something in her head caught at the intent, snagging and twisting the movement of muscles in her arm so that she merely tossed it on the bed. It landed open at another page, another picture, lines of large, clear text.

She climbed on to the bed and crawled to where the magazine was lying. Her body was positioning her to lie on the bed and read from it, but with a tiny core of will she resisted, closing her eyes and holding them closed, knowing that if she opened them she would look directly down into the magazine, into the lines of large, clear text.

WINGS

'When you answered the advertisement you understood that it would not be a usual service?'

'Yes,' she said.

'And you understand now that if you want to leave, now or at any other time, you simply leave?'

'Yes.'

He said nothing for a few seconds. She sat in the chair beside the door, relaxed, looking at him as he looked at her. He was sitting behind a desk and there was a big window behind him, full of light. His head and shoulders cut out a dark outline into it – she couldn't quite make out the expression on his face, though she thought he looked a little like a bank manager or a civil servant, except he wasn't wearing a suit or tie and the surface of the desk was bare. On the wall on each side of the window was a long rectangular glass box full of tropical butterflies.

He shrugged.

'I want to see your cunt,' he said.

'Fine,' she said. As she took off her shoes and started to lift her skirt, he stood up and came around the desk towards her.

'How do you want me?' she asked.

'Stay sitting. Just spread your legs.'

She folded her skirt around her lap and started to pull down her knickers. The rustle of cloth sounded loud in the room. He didn't speak, hardly seemed to breathe, just squatted on his haunches in front of her, watching as the blonde and pink and red of her cunt was uncovered. She could see what expression he had on his face now. None. She rolled her knickers down past her feet, picked them up and held them in her hand.

'Like this?' she asked. She swung her thighs apart, exposing herself to him fully.

'Fine,' he said; then, holding up his right hand, 'May I?'

'Anything you like.'

He moved forwards and put his hand between her legs. His fingers touched her inner thighs, pressed gently, squeezed, left and right. The tendons were taut. His index finger found a pulse, read it for a few seconds, moved on. He touched her *mons Veneris*, stroked her pubic hair, gently touched and pressed apart her labia.

'Good,' he said. He stood up. She glanced at his groin. He wasn't erect. He walked back to the desk and sat down.

'Is that it?'

'No,' he said. 'But please, cover yourself if you want.'

She put her knickers back on, wondering what he wanted, how safe it would be to let him have it. She looked at him. The light behind him was even stronger now. She could hardly see his mouth open when he started to speak.

'You look good,' he said. 'You're what I want. I'll now tell you what I need you for.'

He pointed at the boxes of butterflies on either side of the window.

'You saw these, of course, when you came in?'

She nodded.

'I probably don't need to say that butterfly collecting is a hobby of mine. It has been ever since my teens. Do you like butterflies?'

'Yes,' she said. 'I don't think about them very much but I think they're beautiful. These are very beautiful.'

'Yes,' he said. 'They're very beautiful. I fetishise them. I am sexually excited by the spread wings of butterflies.'

He paused, then said, 'Does that disgust you in any way?'

She thought for a moment, comparing it with what she had encountered in the past.

'No. No, I don't think it disgusts me at all.'

'Good. Will you please stand up and come to the desk?'

She stood up and walked over to the desk. He was opening a drawer in it. He took out a flat leather pouch and leaned forward.

'Have a look at this. Tell me what you think.'

She took the pouch, walked back to her chair, sat down, opened the pouch. It had five or six colour photos in it. She took them out. They were photos of split beaver. Except beaver wasn't really the right word. The vulvas were all shaved, all gaping, all oozing from what looked to have been recent and vigorous sex. The inner thighs were painted with butterfly wings, done with great skill, vivid swirls and eyes and bands of red, green, yellow, orange, black, white, blue, almost as though butterflies had settled there and were feeding from the glistening sex-fluids.

She turned one of the photos over. On the back was written PAPILIO MACHAON. She turned more over. DANAUS PLEXIPUS. HELICONIUS MELPOMENE. MORPHO PELE-IDES. She looked up.

'What do you think?' he asked. 'Please, be honest.'

'It's fucking weird,' she said. She couldn't see whether he was smiling or not, but when he spoke she thought he was.

'I agree. Fucking weird. Does that bother you?'

'No.'

'Good. I am offering you £10,000 to be the next in my collection. *Trogonoptera brookiana*. The Malaysian bird-wing. Your thighs are the perfect shape and texture.'

'£10,000 to have my cunt painted like a butterfly?'

'They are not paintings,' he said. 'Look again.'

She looked at the photos again, looked up.

'Tattoos?'

'Tattoos. There will be no pain. I am able to give you a local anaesth –'

'Look,' she said. 'I'm not sure I want –'

'If you're not interested, please leave. You said you understood that.'

'I did, but –'

'But what?'

She was silent.

'Tell me what's bothering you about it.'

She looked at one of the photos.

'A tattoo is permanent.'

'No. It will be some years before they'll be able to remove them without trace. But it will come. It wouldn't be with you for life. I also offer you medical insurance to cover the cost of eventual removal.'

'I'd lose years,' she said.

'You mean you'd be professionally handicapped? No, you're wrong. I have kept in touch with all of the women whose photos you've got. All of them have found it proved an asset, not a liability. One was even offered a great deal of money by a pornographic magazine afterwards, but I couldn't allow that.'

'Couldn't allow it?'

'By the terms of the contract.'

'I'd have to sign a contract?'

'Yes.'

She was silent again, then said, 'I want to have time to think about it.'

'Of course. Please take as much time as you like. The £1,000 fee we agreed at the beginning is yours whatever you choose. If you like, I can give you a booklet telling you more about what would happen, if you accepted. It would be entirely painless, entirely private. Only you and I would participate. A week later, you would place yourself at my disposal for a day of sex. That would be it.'

A week later she rang him to agree. When she returned to his house for the tattooing, she was surprised

95

to find that she wasn't nervous or apprehensive. She wouldn't have done it without the money, but that was true of most of what she had done in her professional life. She had decided and she was ready.

'Do you want a drink?' he asked.

'Won't the anaesthetic . . .?'

'No, this is only a local. A drink will be perfectly safe.'

'Fine, then.'

'What would you like?'

'A glass of wine.'

He was far more animated now, talking more loudly, smiling, moving quicker. He was wearing jeans and a white T-shirt. His bare arms were tanned, not very muscular, scarred in three or four places. In one corner of the room was a leather couch. There was a trolley beside it with an electrical tool on it, a kidney dish and syringe, little bottles, cotton wool. She tried not to look at it too much. The foot of the couch had ankle-straps attached to it. There was a video-camera on a stand facing down the couch. It would look straight at her cunt. Straight at the tattooing.

He handed her the glass of wine.

'Don't mind me,' he said. 'Stare at the tools if you want. If you've any questions still, ask them.'

'No, it's OK. I know what I'm getting myself into.'

'You make it sound like an S&M session.'

'I suppose it might be.'

He shook his head.

'Pain does nothing for me. Other people's or mine.'

When she had drunk the wine, she took off her skirt and knickers and climbed on to the couch. She spread her legs as he made final adjustments to the camera and switched it on.

'Nervous?' he asked.

'No.'

He left the camera and started to strap her ankles to the couch.

'Try the releases,' he said.

She twisted her foot and it came free from the strap.

96

'OK?'

'OK.'

'When I start tattooing, please remember to make no sudden movement. Get yourself comfortable now, and if you want to move later, let me know first. OK?'

'OK.'

He pulled a stool up beside the trolley and picked up the syringe.

'Turn your head away if you don't want to watch.'

She looked at the wall next to the couch. There was a single framed butterfly on it, green and exotic, its wings wide and narrow. The name-card said *Trogonoptera brookiana*. She felt a sharp, momentary pain in her right inner thigh, another in her left. The syringe rattled as he put it back into the kidney dish.

'OK?'

'OK.'

'Good. Then it's time.'

She jerked a little when he switched on the tattooer. The buzzing sounded very loud, like a giant insect. With a giant sting. She looked away from the wall. He was holding the tattooer above her groin. It had a little silver beak, gnawing away at the air.

'OK?'

'OK.'

'I'll just test that you're numb. Can you feel this?'

He pressed her inner thighs with the fingers of his free hand.

'No, not really.'

'It's numb, yeah?'

'Yeah, it's numb.'

'OK, I'm about to begin. You can still pull out if you want to. Do you want to?'

'No, I've decided. No going back.'

'Right. Good.'

She felt nothing, almost nothing, just a faint pressing, a faint vibration. The hand moved with the silver-beaked tattooer to and from her cunt, to and from the open pots of dye on the trolley. Slowly the white planes of her inner thighs bled lines and bands of colour, started to form the long, narrow, green-denticled wings of the butterfly framed on the wall beside the couch. There was blood, only a little, but constant, wiped away with the cotton wool. Four times she asked him to stop while she adjusted herself or rocked twinges of cramp out of her buttocks. His hand was steady and moved smoothly and precisely. He had an erection, bulging upwards in his jeans. The video camera hummed faintly. It took an hour and a half. He renewed the local anaesthetic twice. When it was finished, she took her feet out of the straps and dressed.

'Do you want another glass of wine?' he asked.

'Yeah, OK.'

'You'll be a little stiff, sore for a few days when the anaesthetic wears off. In a week, you'll be fine. You're OK for Thursday?'

'Yeah. Thanks. I'm OK for now.'

He laughed.

'Yes, I saw. It turned you on?'

'A little.'

'It's happened before. But it's too soon. I don't want it like this. In a week, yeah? We meet, we fuck. Then one more photo, I give you details of the medical insurance, the second half of the £10,000 goes into your account, and that's it. You'll have been collected. Do you like the idea?'

'I don't know. Maybe not. But it's OK. What about the video? That does something for you as well?'

'Sometimes.'

By the time she left the house the anaesthetic was starting to wear off. That night she took a make-up mirror into the bathroom before she showered. She set it up on the edge of the bath and got undressed. When she had showered, she examined herself. The skin beneath and around the tattoo was swollen. When she pressed it or moved quickly, it felt sore. The tattoo was very good. The wings ran from about half-way down her inner thigh to the edge of her labia majora. The colours

98

were skilfully stippled and blended to suggest the vivid, overlapping scales of real butterfly wings. She closed and opened her legs, watching to see how it looked in the mirror. It was almost as though a real butterfly was flexing its wings between her legs. Faster, slower.

The soreness wore off before Thursday. He took her into the same room. The couch and trolley had gone. There was a carpet on the floor, decorated with butterflies. In one corner was a big TV. It was showing the video of her tattooing. The tattooer buzzed on the soundtrack. He was already starting to get undressed. She took off her coat, her jacket, her skirt. He grabbed her by the waist before she was finished and pushed her down on to the carpet. His cock was standing almost vertical with excitement.

'On your back. Spread.'

She obeyed, rolling on to her back, beginning to pull her knickers down. His hands joined hers, more urgent, pulling hard. On the video, she heard her voice saying, 'Hold it for a moment. Cramp.' The buzzing of the tattooer stopped.

He threw her knickers into a corner of the room. He was kneeling in front of her, staring down at her cunt.

'Open and close your legs,' he said. 'No, slower. Open . . . close . . . open . . . close . . . yeah, that's good. Good.'

He put his fingers down into her cunt and started to masturbate her, probing into her vagina with a couple of fingers, moistening her clitoris with her own juice.

'No, keep opening, closing. Yeah, good. Keep doing it.'

Her thighs shut and opened on his moving hand.

'OK, now,' he said. 'You're ready.'

Am I? she thought, opening her legs for entry. But she was. He entered her, was up her. She closed her legs around him and he started to thrust. He started to grunt. After a minute, he asked her, 'What are you?'

He was almost screaming. She was counter-thrusting fiercely against him, grunting with him, timing herself against his orgasm. For a second she couldn't remember what she had to say, how to say it.

'*Trogonoptera brookiana*,' she said, and he started to come, grunting in time with each spurt of semen into her slickened cunt.

Anna became aware of the bedsheet at her cunt, gently brushing against her as she breathed. Her cunt had opened as she read and she had unconsciously pressed it down against the bed. But she could not remember opening her eyes, could not remember beginning to read. She looked at the top of the page she had just finished, turned back to the beginning of the story. Six pages.

She lifted her head, not knowing why for a moment. There had been a flicker of movement in the room. Where? It came again. Not in the room – in the not-mirror on the not-mirror-table. She pushed the magazine to one side and slid forwards over the bed, feeling the bedcover brush at her nipples, resisting the urge to press her cunt down into it again, start slowly thrusting against it, squeezing each nipple in turn as she did so, paining herself above to pleasure herself below, as she reviewed the story: the pinned butterflies in the boxes; the tattooing; the grunts of the fetishist.

She reached the foot of the bed and swung her legs round and down to the floor, stood up, and walked to the not-mirror-table. The screen was alive today, showing the same pale garden under the same bright sunlight. Or was it sunlight? No, this time it was moonlight: the shadows were shallower, harder to make out, and there, twisting her heart with brief shock, was an owl, drifting on wide wings along one of the terraces, a classical symbol above the classical statuary. Had that been the flicker of movement she had seen? Or had it merely been the screen of the not-mirror being switched on?

It had not been the flicker of movement she had seen: this had been: the same figure, at nearly the same spot, but coming back in the opposite direction, doll-tiny with distance, but striding hooded towards the Schloss, not away from it. A woman. A tall woman. Whom she recognised but did not know.

She turned away from the not-mirror-table and looked towards the black curtains. It was night outside – the screen said so – but she was reluctant for a moment to walk towards them, grip them, tug at them to discover where they drew apart. She overcame the reluctance, touched them, drew them apart. French windows. She took hold of the handles and twisted. They opened smoothly and she stepped through them on to the marble terrace outside her room, feeling the woman's name like a seed inside her head, presently unidentifiable, waiting to sprout.

She shivered, but not so much with the cold of air as with the sensation of the marble beneath her feet (her nipples peaked in sympathy). She walked to the railing of the terrace, her feet a little unsteady as she gazed up and out into cloudless black sky and stars scattered across it like splintered gems on black velvet. Her body, thighs and stomach, touched the railing and she looked down almost reluctantly into the garden. Neither the owl nor the woman was there any more, but the seed of the name had sprouted inside her head, putting forth broad green leaves and a wide flower of waxy, sweet-smelling purples and yellows, seeming rooted in a glowing warmth of relief and pleasure at her stomach. Madame Oursor. Here. At the Schloss. Though her sisters were dead.

She heard the cry of a bird that seemed to come from directly beneath her and leaned over the railing, looking down the face of the Schloss. It was not a bird: far below Madame Oursor was standing at the foot of the Schloss, looking up at her, hood thrown back, her face a pale oval with a paler gleam of teeth. She was smiling up at her and Anna smiled back down, her stomach glowing warmer, wider, and a trickle of anticipation starting in her cunt.

Madame Oursor lifted a hand and gestured and Anna frowned, trying to work out what she meant, her hands tightening on the railing. Was she . . .? Yes, she was beckoning. Come to me. Come down here. For a moment she was reluctant to turn away, go back into her bedroom and find the stairs. If she looked away from her, Madame Oursor would disappear. But that was stupid. She nodded, feeling stupid as she said, 'Yes. OK. I'm coming,' knowing that Madame Oursor could not hear her, and turned away from the railing, the glow in her stomach suddenly cooling.

She went back through the French windows and ran across the room for the doorway and the stairs. How would she get out of the Schloss? The marble of the landing and stairs was very cold under her feet: her senses had heightened, her body fuelled by the pleasure and joy of seeing Madame Oursor again. Her feet sounded loud, slapping against the marble, carrying her round and down, round and down as she turned over the problem of how to get out of the Schloss, how to find her way to the spot where Madame Oursor was waiting for her, outside under the black sky and stars.

But the problem did not need to be solved, for Madame Oursor was waiting for her at the foot of the stairs, standing hooded again on the blood-red *fleur-de-lys* in the black mosaic pool. Anna ran to her, her arms opening without conscious will, and the two of them embraced hard, harder, as though trying to crush themselves into one body, one being, Anna's cunt responding happily to the strong arms and the tall body and the feeling on her skin of the dark, soft clothing Madame Oursor wore.

They loosened the embrace and came apart a little, looking into each other's faces, Anna looking up, Madame Oursor looking down, love streaming between them on wide smiles.

'*Ma petite*,' Madame Oursor murmured. Her gloved hands dropped down Anna's back, gripped and squeezed her buttocks. Anna trembled happily. The material of the gloves was soft, smooth, loving, so different to the rough leather on Bärengelt's cruel hands. She almost choked as she started to speak, eyes sparkling with tears.

'Madame, I am so happy to see you. So happy.'

'I had hoped so, little Anna. I had hoped so.'

Her hands tightened on Anna's buttocks, joggling the hemispheres, rotating them, then loosened, lifted away. She broke the embrace, reaching for one of Anna's hands.

'Come, *ma petite*, come with me. We need to talk, before I leave you again.'

'No, madame. Please no. You can't leave me.'

'*Ma petite*, I must. Come with me. I will explain. Down here, it will be safer.'

She tugged on Anna's hand, drawing her away from the mosaics and the doorway to the Black Room, down a corridor Anna had never been down before: she realised she had always walked directly between the foot of the stairs and the Black Room. Like a well-trained sheep.

'In here, *ma petite*.'

Madame Oursor drew her through a curtained doorway into darkness. The darkness of a small room with a high ceiling: Anna could tell from the way their footsteps and the rustle of Madame Oursor's garments sounded within it.

'*Un moment*.'

There was a soft click and on a marble stand a lamp glowed to life, *art nouveau* again, and erotic, lesbian, carved in ivory and crystal: a tall dominatrix, many-thonged whip hanging loose in one hand, stooped to test the buttocks of a just-whipped girl with the other.

'Here, *ma petite*.'

Madame Oursor drew her to a marble bench to one side of the lamp. Anna trembled as her buttocks flattened against the cold surface of the bench, looping one arm around Madame Oursor's firm, slender waist, drawing comfort from the contact. Madame Oursor pulled away from her a little to throw back her hood, sighing with relief, then put an arm around her shoulders.

'Ah, *ma petite*, you are cold. Here, sit on my lap while I tell you my news.'

The skin of Anna's buttocks unpeeled from the marble of the bench, already slightly numbed by it, and slid gratefully on to the warm, soft cloth of Madame Oursor's lap. Her cunt was beginning to ooze at their closeness. Soon yelm would be leaking on to the cloth, staining it. Staining it with love. Madame Oursor would not mind. Anna clutched at her hard, tears stinging her eyes again, whispering huskily, 'Oh, madame, I'm so happy to see you.'

'As I to see you, *ma petite*.'

A gloved hand patted at Anna's knee, squeezed it. Anna sighed, squirming on the warm lap, happy to feel the yelm sliding between her thighs, even happy to feel the tears in her eyes. Warm breath touched her ear and Madame Oursor whispered to her, '*Ma petite*, how I wish I could have an uninterrupted hour with you. As I promise you I shall one day. One day soon.'

Anna's cunt seemed to squirm as though a small animal was loose inside it. The trickle of yelm from her cunt thickened. Madame Oursor kissed her ear lightly and drew away.

'But alas, there is no time. Tell me, quick, what has Herr Bärengelt been doing to you since you came here?'

'Terrible things, madame.'

'Oh, I feared it. I have spoken to him on the telephone and he has seemed to me very strange, *ma petite*, since your arrival. Nor would he let me speak to any one of you.'

Anna clutched tighter, pressing her face to Madame Oursor, the tears in her eyes beginning to flow now, trickling on to Madame's shoulder as, below, her yelm trickled on to her lap. The air of the room was growing thick with the smell of her arousal.

'Two of us are dead, madame.'

'*Comment, ma petite?* I did not hear you clearly.'

Anna lifted her head and looked at Madame Oursor.

'Two of us are dead, madame. Beth and Gwen. In a car crash.'

She swung between horror and elation, her stomach tightening and loosening, as Madame Oursor began to laugh.

'No, *ma petite*. No! It is not true. He was lying to you.'

'Oh, God, madame, is it true? Beth and Gwen aren't dead?'

'No, *ma petite*. *Mille fois non*. Most certainly not.'

'Madame, how do you know?'

'Little Anna, I said only that Herr Bärengelt would not *let* me speak to any one of you. But I have spoken to one of you nonetheless. Yesterday. To Beth. She rang me on the telephone. She too is in the Schloss somewhere, with

Gwen. Was it not clever of her to find a way to the telephone?'

Anna could only nod, her cheek pressed again to Madame Oursor's shoulder, reading the wet patch of her previous tears, but with her present tears coming even harder now from surprise and joy.

'That is why I have come here, *ma petite*. Because Beth could tell me nothing of *you*, only of Gwen and herself. And of course, I was very worried, so very worried.'

'What has been happening to them, madame?'

'To Beth and Gwen, *ma petite*?'

'Yes, madame.'

'They do not know. Beth was very uncertain of how she was and of where she was. She said she had not seen Herr Bärengelt at all, nor you, only Gwen. And she believed it was just the day after you three had set out for the Schloss.'

'Then there *was* a crash, maybe. Look at my scar, madame.'

'I have looked, *ma petite. C'est horrible.* But I do not know whether there was a crash. I do not know how the scar came. I know only that I am very concerned for all of you.'

'Madame. Please. Will you take me away with you?'

'Ah, *ma petite*, I am sorry, but no. I cannot. I must return to England very soon, or else Herr Bärengelt will know I have left and I do not know what will happen.'

'Why can you not take me with you, madame? Please. I want to go with you.'

'Yes, I know, *ma petite*. And I, I wish to take you.'

The gloved hand squeezed again at Anna's knee, patted her leg, and Anna stirred, wanting the hand to climb higher, slip between her thighs.

'Yes, I wish to take you, but I cannot. For what then of your sisters? Where are they? You must find them and then all three of you can escape here.'

Anna said nothing.

'You understand, *ma petite*?'

Anna sighed.

'Yes, madame. I understand. But why can you not stay here and help me?'

'For fear of Herr Bärengelt, little one. I must be in my office in England, carrying out his work and his orders. I can offer no good excuse for not being there and I think even if I could that he would suspect, and if he suspects, he will act. He will take all three of you elsewhere to play these dangerous games.'

Anna shivered.

'Dangerous, madame?'

'Yes, dangerous, *ma petite*. I have told you, Herr Bärengelt has become strange. I do not know now of what he is capable. I cannot believe he will hurt you physically, *mais psychologiquement*? Psychologically? Who knows? That is why you must stay here. Find your sisters. Fight him together. And escape. With my help, from England. When you find Beth, she will tell you how to telephone to me again. You will tell me how things go, and if it is necessary, I will call the police.'

'But why not call the police now, madame?'

'Ah, *non, ma petite*, it is not possible. Herr Bärengelt is so very rich, I am afraid he will have friends in the German judiciary. This present situation you are in, is it criminal?'

'Yes. Yes, it is! He has beaten me, madame. Whipped me. Raped me.'

'No, *ma petite*, think clearly. Where is the evidence? The proof, *ma petite*?'

'Look at my bottom, madame. Just look!'

She half-stood up from Madame Oursor's lap, turning her body, holding her buttocks up for inspection.

'*Mon dieu!*'

'That's proof, isn't it? That he's assaulted me?'

'Oh, *ma petite*. *Ce bâtard*.'

Her gloved hand touched Anna's buttocks gently, stroking at the bruise. Anna shivered at the touch. Madame Oursor squeezed gently, patted, then took her hand away and pulled Anna back down on to her lap.

'Oh, *ma petite*. That is indeed a terrible contusion, but alas, I am afraid it is not sufficient. Can you prove that it was he who beat you so cruelly?'

'Who else could it have been, madame?'

'Someone to whom he will pay a little of his vast money to lie on his behalf, *ma petite*. Oh, my blood boils to think of what he has done to you, but that is all the more reason to do these things with a clear head. We must have proof that he cannot wriggle out of with his terrible wealth. I must make enquiries with the incorruptible British police about how to proceed in this matter. He must not escape the net, *ma petite*. Our case must be secure, watertight, you say? For the time when we sue him.'

'Sue him, madame?'

'But of course. You and I and Beth and Gwen, we shall all four sue him. For what he has done to you and for the involvement he has made me take. You will be rich for the rest of your lives, *ma petite*, and perhaps I . . . but we shall talk of this later. For now, please, I beg you, have courage and stay here, in the lion's den, to find your sisters. We must not act *précipitamment* or we might lose all. Do you understand?'

'I think so, madame.'

'Trust me, little Anna. Trust me. I will not allow you to come to harm.'

'OK, madame. I trust you.'

'Thank you, *ma petite*. But now, I must go.'

She let go of Anna and tried to stand up.

'No, madame. Please. Not yet. I have more questions f –'

'There is no time, *ma petite*. Please, release me.'

She stood up, trying to push Anna gently from her but accidentally tripping her so that she sprawled to the floor, hitting her knees, not caring. Anna clutched for Madame Oursor's feet, caught hold of them, crawled to her.

'No, madame. Please.'

'*Ma petite*, I must. I must go, and quickly.'

Anna was kneeling at her feet, embracing her calves, holding tight, resting her cheek against the warm, smooth cloth.

'Anna, I have no time. I must return to England. Now.'

She tried to turn away, trying to lift her legs free of Anna's clutch.

'No, please. Not now. Give me a few seconds of your time, madame, please. Please. Not until you've hurt me.'

Madame Oursor stopped trying to turn away.

'What is it you say?'

Anna swallowed.

'Don't go. Not for a few seconds. I want you to hurt me.'

Madame Oursor was silent for a moment, then said, 'You wish that I hurt you?'

'Yes, madame. Please.'

Another moment of silence.

'Very well. I give you a few seconds. I will hurt you. For your disobedience. For not allowing me to go as soon as I wished.'

Anna thrilled at the way her voice had hardened, deepened. It had been honey as she started speaking; now it was steel. Cruel and stern.

'Release me, you foolish little girl. Now.'

Anna let go of Madame Oursor's legs and drew back.

'Stay upon your knees. Put your hands behind your head.'

Anna obeyed, her cunt weeping freely.

'Close your eyes and push your *tétons* towards me. *Tes tétons. Vite!*'

Anna closed her eyes and pushed her chest forwards, offering her breasts to the air and the menace of Madame Oursor's unknown intentions. Her nipples had hardened and she was trembling. What would happen? Her blinded senses strained into the darkness. Cloth whispered. Madame Oursor was taking a glove off.

'Now, Miss Anna, what was it you wanted of me?'

Anna licked her lips.

'Pain, madame.'

A moment passed, two, three and then she gasped, pain stinging in her right nipple and areola. Madame Oursor had swung the empty glove hard at it, flicking it with the hanging fingers.

'Was that what you wanted?'

'Yes, madame.'

'Do you want more?'

'Yes, madame. Please.'

She gasped. The glove had swung immediately this time, flicking the same nipple, heightening the pain.

'More?'

'Yes. Please.'

She gasped. The same nipple. It burned, singing a constant note of pain into her. But why did Madame Oursor not maltreat her left nipple? The pain in her right tit was harsh, burning, delicious, but unbalanced.

'Do you want more?'

'Yes, madame. Please.'

'Where?'

'In my left tit, madame. Please.'

'No. You have had enough.'

The glove struck her in the face, but thrown, not swung, and Madame's feet were moving away from her. She opened her eyes, crying out, but the room was already empty. Madame Oursor had gone. Clutching up the glove from where it lay on the floor, she pushed herself to her feet and ran to the doorway. She pushed through the curtains. The corridor outside was empty. Madame Oursor had gone.

She turned back to the room, her hand tightening on the glove, her knees subsiding so that she knelt again on the floor. She pushed the glove down between her legs, rubbing at the folds of her cunt, pinching at her right nipple to heighten the pain that still glowed there, pinching at her left nipple to start pain glowing there too.

Nine

She was walking across the mosaics again, stairs to Black Room, and how differently from the way she had walked across them so shortly before, Black Room to stairs, after the third session with Bärengelt in the Black Room. Then she had been tired and aching, numbed by the news of her sisters' deaths, her thoughts slowed inside her head as though by extreme cold. Now the aches in her body were sharpened, welcome to her, like a seasoning for the pleasure of existence, and two thoughts were repeating themselves inside her head, like twin stars spinning against black sky, red and gold, occulted and revealed again and again: *Madame Oursor has been here* and *He was lying*. Madame Oursor had been inside the Schloss, and her sisters were not dead.

She grinned down now at the abusing Pan, his power over her gone, even her hatred of him drained away inside her. Madame Oursor had been inside the Schloss, and her sisters were not dead. She stepped through the doorway of the Black Room, and paused with shock. There was a woman strapped to the whipping-horse, her head encased in a black helmet, the red brand of a cane-stroke glowing across the rounded curves of her pure white buttocks, a lens glittering greedily on them between the fully opened petals of the black iron flower.

Her mouth had opened and she had felt the muscles of her lips and throat and tongue forming the shape of 'Beth!' when a section of wall directly across the room began to slide aside. Her mouth closed and almost without thought she ducked to one side, lowering herself behind an ebony copy of a Louis Quatorze gaming table. Through its legs she watched as Bärengelt's black-leather-encased legs came into the room: this was the hidden door through which he had taken her to the greenhouse and the butterflies. His legs left her field of vision, striding in the direction of the whipping-horse. She jumped as the speakers inside the room awoke, thinking for a moment that he had seen her.

'Bitch! I am back. How do you feel?'

Here, low to the floor, the bass in his voices was exaggerated, and against her will her cunt responded to it; and then her heart and stomach to the single voice that replied.

'I'm aching all over.'

A pair of fat tears began to leak slowly from Anna's eyes and down her cheeks: Beth's voice. Tired, strained, but as unmistakably Beth's voice as those pure white arse-cheeks, branded with Bärengelt's cruelty, were Beth's arse-cheeks.

'Good!' Bärengelt's voices rumbled. (*It's her first session*, Anna thought; *he's doing to her exactly what he did to me*.) Even as she thought it she heard the buzzing of the vibrator begin, first harsh and then soft, as though it had been pressed into flesh. It had: Beth groaned: he was working it over her cunt: Anna risked a quick peek over the table, up and down, a glimpse of Bärengelt and his victim seized and stored for examination as she crouched behind the table: yes, the bastard, standing there with a hard-on and that black vibrator in his hand (fuck, it was even *more* enormous to look at it than it had felt inside her), working at poor Beth, the bastard, working at her, doing to her what he had done to *her* on that first day, the bastard, making Beth groan and curse, the bastard, and Beth must be leaking by now, Bärengelt must be seeing it, smearing her juice on to the buzzing head of the vibrator and working it into the folds of her cunt-lips, over the swelling hood and nub of her clitoris – and Anna herself swore softly with surprise and self-reproach, realising that her hand had slipped down into her cunt and was slowly

112

beginning to strum on the lips and folds and clitoris in celebration of the abuse of her sister.

Beth groaned, calling out that she was coming, and the buzzing of the vibrator stopped.

'Not yet,' Bärengelt's voices rumbled. 'Not yet. You must suffer for your pleasure first, and I shall not be the one to provide it for you.'

Beth groaned again, pleading for the return of the vibrator to her cunt, pleading for her hands, one of her hands to be loosed; and crouched behind the table Anna groaned too, silently, longing to lower her hand to her cunt again and masturbate: the excitement and fear of her voyeurism were working away inside her, moistening her cunt, hardening her nipples and swelling her tits, sending tendrils of remembered sensation (she refused to analyse it: pain or pleasure?) downwards through her bowels to tweak at her tightening sphincter.

'No!' his voices rumbled. 'You must suffer first. Suffer this.'

Something whistled through the air, the sound cut short by the crack of something hard yet flexible against yielding flesh, with a shriek of surprise and agony from Beth. God. He had caned her again: another red line must be glowing across those pure white cheeks – or (Anna groaned silently again, feeling the whole triangle of her cunt liquefy and burn) had he landed the second stroke directly atop the first, sending a fresh spurt of pain through still smouldering nerves? She longed to peek over the table-top again, snatch a fresh glimpse of the white victim and the black tormentor, but did not dare, and with the failure of her will she groaned again, still silently, feeling her hand drop down to her cunt to renew the masturbation she had dragged it away from a minute before.

No, she told herself; *no, no, no*; but her hand found its way home and began to work at her cunt again, her fingertips reporting the slick warmth of the oozing lips, the hardened, aching nub of her clitoris. Another whistle, another crack of the cane, another shriek from Beth. Why was he caning her again? Why was he not bending over

113

and examining and praising and masturbating himself on to the single cane-stroke he had already inflicted, as he had done that first day with her? The question flared in her mind with another whistle of parted air, another crack of the cane across the white buttocks, another shriek from Beth, with Bärengelt's cruel chuckle rumbling on the speakers (Anna pressed her tits hard against the carpet, her nipples thirsty for the bass flooded into the floor by the speakers). Another whistle, another crack, another shriek, and now, made reckless by the tide of pleasure rising from her cunt into her guts and tits, Anna peeked over the table-top again, to see the white body atop the whipping-horse and the cane-wielding black tormentor that reigned over it, to see the red signs or sign of the black cane on the white buttocks.

Up – no, the strokes had been separate, angled against each other so that the white buttocks bore a scrabble of red lines, like the rusting tracks of iron meteors smashed across the faces of twin moons of white ice – and down, the sight held inside her head to heighten the pleasure of her masturbation as she pressed her tits and nipples hard into the black carpet. Another whistle, another crack, another shriek, and Bärengelt's voices were rumbling away on the speakers, their bass notes tickling at Anna's nipples like fingertips.

'Now, bitch, *now* you shall have some pleasure.'

The vibrator began to buzz again, harsh then suddenly far softer, with a renewed shriek from Beth, as though it had been jammed fully inside her. Bärengelt was muttering to himself, the speakers rumbling an unintelligible mixture of German and English, and there was a faint persistent flap of moist flesh: he was masturbating himself, his hand working at the engine of his cock as Anna's hand was working at the more complex engine of her cunt. And doubtless he was gloating over the red cane strokes, fuelling his pleasure from the abuse he had inflicted on Beth's white buttocks, retrieving the memories of the way they had clenched and writhed as each thundercrack of the cane had injected fresh agony into them.

The thought of it was enough: mouth open, gasping silently, Anna came, crouched behind the gaming table, her hand sticky as high as the wrist with cunt-juice, the black carpet beneath the vee of her thighs sprinkled and damp with it. She lay unable to move, listening to the softened buzz of the giant vibrator buried in her tortured sister's tortured cunt, the multiplied bass of Bärengelt's muttering, the quickening rhythm of his masturbation.

'Bitch,' his voices were rumbling now, 'bitch, are you enjoying this? Do you want to come, you bitch?'

Wailing, Beth answered him, pleading for orgasm, and Anna's ears, sharpened by her own, caught the low splatter of his ejaculation, a heavy warm white sauce thrown, she knew, across the burning red-slashed white cheeks of her sister. Beth would be feeling it trickle over the cane-strokes as *she* had done that second day; feeling it trace the gluteal crease, flow down between her thighs, across her four-chette, on to the lips of her cunt, a moist sensation added to the sensation of the buzzing vibrator.

The buzzing of the vibrator stopped; there was a squelch of released pressure: he had withdrawn it from Beth's cunt, denying her the orgasm she had pleaded for. Straps clicked: he was releasing her. The floor resonated faintly beneath Anna: he was striding across the room, leaving it, leaving Beth aching atop the whipping-horse as he had left *her* on that first day, the single cane-stroke burning across her arse – how much worse it must be for poor Beth, with half-a-dozen red lines slashed into the white, once-perfect globes of her buttocks!

Tears stung Anna's eyes again, but her cunt wept too, excited by her sister's suffering, and she found herself longing to be a *voyeuse* on the second day of Beth's erotic enslavement, watching the continued domination of her by Bärengelt, her subjugation to a will as cruel and dominant, as heavy and unyielding as one of his boots tramped into the tender pillows of a slave's buttocks.

Had he gone? She peeked over the table again. The room was empty. Empty save for her and the white body strapped to the whipping-horse. Unstrapped: he had left

115

her free, but Anna knew that Beth would be aching too much to move, still struggling to rouse nerves and muscles drained by the pain and pleasure she had just undergone. Unconsummated pleasure: how she must be longing to reach down between her thighs and wank!

Anna lifted her breasts from the carpet and began to crawl towards the whipping-horse, keeping in cover as best she could, still frightened of Bärengelt's return, still fearful that he would catch sight of her on the screen fed by the lens among the petals of the iron flower. She crawled beneath another table, two or three metres short of the whipping-horse.

'Beth!' she whispered. The whipping-horse creaked: Beth had heard her: in another moment she would have lifted her head in the black helmet and called back.

'No, say nothing! Stay still! He is watching you!'

She lay beneath the table watching the angle of the flower-lens, calculating what positions it could not over-look. Yes, perhaps by that harpsichord, and from there down beside that *armoire*, yes, she could make it right up to the horse and slip beneath it.

She emerged from the shelter of the table, crawling flat to the carpet, arms and legs splayed to either side, working with elbow and knee to propel herself, her nipples brushed and hardened by the long black pile of the carpet as she circled away from the whipping-horse and returned to it on the opposite side, hoping that her calculations were accurate, that Bärengelt was not watching her from some other camera as she moved towards her abused sister atop the whipping-horse, that he was not delighting in the working of the muscles of her white buttocks, branded by the now purple cane-stroke he had inflicted on her that first day.

She stopped with surprise, breath suspended. The iron petals of the flower were moving – was the camera about to swing towards her? – no, the petals were closing, blinding the crystal eye between them: Bärengelt had tired of Beth's suffering, or had decided to return to view it again in person, perhaps add to it, swing the cane at those

116

white buttocks again. Anna crawled beneath the nearest table to wait, absently squeezing at a nipple in her anxiety, almost crying out as she was surprised again and dug her fingernails into it.

'Anna!'

It was Beth, whispering to her from the side of her mouth, not daring to turn her head.

'Anna! Where are you? What is happening?'

'Shhh!' she whispered back, squeezing at her nipple again to soothe the smart of her fingernails. 'Keep still. There was a camera watching you, but it has been switched off. Perhaps that means he is coming back. Keep still and wait.'

'Who is he?'

'Herr Bärengelt. Our employer. Don't you know where you are?'

'No. I hardly know anything. I only woke up today.'

'In a bedroom, upstairs?'

'Yes. On the thirteenth floor.'

'That's where my bedroom is!'

She suddenly did not care whether Bärengelt was returning or not and slipped out from under the table.

'It's OK,' she said as she ran to the whipping-horse. 'He doesn't seem to be coming back.'

'Are you sure?'

'Well, no. But so what if he does? There's two of us now.'

She unfastened the straps on the black helmet and gently pulled it off her sister's head, feeling the air that had lain against Beth's skin flow past her fingers, warmed and moistened.

'Whew!' Beth said, smiling, eyes still closed. She opened them slowly, carefully, and looked at Anna. The smile fell off her face, dragging her mouth open with it.

'Oh, Anna, darling! What's happened to your hair? And that scar! It's horrible!'

'Like yours, dear.'

'Mine?'

'Yes, yours. Here, feel.'

117

She took hold of Beth's hand and pressed it to her scalp. Beth gasped as Anna's hand guided her fingers over the silky bristles of the stubble (harsher, just slightly, than Anna's, and glowing copper-gold against her white skin). Anna let go and Beth's fingertips found and traced the outlines of the scar she bore in almost the same place as Anna.

Anna said, 'Did you not see it when you looked in one of the mirrors in your bedroom?'

'My bedroom?'

'Your bedroom. On the same floor as mine. The thirteenth.'

'Oh, yes. I can't . . . no, it did have mirrors in it, but I can't remember looking in them. Or can I? I don't know. I feel very . . . strange. And my arse is fucking *raw*.'

'You poor thing. I know. I had *one* stroke from that bastard two days ago, and look! –' she turned to let Beth see '– See? It's turning purple.'

'You poor thing. Does it still hurt?'

Anna turned back, shrugging, shaking her head, gripping Beth's shoulder.

'*You* poor thing – don't worry about me, because your arse will look like that in a day or two, only worse, because he caned you more. Six times, wasn't it?'

'It seemed like a hundred.'

'Wait, I'll see.'

She stepped to the rear of the whipping-horse and bent over Beth's arse, feeling a pang of guilt as her nipples and cunt responded to the sight of the fading red lines of the cane-strokes across the milky, satiny skin.

'Will it hurt if I touch your arse, dear?'

'Try it.'

Anna touched one of the cane-strokes gently. Beth winced.

'Did that hurt?'

'A little. But try rubbing it and it might make it better.'

'I'll rub them as I count them. Like this.'

She ran her fingertip along the line of the cane-stroke, then back again, barely touching the skin.

'That's number one. Does it feel better when I rub it?'

'Yes. Press a tiny, tiny bit harder.'

Anna rubbed the cane-stroke again, pressing a tiny, tiny bit harder.

'Better?'

'Yes. Better. Try one of the other ones.'

Anna picked out one of the other cane-strokes, ran her fingertip along it, once, twice, three times.

'That's number two. Better?'

'Yes. Better. Much better. Do another one.'

'OK . . . this is number three. I'm getting his . . . *stuff* all over my finger. Yuck.'

'I know. That's even worse than the pain – the feeling of his fucking come on my arse. It's dripping down between my legs too.'

'Number four. Shall I try to get it off?'

'Oh, please.'

'Number five. That's the last one, unless the bastard put two in the same place. Wait, I'll see if I can find something to wipe it off with.'

She turned, looking for a cushion or tablecloth.

'No, dear,' said Beth. 'Don't wipe it off. That won't be good enough. Please, dear, lick it off. Then I'll know it's all gone, and your tongue will be *so* soothing on my arse. Please, dear.'

Anna swung back, nausea curdling in her stomach and throat.

'Oh, Beth, you *can't* ask me to do that! *Lick* it off? I'll throw up, I know I will.'

'Please, dear. Lick it off. Then I'll know it's all gone. And my arse is hurting so much.'

'But I couldn't, honestly I couldn't. Even if I wipe most of it off first I'd still be able to *taste* it, and I'd throw up, I know I would.'

'Try it. There's already some on your finger. Lick that and get used to it. It isn't that horrible. I mean, I've never *heard* it's that horrible. Just a bit salty. Don't think about what it is. Hold your breath. Please, dear. For me. For my poor arse. It's hurting so much. I got five strokes, remember. Four more than you.'

Anna raised her smeared finger to her mouth, holding her breath. She opened her mouth and put her tongue out slowly, feeling her throat begin to tighten and the walls of her stomach contract. Then she stopped, withdrew her tongue, closed her mouth. She shook her head, eyes suddenly glistening.

'Oh, Beffy, I *can't*! I'll be sick, I know I will.'

'For me, Ansie. For my poor arse. Just lick at your finger so you get used to it. Just a tiny lick. You won't even taste it.'

'But it's come out of his cock, and I hate him. He's crazy. He only gave me one stroke, and that was bad enough, but he's given you *five*. He enjoyed it. That's why he shot his stuff all over your bum. He *liked* hurting you. He's sick. Evil. How can you ask me to lick his stuff off you?'

'Because my arse is hurting so much. Please, Ansie. Ansie-Pansie. For me, not for him. He wouldn't like to think that his come has been cleaned off me. I know he wouldn't. He'd hate to think that you'd licked it off. I know he would. Just a tiny lick and you'll see how easy it is.'

Anna raised her finger again, opened her mouth, slowly put out her tongue. She tried to move her finger closer, lick at it, but her hand wouldn't move. She wailed.

'*Please*,' said Beth. 'Please. For me. For my poor arse.'

'Oh, darling, I'm trying, but I can't do it. You'll have to help me. You lick my finger first, then I'll know it's OK. It will still be horrible, but I'll do it. You lick my finger first.'

She stepped back up Beth's body, resting a hand on Beth's shoulder. Beth turned her head, sticking out her tongue, and Anna dropped her fingertip on to it. Beth licked, then smacked her lips.

'Nice,' she said. 'Nothing to it.'

Anna let out a half-laugh, half-sob.

'OK, you've done it, so I'll do it. But I'm warning you: if I'm sick, I'll do it all over your arse. Then I'll find that cane and make you wish that bastard were back here again.'

She stepped back down Beth's body and touched her fingertip to the semen-coated cheek of her arse again. She lifted it to her mouth, holding her breath, and licked at it cautiously. She released her breath and inhaled shallowly. Her face twisted and she felt her stomach roll.

'Euuurggggh. It does taste horrible. I wish I had a really, really bad cold.'

'Come on, dear,' said Beth. 'Don't worry about what it tastes like – you'll soon get used to it. Lick my arse and make it better.'

Anna bent over her sister's arse, closed her eyes, put out her tongue, and gave a long, slow lick to one cheek, left to right. She felt the skin quiver and tighten and the gluteal muscles move beneath her tongue. Beth sighed with pleasure.

'Lovely, dear. More, please. Much more. Lick all over. Get it all off.'

Still holding her breath, Anna licked again at the cheek. The coating of semen was half-dried with the heat of Beth's body and she had to work her tongue at it hard to get it off. Even holding her breath she could taste the saltiness of it, and she knew the masculine reek of it would be hanging in her nostrils and mouth, waiting for her to breathe again.

Her stomach rolled, but less than before, and she knew she could do it. But for that bastard's stuff coating Beth's bum it wouldn't have been so bad. It wouldn't really have been bad at all: Beth's skin was so smooth and warm, especially where the strokes of the cane had sunk into it, each side of each stroke raised into a weal that she lingered carefully over, knowing that this was where the pain was worst, where her moist, hot tongue could most soothe her sister's suffering.

Beth sighed again.

'Lovely, darling. Lovely. But lots has dripped down between my legs. It's all over my cunt, darling. Lick there too. You won't mind that so much, will you?'

Anna snorted.

'There's the other cheek to do first, Beth. You slut,' she added daringly, half under her breath. But Beth heard:

121

Anna could tell from the way her buttocks jerked in mock anger.

'What was that, little sister? Did you call me a slut? I will remember that. So will you. When you're telling me about what *you* got up to with that lunatic. I bet you were so reluctant to lick my poor arse not because the taste of his come makes you sick but because you're sick of too much of it. I bet you've been sucking on his cock like it was a fucking lollipop.'

Anna choked with laughter, and bit into the soft flesh beneath her mouth.

'Ow! Stop that, you bitch.'

Anna nibbled, licked again, nibbled. This cheek was almost clean. She turned her head and rested her own cheek against it.

'Cheek to cheek,' she murmured.

'What?'

'Nothing.'

She rubbed her face-cheek up and down over Beth's arse-cheek, side to side, reading the smooth sensitive flesh with her own smooth sensitive flesh. She raised her head and said, 'Beth, I can tell where the cane-strokes are, just by putting my cheek against them. They're hotter.'

'You're fucking telling me. Now do the other side, dear, and between my legs. I can still feel it oozing and dripping and running all down and all over my cunt. Lick it off, quick, there's a dear.'

Anna walked round to the other side of the whipping-horse and bent to begin licking at Beth's other arse-cheek. She put a hand between Beth's legs and felt upwards between her inner thighs, down towards her cunt.

'See?' said Beth. 'I'm fucking drenched in it.'

'Hmm.'

Anna was too busy licking and sucking to reply, too busy working her tongue over the smooth, tainted flesh of that second superb buttock, working her tongue into and up and down each swelling, heated groove incused in her sister's skin by the thunder-crack of each cane-stroke, too busy working the coating of semen up and off the white, quivering skin. Beth sighed, and wriggled her arse beneath Anna's moving tongue.

'Lovely, dear. Lovely. I'm almost glad that bastard went to work on me. Keep it up. Get down between my legs before the fucking stuff dries.'

With a final lick Anna finished the second cheek and stepped directly behind the whipping-horse, directly behind her sister, so she could lean forwards and get to work between her legs. Beth splayed herself, and Anna smelt air charged with arousal rising from the space between her thighs, dense, musky, almost dizzying. She bent her head to the cleft of her sister's buttocks, working her tongue forwards in it as high as the coccyx and its delicate coating of shining red hairs, then back down again, down, down, between the bulges of each cheek, down, where the cheeks began to meld softly into the back of the thighs, down further, to the rim of the rim of the rim of her sister's anus, then back up again, almost having to lap the semen up from where it had collected to run down between Beth's legs.

'Lick me there, too, dear,' Beth told her. 'On my arsehole, dear. I can feel his come drying on it. It's kind of collected there like a little pool. Like I haven't wiped properly. Lick my arsehole too.'

Anna moved her tongue down the cleft again, back as low as she had been before, then lower, past the rim of the rim of the rim of her sister's anus, past the rim of the rim, to the rim, and past it, to the tight whorl of the anus. She could feel the sparse, silky hairs that encircled it as she swirled her tongue left and right, clockwise and counter-clockwise, lapping up the semen that had collected there.

'Ah, God,' said Beth. She squirmed, and Anna felt her sphincter flex beneath her working tongue just in time to pull her head back and watch as the sphincter trembled like an iris and opened (the pink inner walls glistened like wet marble) to give vent to a long, liquid fart. Anna, about to swear at her, closed her mouth and sniffed with astonishment.

'What the hell have you had up your bum?'

123

'Nothing. I'm sorry about that. I couldn't help it. You know I always do it when I'm really excited, and it just felt s –'

'Your fart smells of roses. It smells of perfume.'

She put her nose back down to it, sniffed, probed at it again with her tongue.

'And it tastes sweet. Like honey. What have you had up there?'

'I don't know what you're talking about. Lick lower, dear. Lick over my cunt. Get his come off me – it feels horrible.'

Anna probed at her sister's anus with her tongue, trying to pierce the sealed-again sphincter and gain access to the bowels beyond. She lifted her head.

'Open your arsehole, Beth. I want to taste what's inside it.'

'My *arse*hole, Ansie-Pansie? You've changed your tune, you little tart. I knew you would, once you got going.'

'Shut up and open it!'

The cheeks of Beth's arse trembled and Anna watched as the sphincter relaxed. She put her head down again and pushed her tongue at it, but even as she did so she felt Beth tighten it again.

'Bitch! Open it. I want to know where that smell of roses and taste of honey is coming from. He's been doing something to you while you were unconscious. Shit, he might have been doing something to *me*, too.'

She broke off, struck by a new thought. Beth wriggled her arse impatiently.

'Forget about all that. The important thing is to lick his come off my cunt, so get on with it.'

'No, wait, I've just thought of something and it's *strange*. Really strange. I can remember being here three days now – though that bastard tells me I've been here much longer – and I can't remember *eating* anything. Not a thing. But I don't feel hungry now and I've only felt hungry once. Yesterday. When he wanted me to be hungry.'

'Shut up. I don't care. Get on with licking my cunt!'

124

'No, this is important. Do you remember eating anything?'

'No. I don't remember anything at all about how I got here or about what's happened to me since I've been here except that some nutter has been caning me and spunked all over my fucking arse so it dripped down all over my fucking cunt and it's oozing and dripping there now and feels absolutely fucking gross and my fucking little sister won't do a thing about it even though I keep telling her to. So do it!'

'This is important.'

'*Do* it!'

Anna bent back to her sister's arse, swirled her tongue left and right over the anus for a moment, then dropped lower, over the perineum, following the column of silky hairs that marched from Beth's anus, over to the fourchette, to the cunt, harvesting the still heavy, still liquid coating of Bärengelt's come. She was not holding her breath any more, and the thick salty taste of his come had filled her mouth and throat, disgusting her, but no longer making her think she would throw up.

And here, at Beth's cunt (Beth gasped and began to lift her hips, exposing more of her cunt to the probing tongue), the unfamiliar taste of male sex-juice was seasoned with the familiar taste of female sex-juice: Beth was open and leaking like a ripe fruit split by too much sun. Anna lapped at the cum-and-cunt-juice cocktail, having to lift her head as Beth lifted her hips higher, higher, working her tongue in and out of the cunt-folds, up and down the central slit until her tongue and lower lips brushed and were silkily prickled by the fringes of her sister's pubic hair.

Beth groaned and swore, her cunt pulsing against Anna's mouth and lips, her whole body shuddering. She was shouting something, and Anna obeyed it before she understood the words, standing back, gasping too, her mouth and the whole lower half of her face glistening with mingled cunt-juice, come, and spittle, drops of the stuff sparkling as they gathered thickly and dripped from her chin to her breasts. She lifted a hand, gathered the fluids on a fingertip, and rubbed them slowly into a nipple as she watched Beth reach a hand between her legs and rub fiercely at her clitoris and labia, prolonging her orgasm, screaming. Then her hand fell away and she collapsed atop it, atop her whole arm, lying spent against the whipping-horse, her legs splayed, her cunt and perineum and anus glistening from the attentions of Anna's tongue, the tone of her skin changed suddenly, as though the flesh beneath it had melted with the force and heat of her orgasm. Beth's breath was whistling moistly in–out, in–out, her body rocking as her lungs expanded and collapsed beneath the firm breasts pressed to the whipping-horse.

'Fart again,' Anna told her.

'Wha – what?'

Beth struggled to free her trapped arm, to lift herself up and look back, but her limbs were still too weak, trembling spastically as she tried to move them. Anna swallowed, her mouth beginning to water again as she watched Beth's exposed cunt flex between her moving legs.

'Fart again,' she said. 'Fart again, so I can smell what's inside your arse again.'

Beth coughed. A shudder ran through her body, and the tone of her skin changed again: her flesh was hard and firm again: orgasm had been absorbed back into her body.

'No,' she said. 'Come here and kiss me. I want to taste myself on your lips.'

Anna moved back up the whipping-horse. Beth lifted herself on her hands, twisting her upper body to bring her face to Anna's as Anna bent to kiss her. Her mouth sealed itself to Anna's greedily, sucking, slurping, her tongue forcing itself between Anna's lips, running over her teeth and gums, stabbing at and wrestling with Anna's tongue, withdrawing to pass over Anna's lips, work in her philtrum, probe at her nostrils, the flesh around her mouth, eager for the taste of the fluids Anna had licked from her caned arse and gaping cunt.

She broke away from Anna for a moment, gasping, then clamped her mouth back again, sucking even more fiercely, her tongue working at Anna's skin, almost scraping at it, hot and wet, flexible and muscular.

Then she pulled back again.

'Fuck,' she said. 'That tastes good. Come closer –
there's more on your tits.'

Anna moved closer and Beth dropped her mouth to lick
and suck at her glistening breasts, more slowly and
meditatively now, as though she was pausing to savour the
taste of herself. Anna gasped as her lips closed over a
nipple, sucking hard, teeth nipping, then came loose with
a moist pop, Beth's lips and tongue slowly travelling
towards the other nipple, slipping down into the cleft
between the two firm mounds, slipping up the swell of the
other breast until the summit and nipple were reached and
the mouth closed again, sucking hard, teeth nipping.

Anna's hands closed on the back of her sister's head,
silkily prickled by the stubble on the shaven scalp, pressing
the working mouth closer to her breast, urging the tongue
and lips and teeth to greater effort, greater cruelty,
mingling pain with the pleasure given by Beth's abuse of
her stiff morsel of flesh: she bit her own lips, groaning a
little, her fingers digging deeper into the smooth scalp and
the silky bristles of the stubble, twisting, assaying her
sister's head like a giant nugget of warm precious stone.

And then she stiffened with surprise: one fingertip had
brushed across a patch of longer stubble, too thick to feel
the scalp through. As the pleasure/pain mounted from her
serviced/tortured nipple (Beth was closing her teeth upon
it, drawing her head slowly back to stretch it, releasing it
suddenly, the whole breast shuddering faintly from the
released tension, licking at it, sucking at it, closing her teeth
upon it again) her fingertips clustered on the patch, reading
its dimensions, its shape, its position. It was circular, a little
larger than a fifty-pence piece, centred exactly above the
vertebra of the neck, obviously not accidental: left there
deliberately when Beth's head was shaved.

A thought struck her (she gasped as Beth tugged more
cruelly with her teeth at the nipple, released it, and began
to suck and lick her way back down the swell of the breast
it surmounted for the cleft and the swell of the other breast
and the nipple atop it): she lifted a hand away from Beth's

occiput to pass her fingertips over her own. And yes, there, identically sized, shaped, positioned, another patch of stubble (slightly softer, silkier than Beth's), obviously not accidental: left there deliberately when *her* head was shaved.

'Beth,' she said. 'Stop. Wait a moment.'

Beth's head lifted from her breasts, and she looked up at her, copper-gold eyebrows lifting.

'Don't you like it?'

'Yes. But look –' she took hold of one of Beth's hands and lifted it to the back of Beth's head '– feel that.'

'Feel what? Oh, yeah. What is it?'

'Look, I've got one too. In the same place.'

She turned her head, and after a moment felt Beth's fingers brush over the circular patch of stubble.

'See? When he shaved us, he didn't shave that bit fully. He left it.'

'So? Can I get back to sucking your tits, please? It's very therapeutic, after what I've been through.'

'No, listen. Why didn't he shave those patches? What's underneath them? He's trying to hide something from us. Something that would tell us something he doesn't want us to know. There's something underneath them.'

'What?'

'A scar. Or a . . .'

Her thoughts suddenly turned to the magazine she had read, and the story of the woman whose cunt and inner thighs had been tattooed with a butterfly.

'Or a what?'

'Or a tattoo.'

'A *what*?'

'A tattoo.'

'But that's crazy. If a tattoo is *under* my hair now, it must have been put on when my hair was shaved off before. A long time ago. Before we ever heard of Bärengelt and this crazy shack or whatever-it-is he's brought us to.'

'His Schloss. In the Black Forest.'

'Whatever. So when did I get this tattoo? When did you get yours? We've worn our hair long since we were kids. You can't give kids tattoos. It's illegal.'

128

'OK, but I still think there's something under there. Something important. And I do think it might be a tattoo.'

'Why?'

'I can show you. Something in my bedroom. A magazine. He meant me to see it. Come upstairs and see.'

'OK. I need a piss anyway. There's a bathroom up there, isn't there?'

'There is one in my bedroom – I don't know about yours. I don't know where your bedroom *is*. There's only one door on that landing. Maybe you didn't count the flights of stairs properly.'

'Maybe I didn't. Maybe I did. We'll soon see. Come on.'

Beth swung her legs up and slipped off the whipping-horse.

'Ow,' she said. 'I'm stiff, and my arse is hurting again.'

She looked over her shoulder, turning her hips so she could examine her buttocks.

'Look at them! Look what that bastard's done to me.'

She fingered the fading pinky grooves of the cane-strokes, tugging the cheeks gently apart, swearing softly.

Anna touched the strokes gently too.

'Poor Beth. Come on, come and have a bath. I'll soap and rub them for you. Maybe your arse won't bruise too badly, the way mine has done.'

She lifted her hand from Beth's arse and looked over her own shoulder at the purple stroke bisecting her own arse.

'No,' said Beth. 'I said I needed a piss. Let's get that done first.'

'OK. Upstairs.'

'No. Now. Here.'

'What?'

'Where's one of those fucking loudspeakers? I want to piss on to it. So that it fucking shorts out when he switches it back on again.'

'Don't be stupid – you'll hurt yourself. It might *still* be switched on. You might electrocute yourself.'

'No, I heard them turn off, when he left. He must have turned them off. Where are they?'

Beth strode away from the whipping-horse (Anna swallowed, her eyes drawn irresistibly to the cane-strokes glowing pinkly across the firm buttocks, which were tautened with resolve, bouncing with the energy of Beth's movements as she stooped and twisted, looking beneath one piece of furniture after another as she searched for one of the loudspeakers).

'One of them sounded as though it was about here,' Beth said. 'Maybe – yes, look, bingo.'

She bent and lifted a table out of the way (it was solid teak, heavy, and Anna swallowed again, watching the muscles of her sister's buttocks and rear thighs work beneath the milky, pink-slashed skin, and her sister's cunt gape briefly, a coppery-gold sheen flashing suddenly from her pubic hair).

'Look, Anna, this is one of the fucking things. Look at the fucking shape of it. The childish fucking cunt.'

The loudspeaker was about a metre high, a giant blunt phallus of black plastic, its hexagonally pierced grille fitting snugly over the glans. Beth kicked at it, her foot and shin very white against its black solidity.

'Cunt.'

'Cock,' said Anna.

Beth glanced back, grinning.

'Cock,' she said. 'I stand corrected.'

'*It* stands corrected.'

'Yeah. It'll be standing pissed on in a minute, too.'

She stepped over it, opening her thighs, sitting down on it.

'Is this what you'd like your cock to be like, Bärengelt? Big and black and permanently stiff? In your dreams, you fucking cunt.'

She slowly scraped her cunt and inner thighs over the grille of the speaker.

'Nice,' she said. Her voice deepened as she twisted her hips, grinding herself at the grille. She stopped, peering down between her thighs: 'Look – I could use this to sort out my bikini line. Want one?'

She reached down between her thighs and picked up one of the glistening pubic hairs trapped and torn off her by the hexagonal holes in the grille. Anna laughed and walked towards her, holding out her hand for it. Beth dropped it and it lay curled flat against the palm. Anna lifted her hand to her mouth and licked the hair up. She held it between her front teeth, rolling it slightly. Beth was scraping herself on the loudspeaker-phallus, twisting from side to side, finding the most comfortable angle to begin driving herself at the grille.

Anna said, 'Your pubes, they're so harsh I'd use them for dental floss. Only I don't want to lose my tooth-enamel.'

'Little sister,' said Beth, beginning to grunt as she settled into the rhythm she wanted, 'you're confusing harshness with healthiness. I have healthy, strong-growing pubes.'

She threw out a hand unexpectedly, hooking the fingers hard into Anna's pubes.

'You, on the other hand – and you *are* on the other hand – have the typical pubic growth of a blonde: excessively fine, excessively weak.'

Anna pulled herself away, laughing, squeaking as she left pubic hairs between Beth's fingers.

'See?'

Beth held her trophies up, rocking her cunt at the loudspeaker so hard now that Anna could feel it in the floor.

'Bitch,' said Anna. 'Give them back.'

'No.'

Beth raised the hairs to her mouth, licked at them, closed her teeth on them, and pulled. She spat, holding up her hand again.

'Look: no – tensile strength – at all. – Pull – ah – at them and they – *come* – a–part.'

She was gasping loudly now, her cunt sliding on a grille slick with a thickening film of cunt-juice. Anna lifted a hand and took hold of one end of the pubic hair in her mouth. Holding on with her teeth she tugged at it but it didn't part.

'Jew's harp,' she said, and tried to strum at it.

'Bitch,' said Beth. 'Bitch.'

She came, groaning, grinding her cunt cruelly at the grille, a network of tendons standing out clearly in the creamy surface of each inner thigh.

'Fucking hell,' she said, standing clear of the grille on unsteady legs. 'That was nice. And I've smeared it up nicely for him.'

'For *me*,' said Anna. She stepped towards the loudspeaker and knelt in front of it.

'Fuck off,' Beth said, aiming a kick at her. 'I want to piss on it now.'

'Then piss on it. Piss on me. As I'm licking your juice off.'

'You slut.'

'I know. But I don't care.'

She shuffled near the loudspeaker on her knees and lowered her mouth to kiss the heavy smear of cunt-juice Beth had left on the grille. She could feel the hexagonal pattern through her lips – a black oozing honeycomb – then through her tongue as she began to lick and suck at the black plastic, still warm from the friction of Beth's cunt. Above her Beth grunted and began to piss. The flow struck Anna's forehead and face, hot, almost scalding, splattering off on to the grille, beginning to pour all over Anna's face, dripping from her eyebrows and nose, running to and off the point of her chin as the cocktail of sexjuices had done, but caught on the way by the eager mouth that licked and sucked at the grille. Anna coughed and spluttered with surprise. Beth's piss was warm champagne.

Ten

'But where did it come from?' Anna said.

They were climbing the stairs hand-in-hand.

'Where did what come from?'

'The champagne. Where did the perfume come from, too?'

'What champagne? What perfume?'

'In your bladder. Up your arse. You must have seen Bärengelt on another day. Yesterday, maybe. He's been doing things to you. And when do we ever eat?'

'How do you know he's been doing things to me?'

'Because of the champagne and that perfume. Try and remember how they got there. He stuck something up me.'

They reached the first landing.

Anna said, 'That's the first floor. Let's count them. He stuck something up me. A catheter. When he put the champagne into my bladder. When I pissed on him. Did that happen with you?'

'I can't remember.'

'Try. *Try*, darling. It's important.'

'I can't remember. That's why it's called "can't remembering". Because I can't remember.'

'Nothing at all?'

'Nothing at all. I don't even know there was champagne up there.'

'You tasted it too, darling. Look, taste it again.'

'Gerroff! Leave it alone.'

'Then you touch it. You're still wet. Rub yourself with your finger and lick it. The second floor.'

'Oh, Christ, if it makes you happy.'

Beth paused on the stairs, let go of Anna's hand, splayed her legs ostentatiously, and rubbed at the wet lips of her cunt. She raised the finger to her mouth, licked, sucked, rolled her eyes musingly.

'See?' said Anna. 'It's champagne.'

'It's piss.'

'It's champagne.'

'It doesn't taste much like champagne.'

'It's warm. It must have been inside you for a long time.'

'Not that long. Come on.'

She grabbed Anna's hand again and they continued up the stairs.

'Why not that long?'

'Because if it had been in there a long time it would be piss, mostly. Or I'd already have pissed it out. Champagned it out.'

'That means you admit it. It *is* champagne. Third floor.'

'Yeah, OK, it's champagne. And that bastard must have put it up me sometime not long ago. Today.'

'While he was with you in the Black Room? Before he caned you?'

'Yes. No. Maybe. Look, I don't know. Maybe yes, maybe no, maybe maybe. I can't remember. I can't remember much of what went on. I woke up today and I left the room I was in to find out where I was and I went downstairs – and I *know* it was thirteen floors – and I found that weird black room and Bärengelt was there behind this crazy fucking glass table and he had me roll these crazy fucking dice –'

'Just like me. Fourth floor.'

'And I lost – just like you, yeah? – so he could tell me what to do.'

'You had to rub yourself on the glass table? While he tossed himself off underneath it? And when he came, you had to get underneath the table and lick his stuff off and if any went on the floor he was going to punish you and some did go on the floor?'

'Yes. I think. It's a bit . . . blurred. I remember the cane. Because that hurt. A lot. Kind of. It's still hurting.'

'I know. Fourth floor. But what do you mean "kind of"?'

'It hurt a lot, but it kind of didn't too. You know?'

'No, I don't know. What?'

'It made me leak. I got a wide-on.'

'Because he caned you?'

'Yeah. I liked it. I wanted him to carry on. Carry on till my arse bled. But at the same time I hated it.'

'He's corrupted you already. Perverted you.'

'I know. That's why I want to get my revenge on him. I want to see how *he* likes it, strapped to that fucking whipping-horse, taking half-a-dozen strokes on the arse –'

'Or a dozen.'

'Yeah. And then taking something *big* UP the arse. That fucking dildo. On maximum revs. Buzzing like a fucking giant wasp.'

'Like a giant hornet. Fifth floor.'

'Like a nest of giant hornets. So that it shakes his guts up. So that he feels it all the way up his spine and in the back of his head. So that it makes his balls ache like they're going to fucking explode.'

'And when he comes, he comes so hard he feels as if his balls *have* exploded.'

'Stop it – you're making my nipples stiff.'

Anna giggled.

'Mine already are. Feel them.'

They paused again, swung together, belly-to-belly, and fingered each other's nipples.

Anna said, 'Rub the left and squeeze the right. Scratch it too. Twist it. Like this.'

She demonstrated on Beth's tits.

Beth shuddered.

'Nice,' she said, adjusting her fingers on Anna's nipples to return the favour. 'Where did you pick this up?'

'Bärengelt did it to me. I'm calling it the four T's.'

'Yeah?' said Beth, the tip of her tongue protruding slightly as she concentrated on rubbing Anna's left nipple

135

and squeezing and scratching her right. 'What does that mean?'

'Tender-tit, tough-tit. Stroke one, torment the other.'

'It gives me an idea. I'd like to try PPTT.'

'What's that?'

Their voices were unsteady now as they worked at each other's nipples, their right hands growing gentler as their left grew harsher.

'Pleasured pussy, tortured tits. But it would need three – aaaah, you vicious little bitch – one to submit, one to pleasure her pussy, one to torture her tits.'

Anna let go of Beth's right nipple, then her left.

'If we had Gwen.'

Beth stopped too.

'Yeah. If we had Gwen. Where is she?'

Sobered, they swung apart, only a gleam of liquid between the slightly gaping lips of their cunts to show what they had just been doing, and clasped hands again to continue up the stairs.

Anna said, 'Bärengelt told me you were both dead. In a car crash that only I survived. With head injuries. Which is where the scar came from. But you've got the same scar. In the same place. Sixth floor.'

'Which is two out of three. So maybe Gwen is here somewhere too. With the same scar, in the same place.'

'I know she's here somewhere.'

'How?'

'Two reasons. First is that Madame Oursor told me that she's here. Or told me that *you*'d told *her* that she's here.'

'When?'

'When what? When did Madame Oursor tell me or when did you tell her?'

'When both.'

'About half-an-hour ago. She was here. She came over from England because she was worried about me. She said she'd spoken to you on the phone an –'

'I don't remember that.'

'You don't remember a lot but that's what she said. She said she'd spoken to you and you said that you'd seen Gwen. Here.'

'I'll take your word for it.'

'And I'll take Madame Oursor's.'

'And she takes mine. Isn't that arguing in a circle?'

'Yes. But who cares? Gwen *is* here. I know it because Madame Oursor says so and because I've seen Gwen myself. The way I saw you.'

'When? You saw her today, like you saw me? Down there, you mean?'

'No. I've seen both of you in the mirrors in my room. It's full of antique furniture. Lots of mirrors.'

'I think my room is too.'

'Have you seen me or Gwen in one of them?'

'I can't remember. I've seen you. Today. But downstairs. When you saw me. I think. It's this scar: it makes my head feel . . . metallic. The car crash you said we were in.'

'No. Seventh floor. The car crash *he* said we were in. But our scars are all the same. All in the same place. Yours – and mine – and Gwen's. That's impossible. In a real car crash it couldn't happen. So it was him again. Something to do with the tattoos.'

'What tattoos?'

'Behind the unshaved patches of hair. The not-properly-shaved patches. Here.'

She lifted her free hand across to touch the back of Beth's head, but Beth shook her head, swinging her free hand to ward Anna's off, saying, 'No, you only think there are tattoos there. Maybe there aren't.'

'Maybe there are. We'll see. When we get to my bedroom. Or yours. Eighth floor.'

They climbed in silence interrupted only at each new landing by Anna's 'Ninth floor . . . tenth floor . . . eleventh floor . . . twelfth floor . . . Thirteenth floor. This is it. Where's your bedroom door?'

'Where's *yours*?'

'That's mine. There.'

'No, that's mine. It can't be yours.'

'It's mine – I've been sleeping in there for three days.'

'It's mine. I remember it. Thirteenth floor. That door. My bedroom.'

137

Their clasped hands momentarily loosened, as though about to let go, and then tightened again.

'Let's see,' said Anna.

They walked towards the door, through it, and screamed. Or Anna screamed. Beth had disappeared. Anna's left hand tingled with the memory of Beth's right, then went quiet. But there, ahead of her in one of the mirrors, was Beth. But Beth was not in the room. She panicked and ran out of the room, back on to the stairs, and was suddenly sprawling on the cool marble, limbs tangled with someone else's limbs, her shriek echoing in her ears with someone else's shriek. Beth's limbs – Beth's shriek.

They sat up, looking at each other.

'Wha –?' they both started to say, and laughed.

'What happened?' said Beth.

'You disappeared.'

'No, *you* disappeared.'

'When we went into my bedroom?'

'No. When we went into *my* bedroom.'

'So what happened?'

'Let's try it again. Holding hands really tight this time.'

They took hold of each other's hands again, squeezed hard, looked at each other, smiled.

'Big breath,' said Beth.

They walked towards the door of the bedroom – and screamed again. Or Anna screamed, though not so loudly as before. Beth had disappeared again. No, there she was – ahead of her, in one of the mirrors, standing almost next to her, the way she should have been just after they came into the room. A thought struck her. She began to wave at Beth's reflection. After a few moments the reflection began to wave back, then make gestures, as though asking her to do something.

Anna frowned.

'I don't un – ah, yes.'

Beth was gesturing for her to leave the room again.

She did so, carefully, but still nearly bumped into Beth again. They grabbed at each other.

'Did you see me waving in the mirror?' Anna said.

'Yeah. We can see each other in the *mirrors* in the room but we can't see each other *in* the room. This is very weird. Fucking surreal.'

'Maybe . . .' Anna said.

'Maybe what?'

'It's him again – Bärengelt. He's playing games with us. I've heard of something like this before.'

She frowned, bowing her head in concentration, then jerked up hard (the loss of her hair struck her again), looking at Beth, smiling.

'Yes! I remember now. Remember when we were taking the secretarial course, before we came out here?'

'Uh, yes. I think so.'

'The shorthand. We had to type up someone else's shorthand notes. Mine were from a psychologist. Preparing for a lecture. Something about hypnosis. What you can do with it. That's what Bärengelt's done. He's hypnotised us.'

'I don't remember that. I remember the shorthand, but I didn't type up that. Mine was a scientist, preparing notes on insects or something. Mosquitoes.'

'Maybe we all did something different. Mine was definitely a psychologist, talking about hypnosis. The way you can use it to make people see what you want them to see. Or *not* see what you don't want them to see. That's what he's done. He hypnotised us so that we don't see each other inside that room. Except in the mirrors. So when I saw you and Gwen, you really were there. In the room with me. No, wait, I think we must all have been sleeping in the same bed. But we just didn't know it.'

'That's impossible. We would have bumped into each other. We'd have felt each other even if we didn't see each other.'

'No, it doesn't make a difference. You can blank out any sense. Sight or touch. Hearing, smell, taste.'

'But how? I don't believe it's possible.'

'But you saw it. We can't see each other when we go inside that room. We can't feel each other. Or smell or taste or hear each other.'

'But now we know what's going on. We'll know we're really there. Look, let's hold on to each other as we go in. *Really* hold on to each other. Go in screaming at the top of our voices. OK?'

'OK. I don't think it will work, but OK.'

'Believe that it won't work, and it won't work. Believe that it will, and it will. So believe. Be a believer.'

'I'm a believer.'

'You're going to be in for such a spanking when Gwen turns up, madam.'

'No, please. Not on my bruise.'

'On your bruise. A really stern spanking. I'm looking forward to it. Now, get hold of me.'

'Let's go in like tango dancers. Cheek to cheek, arms outstretched.'

'OK. If you know how, show me.'

'Like this.'

Anna took hold of Beth.

'See? Bodies together – like this. Then clasp hands – like this. Hold them out – like this. And step in time – like this. Come on – like this.'

'*Where* did you learn all this?'

'When we were in America. Yeah, good. That time I was ill and spent a lot of time by myself in the hotel room. Those big TVs and all those channels. When we were down south. Good, that's the way. I could pick up South American TV. That's where the tango comes from. Watch my feet. Good. From Argentina, actually, dear.'

'And a history lesson is thrown in, too. Great. Are we ready now?'

They were tangoing back and forth across the landing outside the bedroom, torsos sealed together, hip spearing hip, hearts beating with heavy asynchrony in the single mound formed by their left-and-right breasts pressed together, creating a single shell of body heat and odour (the dried sweat and sex-juices of the Black Room).

'Yeah, I think so.'

'Then hold tighter. Really tight. And we've got to go in yelling.'

'What?'

'Up yours, Bärengelt.'

'Good. He might even be watching.'

'I hope he is watching. Ready?'

'Yep.'

'OK, on the count of three . . . one . . . two . . . three . . .'

In three swift simultaneous strides they reached the door of the bedroom, arms spearing the air in front of them, yelling at the tops of their voices:

'Up yours, Bä –'

And Anna wailed this time, a little, with disappointment. Beth – the smell, the sound, the touch of her, everything – had disappeared as soon as they passed over the threshold. She looked towards the mirrors, and saw Beth gesturing to her, sticking out her lower lip with annoyance. She left the room, and Beth seemed to materialise out of bare air as she walked.

'I told you,' she said.

'I told you,' Beth mimicked. 'I might spank you now. On your bruise. Now!'

But Anna had been expecting the lunge and jumped back, sticking out her tongue. Then she sucked it back in, lifting up a hand as Beth crouched and moved menacingly towards her.

'No, Beth, wait. I've had an idea. About Gwen.'

'What?'

Beth straightened, suppressing a yawn, rubbing at a nipple, scratching at her pubic hair, her fingers making a faint, silky rasping.

'Hurry up,' she said. 'What about Gwen? I'd like a bath.'

'Well, isn't it obvious? If you were there with me –'

'No, if *you* were there with me.'

'Whatever. If we were there with each other, why not Gwen, too? She might be in there now, and we'd never know. Except if she comes out.'

'But wouldn't she see us from inside?'

'I don't think so. Hold on, you stay here and I'll go in and see if I can see you.'

She trotted into the room, turning once she was inside and looking out. The landing seemed to be empty. She trotted out again.

'I didn't see you. Did you see me?'

'No. It was fucking weird, the way you just *faded* as you went through the door. Like you were melting apart – no, it's hard to say what happened. I can't say how it happened.'

'So Gwen may be in there now.'

'Maybe. Maybe.'

'We'll see her in the mirrors. If she's there.'

'Why?'

'Bec – oh, yes. You're right. You mean Bärengelt might be playing another game?'

'Yeah. *We* can see each other in the mirrors in there. And without the mirrors we can see each other out here. But what about her? You've seen her in the mirror but maybe you only see in the mirrors. Not anywhere else. Maybe she's here with us now, and we don't see her. Even if she can see us.'

'This is very strange.'

'What do you remember about that shorthand – the psychologist, talking about hypnosis?'

'Why?'

'Because maybe we can dehypnotise each other. Dehypnotise ourselves so that we can see Gwen, wherever she is.'

'Yes. I see. Um, I don't remember much.'

'How do you hypnotise someone?'

'Get them relaxed. Then do the traditional thing, like with a swinging watch or just moving your finger, or tell them to visualise. Tell them they're walking down a set of stairs, getting deeper and deeper into . . . it. The hypnotic state, I suppose. With some people it's very easy, with some it's very hard.'

'How do you tell?'

'You try it.'

'OK. I'll try it with you.'

'I'm not relaxed.'

'Then relax. Lie on the floor.'

'It's cold.'

'Then sit on it. It'll soothe your bruise. Adopt the position. You'll like that.'

'What position?'

'The lotus position.'

Anna sat on the floor and carefully folded her legs into the lotus position.

'Like this?'

'Yes. Like that,' Beth said, sitting on her haunches in front of her. 'But what do I do when you're hypnotised?'

'Try to find out what Bärengelt did in the first place. You can remember things when you're hypnotised that happened when you were hypnotised before. So maybe I could remember what he said when he hypnotised me. Unless he's put a block on it.'

'OK. I'll try that. So get ready to go under. The traditional approach first. Watch my finger.'

She began to move her right index finger back and forth in front of Anna's face. After a couple of moments Anna's face began to crease, then it split into a smile, a laugh.

'What's wrong?'

'I can't concentrate. Your tits are right behind your finger. It looks like you're stroking your nipples. If I squint.'

'Then don't squint. Concentrate.'

'No. Waggle your tits instead. That will be much more fun.'

Beth shook her head.

'You want to be spanked, don't you? Don't worry – you will be. I'm going to tell Gwen all about this.'

'I pick the right. I'll watch it, you waggle.'

Beth blew out her cheeks and sighed.

'OK, young lady. You've been warned, so suffer the consequences when they come. Watch my right tit, and relax.'

She began to rock her upper body, slowly allowing the movement to bleed into her tits, which began to swing, the nipples describing lazy arcs. Anna thought they looked like cherries sitting on scoops of coconut ice-cream on a table during an earthquake.

'Or while someone is having sex on it,' she said. 'Before dessert. The ice-cream is still firm, but it will start to melt soon. Maybe they'll rub it into each other.'

'Shut up. Concentrate. You're getting sleepy. Sleepy.'

'I'm getting hungry. I want to get my teeth into something.'

'Shut up. Concentrate. Watch my right nipple swing. You're getting sleepy. Sleepy. Sleepy.'

Anna began to speak, then stopped with her mouth half-open.

'You're getting slee – Stop it, you silly little bitch. This is meant to be serious.'

But Anna's mouth stayed half-open. Her eyes had suddenly focused beyond Beth's breasts, beyond the ripe cherry of the right nipple atop the firm scoop of coconut ice-cream, and the tone of her skin had changed, as though it were snow lying beneath suddenly changed sunlight.

'Anna? You'll get that spanking now if you're fucking me around. Now, girl!'

She raised her hand, moving as though she were about to lean forward and slap at Anna's bare legs. Anna didn't move. Beth waved her fingers in front of her face.

'Anna? Are you hypnotised? Tell me if you're hypnotised. Say "Yes".'

Anna's mouth moved.

'Yes.'

'Are you hypnotised?'

'Yes. I'm hypnotised.'

'Bingo.'

Beth moved her legs forwards and knelt in front of Anna.

'Now, listen to me. Can you remember anything about Bärengelt hypnotising us?'

'No.'

'Why not?'

'I can't remember anything about him hypnotising us, only about him hypnotising me.'

'Ah. Yes. OK, what did he do when he hypnotised you?'

'He told me some things.'

'What things?'

'I can't remember some of them. I'm not allowed to remember.'

'Try.'

'I can't. It's impossible. He has to tell me to remember; no one else can.'

'OK. What about the things that you can remember? What about the bedroom? Did he tell you that you couldn't see me inside the bedroom?'

'Yes. I wouldn't be able to see you, or hear you, or touch you, or smell you, or taste you. You would not be there, even if you were.'

'And what about Gwen?'

'I can't remember.'

'He didn't say you wouldn't be able to see Gwen in the bedroom?'

'I can't remember. I'm not allowed to remember.'

'Try.'

'I can't. Only h –'

'OK. I know. Only he can let you. Now, listen. I'm telling you something. Me. Your sister, not Bärengelt. I'm telling you that when I'm in the bedroom, you'll be able to see me. OK?'

'Yes.'

'Repeat this after me: "I will be able to see you inside the bedroom".'

'I will be able to see you inside the bedroom.'

'Good. Now – shit. You didn't tell me what to do at the end. What do I do? Tell me what I do now.'

'You tell me to wake up. Say: "Wake up, Anna. It's over."'

'OK. Wake up, Anna. It's over.'

Anna blinked, licked her lips, said, 'What happened? Did it work?'

'I hope so. The hypnosis worked, anyway, or seemed to. You weren't fooling, were you?'

'No. Promise. I kind of remember what you said. Kind of. Shall we test it?'

'OK. I'll go in, you come in after me.'

'OK.'

She watched Beth walk into the bedroom – and not disappear. Smiling, she ran in after her, and she was there.

'It worked! Beth, it w – oh, yeah.'

She walked out of the room and watched as Beth stood just beyond the door for a few seconds and then walked out as well.

'Did it work?'

'Yes. I could see you perfectly. For a moment I thought you must be able to see me too, so I tried to speak to you. But you've not been dehypnotised.'

'Nope. Do you want to try it?'

'OK. The same way?'

'Yes. Now I get to watch your right tit swinging.'

Beth sat on the floor and folded her legs into the lotus position; Anna sat on her haunches in front of her.

'Ready?'

'Yep. Start swinging.'

Anna started to sway her upper body, watching her tits to see how well they were responding.

'Watch my right nipple. Watch it swing. Feel your mind start to get heavy. Very heavy. It's starting to sink. Sink down through warm, deep water. Deeper and deeper. Darker and darker. Deeper and deeper. Darker and darker.'

'You're good at this.'

'Shut up! Listen.'

'Good, but not good enough. I don't think it's going to work.'

'Try it again. Watch my right tit. Watch it swing. Your mind's getting heavy. Heavy. Very heavy. It's starting to sink.'

Beth burst out laughing.

'No, sorry. It's not going to work.'

'Then I give up.'

'Good. It wasn't going to work. I'm not – what's the word? – a good something.'

'Subject.'

'Yes. I'm not a good hypnotic subject.'

'Because you don't want to be.'

'I do. Take that back. Now.'

'No. You're just being stubborn. You don't want to submit to me, the way I submitted to you.'

'Rubbish. I've just got a strong mind, that's all. Not like yours. Weak. Wishy-washy.'

'You mean you're just a stubborn bitch. Pigheaded. Muleheaded.'

'Right. That's it. I'm not waiting for Gwen – you're getting that spanking now.'

She lifted her legs from the lotus position and stood up quickly. Anna pushed herself off her heels backwards.

'But my *bruise*, Beth.'

'Fuck your bruise. You're going to get a spanking.'

'I'm not.'

'You are, young lady.'

She darted at Anna, grabbing for an arm. Anna ducked with a squeak, and they had swapped places, Beth with her back to the stair-railing, Anna with her back to the door of the bedroom. Anna glanced over her shoulder.

'Aha!'

She ran into the bedroom. Beth shouted from behind her.

'Cheat!'

Laughing, panting, Anna slowed to a walk as soon as she was inside the room, knowing she was safe now: Beth could not see her inside, but she could see Beth inside or out. She began to turn to watch the door, then stopped. There was someone sleeping in the bed: a shaved head that would have been almost invisible against the white pillow but for the scarlet crescent of a scar and the fuzz of black hair that was beginning to grow again on the white scalp. Gwen had been here all the time, but was only here now. Anna laughed with delight and ran towards the bed. She jumped on to it, landing on her hands and knees and beginning to crawl as she bounced forward, hurling herself around Gwen's neck as she reached the final couple of metres.

Gwen woke with a gasp.

'Wha –?'

But her eyes focused beyond Anna, not seeing her, not seeing Beth as she came into the room shouting out for Anna.

'I know you're in here, you cheeky little bitch. C'mere or I'll get angry.'

Anna blew a raspberry, bouncing herself on the bed to land over Gwen's stomach. Air whooshed out of Gwen's mouth but she only looked puzzled, not angry.

'Anna!' Beth shouted. 'Anna, c'mere! Now!'

'Go fuck yourself, cuntbreath,' Anna said. She was starting to enjoy this. Gwen was trying to sit up in bed, not seeming to understand why it was an effort to do so. Anna drew the sheet down to expose Gwen's breasts. She took hold of a nipple, tugged it, twisted it. Gwen's face creased with pain mixed with puzzlement and she rubbed at the nipple, not seeming to notice Anna's fingers working on it. Anna switched to the other nipple, twisting it like a radio dial.

'Hello!' she said. 'Calling Ms Gwen Camberwell! Are you receiving me, over?'

Gwen tried to cover her breasts with her hands, pushing herself further down in the bed. Anna slapped one of her hands away and tugged at a nipple again.

'Let's try longwave,' she said. 'Come in, Ms Camberwell. This is Radio Anna broadcasting on an emergency frequency to Ms Gwen Camberwell's left tit. Are you receiving me, over?'

Gwen slapped out but Anna swayed back and the blow missed her easily. Gwen was frowning.

'What's fucking going on?' she shouted. 'Who's there? Who's fucking doing this to me?'

Anna laughed.

'Only me, Ms Camberwell. You do seem to be receiving me, but not fully. Can't you feel me too?'

She took hold of one of Gwen's hands and pulled it towards her, fanning it out over her left breast. Gwen tugged back at her captured hand, looking even more puzzled. Anna laughed again.

'It's me, Gwen! Anna. Your little sister. Finally getting a bit of revenge for the way you've mistreated her all these years. Revenge like this.'

She plucked at one of Gwen's nipples again. Gwen gasped and grabbed at her tit. Anna plucked at the other.

Gwen clutched at herself with both hands again and tried to sink under the bedclothes.

'No!' said Anna. 'Not so fast, Gwennie.'

She lifted herself forward and sat on Gwen's face, folding her legs around her head.

'Savour my flavour,' she told her. 'Savour it, you bitch.'

She started to rock backwards and forwards, feeling her cunt begin to moisten and swell as she rubbed it over the planes and edges of Gwen's face.

Then she shrieked.

Gwen had licked her cunt. As if she knew exactly what it was.

'Had enough?' Beth's voice said from behind her.

Anna twisted to face Beth. Gwen's palm caught her across an exposed cheek of her buttocks and she threw herself off, kneeling on the middle of the bed, head turning quickly between her two sisters, both of whom were smiling at her. She knew those smiles. Her stomach began to tighten.

'Y – you've been able to see me all along,' she said.

''Fraid so, sis,' said Beth.

Gwen's smile broadened.

'All along,' she said. 'You were the only one hypnotised. Bärengelt did it to you ages ago. But not to us. We've been playing along with him. For our own amusement. He can be quite amusing at times. Though not amusing as you, little sister.'

'Bitches.'

'Bitches? Us? Did you hear that, Beth?'

'Yes. Do you really think she means us?'

'I really think she does. And isn't it terrible? To call us that, her own lov –'

Anna had sprung to the far side of the bed, bouncing once on it before landing on the floor and starting to run for the door. Beth intercepted her easily, tripping her up with a deft tap of her ankles. She tumbled to the floor, banging painfully into an *armoire*, a knee and palm glowing with carpet-burn, and turned panting on her hands and knees to face her sisters again.

'That's better,' said Gwen. 'That's the way we like you. On your hands and knees. Ready to plead with us.'

'Piss off,' said Anna. She was trying to adjust herself imperceptibly to jump up and start running again, but she suspected (knew) from Beth's grin that she was quite aware of what she was up to. Gwen had snorted when she swore.

'Dear oh dear oh dear. Did you hear that, Beth?'

'Yes.'

'What can be done with her, do you think?'

'Lots of things. Would you like to hear a few?'

'No. Let's not be precipitate. We're grown women, or least the two of us are, so let's try and resolve this in a gentle, civilised manner.'

'Fairly gentle. Fairly civilised.'

'No, *perfectly* gentle and civilised. If she apologises to both of us properly then we won't hurt her.'

'Won't hurt her much.'

'Won't hurt her at *all*, Beth. We have to set her an example. No brawling. No beating. No S&M.'

'No fucking fun.'

Gwen sighed.

'Oh, dear. You're right. I'm afraid the sight of the little beast kneeling there on the carpet with her tits jiggling is arousing all my baser instincts.'

'And mine. In f –'

Anna jumped up again, feinted left, dodged right, and was tumbling on the floor again, squealing.

'Get her on her feet, Beth. Bring her over to the bed. Let's get this over with. Or let's get the start of this over with, at least. I fancy we're in for a long session. I really can't bear to let those tits go unmolested any longer. I've been holding back too long and I'm sure it's not healthy. What is it Blake says?'

'Spare the rod and spoil the child.'

'Well, something like that. Do we have a rod handy?'

'No, but we can improvise. Look out – she's trying to bite.'

'Give her a slap. There. Good. She'll quiet down quickly.'

'I hope not.'

'If she does we can start something else. Ah, that's better. I've got my hands on them at last. They're really remarkably well-developed for someone so young. Hold her arms behind her back. Yes. Kneel on her legs. Good. Now, let's see: left or right? Or both? A tweak-tweak here and a tweak-tweak there, or a tweak-tweak *here* and a tweak-tweak *there*?'

'The latter. The latter. As Xenophon said.'

'He did? I'm thinking more of Richmal Crompton myself, at the moment, I must admit. I feel like a little girl left alone in a sweet-shop and not sure how long I have before the owner comes back. Do I gobble as much as possible as quickly as possible, or gobble as much as possible of just my favourite?'

'Is she hardening?'

'Nicely. Look. They're . . . sronging. Like this. That is the word, isn't it? Sprong.'

'Do it to her again . . . Hmm, it's either *sprong* or *sprongle*. Try the other one.'

'Sprong. Sprong. Sprongle. Sprongle.'

'Maybe it's both. Try some twengling and see what happens then.'

'You try it. It's best done from behind. I'll hold her arms down.'

Anna gasped and struggled as Beth and Gwen swapped roles. Beth wriggled her fingers.

'Warming up,' she said. She put her hand carefully to Anna's left nipple, holding it loosely between index and forefinger.

'Try an arpeggio,' said Gwen.

'Too complicated for now.'

She closed her fingers on the nipple, then, 'One . . . two . . . three,' and jerked her fingers away. Anna squeaked. Gwen clucked her tongue.

'There was a definite sprong there. I was watching closely.'

'What about now? I'll try a different angle of attack.'

Anna squeaked. Gwen sucked at her teeth.

'Hmm. Yes, that *was* a sprongle. Kind of. It wasn't quite a sprong, anyway. Try it again.'

Anna squeaked.

'Yes, that *was* a sprongle. A definite sprongle.'

'Is she juicing up?'

'Hang on. I'll sniff ... Yes, there's a *slight* whiff of slut-juice. Or maybe not so slight. Try fingering her.'

Eleven

Anna ached. All over. All under. Beth and Gwen seemed to be sleeping, breathing deeply and regularly, murmuring occasionally. But were they really sleeping? Was it another trick? Would they pounce on her when she moved? When she tried to slip off the bed?

'Beth?' she whispered.

Nothing.

'Gwen?'

Nothing.

But they wouldn't answer her if they were pretending to be asleep, would they? Anna flinched as Beth shifted, saying something out loud, her feet rolling over Anna's aching arse. How long had she been lain here under the sheets with their feet resting on her, their dried piss sticky in her scalp-stubble, the feeling of their departed fingers still humming in the nerves of her nipples and cunt, earlobes and buttocks? An hour? An hour-and-a-half? Or was she overestimating, seething with the humiliation and pain they had subjected her to?

'Beth?'

No response.

'Beth? Did I ever tell you something? That you're a –' she dropped her voice to the passing whisper of a butterfly's wings '– a bitch?'

Nothing. Then Gwen murmured in her sleep and Beth seemed to murmur back. Anna stiffened, stifling a spurt of nervous laughter, then began whispering again, a little louder.

'You're a fucking slapper too, Beth. A slack-cunted, sag-titted, cock-sucking, come-slurping slapper.'

She stopped again, listening, heart beating faster, nervous laughter in her throat again. If they were awake she had had it now. Any moment now they'd pounce. Any moment. Any moment. Any moment. Any m –

'You could take an oil-tanker up that cunt of yours, Beth. Gwen could too.'

Gwen's feet began to shift on the small of her back and she almost screamed. But then they stopped moving. Gwen was just shifting in her sleep.

'Because you're a fucking slapper too, Gwen. You could take a fucking fleet of oil-tankers up *your* cunt. They could steam in three abreast and not even touch the sides. Never to be seen again. Though you'd prefer them up your arse, wouldn't you? They could go in six abreast there. That's how much of a slapper you are.'

She stopped. They were asleep. Surely they were asleep. Slowly, cautiously, she began to slide out from under their feet. God, how she wanted a bath. Hot water and a little time to herself. Gwen muttered, shifted her feet, and Anna stopped, holding her breath. Just a few centimetres more. Beth settled and she began to move again. But maybe it would be quicker if she pushed Gwen's feet off her. Very slowly. She lifted an arm away from her body and reached back with it, wondering. When she first touched them, should it be gently or firmly? Because a gentle touch might seem unnatural, purposeful. Or would it?

Perhaps. But if she touched them firmly, how firmly? She brought her arm back while she thought. She didn't know. Maybe gentle was better after all. Maybe Gwen wouldn't even notice if she was gentle enough. But how could she be gentle enough if she was moving the feet off her legs? Christ. She didn't know what to do, but she had to do something. Now.

She reached out again and touched one of Gwen's feet with the tip of a finger, holding still to see what happened. The foot twitched and Gwen's breathing stopped for a moment, then began again. Maybe if she tickled them they'd move of their own accord. Or scratched them. Gently. She scratched the side of the foot gently. Very gently. It twitched again and moved a centimetre away from the finger. Good. Maybe – no, now it had moved back again. Shit. Shit.

And Beth's feet would be even more of a problem too. The heel of one of them had slid into the groove of her buttocks. She would have to roll and twist and slide away from them once she got Gwen's feet off her. Or maybe she should try to get Beth's feet off first. Jesus Christ. Those bitches had known this was going to happen. That's why they made her crouch down at the bottom of the bed with their feet on her while they went to sleep. They'd known how uncomfortable it would be. How cramped she'd get. How the aches they'd given her would settle into her flesh and grow. How she would long to slip away for a bath. How she wouldn't be able to do it. Though she *was* going to: she was fucked if she was going to let them get away with it. But then they'd already got away with it. And were going to get away with it again.

And even if she *did* get away, how was she going to get back? She'd have to get back, after all, because if they woke up in the morning – or what passed for the morning – and found her not lying in the same position, under their feet, she would be in for it again.

Jesus. Oh, Jesus. What a life. If it wasn't that mad cunt Bärengelt, it was her own sisters. What had she ever done to deserve this? Well, who cared? She was going to get out from under their feet, and she was going to have a bath.

She reached her arm down again, touched Gwen's foot, started to scratch it.

'*Move*, you horny-footed bitch,' she whispered – and froze, her heart in her throat. Gwen had grunted and – from the sudden shift of tone in the muscles of her feet and calves – woken up. Anna's ear, straining into the darkness, caught a faint rasping sound. Gwen was rubbing her scalp. Then she had rolled over, the heel of one foot digging into another of Anna's aches, and was speaking to Beth, shaking her (Anna felt the faint tremors in Beth's feet).

'Beth. Beth.'

Her voice was low, husky, sleep-drunken. Anna strained to analyse its tone. Had she realised what had woken her up? Was she waking Beth so they could start another session on their little sister? Christ, no, please. Not another one, you bitches. I'm aching all over. All under. Leave me alone.

Beth was waking up.

'Uh? What?'

'I want another fuck. Come on.'

'Oh, Gwen, no. Not now. Let me sleep a while. Have that bitch give you a blow-job instead. I'll rub your nipples. It's all I'm capable of. Christ, I'm still aching from what that bastard did to me in the Black Room.'

What about me? Anna wanted to shout. *I'm aching from him and from you. Bitches. Fucking bitches.*

Gwen grunted.

'OK. Anna!'

She lifted her heel and let it drop sharply on to Anna's back.

'Anna! Wake up, you silly little bitch. Blow-job time.'

Anna pulled a face towards her in the darkness.

'I'm awake. I've always been awake. How do you ex –'

Gwen coughed sleepily and said, 'Shut up, Anna, you slut. We're not interested. Get your arse up here and get sucking.'

'Get your feet off me first. Ow!'

'Shut up. We give the orders. Get your arse up here. You kick her too, Beth.'

'Delighted.'

Anna yelped again and began to struggle up the bed. Gwen rolled on to her back, opened her legs, groped down for her little sister, gripped her ears, hauled her up, twisted her, dropped her with a sigh of contentment on to her cunt.

'Shut up and suck. Savour my flavour.'

Her thighs rose around Anna's head, the softness and smoothness of their skin a strange contrast to the strength of the muscles beneath as they clamped her into place, crushing her ears flat. Anna struggled for an extra cen-

156

timetre of space to breathe in, working her mouth for spittle. A minute ago she had been hoping to get away; now look at her. Out of the frying-pan into the fire. She pressed her lips against the hot, moist, musky folds of Gwen's cunt.

Bitch, she mumbled into them, *bitch, fucking bitch*; and started to lick, suck, work her tongue under a fold of flesh, up it, down it.

'Mmm.'

Gwen's voice was barely audible through the soft prison of thigh-flesh in which her ears were locked.

Beth asked something, but Anna couldn't hear what it was.

Gwen, her voice louder, reaching Anna's ears partly through Gwen's body, said: 'Yeah. Get rubbing my nips, the way you promised.'

Anna felt fingers – Beth's fingers – on the back of her head. They pinched her maliciously, then lifted away. A moment later Gwen's thighs trembled and tightened: Beth had started to rub her nipples. Her cunt was starting to respond to Anna's tongue, beginning to ooze, leak. Anna strained her neck backwards, trying to win herself the space to spit in, but Gwen wouldn't let her. She'd have to dribble spittle in. But at least she could swear at her and not be noticed. She heard the thigh-dimmed sound of laughter. The bitches were laughing. At her. At what they were doing to her.

Cunts, she mumbled into the wakening cunt of her elder sister, *fucking cunts*. She licked, dribbled, sucked. *I'd like to bite. Your fucking slack-walled. Quim. Gwen. You fucking slag. That would. Get you. Squealing.*

Gwen's thighs trembled, tightened, relaxed, tightened, relaxed again. Gwen was enjoying this. *Stupid fucking. Bitch. You don't know. What I'm saying. Do you? Bitch.* Anna licked again, sucked, despite herself beginning to savour the flavour of her sister's cunt. *Bitch. Fucking bitch. I'd love to sink. My teeth into you. Bitch.* She struggled a little higher, trying to get her tongue over Gwen's clitoris, feeling her chin slide over the oozing surface of Gwen's cunt-lips. The two of them were laughing again. Anna imagined biting the cunt in front of her. Sinking her teeth into its succulent folds. Like biting into a huge fruit warmed to blood-heat by the sun. That would make Gwen sit up and take notice.

Her neck was aching badly now with strain and it was hard to breathe. If the bitch would only loosen her thighs. It would be better for her, too – Anna would be able to cunnilingue her more freely, more subtly. But no: what was better for her was the thought that Anna was having to struggle to perform something she was unwilling to perform in the first place. Anna snorted, trying to clear her nostrils of cunt-juice. But the smell remained. She was starting to feel dizzy. There seemed more cunt-juice than air in what she was trying to breathe. It was like trying to breathe underwater. In a sauna. The air thick with steam and musk.

Bitch! She scream/mumbled into the gaping, oozing flesh in front of her. *I can't breathe. I can't. Breathe. You fucking bitch. Bitch.* She licked. *Bitch.* Sucked. *Bitch.* Drank. Gwen was speaking again, her voice coming dully to Anna's ears as though through water or miles of overheated humid air. No, Gwen was groaning. And her thighs were flexing and trembling against Anna's ears. The angle of her pelvis changed, tilting, as she lifted her legs, feet locked together, beginning the slide to orgasm, thrusting her swollen cunt against Anna's mouth and lips and tongue in a quickening rhythm, galloping her cunt beneath them, a cunt-horse spurred by Anna's soft, probing tongue, galloping head-long – clit-long – into its own liquefaction, lubricating its race with a self-generated juice of pleasure, slipping, sliding, slithering, sliding, slipping, slithering.

And now Anna was able to cunnilingue no longer, could only hang on and hope to emerge (indeed!) unscathed, for Gwen was bucking against her, gripped by full orgasm, grinding her cunt at her little sister's face, treating its surfaces and underlying bone and cartilage as a mere aid to her own pleasure: no longer a face but a thing, a living dildo-head, her thighs tightening around Anna's head as though she wished to cave in Anna's skull (and Anna truly couldn't breathe now: there was a glowing sediment of pain in the base of her lungs, beginning to rise), crush the whole of Anna's head and continue crushing it, like a vast machine crushing a lump of black carbon to a sparkling point of diamond – the image was flashing through Anna's oxygen-starved brain and she was screaming airlessly for breath, almost desperate enough to begin biting, sinking her teeth into the sun-warmed fruit-flesh of Gwen's cunt.

But the vigour of the rhythm of Gwen's bucking pelvis was fading: the wave of orgasm was seething out on the sands, sparkling in the moonlight, sparkling on black volcanic sands, its rush up the beach here and there beginning to slow, pause, and be sucked back into the sea. Anna found a thread of air in her nostrils and drew on it with the full force of her lungs, feeling the grind of Gwen's cunt against her face slow and die, the thighs clamped on her ears and head begin to relax.

Suddenly, it was over. Gwen's thighs trembled, began to move apart, and then were splayed lazily, and Anna's head was resting between them unimprisoned at last, her whole face wet and reeking with the juices of the cunt beneath it. Her neck was aching fiercely and she could barely find the strength to lift herself up. Gwen laughed, her voice rich with pleasure and self-satisfaction.

'Christ, that felt good. Really fucking good.'

A hand slapped down carelessly at Anna's head, one finger catching her scalp stingingly.

'Get off me, you silly little bitch. Fuck off somewhere till you're needed again.'

Anna raised her head and drew a deep breath. *Bitch*, she thought. *Bitch.* She pulled herself back quickly as Gwen rolled over, reaching out for Beth, swinging a knee at Anna, kicking at her. Anna was at the side of the bed now, free, feeling the bed begin to tremble beneath her as Gwen grappled with Beth.

'Wake up. I've a bone to pick with you.'

'Get off. I'm tired. Sleep. I need sleep.'

'What have you got between your legs? Fucking balls? I've just had some fun with our little sex-slave but I need

159

more. A girl's all very well for foreplay but it takes a woman to satisfy a woman. So show me which you are.'

Anna had one foot on the floor now, reading the movement of the bed in her buttocks. It was still trembling, but irregularly: Beth was struggling, pretending to resist Gwen's advances, panting, swearing at her: when it started to bounce regularly Anna would move fully off the bed. They wouldn't notice her. Bitches. Beth squeaked, panted.

'No, stop. What was it you said you wanted to pick with me?'

'A bone. Because you fell asleep while you were supposed to be rubbing my nips.'

'Well, get picking. But I know something better than a bone you can pick.'

'Oh, yeah? Show me.'

'Find it for yourself.'

The bed trembled harder. Beth was giggling: Gwen would be swinging atop her back in a moment and the regular rhythm would begin. Anna waited, feeling a jealous tickle of arousal in her cunt, scowling, squeezing at one of her nipples. Bitches. The regular rhythm began: Gwen was riding Beth, swelling cunt sliding on caned buttocks, slick pink lips kissing purple-striped flesh, black pubic hair pricking soft white skin.

Anna slipped off the bed, getting down on her hands and knees. She waited. Had they noticed? The bed was squeaking now, and Gwen was starting to pant as she began her second gallop to orgasm. Her hands would be gripping Beth's breasts, fingers sternly kneading the firm flesh of the two symmetrical mounds or rhythmically twengling the rigid nipples, cunt grinding harder at the upthrust curves of Beth's arse in classic tribadism, smearing it with hot, sticky cunt-juice.

Anna's lip curled with a contempt she tried hard to truly feel. Bitches. Unimaginative bitches. If *she* had Beth's body at her disposal, she'd make much better use of it than that. If. She began to crawl away from the bed. They hadn't noticed her departure and certainly wouldn't do so now. Even if she shouted at them what she was doing. They were too busy with each other. Beth was gasping now, no doubt thrusting her arse backwards to meet each cunt-grind Gwen made against it, savouring the flavour of the pain crushed out of it by Gwen's cunt-lips against her bruises, her own cunt oozing freely on to the bed, its lips gaping greedily for fingers that any moment now Gwen would supply as her gallop to orgasm reached the final stretch, sliding to the brink of the briny abyss into which she the rider and Beth the mount would both plunge, sweating, pulsing, oozing, gasping, wailing.

Anna shook her head to clear it of the imagined sensations, the tastes and scents and feelings of the audible fucking. She was halfway across the room now, crawling carefully between the furniture, guided by her memories of the room, groping out in front of her with a hand where she was uncertain. She was uncertain again; lifted her hand forwards; and nearly fainted with fright, the black world suddenly blooming blank scarlet, her heart (or so it seemed) leaping like a small animal into her throat where it scrabbled frantically for escape, warm piss trickling down her thighs.

She had touched leather. Leather encasing a leg. Bärengelt's leg. He was standing silently there in the darkness as the squeaks and gasps and slaps of Gwen's and Beth's fucking filled the room. Anna's hand had gone cold where it rested against the leather. She began to withdraw it and hissed with pain as a gloved hand clamped down hard over her wrist. He could see her quite plainly, she realised. Could no doubt see the bed and her fucking sisters. The fucking bastard. The fucking voyeur.

But no, not fucking: wanking, she learned as his gloved hand tightened and drew her to him, lifting her easily from her knees to stand in front of him: she could sense the bulk of his body before her, the scent of the warm leather, the warmth radiating from it. And from his erect, exposed cock, over which his left hand was slowly, silently, cycling. He dragged her hand to his cock, ran her fingers down its length. For a moment she tried to pull herself back, but his hand tightened even further, biting into her wrist like

161

sharpened iron, sending threads of dull, metallic pain running up the nerves of her arm, and she gave in, allowing him to do as he would.

He stopped masturbating and dragged her wrist downwards, forcing her back on to her knees, his freed left hand finding the back of her head, twisting her head into position at his groin. He wanted her to suck him. Now. The head of his cock brushed her lips, smearing them with pre-come, and she sighed, giving up hope of a bath for another ten, twenty, thirty minutes, while she serviced another of her tormentors. She opened her mouth and let him slide his cock inside. He rewarded her by releasing her wrist, lifting his freed right hand to join the left on the back of her head, pulling her nearer to him, allowing his cock to slide deeper, the head hot and blunt and bald.

She sucked hard, wanting to heighten his pleasure quickly, her lips sealing around the shaft as it slid into her mouth, smearing it with the pre-come with which they were coated, then unsmearing it as he drew the shaft slowly out, paused, slowly thrust it back in again: a piston, beginning its run, in-stroke, out-stroke, in-stroke. She had time to run the blade of her tongue over the head as, on completion of the out-stroke, it paused in the vestibule of her mouth before beginning the in-stroke, sliding deeper, out of range again. Beth and Gwen were nearing climax behind her, swearing at each other, urging each other on, their voices thick with pleasure.

The out-stroke began again, a piston of hot meat lubricating its own chamber, its movement beginning to quicken, pausing again at the vestibule to allow her to sample the hot, blunt, bald head with the blade of her tongue, tasting the salty pre-come leaking freely from the cock-slit and the contrasted sweet of her own saliva. The in-stroke began, the piston of hot meat sliding into its self-lubricated chamber, a little faster now, and as his gloved hands tightened on the back of her neck, clutching her harder to him, she lifted her arms around him to clutch his leather-clad buttocks, clinging to him, hating him for the humiliation of the fellatio he forced upon her, but

162

simultaneously pleasured by her punishment, delighting in her degradation, happy in her whoredom.

His buttocks were working under her fingers now, waves of muscular effort washing through them as he thrust his erect penis at the moist chamber of her mouth, and the bulb of the head was sliding across the entrance to her throat now, its slit leaking thin pre-come that seared her faucal tissues like brine. She was having to adjust her breathing to his thrusts, her heart beginning to beat faster with the fear that he would get carried away, sliding deeper and faster into her, forcing himself on her to the limit of her capacity to accommodate him and beyond, choking her with the delighted meat of his cock, to synchronise his final, triumphant thrust and spurts with her gasps of asphyxiation.

She would have to bite at him, bite at the blood-engorged rod of his cock, sink her small white teeth into its swollen red tissues, but she did not know that she would have the will. Perhaps she would welcome being choked like this, murdered by her master's cock, surrendering her life to the satisfaction of his pleasure. Her head and whole upper body were rocking with the force of his thrusts now, her fingers digging deep into the smooth leather that sheathed his buttocks, dragging her nearer to him as his grip strengthened on the back of her head. Her breaths were snatched in half-seconds now, slices of self-preservation carved from her almost single-minded concentration on giving her master absolute pleasure, absolute obedience, absolute submission.

And then he stopped. Dead. At the limit of the in-stroke, his cock thrust to its maximum in her mouth. She blinked foolishly, her body prepared to move with the out-stroke that had not come, as though her foot had dropped for a step that wasn't there. She groped for thought, unable to breathe, uncaring that the sediment of pain was re-collecting at the base of her lungs as it had done when she cunnilingued Gwen. He was going to come now. Start spraying thick gouts of semen into her, his cock like a heavy gun firing heavy, liquid shells that would explode on the back of her throat and slide down into her, deeper, feeding her, saluting her, choking her.

But no: even as she thought it his cock began to slide out of her and his hands left the back of her head and landed on her arms, pulling at them, urging her to release her hold on his arse. She let go of him, wonderingly, as his cock came out of her mouth with a pop, the moistened heat of it tangible on her face. He released her arms and took hold of her head again, adjusting it, tilting her face up and back. He let go with one hand and she felt him lifting his cock to her face. It bumped against her upper lip, touched her philtrum, and was settling against her left nostril. Now his other hand fanned on the back of her head again, gripping hard, holding her in place as he held his cock to her nostril, pressing it deeper, rubbing it against the rim of the nostril.

The hot smell of it, mingled cockhead, pre-come, and Anna-saliva, was rising into her when suddenly she felt a puff of compressed air, injected into her nostril as though by a syringe, inexplicable for a moment until, as the first spurt of his semen smashed against the sculpted inner chamber of her nostril, she realised it was the air forced out of his urethra by the ejaculate itself, a liquid piston rising in a narrow meat-chamber.

And the ejaculate hurt, a thick musk/salt fist smashed against her sinus, exploding against nerves that simultaneously smelled it, like a blow that sang or glowed; and the musk/salt fist swung and smashed again, and hurt; and swung and smashed again, and hurt; and swung and smashed again, and hurt; and swung and smashed again, and hurt; until the sensations of it blurred and she was unaware when he had ceased to ejaculate into her.

His cock dropped from her nostril, but he had not finished with her. His right hand cupped her chin and touched her face, exploring it, its fingers sliding to her nose, pressing her right nostril closed as his right hand tightened on her chin, clamping her jaw shut, holding her head steady as he waited for her to have to breathe in through her left nostril, sucking the semen clogging its passages and chambers over the more sensitive tissues deeper within. She held her breath, not wanting his occupation of this part of her to become final, not wanting him to complete his victory over half her nose, but moment by moment her need for air grew, and the glowing sediment at the base of her lungs reignited and began to burn, sending tremors through the swollen flesh of her breasts, reawakening a trickle of treacherous sensation in her cunt. She shook her head, trying to free her jaw just a fraction, just a sliver, for a hissed intake of breath, but his hand was too strong, fixed to her jaw, the leather encasing it already grown warm against her skin.

She groaned inwardly. He was hurting her, dominating her, and it was pleasurable. Her emotions swung and mutated, thrown back mirror-reversed from the silver of her pain, and now she was holding her breath to prolong the torture he inflicted on her, wanting to please him with her own pain. Then she surrendered and tried to breathe, her lungs dropping away beneath her applauding heart. For a moment her nostril seemed too thickly blocked, the thick semen too well clogged in the narrow passage and chambers into which he had spurted it, and an asphyxiatory panic flooded her body, but in the next instant the nostril uncorked and his semen spurted deeper inside her, a second, self-initiated ejaculation, searing over new surfaces, pouring into her throat, thick, warm, salty, his come, for her to gulp, retching at the taste of it and the pain it caused her, but leaking too down under, glad to be mistreated, glad to be turned into a whore by him, glad that he had conquered a third orifice, adding her nostril to her mouth and arsehole.

As he felt her inhale his grip relaxed, and a second later he let go of her, then casually pushed at her so that she fell away from him. He had satisfied himself with her and for the time being she was useless to him. It pleased her to think that she was an object, a warm, girl-sized sex-doll whose attraction for him rose and fell with the rising and falling of his cock. He was walking away from her, she could feel it in the floor, a faint tremor rising into her skin as the post-coital murmurs of Gwen and Beth fell into her ears from behind her. She savoured the semen that was still trickling from the spaces of her left nostril into her throat, dropping a hand to her warm, oozing cunt and beginning to masturbate, thrumming and stroking the folds and nubs of her cunt as she told herself over and over, *Slut, slut, you're a slut. A slut. A slut.* As she started to come she had to bite at her lip to keep from screaming out aloud into the darkness.

Which was suddenly no longer darkness. The lights had come on, shining more brightly than she had ever seen them before. Anna rolled over, orgasm arrested inside her, looking toward the bed. Beth was sitting up in bed, blinking, one hand held protectively over the sleeping Gwen. Bärengelt was standing by the door, his cock returned to his trousers, the black cane twitching gently in his hand. Anna crawled into the cover of a table, peeping out at the bed and Bärengelt, hearing speakers hidden all over in the room come awake, singing with over-amplified silence. Then Bärengelt's voices came rolling and crashing into the room.

'Girls! Good morning to you. Time to rise and shine. You have a busy day ahead of you.'

Gwen struggled up in bed, pushing Beth's hand away.

'Oh, fuck off, Bärengelt. We don't answer to you any more.'

Bärengelt waited a moment, a moment more, as though to let the flavour of Gwen's words soak deeper, a moment more.

'A good beginning, Gwen. Very good. This is what I have been looking forwards to for some time. Our contest of wills. So now, get on your feet. If you beg my forgiveness *now*, I may be lenient. Quick. Your chance is about to be lost for ever.'

'No. Just fuck off. I've already told you: we don't answer to you any more.'

'OK, your chance is lost for ever. But I'm still prepared to have a little bet with you. I'll bet you that you'll be sucking my cock within ten minutes.'

Gwen snorted.

'No, I won't. I might make you suck Anna's cunt, though, if you're lucky. Before we all piss on you and say our goodbyes.'

'OK, it's a bet. But I forgot to tell you the stake. It's your arse. If I win, it's mine. To do with as I will. If you win, it gets out of this intact. But you won't win and it won't get out of this intact.'

'We'll soon see, Bärengelt.'

'We will.'

He lifted the cane in salute and started to walk towards the bed, swishing the cane idly at the air, left, right, idly, casually. Gwen lifted her legs free of the bedclothing and jumped to her feet, the mattress bouncing beneath her, sending tremors through her breasts. Anna felt her mouth go dry and cunt begin to move with arousal again. Gwen looked splendid. Boudicca-like. Glowing with defiance and dominance. Now she was lifting a hand and flicking at a lock of dark hair that was no longer there, her breasts starting to rise and fall with impending effort.

'Beth,' she said. 'You go left, I'll go right. Anna, where the fuck are you?'

Anna wondered whether to answer. Bärengelt was going to win. He'd be angry when he did. Bound to be. And if she'd been part of the rebellion, he'd be angry, specifically, with her. Which would be painful. Very painful.

'Anna! Answer me.'

Gwen couldn't see her, she realised. She could slip away now. Hide until it was all over. But when would that be? How long would she have to hide?

For ever. She crawled out from under the table and stood up.

'Here I am, Gwen.'

'Get over here, quick. If we stick together we can beat this bastard, no problem.'

Twelve

'Kiss the rod. Now.'

They were crouched on hands and knees on the landing outside the bedroom, three points of an equilateral triangle whose centre was Bärengelt. His voices were rumbling through the bedroom door, dislocated from his leather-clad presence, echoing coldly from the marble walls.

Gwen turned her head aside as the cane was presented to her lips, and its black length jumped backwards, upwards, across, up, and swished and cracked across her buttocks in one flowing movement. Her face tightened with pain and Anna licked her lips, feeling the lips of her cunt stir and begin to moisten.

'Kiss it.'

The cane – warmed by the firm flesh it had already kissed five times? – was back at Gwen's lips.

'Kiss it.'

Gwen closed her eyes. The cane leaped, swung, swished, cracked. Gwen's eyes closed harder. Anna could feel the smile of her cunt widen, widen to an idiot grin. A dribbling idiot grin. Yokel-cunt.

'Kiss it.'

Gwen opened her eyes. They were shining. Shining with tears. The cane was back at her lips. If it leaped, swung, swished, cracked one more time, then tears would begin to slide down her cheeks, an answering fluid for the fluid flowing down the inside of Anna's thighs. Gwen's lips twitched. Bärengelt was about to swing the cane back, up, across, up, down. Gwen licked her lips, then leaned forwards and kissed it. Kissed the rod.

'Good girl. Now, my cock. Suck it.'

A zip rasped and Bärengelt's cock jerked out of his trousers, erect and ticking to his heartbeat. Anna watched it, fascinated. The lens of the fibre-optic camera glittered as he rolled back the foreskin to expose the broad purple bulb of the head. He pushed it towards Gwen's lips. Her face would be huge on the camera now. But she would never close her mouth over the camera. And over the head of his cock. Never.

'There are two minutes and twenty-eight seconds left. Suck it.'

Gwen shook her head.

'Suck it.'

The cane twitched and Anna winced in anticipation of the smooth, fluid sequence of movements that would end in another swish through the air, another crack across Gwen's striped buttocks. The pain must be hellish now. Shrieking. Sizzling its way deeper into her arse second by second. How could she stand one stroke, let alone seven? Let alone eight? But Anna knew Gwen would never suck Bärengelt's cock. Never. So he would lose the bet.

'One minute and forty-nine seconds. Suck it.'

Gwen shook her head again. The cane twitched but Anna suddenly knew that Bärengelt was not going to use it. His free hand was fumbling at the breast of his bodysuit, opening a pocket, pulling something out. Something that dangled. A tiny pair of black earphones. Dangling from a wire attached to Bärengelt's suit.

'Anna.'

Anna swallowed.

'Yes, master?'

'Put these on her, then get back where you were.'

Anna jerked guiltily. If she went near Gwen ... But she was already on her feet, stepping forwards to catch the earphones as Bärengelt dropped them to her, bending over Gwen's head, her stomach dissolving as she saw Gwen's nostrils twitch and anger flow into her face. She put the earphones on her sister, adjusting them carefully before stepping back and getting back down on her hands and knees, watching. Oozing.

There was silence. Bärengelt must be speaking to Gwen through the earphones. Now Gwen was moving. Lifting the upper part of her body. Kneeling in front of Bärengelt. Reaching up for his cock. Guiding it into her opening mouth and beginning to suck it, the black wires of the earphones swinging against her white skin as she moved. Anna's mouth fell open with surprise. Gwen was sucking him. Gwen was sucking Bärengelt's cock. Without being caned any more. Without anything but words.

Bärengelt's hand dropped to the wires of the earphones and yanked at them, pulling them cruelly free of Gwen's ears. His voices rumbled through from the bedroom again.

'That's enough. You lose the bet. Your arsehole is mine. On your feet, all of you and get downstairs.'

Gwen's mouth unsealed from his cock, leaving it moistened and glistening for a third of its length, and she got unsteadily to her feet. Anna was still crouched, staring at her sister's face, trying to read the expression there, trying to tell what Bärengelt might have said to her.

'Anna, you're too slow. Two squats, now!'

She scrambled to her feet, not sure what he meant her to do.

'I said *squats*! Now! You can do an extra three for insubordination.'

'Master, I'm sorry. I don't understand wh –'

'An extra two for ignorance. Beth, show her what to do.'

Confused, Anna felt Beth's hands on her body, tugging her down, showing her how to do what Bärengelt wanted her to do. Squats. She understood now. Squats. She positioned herself for the first, arms outstretched, knees together, tightened the muscles of her thighs and stomach and started to rise. The tip of the black cane flicked at her knees.

'Stop. Do it again. Knees apart. Well apart. I want to be able to see your cunt at all times. So do it slowly. Gwen, watch.'

Anna resumed her position. She was reluctant to open her knees, to expose her glistening cunt and inner thighs to Beth's and Gwen's gaze. Particularly Gwen's. She opened her legs, not daring to look at Gwen, but knowing that her face would have tightened with anger.

'Do you see, Gwen? This is how your little sister reacts to your pain. With pleasure. She oozes as you bruise. But you had already smelled it, hadn't you? Anna: begin. Eleven squats.'

'But, ma –'

'Thirteen. Begin.'

Anna bit her lip, tears stinging her eyes, and began, rising from her squat, slowly, arms outstretched, knees apart, glistening cunt and inner thighs exposed to the greedy gaze of Beth, the cold gaze of Gwen, the cruel gaze of Bärengelt. And her cunt and nipples responded. Began to swell and open again, to harden and lengthen. Christ. Oh, Christ. Beth snickered. The black cane leaped, swished, cracked, and Beth sobbed once with pain, rubbing at her stinging arse.

'One,' Bärengelt's voices rumbled as he counted off the first squat. Anna, sinking back to begin the second, was careful to keep her pleasure at Beth's chastisement out of her face. The muscles of her thighs were already starting to ache with anticipation but if she wavered for a moment, looked tired, resentful, she knew Bärengelt would add to the total again.

'Two.'

Anna nearly overbalanced, thinking he *was* adding to her total again, but he was merely counting off the second completed squat. Christ. Only two. Eleven to go. The ache of anticipation in her thighs was slowly being leached out by the ache of actuality. This was going to hurt. Hurt a lot.

'Three.'

Her cunt-juice had trickled to the back of her thighs now, was clamped stickily against her calves as she settled into the squat, thigh-skin pressed against calf-skin, the two moistened surfaces coming apart with an uncorking kiss, counting the squats too but with a single unvarying liquid syllable.

'Four.'

And the ache in her thighs and knees was fully ripened now, settling around the muscles and tendons like grains of splintered metal. Silver. Poisonous silver. Heated silver. Insinuated into the delicate meat of her thighs and knees to prick and irritate, to irrigate the ache as though they were constantly melting into it and being replaced, recrystallising grains of poisonous silver.

'Five.'

Melting into the rising ache. That her greedy cunt was lapping at, wrapping itself in it like a stripped courtesan wrapping herself in a vast polar-bear's pelt as she waits in the antechamber of an ice-giant's thalamion. Waits and hopes her cunt will be hot enough to save her from frost-bite as his vast icicle-prick prods at her folds and slides inside her. A cocksicle. Huge and searingly cold.

'Six.'

She closed her eyes for a second, pushing the image away, frightened that she would lose concentration. Her thighs clamped against her calves, the skin of each sealing and unsealing, *psok*, *shtok*, the coating of cunt-juice there growing thicker each time she rose and fell. Gwen's eyes were fixed between her open thighs, smouldering with anger. Anna could feel the heat of them. So could her cunt.

'Seven.'

Her cunt was beginning to swim in its own juices now. Unashamedly leaking its pleasure at her punishment and humiliation. Basting itself like a fat wad of fruit and berries wrapped in pastry and stewed in sugar and cream. Steaming juicily, bubbling and popping, filling all mouths within waftage with warm, clear saliva.

'Eight.'

Leaking cunt. Like a huge, vertical eye-socket weeping delightedly that it contained no eye. Blind with pleasure. Blinded for pleasure. Willingly. Like the Cyclops' eye stabbed by the glowing trunk-prick of Odysseus. Seething, bubbling, quenching and softening the stiff wood so that miraculously it emerges drooping, flaccid, dripping with steaming fluids.

'Ten.'

And the Cyclops groans with pleasure, not pain. In rumbling bass, like Bärengelt's voice. But with spits of static. Like the snap and crack of dry pine-wood burning in bright sunlight. With a beaten silver cunt-dish laid upon it. With lumps of yellow and orange resin dropped into the dish. Beginning to melt. To ooze and drip from one open end of the cunt-dish.

'Eleven.'

Dripping into the fire. Burning with aromatic flames, purple, green, and gold. Like transparent flowers. Like flowers springing from the ash of the dead fire as a dryad stands above it and masturbates, resinous juice dripping from the green, translucent folds of her cunt. Dryad-cunt. Tightening like roots around the hircine cock of a hirsute satyr. Around the hircine cock of hirsute Pan.

'Twelve.'

The cock of the Pan on the mosaic far below her. Bärengelt's cock. Which she wanted up her. Now. Filling her. She wanted Beth's mouth at her cunt. Drinking her. Sucking the bud of her clitoris. Gwen's fist. She wanted it pushed up her. As far as it could go. Bärengelt's cock. Up her. Beth's mouth. Sucking her. Gwen's fist. Up her.

'Thirteen.'

She fell forwards on her knees, breath whistling out of her mouth, breaking the voyeur-silence that had settled around her as she rose and fell, knees apart, cunt glistening. The air was thick with the smell of her yelm. Beth's nostrils had widened, drawing the smell in, and one corner of her mouth was leaking saliva. Bärengelt lifted his cane.

'Clasp your hands behind your head. Then stay still. Very still.'

Anna lifted her arms and clasped her hands on the back of her head, her tits jutting forwards on to the yelm-thickened air. The cane swished: and suddenly the tip of her left nipple was stinging, flicked by the tip of the black wood; and the cane swished again: and the tip of her right nipple was stinging. The pain was sharp, clear, nailing her tits to her body, singing into her, strengthening second by second, shining through the dull ache of her thighs and knees, sinking like a shower of gold coins through the jade-green water of a well, welling up from her cunt, swelling up from her cunt. She felt as though she were rocking on the edge of an abyss and gasped in pain as a tendon tightened in her thighs. She had seen a red tropical flower bloom in seconds by camera trickery once, its yellow stamens stabbing out through the soft, undraping folds of its petals, opening its wide mouth and then falling back into real time, full-bloomed, quivering as a huge bee landed on it and crawled heavily inside its scented throat to suck its nectar.

She fell into the abyss, into the flower-throat, her cunt pulsing between her thighs, that red tropical flower spilling its excess of nectar, her stung nipples hardening painfully as the tide of orgasm rose in her body, washing out the chemical ash of exercise from the chambers of her body, dissolving them in its warmth, tightening her tendons and muscles like fingers tightening the strings of a harp, overtightening them, painful as it was pleasurable, more pleasurable as it was more painful, more painful as it was more pleasurable. She gasped, every second inhalation jerking shallowly as the rhythms of her cunt and heart swung together, alloyed, and broke apart.

She squeezed her eyes shut and rode the last few seconds of it, biting her lip. Then she opened her eyes and looked at Bärengelt. He moved his head as though about to shake it, then shrugged.

'On your feet again.'

Anna unclasped her hands and rose shakily, thighs and calves unsealing for the final time with the uncorking kiss of compressed cunt-juice. Gwen and Beth had left the apices of the triangle, ready to precede Bärengelt downstairs to the Black Room and the further tortures that awaited them.

'No,' Bärengelt's voices rumbled.

'Master?' Beth said. Gwen said nothing, merely looking at him, hatred and anger veiled in her face.

175

'No. We are not finished here. Anna is coated with yelm. Look at her. She needs to be cleaned at once. A tongue-bath. From both of you. You, Gwen –' his cane swung to point at Anna's cunt '– see to that. Beth –' the cane dropped and jerked left and right to indicate Anna's thighs and calves '– clean those. Now.'

Anna nearly folded to the floor, feeling her knee-joints soften like melting wax. She thought she would come again as soon as Gwen's tongue touched her cunt. But her whole body felt like a cunt: the strain and aches of the thirteen squats were swelling inside her, growing hotter, thicker, richer, so that she wanted to fold herself apart and allow the world to slide into her like a cock, as though she were the world-cunt of a goddess. She noticed that Gwen had knelt in front of her. To worship her. With mouth and tongue at the altar of her cooling, oozing cunt.

'Begin.'

Anna gasped with shock as a tongue touched the back of one of her calves and licked upwards – it was Beth's. Beth was kneeling behind her. Like Gwen in front of her. When was Gwen going to lick her? Bärengelt's cane swished and cracked.

'Begin, Gwen. Now.'

Gwen's breath tickled at Anna's inner thighs, feeling warm, moist, scented. Tickled. But came no closer.

Swish, and crack.

'Lick her. Now.'

The tip of Gwen's tongue touched an edge of a fold of the lips of Anna's cunt. Anna trembled. The tongue-tip moved, pressed harder against her flesh. And Gwen licked her. Anna could feel the heat in her tongue. The anger. Beth's tongue was sliding thickly over the rear of her calves, pleasant, but not pleasurable. Not truly. It was like a candle burning as dawn broke: Gwen's tongue was the rising sun. Promising a flood of light and warmth. But dawn was slow in breaking. Gwen's tongue was touching her but not pleasuring her. Not fully. Not yet.

The black cane descended slowly in her line of sight and rested on Gwen's buttocks. Anna felt Gwen stiffen with anticipation, hardening her body and mind to the next stroke of the cane.

'Gwen,' Bärengelt's voices rumbled. 'I will count to three. If you have not started truly licking her on three I will cane you again. Then I will count three and cane you again. Until you start licking her. One. T –'

Gwen lifted her hands and Anna felt them grip her buttocks a moment later. Gwen pulled at her, sealing her mouth and lips to her cunt, and began to lick at her slowly, firmly, lingeringly. Deliciously.

'Good. Very good.'

Anna could feel her cunt begin to waken and respond to the heat and moistness of Gwen's tongue. The firmness of it. The strength. For the tongue is a muscle. Her cunt seemed to break through a crust of exhaustion and begin to leak a new trail down which it would slip to fresh orgasm, like an octopus-goddess slipping from a ceremonial tank to the sea. She shivered. Gwen's tongue was working deeper inside her, parting her cunt-lips to penetrate the chamber of her cunt. Gwen half-sucked, half-slurped, drawing in Anna's fresh juice, the fresh yelm welling from her re-excited tissues. Orgasm was coming again, swelling up inside her like a vast note throbbing in the pipe of an organ, climbing from gut-shuddering infrasound into the audible register and up through it to the clear, high, thin bat-shriek that would shatter suddenly into sensation.

Anna began to shudder, gasping again, rocking with orgasm as Gwen's tongue lapped at her cunt like the tongue of a bear at wild bees' honey trickling down a tree-trunk from a violated hive. The air, cool above the smooth marble of the stairs, had been warmed by the heat of all three sisters' bodies, but mostly Anna's: brought to orgasm twice (Bärengelt's whip, Gwen's tongue) and now sliding towards orgasm again, helplessly, as Gwen's tongue dipped into the soft thigh-hollows on either side of her cunt, tickling the milky, satiny, yelm-smeared skin, less sensitive than the mucous tissues and clitoral bud of her cunt but awakening sympathetic sensations in it, like a

177

drum being beaten beside a harp, its rougher notes wakening trembling note-fragments from the strings.

Anna shuddered and gasped again, reaching her third orgasm as Beth's tongue touched the back of her thighs and Gwen's flickered into her gluft, cleaning and smoothing the soaked pre-swiff that paved it so that the golden hairs lay flat to her skin. Gwen's nose pressed into her cunt, the musk of her cunt surely deep in Gwen's nostrils.

'Enough,' Bärengelt rumbled. 'Enough. The little bitch is oozing harder than ever. Leave her.'

Gwen's tongue paused and then withdrew, her hands unclasping from Anna's buttocks, her fingernails leaving a pattern of red crescents in the white skin. Beth licked one last time and then withdrew.

'I wish I could cane you, Anna, to teach you not to waste my time by oozing so heavily, but your arse is, alas, inviolable for the present. The bruise must develop. But please remember that I am forgetting nothing: your strokes are deferred, not forgone. Remember it.'

Anna's body, still trembling in the afterglow of orgasm, was stiffened and cleaned as the length of the black cane tapped against her arse, then slid down it, tracing its curves, and lifted from her skin.

'But you, Gwen, and you, Beth, are not so privileged. Your arses are mine at the moment of your disobedience. Do you understand?'

'Yes, master.'

'Yes, master.'

'Good. Let us be on our way. Now. In a line: Anna, Beth, Gwen.'

They formed the short line and began to walk down the stairs, Anna, Beth, Gwen, with Bärengelt bringing up the rear, muttering to himself, the sound of his voices slowly dwindling overhead. He seemed to be testing rhymes: Anna caught the sound of her name, Beth's, Gwen's. Was he composing poetry? After they had descended three flights Bärengelt said, 'Stop.'

His voices were soft now, filtering down through the door of the bedroom from three flights above, and Beth walked into Anna's back, tits brushing shoulders, thighs brushing arse.

'Beth and Gwen: stand side by side and bend over. I need inspiration. I will seek it in your pain. An arm's length apart. Gripping your ankles. Legs straight. Anna, come here. You will suck me as I cane them.'

Anna walked to him and knelt in front of him as he unzipped his trousers and pulled out his cock. Beth and Gwen, trying to keep anger and resentment out of their faces, stood an arm's length apart and bent over, long legs stretching, cane-striped arses bunching and tightening as they gripped their ankles, the shell-like halves of their cunts peeping through their crotch-gap, Beth's fringed with coppery hair, Gwen's, more delicately, fringed with black.

'I am not sure,' Bärengelt's voices came from above, 'whether the cunt is more beautiful viewed from the front or from the rear.'

Anna, kneeling ignored for the moment on the floor, watched as he lifted the cane and pushed the tip into Beth's crotch-gap, tickling it between the lips of her cunt. Beth shivered, the striped skin of her arse seeming to dance above the soft, nervous flesh that underlay it.

'A cunt seems so symmetrical glimpsed like this from the rear. Like a shell. A pearly-lipped shell.'

He withdrew the tip of the cane and lifted it so that light gleamed off the fluid that had coated it.

'Are you excited by the prospect of the pain that I am about to give you, Betchen? It seems so. And you, Gwen? Are you excited also?'

He wiped the tip of the cane clean on Beth's arse and lifted it to Gwen, slipping it through her crotch-gap, tickling the lips of her cunt, probing between them. Gwen did not move.

'Ah, ever the Stoic, Gwen. But I fancy that your cunt is more forthcoming than you are.'

He withdrew the tip of the cane and lifted it to the light.

'Yes. Good. You cannot disguise your excitement at what awaits you.'

He motioned to Anna and she shuffled closer to him, rose a little on her knees, and began to lick the head of his cock, which was still hanging crescent-shaped, half-erect. The head was soft, shrunken, only the hard stub of the lens of the fibre-optic camera resisting the passage of her tongue.

'What two fine perverts I have here before me. Two refined young Englishwomen whose cunts now seethe and boil at the thought of –'

The cane swished and cracked and Beth cried out.

'At the thought of being caned. Being punished. Being *pained*.'

His cock had sprung to full erection as the cane landed, and Anna drew more of it into her mouth, sucking harder. The cane swished and cracked again, with an accompanying throb from Bärengelt's cock but without a cry from the victim, and Anna knew it had landed on Gwen's arse this time. Bärengelt's hand gripped the back of her neck and pulled her closer to him, her knees sliding on the marble of the stairs, his cock sliding deeper into her mouth, deeper, to the back of her throat, and he began to mouth-fuck her, casually rotating his hips clockwise, counter-clockwise, clockwise, counter-clockwise, sliding his cock in, out, in out.

'Inspiration. I need inspiration. Light, in my darkness.'

The cane swished and cracked and his cock slid to its deepest in Anna's mouth.

'Inspiration. Purchased with female pain. Your pain, Gwen.'

Swish and crack.

'And yours, Beth.'

Swish and crack.

'Ah, and I believe I am on the verge of receiving it. Sing for me, Gwen.'

Swish and crack.

'Sing, you bitch.'

Swish and crack.

(In the silence that followed, listening hard for Gwen's voice, Anna heard Bärengelt's breath boom faintly on the speakers three flights above. The effort of beating Gwen was making him breathe faster.)

180

'Sing. Bitch.'

Swish and crack.

(Another intake of breath on the speakers three flights above. Poor Gwen! – he was beating her so hard that it made him pant. Or else he was panting from excitement, from the pleasure of paining Gwen.)

Swish and crack.

(Or both. Effort and ecstasy. Swelling his lungs. Hardening his cock as it shuttled in the warmth and moistness of Anna's sucking mouth. In and out. In and out. I –

Swish and crack.

And, yes, after a second Anna caught a faint suppressed gasp of pain from Gwen, as the pain melted the iron of her will to remain silent. Her arse must be on fire by now, eaten by pain, screaming silently into her nerves. Bärengelt's chuckle came down to them faintly from the speakers in the bedroom three flights above. His cock slid to the back of Anna's mouth again and suddenly began to spurt thickly. Anna gulped at his seed, holding her breath as she tried to avoid choking. His cock slid out of her mouth, still dripping, the flavour and thickness of his seed still burning in her throat, beginning to slide like warm, curdled cream into her stomach.

'Gwen, you have a will of iron but an arse, alas for you, of softer stuff.'

He pushed Anna away from him and stepped over to Gwen, reaching greedily out for the broad platter of her arse. Anna tried to peer around him to examine it but could not see it properly and sat back on her haunches, licking at a dribble of Bärengelt's seed at the corner of her mouth, her eyes widening as she examined Beth's arse instead with a by-now skilled eye. Broad red strokes fading to pink across the bruised tapestry already laid down there. How they must burn! Poor Beth!

'Of much softer stuff.'

Bärengelt had gripped Gwen's arse, begun to knead and rub it, his body blocking it from Anna's gaze.

'Beautifully soft. And so sensitive. So exquisitely sensitive. But what a pity that beating it must bruise its snowy

181

whiteness. I am not greedy, girls: one bruised arse is enough for me. Anna's arse. That would have sufficed. The day-by-day – hour-by-hour – chromatic shifts of a bruise on the snowy-white arse of one young girl would have been enough. But I am forced to discolour your arses too. How else can I give you pain? I must beat, and so, I must bruise. It is barbarous of me. I freely confess it. Very barbarous. But I hope you will be able to forgive me for it one day.'

With a final squeeze he left Gwen's arse and stepped to grip and rub Beth's. Anna gasped, seeing Gwen's arse fully now, stretched and tautened as Gwen held the position Bärengelt had ordered her into. At first sight it seemed to have barely been touched by the cane: a single red stroke glowed across its satiny, bruise-striped creaminess. But Anna had heard the cane land seven times on the soft target of its twin hemispheres, and she could see the way the edges of the stroke had sunk into the arse-flesh.

There was only one explanation, and her own arse quivered and tightened in sympathy. Bärengelt had been crueller than she imagined him capable of being: he had caned Gwen once, planting a single red stroke across her bruised/white arse. And then he had caned her again, landing the second stroke precisely on top of the first. And then caned her again, landing the third stroke precisely on top of the second. And then caned her again, landing the fourth stroke precisely on top of the third. And then caned her again, landing the fifth stroke precisely on top of the fourth. And then caned her again, landing the sixth stroke precisely on top of the fifth. And then caned her again, landing the seventh stroke precisely on top of the sixth.

And almost straight after the seventh stroke Gwen had cried out. *Almost* – how pathetic the qualification was! The pain of the seventh stroke had not broken her will at the very moment it had flared in the tortured cheeks of her arse, but a moment later. The pain must have been heightening each time, the momentary flare of each stroke having an evil afterlife, like the echoes of a demonic chuckle in an obsidian-walled valley, rumbling away into the distance, starting avalanches whose voices add to the uproar, until the whole valley is a pandemonium of sound, shrieking, groaning, crackling.

Like Gwen's tortured arse. Anna's eyes shone with tears as she gazed at the abused buttocks before her. Gazed at the edges of the single stroke-mark sunken into those perfect semi-globes by seven cane-strokes. How clear and straight the edges of the stroke were, as though they had been ruled out! And they were white, bloodless, running beside the floor of the stroke, which glowed, suffused with blood like a white silken ribbon soaked in wine.

And what agony poor Gwen must still be suffering! Worst of all, perhaps, was the thought that the pain was merely the first crushing of grapes for a vintage Bärengelt intended to continue pouring into her for the rest of the day. Perhaps in another hour, another half-hour, when the pain of the seven strokes had sunk to a low, acidic seething, he would cane her again, an eighth stroke falling precisely where the seventh and sixth and fifth and fourth and third and second and first had fallen. And then a ninth, and a tenth, and an eleventh, a twelfth and thirteenth!

Poor, poor Gwen! It would be like having one's arse turned into a personal hell, a portable inferno of tortured nerves and tissue. A tear gleamed at the inner edge of Anna's right eye and slowly trickled down her nose, along the curve of her lip, down her chin. Poor Gwen. But below, in the chamber concealed by the pink-lipped slit of her cunt, the thought of Gwen's pain was also at work. Anna's cunt too was weeping, but the fluid that emerged from it was stickier. Muskier. More copious. It trickled down the smooth surfaces of her inner thighs, a libation poured in tribute to *Callipygé Algión*: the Beautiful-Buttocked Goddess in Agony.

Bärengelt gave a final squeeze to Beth's arse too and turned away from it. Beth's and Gwen's inverted faces were scarlet now, swollen with blood as they held their position, hands gripping ankles, abused arses bare and exposed.

'On your feet, Anna. You cannot sit gloating over Gwen's arse all day.'

'Mas –' Anna started to protest, but Bärengelt lifted the cane aloft warningly. She closed her mouth, heart beating faster with anger and frustration, and got to her feet, very conscious now of the glistening fluid that coated her inner thighs.

'Beth, Gwen, up you get. Let's get downstairs to the further fun and games that await us. *In meinem schwarzen Raum*.'

Beth and Gwen released their ankles and straightened up, their lifted faces suffused for a moment more with blood, Gwen's still suffused with anger as she glanced towards Anna, eyes and mouth narrowing as she saw the further evidence of her arousal. Bärengelt's laughter came down to them from three flights above.

'I would not be in your shoes, little Anna. But then, you have not worn shoes, have you, since you began to enjoy my hospitality?'

He swished the cane, gesturing them back down the stairs. They lined up again, Anna, Beth, Gwen, and started to descend the stairs. He was in a good humour all of a sudden, Anna thought. Was it simply because he had been using his cane or also because he had got the inspiration he was looking for? Did he have rhymes now for those poems he was composing? Had he been inspired to find them by beating Beth and Gwen? Poor Gwen. And poor Beth.

But poor Anna, too. That bastard. How she hated him. Because she knew he was setting her up to be punished by Gwen later in the day. When they were alone again in the bedroom. Gwen would never believe her when she said that she had felt sorry for her, that she couldn't help the way her cunt had responded. Bärengelt had corrupted her too, the way he had corrupted all of them. Trained them to respond with pleasure to their own suffering, and the suffering of others. Particularly the suffering of others. For she knew now that she would never accept punishment again as readily as she would inflict it. A lesbian slut still, but a masochistic lesbian slut no longer. Not *pur sang*. Because she was a sadistic lesbian slut now too.

She whispered it to herself: 'Sadistic lesbian slut. Sadistic lesbian slut. Sadistic slut. Lesbian slut. Sadistic leszzzzzzzzbian slut' and then nearly fainted, nearly soiled herself, with fright, for rumbling up from speakers of the Black Room five flights below came Bärengelt's voices.

'Shut up and walk, Anna.'

She shut up and walked, hearing only the slap of her own and her sisters' bare feet on the marble of the stairs, the stamp of Bärengelt's boots. She could hear the rhythm of each pair of feet and the rhythm of his boots overlapping, merging, coming apart and the rhythms of each combination of pairs of feet (hers and Beth's, hers and Gwen's, Gwen's and Beth's) overlapping, merging, coming apart. She wondered what it would sound like as music, each pair of feet a different light, feminine instrument: violins or flutes or harps; his boots a dark masculine one: a bassoon or an oboe or a bass cello. How the rhythms would run and sway!

Or what it would look like as waves of colour washing together, each pair of feet a light feminine colour: pastel greens or blues or yellows; and his boots a dark masculine one: black or hot gold or blood-and-wine purple. How the waves would flicker, collapse, and grow, fusing together, now dominated by male darkness, now by female light!

Or what it would smell like as puffs of smell wafting from a strange, gleaming machine of brass and ebony in a warm, silk-lined room, each pair of feet a light, feminine scent: sandalwood or mint or lemon; and his boots a dark masculine odour: pulverised coal or burning ivory or the fumes of a molten metal. How – but she thought that on the whole the shifting combinations of smells would not be something to marvel at. And now they were at the foot of the stairs, walking across the mosaics towards the door of the Black Room.

'*Willkommen, Fräulein!*' Bärengelt's voices rumbled to them from within it. '*Willkommen, und dreimal willkommen!*'

They crossed the threshold, the marble-cooled soles of their feet sinking into the dense black carpet. Anna looked at once for the hidden speaker that Beth had pissed on to. Surely it would be sparking, crackling, smelling of burning circuitry and plastic. But no, it wasn't: instead it was on open display, a black, hexagonally grilled stump now surmounted by a gleaming saddle of black leather with dangling stirrups and rein and a curiously elongated and swollen pommel. Two other speakers formerly hidden were on display now too, surmounted by the same saddles, one speaker a little distance into the room, one near the door through which they had just come, overlooked by Anna at first in her eagerness to see the pissed-upon one. All three saddles were facing towards the door, towards the space Bärengelt would shortly occupy. She turned, looking for him and an explanation. He was stepping through the door of the room, cane lifted.

'Welcome, girls. I have prepared a special treat for you today. You are not to be ridden by me, but to ride for yourselves. My cock can wait: your cunts cannot. At least, I say they cannot, and I do not think they will contradict me. So please, quick, mount. Into the saddle. You, Anna, take that one –' the speaker furthest into the room '– you, Gwen, that one –' the speaker nearest the door '– and you, Beth, that one. Quick, come on.'

Beth had been given the speaker she herself had pissed on. Thankful it had not been given to her, Anna trotted to the speaker that had been. The saddle was at about pony-height, she supposed, and it was easy enough to swing herself into it and settle into place, slipping her feet into the stirrups, though she had to hold on to the reins with one hand and fend herself off from the pommel with the other. The pommel seemed badly positioned, taking up more space than it should, jutting towards the rider's groin. Then she realised it was not badly positioned at all. Not for Bärengelt's purposes.

She tested her feet in the stirrups, her mouth quirking as she felt cold metal bite into the soles of her feet, and looked towards Bärengelt. He was standing still, the blank surface of his helmet-mask tilted towards Beth, who seemed reluctant to swing herself into the saddle atop her speaker.

Waiting to see what would happen, Anna ran a fingertip over the pommel of her saddle. It was soft leather over some harder, firmer substance, and thickly coated with something slick. She had been right. It was already prepared for her. Just like Beth's, she knew, and Gwen's. The speakers still hidden in the room came to life again, rumbling as Bärengelt spoke. But not the speaker she was sitting on. Nor Beth's. Nor Gwen's. Not yet.

'Come on, Betchen. What are you waiting for?'

Beth was silent a moment, then said, almost inaudibly, 'What do y –'

She cleared her throat and began again (Anna could hear her trying to keep fear and guilt out of her voice. Would Bärengelt?).

'What do you want us to do, master?'

'What I want *you* to do, Betchen, is to get into the saddle and prepare to ride. Quickly. Your sisters have done it, so why not you?'

Beth swung herself into the saddle, her pubis shining foxily between her legs as she opened them and gripped the saddle with her thighs, looking unhappy and apprehensive.

'Feet into stirrups too, Betchen. And get hold of the reins.'

'It's difficult, master. This thing gets in the way.'

'That thing is called a "pommel", Betchen, and if it gets in the way there is an obvious solution, is there not?'

'Master?'

'To get it out of the way. Anna will show you how, won't you, Anna?'

Anna's heart thudded.

'Yes, master,' she said.

'Then go ahead. Get it out of the way. Now.'

Anna let go of the reins and took hold of the pommel with both hands, running her fingers over it, judging its size and thickness by touch too, pulling and pushing at it, trying to decide whether it would move or bend as she lowered herself on to it, her fingers turning slick with the lubricant that coated it.

'Now, Anna. Quickly. Your sister is waiting for you to show her the way.'

Anna rubbed the fingers of one hand on her cunt, smearing the lubricant over it, and then put the hand on to the saddle and lifted herself, trying to present her cunt to the end of the pommel at the right angle, smearing more of the lubricant on to the lips and vestibule of her cunt with her other hand, fingering the lips apart, frightened that she was going to injure herself as she lowered herself on to the black leather.

But her cunt was more prepared than she was and confidence suddenly flowed into her as she sank down on to the pommel and her cunt accepted the first inch of it easily, like the head of an undersized cock. She grunted twice as the pommel rose inside her, as she sank over it, the walls of her cunt stretched by it but not painfully, pleasurably. And now she was sitting firmly and comfortably in the saddle with the pommel buried in her cunt, a finger-like projection on its base pressed firmly to her clitoris.

'*Brava*, little Anna. *Bravissima*. A bravura performance, one might say. So please copy it, Betchen. At once. You too, Gwen.'

Still reluctant, Beth began to smear the lubricant on her pommel on to her cunt, tugging the lips apart, but shaking a little, Anna could see. Gwen, her face still full of resentment and anger, lifted herself without any preparation other than a fanned hand to hold her cunt-lips apart and sank on to her pommel in silence, her face suddenly growing expressionless, sphinx-like.

'Quickly, Betchen. My patience is growing thin.'

'Master, I'm sorry. I am too dry. This thi – the pommel is too big for me. I –'

'Silence. I do not want excuses but action. Now.'

'Master, please! I –'

'Silence. Lie forward on the saddle with your arse in the air. You have just told me your cunt is too dry. We shall see if we can moisten it for you. Lie forward, I said. Quick. OK, that is it. Arse a little higher. Good. Now, put your hands together, under your *mons Veneris*. Your cunt-mound, you silly little bitch. You can work out where that is, can't you? Rest your cunt-mound on your hands.'

He stepped forward, cane twitching. Beth was leaning forwards on the saddle, balanced uncertainly, the pommel prodding uncomfortably at her stomach and breasts, and her already striped arse raised for further punishment (a *moue* of disappointment flickered across Anna's face: Bärengelt's body would obstruct her view and she would not be able to see Beth's buttocks clearly, would not be able to watch as they striped anew and began to glow under the cruel strokes of the cane).

Bärengelt circled Beth, tapping first one boot with his cane, then the other. He suddenly stooped and seized the reins Beth had let fall as she leaned forwards, and looped them over her body before fastening the ends tight to a projection at the base of the speaker. Anna glanced down at the same spot on her own speaker: there was nothing there. Bärengelt had stepped back down Beth's body now and was standing behind her. He lifted the cane and inserted it between her legs, tickling the lips of her cunt as he had when she had been bending before him on the stairs. He lifted the cane away and examined the tip, turning it from side to side to catch the light.

'You were right, Betchen. Your cunt is dry. Are you suffering from nerves? How strange that they should afflict you and not little Anna. But perhaps it is something about the *Lautsprecher* you have been allocated. The loudspeaker, *Liebling*. Could that be it? We shall see. First, however, we must see to that cunt of yours. A dry cunt is a terrible thing, but I believe I know an effective cure.'

He stepped back and away from the rear of the saddle, rotating the shoulder of his caning arm as though to loosen it.

'Are you ready, Betchen?'

'Yes, master.'

'Then remember to thank me after each stroke. We shall commence with three, then see whether my little cure has had any effect. If not, we shall see what another three can do. Very well?'

'Yes, master.'

'Good.'

189

He swished the cane experimentally through the air once, twice, three times, gripping his caning shoulder with his free hand, then stood still for a moment, feet together, bowing his head as though in prayer or meditation. Anna waited. Waited. Swish, and crack. Anna jumped, the pommel sucking an inch out of her cunt before sinking back in again: he had delivered the first stroke out of a clear sky, his feet suddenly moving apart to provide a firm base for the movement of his upper body as his arm flashed up, around, and down, swish, crack, upon Beth's tense, trembling arse.

Beth's voice, tightened with pain, broke the silence.

'Thank you, master.'

The cane leaped up, around, down again, swish, and crack, and Anna imagined a second crimson stripe burning across the creamy-and-bruised satin of Beth's arse-cheeks (her cunt was beginning to ooze around the thick leather of the pommel, excited again by the pain of another).

'Thank you, master.'

Beth's voice was nearly cracking, embrittled by the agony of the second stroke.

Swish, and crack.

'Thank you, master.'

Beth's voice was barely audible this time. Perhaps Bärengelt was doing to her what he had done to Gwen, landing each successive stroke exactly atop the previous, incusing a single crimson ribbon of agony into her shrieking arse. Poor Beth. Poor Beth. But Anna's cunt, no hypocrite, oozed more quickly at the sounds and imagined sights of the caning, accepting the pommel further into itself, anointing the already slick leather with fresh yelm.

Bärengelt was standing behind Beth again, the black length of the cane stretching from his black gloved hand to her white buttocks, its tip probing between her cunt-lips again. He lifted the cane away, raising it, examining the tip. This time it gleamed: Beth had responded to the caning: her cunt was oozing its pleasure at the pain suffered by her buttocks. But Bärengelt had tutted, and was stepping back to his caning spot!

'Still dry, alas. A further dose is in order. *Da capo*, Betchen.'

Words choked in Anna's throat. He was going to cane her again, even though he had seen that her cunt was oozing. The bastard – but a thought struck her and she caught her breath. Beth must know, too. Beth must know that her cunt had responded. And Beth was saying nothing. For fear of being beaten even more?

Swish, and crack.

'Thank you, master.'

No, it wasn't that.

Swish, and crack.

'Thank you, master.'

The answer was in Beth's voice.

Swish, and crack.

'Thank you, master.'

Faint but unmistakable.

Gratitude.

For pain given and pain received.

Bärengelt was probing with the cane between the lips of her cunt again. He lifted the tip up, turning it in the light.

'Good. You are ready. The pommel awaits you.'

Beth lifted herself upright on the saddle. She had been crying and knuckled her wet eyes with one hand as she gripped the pommel with the other, seeming to judge its size and flexibility as Anna had done, her breasts jerking as she fought back further tears from the beating. Bärengelt was still standing close to her, but now, as she raised her hips and positioned her cunt to slide it over the pommel, he stepped back. Anna watched the black length of the pommel as it touched the pink lips of Beth's cunt. How big it seemed, how small the hole it had to enter!

But as Beth sank on to it her cunt opened easily, swallowing it in one smooth movement, the shining walls of her cunt-chamber visible for an instant around it before she was sitting firmly atop it, a faintly pleased, faintly bored expression on her face: a woman with a large but inactive object up her cunt.

'Good.'

Bärengelt turned away from her, the blank, black surface of his helmet-mask gleaming towards Anna.

'Now we can begin. Anna, are you sitting comfortably?'

'Yes, master.'

'And now?'

She gasped a little. The pommel had quivered inside her cunt and was now buzzing quietly to itself.

'Yes, master. I am still comfortable, master.'

'And now?'

She jerked this time: the speaker beneath her had been switched fully on and his voice had risen from directly beneath her, the bass notes of it vibrating through the pommel. Into her cunt.

'Yes, master. I am still comfortable. But the pommel is . . . vibrating, master.'

'Speak up. What is the pommel doing?'

His voice was buzzing, humming inside the pommel deeper than ever, the sensations of it almost powerful enough to distract her from the sound of it reaching her ears from the loudspeaker itself.

She swallowed and said more loudly, 'The pommel is vibrating, master.'

'Good. Very good. Then we are ready, I think.'

He was increasing the volume somehow, lowering the frequency, down, down, deeper and down, almost to infrasound, like notes from the largest pipe of the largest organ in the world.

'I said, we're ready. Aren't we? Are you ready, Anna?'

Her mouth fell open and she gasped with pure pleasure: the notes of his voice were rippling through the walls of her cunt like steel-fingers-in-velvet, and the projection at the base of the pommel was shuddering against her clitoris. She could only nod in reply to his question, gripping hard to the saddle with her thighs, clenching the reins as she waited for him to speak again, feeling her cunt ooze thickly around the thick pommel it had engorged.

Bärengelt's voices began to speak. To declaim. To *chant*:

'There was a young lady named Anna,

Who tightened men's nuts like a spanna:

'Twas partly a stunt
She did with her cunt,
But mostly her virginal manna.'

She had begun to orgasm by the third line, the infra-bass notes of his overamplified voice throbbing through the walls of her cunt, shuddering against the turgid nub of her clitoris, the vibrations of it reaching as high as her breasts and her hardened, aching nipples, loosening her like an oyster and lifting orgasm out of her like a pearl, giant and glistening and priceless, dropped fizzing into an amethyst goblet of yellow Samarian wine and dissolving into an ambrosial elixir drained to dregs that she licked fiercely for with a probing, aching, swollen tongue.

'Did you enjoy that, little Anna?'

She was swaying in the saddle, the muscles of her thighs jelly-like from the force of her orgasm, mouth slack, a thread of saliva gleaming down one side of it, eyes unfocused. She shook her head, trying to clear it. He had switched off the loudspeaker beneath her and the pommel was huge and inert in her cunt again.

'Yes, master,' she managed to say. 'Yes.'

'Good. Now your turn, Beth.'

But Beth, the pommel coming free from her lubricated cunt with a liquid *thlup*, was sliding backwards off the saddle, shaking her head, a look of defiant desperation on her face. She stood on the black carpet looking towards Bärengelt, her breasts rising and falling with barely mastered panic. He lifted the cane and pointed at her with it.

'Betchen, what is wrong? Admit it to me, for your own sake. You are going to be punished severely for this, but your co-operation will be taken as part extenuation. If it is given quickly and willingly.'

Beth shook her head. The half-dried tracks of the tears she had shed before as he caned her were beginning to shine again as fresh tears leaked into them.

'Betchen, be quick now. Tell me what is wrong. Why do you not wish to undergo the exquisite pleasure that Anna has just willingly undergone, that Gwen will willingly undergo? Quickly. Tell me.'

193

Beth started to shake her head again and then stopped as her tears started to flow fully, falling to splash on her breasts. She slowly collapsed, her knees bending under her so that she finished kneeling on the carpet, holding out her hands towards him in supplication.

'Master, master, I am sorry. I was frightened. I can't do it. I'm frightened.'

'Of what, Betchen?'

'The loudspeaker, master.'

'But why, Betchen?'

'Yesterday, master. I – I did something to it. Something that makes it dangerous. I'm frightened of being electrocuted by it.'

'Electrocuted? But what have you done to it? Have you interfered with the wiring?'

'No, master. I did some – something dirty to it.'

'What, Betchen? Come, tell me. Tell your master. He will understand. Perhaps he will even forgive you. Tell him.'

'I – I puh – puh –'

She choked and fell forwards, burying her face in her hands, tears coming harder than ever, sobs shaking her body, the pink soles of her feet sticking out beneath her exposed arse. Bärengelt walked towards her, cane swinging gently in his hand. He stood over her, watching her for a few moments, then reached out with the cane and began to tap gently at her buttocks.

'Betchen, tell me. You did something dirty to it. Something starting with "p". What was it? Tell me. I think I can guess, but I want to hear it in your own words. Tell me. Look up at me and tell me.'

Beth slowly lifted her head. Anna could see her face was shining with tears. Beth licked her lips, opened her mouth, closed it, opened it.

'I – I pissed on it, master.'

'Ah. So that was it. What a foolish little girl you are. A very foolish little girl. How could you think for a moment that I would be unaware of what you had done? I could almost believe that you knew perfectly well – that you wanted to be punished. If so, I am sure you will not want it again. Once you know what your punishment is. Once you *feel* what your punishment is. Stand up.'

Beth got slowly to her feet, head bowed.

'Clasp your hands behind your head.'

She lifted her hands and clasped them behind her head, her elbows pointing out in front of her. Like her breasts. Anna licked her lips and shifted in the saddle, feeling her cunt begin to shift around the pommel that filled it.

Bärengelt began speaking again: 'Now listen. You cannot unclasp your hands until I release you with the command "Unclasp". Repeat.'

'I cannot unclasp my hands until you release me with the command "Unclasp".'

'Good. Now try to unclasp your hands.'

Anna licked her lips. Beth was straining to unclasp her hands but couldn't. Her breasts quivered with the effort she was making, hemispherical seismographs for the continent of her body.

'Stop. Stand up straight. Feet side by side. Good. Now, your feet are fixed to the floor. You will remain standing in that precise spot until I release you with the command "Unfix". Repeat.'

'My feet are fixed to the floor. I will remain standing in this precise spot until you release me with the command "Unfix".'

'Good. Now try to move your feet.'

Anna watched, fascinated. Beth's breasts were quivering again. She was trying to move her feet. Trying very hard. But she couldn't move them a millimetre.

Bärengelt walked towards Beth and stood in front of her.

'Tell me, Beth, how sensitive are your nipples?'

'Master? I –'

'Shut up. I will see for myself.'

He reached out and touched one of her nipples, black reaching to pink on white. He squeezed it, gently at first, then harder. Harder. Harder. Beth gasped. He let go. Anna noticed that the nipple – both nipples – had started to swell. Beth had enjoyed the pain. Enjoyed the punishment.

Bärengelt was opening a pocket in the breast of his bodysuit, pulling out the pair of earphones attached to wires again. Only they weren't earphones. Not this time. Anna couldn't quite see what they were, but he was attaching them to Beth's nipples and stepping back, the hanging curve of the wires stretching. Clamps? No, not clamps. Electrodes.

Beth's body suddenly jerked and stiffened and started to shiver violently and she wailed with pain, the tendons and muscles in her shoulders and legs standing out as she tried to unclasp her hands and pluck the electrodes off her nipples, to move her feet and step backwards. But she couldn't move her hands or her feet. Not a millimetre. Her shivering slowed and her body seemed to slacken and shrink. Bärengelt had switched off the current. He stepped towards her, unclipped the electrodes, tucked them and their wires away in their pocket, stepped back.

'Unclasp.'

Beth groaned, unclasping her hands and clutching at her breasts.

'Unfix.'

Her knees sagged, buckled, collapsed, and she folded to the floor, still holding her breasts, rolling over to shield them with her body, her buttocks swinging to point ceilingward, the round bruise-striped cheeks still shivering from the effects of the torture. Bärengelt stepped back towards her and planted a boot on her buttocks, pressing down hard, dominantly, before working the toe downwards, over her arsehole, down towards her cunt.

'I have punished you now, Beth. How did it feel?'

She groaned.

'Open your legs.'

Her legs swung open, jerking spastically, and Bärengelt pushed the toe of his boot into her cunt and started to rock it back and forth.

'Did it hurt?'

'Yes.'

He withdrew his boot. Anna could see that it was glistening with yelm. Bärengelt straightened.

'You have soiled the toe of my boot. Lick it clean.'

Beth rolled over, still clutching at her breasts, and wormed her way to Bärengelt using her elbows. She put her head down to the toe of his boot and started to lick it. Bärengelt's helmet tilted downwards, seeming to watch her.

'Enough. Stand up and get back into the saddle. Put the pommel up yourself. Now.'

Beth slowly got to her feet. Her face was glistening with fresh tears but Anna saw that her lips were swollen. She climbed back into the saddle, still shielding her breasts with one arm, and pushed her feet into the stirrups. She gripped the pommel with her free hand and swallowed. She looked towards Bärengelt.

'But, master . . . I pissed on the speaker.'

'It is safe, Beth. I knew what you had done. Always remember that. I knew what you had done. I always know what you have done. What all of you have done.'

Beth lifted herself awkwardly into the saddle, settled her cunt on to the pommel, and slid slowly down over it with little gasps whose tone Anna could not quite read. Uncertainty? Fear? Pleasure? All three? She clutched the reins with one hand, shielding her breasts with the other.

'Good,' Bärengelt's voices rumbled. 'Now listen.'

Anna watched Beth's body jerk and stiffen with powerful sensation again, but this time from her cunt and clitoris, this time pleasure. The loudspeaker beneath the pommel had come to life and the pommel was vibrating thickly inside her.

Bärengelt's voices started to speak. To declaim. To *chant*:

'There was a young lady called Beth,'

(Beth's mouth had fallen open and she was gasping.)

'Who sucked seven men half to death;'

(The arm shielding her breasts suddenly released them. They fell free, bouncing a little, heavy and swollen.)

'With a murmured "Yum-yum",'

(She started to finger the nipples, rubbing them, squeezing them, her head falling back and mouth groaning to the black ceiling.)

'She swallowed their come,'

(Her feet started to lift in the stirrups, swinging to point ahead of her, toes bunching.)

'And scarcely took pause to draw breath.'

She came, legs straightening, lengthening an impossible couple of centimetres more, then slumped back into the saddle, her cunt-lips glistening around the base of the pommel as it held them and the walls of her cunt apart: the pink corona of a sun around the black bulk of a moon. Anna oozed with thick sympathy, knowing the afterglow of orgasm that seethed in Beth's cunt and thighs, nipples and lips and throat.

Bärengelt had turned away.

'Your turn, Gwenchen.'

Gwen's face was still expressionless, but a tremor ran through it as the speaker beneath her came alive and Bärengelt asked, 'Are you ready?'

Gwen blinked, shaking her head slightly. Her breasts shook. Anna knew that she was trying hard to contain the sensations rippling through her cunt.

'I think so, master.'

'Do not think so: know so. Are you ready?'

Feedback was rumbling from the speaker, *grumbling* from it, almost too deep to be audible, trembling on the threshold of infra-sound, and Gwen's expression of expressionlessness was creasing, breaking, as the pleasure of the notes in her cunt mounted.

'Yes, mast – ah!'

She gasped. Bärengelt had varied the volume and frequency of the speaker, searching for the range to which Gwen's cunt was most sensitive, allowing the feedback to hunt down Gwen's pleasure. Now that he had found it, he could begin.

'There was a young bull-dyke called Gwen,

'Who dreamed of a world without men;

'But her separatist front

'Was betrayed by her cunt,

'Which liked a stiff cock now and then.'

Gwen had fought hard but she was sliding towards the brink of orgasm, a careful skier mistaking her way and finding herself sprawling, sticks lost, skis tangled, on a patch of sloping ice whose edge falls away into mist. Bärengelt walked towards her, the black cane lifting in his hand. He flicked delicately at her nipples with the tip, wrist working like a fencer's, and Gwen lost her fight, the skier sliding to the edge of the sloping ice and into the mist, her scream dwindling into the abyss that it conceals, echoing weirdly from walls of rock and ice, answered by the rumbles of avalanche.

Bärengelt stepped back, the cane jerking upright in his hand.

'Dismount. All of you. Now.'

Anna began to ease herself off the pommel.

'Now!'

She slid herself off more quickly, wincing at twinges of cramp, feeling the leather of the pommel rub at the walls of her cunt. She lifted her feet from the stirrups and swung herself to the ground, almost falling over in her haste.

'In a line, here. Quickly.'

She ran across the room to line up with Beth. Gwen was still dazed by orgasm, still sliding cautiously off the pommel.

'Gwen, hurry the fuck up. Now. Line up.'

Gwen's cunt slurped as the pommel slid free of it. She struggled out of the saddle and ran, almost tottering, to join Anna and Beth.

'At last. Now, stand an arm's length apart. When I say "Go", I want you to start high-stepping on the spot. Keep your knees up. Keep synchronised. Go. Go!'

The cane swung into and across the space between Beth and Gwen, swish, crack, catching Gwen neatly on the edge of one buttock-cheek. She clapped at the reddening mark, already starting to copy what Beth and Anna were doing: high-stepping on the spot, knees jerking up high, breasts bouncing, cunts flashing between working thighs. Bärengelt stalked up the line, Anna, Beth, Gwen, down it, Gwen, Beth, Anna, walked behind it, up it, Anna, Beth, Gwen, down it, Gwen, Beth, Anna.

They were starting to sweat, Anna feeling the dreckle of it between her breasts, in the cleft of her buttocks, savouring the commingled tang of her own and her sisters' heated skin, the musky scents wafted from the enclosed surfaces of her and their armpits, inner thighs and cunts, elbows, naxters, from her and their areolae. Bärengelt stepped out in front of them again.

'Stop. That is thirty-seven. Now squats. Begin when I say "Go". Prepare yourselves. Quickly. Quickly! Go.'

Anna smothered a groan as they began, her muscles instantly commemorating her session on the stairs with an ache that hardened and sharpened like splinters of glass in her muscles and around her joints and tendons. She was counting this time, hoping it would be thirty-seven again, fearing it might be seventy-four. She wondered – and wondered harder, finding that it distracted her mind from the pain of the squats – what significance Bärengelt attached to the number. Thirty-seven. Was it a prime number? Three plus seven was ten, so three wouldn't go into it, and neither would five, which left seven and seven times seven was forty-nine and seven times six was forty-two and seven times five was thirty-five, so it was a prime number. But so what?

'Stop. That is thirty-seven. Get down on the floor and when I say "Go", start push-ups. Down on the floor. Quick.'

Gasping, sweating, Anna smothering a second groan. They knelt, then stretched out on the floor, positioning their hands, ready for the command to go.

'Go.'

Anna started her push-ups, squeezing her eyes shut as old strains awoke in her arms and shoulders, balancing them against the relief of rest in her legs, a pain of actuality balanced against a pleasure of absence. Thirty-seven again? How many had she done? This was the worst of all, for her buttocks were raised to the constant threat of Bärengelt's cane as he stalked up and down the line they formed, Anna, Beth, Gwen, Gwen, Beth, Anna. Anna's breasts pressed into the carpet as she lowered herself from each press-up, relieving her of a little weight that did not seem so little as she started the next. Perhaps it would be better to be an amazon, a breathless one, bec –

'OK, stop. On your feet. Now!'

Anna had collapsed against the floor, feeling the bass of Bärengelt's voices trembling faintly in it, sparking pleasure in her nipples where they were pressed hard enough to the black carpet for her to feel the solid floor beneath. For a moment she couldn't move: her muscles ached too much; then they seemed to split and burn as she rolled over on to her back, sat up, knelt, pushed herself up on one leg, got up on two. She could feel sullenness in her face and flexed her lips, trying to smooth it away. If Bärengelt saw it he would punish her for it.

'Good girls. Good. Now, it's time for lower orifice inspection. Stand in a line. An arm's length apart. In a line, Gwen! Don't tempt me too soon. Good. Now, bend over. Legs straight, gripping your ankles. And keep still. Very still. I want to see that you are keeping your lower orifices in good condition for me.'

Anna bent over, feeling the sullenness return to her face, but hoping that Bärengelt wouldn't notice it. Her face was upside down, after all, becoming puffed as gravity drew blood into it. She flinched as Bärengelt laid a gloved hand on her arse.

'Keep still, Anna. Concentrate on it. Concentrate on keeping very, very still. Do you understand?'

'Yes, master.'

'Good.'

He took a fold of her buttocks between his fingers and tugged at it, then pinched hard. She didn't move.

'Good. Very good.'

He released her, patted her arse, and moved on down the line to Beth.

'Is your arse in good condition, Beth?'

'Yes, master.'

'And yours, Gwen?'

'Yes, master.'

'And yours, Anna?'

Anna tried to swallow and couldn't for a moment. She was growing dizzy, her vision starting to blur from blood pooling in her head.

'Yes, master.'

'And your cunts, all of you? In good condition? Kept clean, ready for immediate use?'

'Yes, master,' they chorused.

'Good. Then I hardly need to go on with the inspection, do I? Gwen, what do you think?'

'No, master.'

Bärengelt laughed.

'Thank you, Gwen. It would be a very dull session – in some ways – without a typical piece of your audacity and insolence.'

His cane swished through the air and cracked against the firm flesh of an arse in almost the same instant. Anna caught the sound of breath hissing into Gwen's mouth at the pain.

'Anna, what about you? Do you think I need to go on with the inspection?'

Anna struggled to clear her head. She was dizzier now, starting to forget where she was. For a moment she was fumbling for the words, then they came and she almost gasped with relief.

'I – As you will, master.'

'Good, Anna. Very good. And you, Beth? What do you think?'

'As you will, master.'

'Good. That is the correct answer. As I will. You have told me that your cunts and arses are in good condition, clean and ready for immediate use and so it might seem that an inspection is no longer necessary. But there is a hidden assumption, isn't there? Gwen, can you tell me what it is?'

Silence for a moment. Anna was starting to drift away again. The swish and crack of the cane brought her mind back into focus.

'Gwen, Gwen, how many times will I have to do this to you before you learn obedience? What is the hidden assumption? When it seems that an inspection is no longer necessary? Answer me. Quickly, please. You have three seconds: one . . . two . . . thr –'

Gwen said something, but too low for Anna to catch.

'Thank you, Gwen. That is correct. But please, say it again. Repeat your answer for the benefit of your sisters. What is the hidden assumption?'

'That you can trust us. Master.'

'Good. Very good. Yes, that I can trust you. If I can trust you, then your assurance that your cunts and arses are clean is sufficient, and an inspection is no longer necessary. But can I trust you? How do I know? Can I trust *you*, Beth?'

'Yes, master.'

'What about you, Anna?'

'Yes, master.'

'And you, Gwen?'

A pause, then sulkily:

'Yes. Yes, master.'

'Such sincerity, Gwen. So you all tell me I can trust you. And if I can trust you when you tell me that I trust you, I can trust you when you tell me that your cunts and arses are clean. But can I trust you when you tell me that I can trust you? How do I know? Can I trust *you* when you tell me that I can trust you, Beth?'

'Yes, master.'

'And y –'

But Bärengelt broke off, laughing.

'Do you see my difficulty, girls? I am on the brink of an abyss of infinite regression. Staring into it. *Und wenn du lange* ... Can I trust you when you tell me that I can trust you when you tell me that I can trust you when you tell me that I can trust you – *ach*, it would never end. So I have to decide: do I trust you? I have to ask *myself*: do I trust you? Do I? And the answer is, of course ... no. No, I do not. No, I do not trust you. Not all of you. Not one of you. So the inspection goes ahead. And you, of course, are first, Gwen.'

Anna had barely heard what he was saying; now, knowing that Gwen would be first to be inspected, she allowed herself to slip away fully, into the pulse of blood in her head, the dizziness and high, clear humming in her ears. Then she gasped and nearly fell over. The tip of the cane was wiggling between the lips of her cunt, inserted from the rear. Bärengelt must have walked quietly up behind her.

'What a shame, little Anna, that I could not bring the cane down upon your buttocks. That would truly have been an awakening, *nicht wahr*? But I must not disturb your ripening bruise – I have great plans for it.'

The tip of the cane slipped out of her cunt, slid along her gluft, traced the lower cleft of the buttocks, tapped for a moment at her arsehole, traced the upper cleft of her buttocks, was lifted away.

'Such beauty of body, such weakness of mind. Did I not tell you to concentrate?'

'Yes, master.'

'And did you promise me that you would?'

'Yes, master.'

'Have you kept your promise?'

'No, master.'

'Why not?'

'I – I couldn't help it. I was thinking, master.'

'Thinking? About what?'

'About yesterday, master.'

'Ah. About yesterday. I understand. Then please, think about yesterday. Think about it now.'

'Master?'

'Think about yesterday. Now. Think about it.'

'I – it's hard, master.'

'Why?'

'Be – because you are standing near me.'

Bärengelt laughed again.

'Ah! Good! The proof I needed. I *ask* you – I won't go so far as to say I *ordered* you – to concentrate and you promise that you will, and yet as soon as you think I am safely away from you, intent on inspecting Gwen's cunt and arse, you break your promise. You do not concentrate. What other proof do I need that you, Anna, cannot be trusted? Faithless little bitch that you are?'

'I'm sorry, master.'

'Sorry? She is sorry! Anna is *sorry*. She breaks her promise, disobeys me, and she is sorry. Sorry. But *why* is she sorry? Anna, why are you sorry?'

Anna tried to speak and choked. Tears had started to trickle from her eyes, running strangely downwards *up* her face, over her eyebrows, across her forehead, on to her scalp, warm and tickling, to gather and drip from the shaven top of her skull.

'Mmmma –' she hiccoughed, swallowed, choked '– Master, I don't know. I'm sorry.'

'Beth, can you tell me? Why is your little sister sorry? Why are tears streaming down her face? Or, as she might say, up it?'

'Because she was caught, master.'

'Wonderful. You have encapsulated it perfectly. But please, say it again, a little louder, in case Anna – who is expressing her sorrow quite noisily – did not hear you properly. Beth, tell me again, why is your little sister sorry?'

'Because the silly little bitch was caught, master.'

'Oh, dear, Beth. Oh, dear, oh, dear. "The silly little bitch"? Did I ask you to provide a commentary?'

Beth was silent for a moment.

'No, master.'

'Then why did you call your sister a "silly little bitch"?'

'Be – because I – I'm not sure, master.'

'Are you sorry that you did so now?'

'Yes, master.'

'How sorry, Beth?'

'Very sorry, master.'

'Indeed?'

The cane swished and cracked and Anna, her whole forehead wet with tears now, felt her lips quirk with amusement at the hissing intake of Beth's agonised breath.

'And how sorry are you *now*, Betchen?'

Beth was silent for a moment again (Anna imagined her working her lips, trying to ride the still towering wave of pain in her buttocks sufficiently to speak without her voice trembling).

'Very sorry, master. Very sorry.'

'More sorry than before?'

'No, master.'

Swish, and crack.

'You were lying, weren't you, Beth?'

Another pause, slightly longer.

'Yes, master.'

'Anna?'

'Master?'

'Using your own experience, tell me why your sister was sorry that she provided a commentary in her explanation of why *you* were sorry for disobeying me?'

'She was sorry because it displeased you, master.'

'Good. But how sorry was she?'

'Not very, master.'

'Good. And how sorry was she after my black cane landed across her white buttocks? Though not *entirely* white, today, I am pleased to say. Hmm?'

'She was very sorry, master. After that.'

'More sorry than before my black cane landed across her white buttocks? Reddening nicely now, I note.'

'Yes, master. Much more sorry than before that.'

'Good. And how sorry do you think she is now?'

'Even more sorry, master.'

'And why?'

'Because she had learned the consequence of displeasing you, master.'

'And what is that, little Anna? From your own experience, mind?'

'It is pain, master.'

'A little louder, Anna. I have a feeling that Beth is somewhat distracted by the pain in her arse. Again, what is the consequence of displeasing me?'

'Pain, master. The consequence of displeasing you is pain.'

'Excellent! Then you understand exactly why –' Anna gasped as his gloved hand slipped between her thighs and tugged and twisted at the lips of her cunt '– I do this.'

'Ah! Yes, master.'

'Tell me why.'

'To hurt me, master. To give me pain.'

'Good. But is there anything else beside pain?'

'I – ah! – I don't know, master.'

'Beth?'

'Humiliation, master.'

With a final tug and twist at Anna's cunt-lips Bärengelt's hand withdrew.

'Very good, Beth. An excellent answer. Pain and humiliation. Those are the consequences of displeasing me. And what displeases me? Anna?'

'I think . . . what you will, master.'

'Beth?'

'What you will, master.'

'Gwen?'

'What you will, master.'

'What excellent students you are! So ready in theory, so – dilatory, shall we say? – in practice. I pain and humiliate her who displeases me, and what I will displeases me. Beth has displeased me, and has been pained. Only half-complete. Anna has displeased me, and has been pained. Only half-complete. Neither, as yet, has been humiliated. But humiliation is less easy to administer. Pain, mostly, is a matter of soma; humiliation, almost entirely, of psyche. As I hope I have demonstrated abundantly to you all by now, I understand the soma – the body – of a young woman well. Intimately. I can wring great pain from it with the twitch of a fingertip. A body is a body is a body. It is less dependent on the context of individuality.

'But the psyche – the mind – of a young woman. Not so easy. Here context is a very great deal. Take and mistreat the nipples of any young woman and you are, I believe, guaranteed to waken pain in her –' Anna squeaked '– but what emotions do you waken? Does she hate you for it? Does she worship you for it? Does she seek to hurt you in return, or ask you to do it again? Is she paradoxically pleasured by it? Is she humiliated by it?

'Without a context – without an individual – who can say? I have three young women here, three fine sets of nipples supplied with healthy nerves, three opportunities for endless symphonies of pain. But how would young woman number one react to tit-torture? How would young woman number two? Young woman number three? As yet, only she would know for sure.'

He was silent for a moment.

'Nevertheless, that is not to say the experiment might not be as useful as it would be enjoyable. Perhaps I shall perform it one day. Perhaps today, perhaps within the hour, who knows? But for the moment I have the problem of having only half-completed the punishment for Anna's and Beth's having displeased me. I have pained them both: I must now humiliate them both. But I do not, as yet, know either of them well enough to know quite how to go about it. Perhaps with Anna I could make a very good guess, but Beth remains an unknown quantity. What shall I do? Gwen, have you any suggestions?'

'No, master.'

'None at all?'

'None, master.'

'I do not believe you, Gwen, but I prefer not to waste time – at present – forcing an answer out of you. So I will fall back on my own resources. So how shall I humiliate Anna? Chain her up and piss on her? Chain her up and beat her? Chain her up certainly, I think. And Beth too. And why not Gwen? All three of you.'

Thirteen

The corridor ended in a narrow, arched doorway beyond which a steep set of steps curved up and out of sight. Anna stopped, uncertain, and felt Beth's chin hit her buttocks. The chains linking them clinked and swung, cold against the back of her thighs.

'Climb,' Bärengelt's voices rumbled. Anna heard a crack and gasp as his gloved hand (she imagined the leather warm from the spanking he had administered to Beth) landed atop Gwen's buttocks.

Already fearful of what Gwen would do to her in their bedroom afterwards, fearing worse if she delayed further, Anna crawled on to the steps and began to climb. The clink of the chains echoed between the narrow walls, curiously gentle as the edge of each step bit into her knees and the muscles of her thighs and shoulders trembled with the strain of the climb. The steps were unlit, steep, climbing widdershins in a tight spiral between smooth, cold marble (it had been white at the bottom, in the light, and might be white still: her haunches and flanks brushed against it and she shivered, adding delicate rhythms to the clinking of the chains).

She was beginning to pant with effort, climbing in darkness that she knew was calculated to allow her body the full flavour of the pain the climb induced in her. Sweat was already running down her flanks and thighs, between the cleavage of her swinging breasts, along the groove of her spine, down the cleft in her buttocks. The pain in her knees as she lifted them to each new step, the ache in her wrists as she strained to ease the pain in her knees, were beginning to moisten and heat her cunt, and she moaned, wondering what tortures awaited them at the top of the steps, wondering if there were a top to the steps or if Bärengelt had devised some way to keep them climbing for ever, higher and higher, until the air began to grow thin, drawing the blood to the surface of their white skin, making their tits and nipples and the lips of their cunts swell harder and harder with painful pleasure.

'I hope,' Bärengelt's voices came rumbling up after her, drowning the clinking of the chains, 'that you have all been counting the steps, for there will be a test at the top and severe punishments for ignorance.'

Anna groaned, hearing Beth and Gwen groan too, and knew none of them had been paying any attention to how many sharp-edged steps they had crawled upwards over. Why had the bastard not warned them at the bottom? But she already knew the answer to that.

'Faster!' Bärengelt's voices rumbled, and there was another crack of his gloved hand on Gwen's buttocks and another gasp from Gwen (Anna heard anger and resentment in the gasp, and knew Gwen's thoughts would be dark with thoughts of retribution in their bedroom afterwards: she began to climb faster). Suddenly it became easier, for the light ahead of her had changed and she knew she – they – were almost at the top. The edges of each step were cutting into her knees almost like knives now, and as she dragged herself over the last and into the circular room that awaited them, she glanced down and along her body (breasts swinging) at the floor, half-expecting to see her knees leaving smears of blood.

She crawled towards the centre of the room (white marble floor, where three strange shapes swathed in black velvet were sitting, erotic tapestries in yellow, purple, and red silk along the walls), feeling the chains tug and loosen on her shoulders as Beth came off the stairs too. Gwen would be following next, and Bärengelt had only struck her tw – no, his voices were rumbling up the spiral of the stairwell again: 'Faster, Gwen, you bitch!'; and for the third time his glove had cracked down on Gwen's buttocks, for the third time Gwen had gasped. Anna bit her lip, knowing Gwen had done nothing to deserve the third spank, knowing that Bärengelt was merely stoking Gwen's resentment and anger, his cock stiffening no doubt with anticipation of the punishment he would gloat over when the sisters were gathered alone again in their bedroom.

Chains clinked and Gwen was in the room; boots thudded on the floor and Bärengelt was in the room too. Speakers hummed along the walls and his voices began to rumble from them.

'*Willkommen, Fräulein.* Are you ready for what awaits you? Well, an answer, please. Quick!'

Beth answered for them (Anna was too aware of Gwen staring angrily at her, one of her slim white hands rubbing at a burning left buttock, too aware of the three strange shapes swathed in black velvet).

'But what awaits us, master?'

'An obvious question, my little Beth, but an important one. I will show you.'

His boots thudded again as he walked to the nearest swathed shape. The velvet came off it in a harsh whisper, like a low promise of extreme pain in a honeyed voice, revealing the glittering steel tubes and polished black leather straps of an oddly shaped chair.

'This awaits you, little Beth. And this –' his boots thudded across the floor to a second shape, his black glove pulled away a second harshly whispering velvet swathing to reveal a second chair of glittering steel and gleaming black leather '– awaits you, little Anna. And this –' thudding; harsh whisper of velvet; glittering of steel, gleaming of black leather '– awaits *you*, little Gwen.'

Anna groaned. Bärengelt turned on her instantly, the toes of his boots lifting, his heels swinging with a squeak that was cut short by the click of his toes landing on the floor again.

'Ah, Anna, I see that the prospect excites you, so you shall be first into your chair. On your feet, *Liebling*. Quickly now. Quickly.'

Anna got up on one knee and tried to stand.

'Quick!'

The sound of his boots advancing towards her across the marble floor galvanised her and she managed to straighten, lift herself to her feet, choking a little as the chains tightened around her neck.

'Good, *Liebling*. Very good. Let's get your chains off you so that you can settle comfortably into your personal chair.'

She shivered as he busied himself with the chains around her neck, the smooth leather of his gloves pressing and stroking against her skin as he loosened and undid the catches and dropped the chains to the floor. Then his right hand clamped over her left shoulder, digging into her flesh, rays of numbness shining out along her arm where his fingers had landed atop nerves. But she knew better by now than to cry out.

He pushed her at the chair and she tried to sit down on it.

'Dearest –' his voices had gone dangerously quiet, and she flinched in expectation of a sudden blow '– not like that. You do not sit upright in this special chair. You sit head downwards, arse in the air. Like this.'

His hands grabbed at her, forcing her into the chair head-down, arse in the air, legs folded, thighs tucked to her stomach, ankles pressed against the lower halves of her buttocks. Upside down, she could see tapestries along the far side of the single curving wall and the other two chairs as a backdrop against which the lower half of his body moved (boots gleaming; a long bulge at the groin of his black leather bodysuit). One of his hands hung loose, clenching and unclenching as the other lifted and dropped to a lever, seized it, tugged it. The chair folded around her, kissing her skin with long lips of cold steel. She hissed at the sensation; gasped as leather straps were thrown around her and bit into her, tightened hard; moaned a little in fear as his gloved hand stroked at her arse, tracing the cleft and pressing a stiff fingertip into her arsehole.

'Beautiful,' his voices rumbled. 'Quite beautiful. I have not decided which of you possesses the most beautiful arse of all, but I reserve a special place in my affections for yours, little Anna, because it was the first that I knew. The first I beat. Look at the glories of this bruise! –' his gloved hand moved to squeeze at the flesh over the bruise, to trace its outlines left and right '– Beth, Gwen, look! Look at this! How the old masters would stand in awe before it, despairing of ever paying sufficient tribute to its delicacies – its *morbidezza, Liebling* – with pigment and canvas, strain they their genius never so hard. Yet how they would *stand*, Annalein, at the thought of saluting you in some other way, depicting you with a living brush *à la moderne*, hurling a self-manufactured pigment at an arse that formed its own canvas. Ah. I myself stand – harder – just at the thought of it. To perform it again would be very heaven. But not tonight. Alas, not tonight. Tonight I reserve your arse for something other, though still art. Arse *gratiâ artis*, Annalein.'

With a final stroke of its bruise-bisected satiny cheeks and tweak at its pink hole (she gasped involuntarily, feeling the sphincter tighten, firing a shaft of pain up the walls of her rectum) his hand left her arse and he turned to get Beth on to her feet and into the second chair. Anna was already beginning to feel dizzy, her head suffused with blood, and she was trembling with the humiliation of her position and the fear of what Bärengelt was planning for her – for them (the chains were clinking as he urged Beth to her feet). Heads down, arses in the air: surely he intended some orgy of flagellation: she had already noted how the chairs all faced inwards to the centre of the room, within easy striking distance of a cane or whip. Would Bärengelt stand there, cock out, tugging at himself, slashing out at them, each white, tender arse an apex of an equilateral triangle of agony?

Beth was being forced into her chair now, face tight with ill-suppressed anxiety, her arse lifting, its cheeks livid with the cane-strokes Bärengelt had already slashed into them, like violent brushstrokes on white canvas. Perhaps Bärengelt would beat Beth's arse again, and Gwen's, leaving hers unmolested, anxious to preserve the single bruise that bisected it. Perhaps he would merely come to her at the end of the session, to rub the glowing head of his cock over her arse, grunting, soliloquising its charms as he masturbated himself to orgasm and flooded it with his warm seed, a self-manufactured pigment for an arse that formed its own canvas.

She prayed not: Beth and Gwen would keep a careful ledger of each stroke they received, entering it in red under their little sister's name, a debt to be demanded in full and with interest from her in the privacy of their bedroom, while the voyeuristic mouths of Bärengelt's hidden cameras feasted on the scene. Gwen was being forced into her chair now, her arse livid too with Bärengelt's cane-strokes, her face full not of anxiety but of anger and stubbornness. Anna caught her eye across the room and tried to smile at her ... and felt her stomach dissolve in fright as she received merely a flash of Gwen's amber eyes in return: Gwen was already angry, wading thigh-deep out into a sea of rage that would not drain until she had avenged herself on the one whom she blamed for her pain: Anna.

Anna shook her head, trying to mouth apologies at Gwen, signal somehow that it was not her fault, but Gwen had looked away, staring with stony resolution at the wall opposite her, no doubt vowing not to give Bärengelt the satisfaction of crying out as the cane-strokes rained down upon her elevated and supremely vulnerable arse. Bärengelt strode to the centre of the room, equidistant from the arses of all three of them.

'Fräulein, the first half of your preparation is over and you are ready for the second. Can you guess what it shall be? You, Beth? Can you guess? Or you, Gwen? Or you, little Anna? No, I think not. I think you are all dreading – even you, Gwen, sturdily as you try to deny it to yourself – that I have brought you here to cane or whip you. Why else, you are asking yourselves, should he have trussed us like this, shaven heads down, tender arses in the air and tremblingly at his far from tender mercy?

'Take heart, my little ones: appearances are deceptive. Your tender arses are indeed at my mercy, but I shall not inflict pain upon them. Not tonight. Tonight I reserve them for something other. I reserve them for a display in – darkness.'

All lights in the room went out as he spoke the final word, an almost literally plunging into darkness, for Anna seemed to feel herself lurch downwards, the thudding of blood in her ears suddenly louder, the pressure of blood in her face and nostrils increased, the crawling anticipation in the skin of her buttocks and thighs sharper as the tap of one of her senses was twisted off. She jumped as Bärengelt's voices began to rumble again: 'This is better. More intimate. And far more suitable for the display I have in mind.'

And Anna shrieked with surprise and fear, for his gloved hands had closed again on her buttocks, kneading, tugging: the speakers had given her no indication that he had moved from the centre of the room, and he must have crept to her, careful to make no noise with his boots on the marble floor.

'Open to me, little Anna. Open your arsehole to me, quickly, or I *will* be forced to beat you.'

His gloved fingertip was pressing again at her anus, and there was something with it, a beak of plastic or ceramic.

'Open, Anna. Open. Little pig, little pig, let me come in.'

Reluctantly, fearfully, Anna relaxed and allowed his gloved fingertip to enter her anus, to tug it wider for a second fingertip to enter, for the two fingertips to prise it apart for the beak of plastic-or-ceramic to slip between them and inside her. She moaned and Bärengelt laughed.

'Are you fearful of what I am about to do to you, little Anna? Well, here it is.'

Anna screamed. Something was pouring into her, a cold, thin, astringent fluid, prickling at the walls of her rectum, tightening them. A moment later a pleasant scent reached her blood-suffused nostrils, almost dizzying her with its strength. Musk and roses. He was pouring perfume into her.

'Do you smell it, little Anna? My specially prepared scent, specially prepared to fill your beautiful arse? Hold it

215

in, *Liebling*. Warm it with your body. Keep it ready for the display I will shortly command you to put on. There –' the pouring stopped, leaving her arse full of the fluid (its cold made the walls of her arse ache and her eyes and cunt leak) and the beak of plastic-or-ceramic withdrew '– all done. Tighten your arsehole now, dear. Don't allow any of it to spill prematurely.'

His fingers withdrew and she tightened her anus, resisting the urge to purge her congested bowels of the fluid. The perfume. It would squirt forth freely if she did and she imagined it spilling down her thighs and stomach, running over her breasts and face, freezing her skin as it evaporated, filling her nostrils and sinuses, dizzying her with its strength. But she dared not. Bärengelt had moved to Beth now ('Little pig, little pig, let me come in'), and Beth too had gasped and then screamed as perfume began to pour into her bowels.

'Do you smell it, Betchen? My specially prepared scent for you, too? Hold it in, *Liebling*. Warm it as Anna is warming hers. Ready it for the command I shall give the two of you. There. Tighten your arsehole. Tight, tight. Hold it in.'

He must have crossed to Gwen, his feet still silent on the marble floor (had he taken his boots off?), for his voices began to rumble again on the speakers (the bass trembled in the rims of Anna's nostrils, the sensation of it mingling with the dizzying scent of the perfume, and Anna felt as though she was on the verge of hallucinating): 'Little pig, little pig, let me come in.'

But there was no gasp and scream from Gwen, and suddenly Bärengelt's voices were repeating, 'Little pig, little pig, let me come in.'

There was a slap, but no sound from Gwen.

'Open, Gwen. Quick. Now.'

Another slap.

'Open, you silly little bitch. Now.'

A double slap this time then a period of silence (what was he doing to her?), broken by a sudden gasp from Gwen (what had he done?).

'Open your arsehole, Gwen. Open it.'

Another period of silence broken more quickly this time by a gasp from Gwen. Anna could hear the anger and stubbornness in her voice.

'How foolish you are being, Gwen. How very foolish. I have unlimited supplies of pain to bestow upon you, and in the end you *will* give in, having achieved nothing for yourself while giving me a great deal of pleasure. A very great deal of pleasure. Feel this. Feel how stiff you have made me. Feel me stiffen even further as I do this to you and hear you –' Gwen gasped again '– gasp in acknowledgment of my skill at the infliction of pain. Give in, dear Gwen. Give in now. Save both yourself and me something. Save yourself a great deal of pain and me a little expenditure of energy. Each time it will be worse for you, better for me. More pain for you, more pleasure for me.'

Gwen gasped again, and Anna could read in the harmonics of her voice that her resistance was weakening even as her anger grew. What *was* Bärengelt doing to her?

'Ah, Gwen, that is better. Good. I felt you loosen for a moment then. So loosen fully. Let me in, let me fill you, let the display commence. Quick. The next time you will know that I have only been playing with you thus far. Oh, dear. Oh, dear. I am being very patient with you, Gwen. Do not disappoint me. Open yourself. Now.'

Gwen grunted, almost barked, with pain this time. Anna had started to sweat, imagining all manner of horrors taking place in the darkness a few metres from her. What *was* he doing to Gwen? Her bowels were beginning to stir with unease and she had to suppress an urge to fart, sweating even more at the thought of what Bärengelt would do to her if he heard such audible defiance of his injunction to lock the fluid tight inside her, warming its cold with the heat of her bowels.

Bärengelt chuckled.

'But I spoke too soon, Gwenchen. Far too soon. Shall I tell your little sisters what I have just discovered? How you are re – ah, that is better. Open wide. Good. Very good. Can you feel it pouring inside you? Filling that tight, hot

217

arsehole of yours? An arsehole fit for the gods, *Liebling*. Ganymede himself could not have boasted a finer. Such muscular tension in that sphincter of yours. I believe you could have held out against me, had I not discovered the means to compel you to obey. Good. Very good. Now, hold it in. Warm it with your body. I fancy that Beth and little Anna will already be discovering the special properties of the potion that I have poured into each of you. Are you, my little ones?'

Anna realised that the swelling discomfort in her bowels was not fear, not horror at what Bärengelt had been doing to Gwen, but some flatulent effect of the perfume he had filled her with. She was having to strain to keep her arsehole closed, knowing that if she relaxed it for a moment the room would fill with the clear, high note of one of the longest farts she had ever produced. She heard Beth whimper and swear, and knew that her bowels too were filling with gas. Soon Gwen would join them, and three white arses would point upwards in the darkness straining to hold in what already felt to her like litres of gas.

She whimpered too, closing her useless eyes and clenching her teeth in concentration, cursing Bärengelt silently in her head. Was this one of his new tortures, to force them to hold in bowels against an ever-growing volume of wind? Was he waiting for one of them to weaken and fart, so that he could punish her? Bastard, she said to herself, bastard, bastard, bastard. I won't give in. I won't give in. It won't be me. Bastard.

She screamed, almost letting her sphincter go with fright, for Bärengelt's leather-encased fingertip was probing again at her anus, resting upon it motionless, reading the activity within.

. 'Are you swelling, little Anna? Bloating with gas? I can feel that you are, *Liebling*, so don't deny it to me. Tell me the truth. Do you want to fart, little Anna?'

'Yes, master.'

'Ah, you say it through clenched teeth. How delightful. You are holding it in for love of me. Or for fear of m –'

His voices were interrupted, cut clean through by the clear, high note of a fart, sounding for what seemed like seconds, released through a half-tensed sphincter that added (Anna caught herself just in time to stop laughing) an unmistakable vibrato of contempt. Gwen – she was sure it was Gwen – had farted. Had shown Bärengelt just what she thought of him.

But what was this? Bärengelt was *laughing*.

'That was you, wasn't it, Gwen? Thank you.'

The speakers made a strange noise that Anna realised was a sniff. Beneath his helmet Bärengelt was sniffing, sampling the air.

'Yes, it was you. I detect the undertones of certain aromatic herbs that I added to your mixture. Delightful. Please, fart again as soon as you like. There is little chance you will be able to exhaust the supplies of gas that are building in that delightful alembic of yours. I even intend to, at one point, with one of you – stir up the sediment with a pestle. My pestle, *Lieblinge*. I think you can guess what that means.'

Another fart sounded – from Gwen's direction again – but there was an uncertain note in it this time, and the sphincter was slack, adding no contemptuous vibrato to the note. Then another fart, from Beth this time, unadulterated, a sheer release of pressure that Anna, the building of gas in her bowels almost painful now, knew she would have to imitate in another few seconds.

Bärengelt sniffed.

'And you, Beth. You have joined your sister. But I suspect yours was not a deliberate act of defiance. The pressure is growing, is it not? So fart too, if you wish, Anna. You were wrong if you thought that is not what I intended you all to do. I want you all to fart as freely and as hard as you can. I want you to *compete* against each other.'

Anna relaxed her sphincter and what seemed like a gale of wind poured through it, slightly moist, still slightly chilled, but warming even as the flow continued. The scent of it filled her nostrils, dizzying her truly this time. Musk and roses.

'Thank you, Anna. That was a truly generous contribution to the delightful atmosphere the three of you are creating here. Another contribution would be welcome from Gwen, but I suspect now that she is struggling *not* to fart, now that she knows I wish her to do so. Oh, so stubborn. But you will have to fart, sooner or l –'

He paused as Anna vented a second enormously long fart that was joined halfway through by another from Beth, the two notes harmonising in a way that added to the dizziness Anna was experiencing, as though it were sounding beyond the dimensions of the room.

'Listen!' Bärengelt's voices rumbled. 'A feast for two senses now. The nose –' he sniffed deeply again '– and the ears. One can tell you are sisters by the way your farts harmonise. Come, Gwen, when they start again, please add your voice. I am sure we can achieve a three-point harmony. How delightful to think of those three pink sphincters relaxed and singing in the darkness, creating one of the most natural, unaffected melodies of which the female body is capable.'

Beth farted again and Anna joined her, trying to relieve the bloated feeling in her bowels. The flow of wind was at blood-heat now: the mixture Bärengelt had poured into her had been warmed by her bowels as he had wished and the full scent was being released, making her feel as though she was slowly suffocating. She tried to breathe through her mouth but the scent lay thick on her tongue and fauces and she gagged. Bärengelt waited for the two-part harmony of the two sisters' bowels to end and tutted sorrowfully.

'There was your chance, Gwen. You did not take it. I am disappointed in you. Must you always seek to thwart my will? Fart again, please, *Liebling*. The pressure must be building considerably now. You do not wish to injure yourself, do you? I should hate to think of the gas building inside you to such a pressure that it bursts past your delightful sphincter despite your efforts to hold it back. If your sphincter is injured, it may reduce the pleasure I take in buggering you. That is, should you bring up the rear in the competition I am about to set under way between the three of you. Though an injured sphincter will certainly increase the pain you suffer. An injured sphincter is no good to either of us. So fart, dear.'

Anna thought she caught a snarl of frustration from Gwen's direction in the slice of an instant before Gwen farted again. It seemed to last for thirty seconds or more – what a pressure she must have been holding back! Perhaps Bärengelt had not been joking when he said that trying to hold the gas in would result in injury to the sphincter. She farted again herself, Beth joining her this time halfway through.

'Good,' Bärengelt's voices rumbled. 'Good. Very good. You are all farting freely. Now I can set up the competition between you.'

Anna was farting again and the note of it suddenly shot up in pitch as she screamed and her sphincter tightened in panic: Bärengelt had laid his gloved hands on her arse again, gently probing the sensitive skin around her anus.

'Delightful, little Anna. I can feel the fluttering of your sphincter as the gas flows through it. And how well you have warmed it in that delightful anal alembic of yours. The full bouquet –' a deep, lingering sniff sounded on the speakers '– has begun to emerge. But now, *Liebling*, it is time for a little raising of the stakes.'

His hands left her arse and she felt the chair tremble faintly as he made some adjustment to it. Suddenly the darkness lightened fractionally: something was glowing, red and intense, just above her arse and she felt heat on the cheeks of her buttocks. The metal in the chair rattled as she jerked in panic. Bärengelt's gloved hand rested again on her arse, squeezing the left cheek firmly.

'Anna! Stop that. What do you take me for? I am not going to brand you. This is part of the competition I am setting up for you. Fart again and see what I have done.'

Even in the ten seconds or so since she had last farted the gas had built up strongly again in her bowels and she was glad to obey him. She farted, and again the note shot up in pitch as she screamed in surprise. The whole room had lit up with a sudden spurt of yellow flame burning somewhere behind her, and she felt the skin of her buttocks tighten as it was struck by an intense puff of heat and gave up a little of its moisture.

It took her a moment to realise, her heart pounding in her throat, that her fart had been ignited by whatever glowing object it was that Bärengelt had set up above her arse. She tried to look behind her and though she couldn't move her head far enough Bärengelt was obviously still there, watching her movements.

'Don't worry,' his voices rumbled. 'I will be putting your helmet on you soon, so you will be able to see all the details. But you must be patient, for Beth and Gwen still have to be prepared.'

Anna farted again and flinched as the room was lit by a second spurt of yellow flame, followed by the same intense puff of heat on the skin of her buttocks. The musk and roses of the perfume emerging from her bowels had burnt undertones now, and she had started to sweat in reaction to her fears of what Bärengelt had been about to do to her, the odour of her sweat mingling with the burnt perfume and adding to the dense, jumbled dizziness that seemed to swoop inside her blood-suffused head.

Bärengelt was talking to Beth now, and suddenly the room lit again, this time with an oddly sinister red light: Beth must have farted on to the heated apparatus he had set up for her. What was the competition Bärengelt had spoken of? Were they to compete to see who could fart hardest, or longest, or brightest? Or all three?

She farted again, realising suddenly that Bärengelt had colour-coded their farts in some way, so that she, a blonde, farted yellow flame and Beth, a redhead, farted red. What colour would raven-haired Gwen fart? Blue, she thought: black would be impossible. The room lit sinisterly again with the red flame of one of Beth's farts, and Bärengelt was talking to Gwen: in a few more moments she would know what colour Gwen's farts were. Unless Gwen was stubborn again – but no, for the room had suddenly flashed red and then blue, as Beth and Gwen farted almost simultaneously. What would happen if two of them – or all three – did fart simultaneously? Would the room turn orange (she and Beth) or purple (Beth and Gwen) or green (she and Gwen) or white, maybe (all three of them)?

She farted again herself, hardly flinching at all now as the puff of heat hit her buttocks. The room lit red as Beth farted, then blue as Gwen farted. Anna was feeling strangely indifferent, her head suffused with blood, buzzing with the heat and scent of the room. Bärengelt was suddenly back with her, fixing the video-helmet over her head. The red flare of one of Beth's farts was cut off and she stared into darkness. Bärengelt left her with an oddly disturbing – proprietorial? avuncular? – pat of her buttocks. She waited, farting as the gas built up in her bowels, feeling the puffs of heated air strike her buttocks, enjoying the sensation of indifference that had slowly come over her.

'Girls!' Bärengelt's voices rumbled. 'Now it is time for the competition. First, I am sorry to inform you that there is no prize for the winner. As I hope you have realised by now, I am not one to encourage by rewards, so there will of course be only a penalty. A penalty for the loser: the one who, as I remarked before, brings up the rear. Her penalty for bringing up the rear shall be that I come up her rear. I intend to bugger her through that same orifice with which she has failed in the competition I am about to set you. Is that understood?'

Anna had to swallow and lick her lips before she could answer.

'Yes, master,' she said. Beth muttered something too, but Gwen remained silent.

'Is that clear, Gwen?' Bärengelt's voices rumbled menacingly. 'An answer, please, or I will disqualify you before the competition even begins.'

'Yes.'

'Unsatisfactory, Gwen. Answer in the prescribed fashion or disqualification will be automatic.'

'Yes, master.'

'Good. I shall overlook your tone, because I am anxious not to be unfair to any one of you. I want this competition to be free of any interference from my bias, conscious or otherwise, for I am truly undecided as to which one of you should be the best to bugger. Anna's exquisite arse I have already sampled, but I should not be so dogmatic as to affirm that its heat and tightness are unsurpassable, likely though that seemed to me at the time. No, your own efforts shall decide whom I enjoy tonight. And you are of course waiting to see how you shall make these efforts. Like this, *Liebling.*'

Anna jerked, rattling the metal of her chair as the screen in her helmet sprang to life, and she knew from the answering rattle of metal from Beth's and Gwen's chairs that their screens had been switched on too: they were all watching the room (Anna from a position somewhere in the centre of the ceiling). Anna could see herself and her two sisters in the chairs, their white arses glimmering beneath an eye of glowing metal held above each on what she guessed to be a metal arm too slender to be seen in the gloom.

'Fart, one of you,' Bärengelt's voices rumbled. Beth obliged, and a shaft of red flame leaped into space from the glowing eye of metal that sat above her white buttocks. It was curiously feathered, extending for what seemed like two or more metres and Anna, anxious suddenly to see how her one would look, tightened the muscles of her stomach and farted hard herself, and was delighted with the shaft of yellow flame that shot into the air. Gwen, deciding not to be stubborn any more, or to practise for the competition Bärengelt had mentioned, farted almost straight after her, sending a blue shaft of flame higher into the air than either Beth or Anna had done, and Anna swallowed, realising that Gwen had decided to play hard and to win, doubtless hating the thought of being buggered by Bärengelt most of them all.

'Excellent,' Bärengelt's voices rumbled (he was now standing in the centre of the room, his leather bodysuit gleaming softly in the glow of the metal eyes, glittering suddenly as each shaft of fart-flame leaped into space). 'You are almost ready to begin. But a warning, *Lieblinge.* I am sure each of you will be trying to fart as hard as she

224

can, but beware of suck-back. If the vacuum created within the lower reaches of your bowels by your expulsive efforts is too great and your arsehole is not sufficiently tightened as you end the fart, you may suck a fragment of flame back inside yourself and ignite the gases lying deeper within.

'This will certainly be painful and will possibly be dangerous, and I am afraid that while it will automatically disqualify you from the competition, it will not prevent me from buggering you as the disqualified loser, which will doubtless increase the pain you are already suffering. So, your motto must be: guard against suck-back. Expel freely and hard, but seal your arsehole forcefully the instant you have discharged. Do you understand?'

Anna licked her lips and said, 'Yes, master.'

'Yes, master.'

'Yes, master.'

'Excellent. Excellent. Then we are almost ready to begin.'

Anna saw him gesture – breaking an infra-red beam projected by some hidden apparatus? (but how had she known to think that?) – and a curious series of shimmering white lights took to the air and began to spiral around the room. No, not lights – it took her a moment to realise that they were not lights, but butterflies lightly coated with some kind of phosphorescent paint.

'This is your competition, girls. Reach out with your hands and you should be able to find and grasp a handle with each hand. Pull on it and you will find you are able to control the movement of your chair. You must try to shoot down the butterflies with your flaming farts. The helmet-screens will switch to a suitable perspective view once I have prepared each of you in a moment. Once you are ready, begin farting and try to outscore your sisters. The one with the least satisfactory score – from her point of view – will lose, and I shall bugger her. Any questions?'

Beth's chair rattled.

'Yes, master.'

'What is it?'

'How will you be sure which of us has hit which butterflies?'

'A good question, Betchen. As you see, the butterflies have been coated with a phosphorescent paint of my own manufacture. A special paint that will react to the chemicals unique to the flaming gases of the farts of each of you. To the yellow farts produced by you, Anna, the paint will react by turning red; to the red farts produced by you, Beth, it will react by turning blue; to the blue farts produced by you, Gwen, it will react by turning yellow. This will mean what, Anna?'

'Master? I –'

'A butterfly that burns orange when hit will have been hit by whom?'

'By me, master.'

'Good. And one that burns purple? By whom will it have been hit?'

'By Beth, master.'

'Good. And one that burns green? By whom will it have been hit?'

'Gwen, master.'

'Good. Very good. The competition will be videoed and I assure you that I will be scrupulously fair in my scoring, and will consult the video evidence if necessary. Very well? Are you all prepared to begin? Has each of you found her handles?'

'Yes, master.'

'Yes, master.'

'Yes, master.'

'Excellent. Then one thing remains.'

Then was a moment, two, of silence, and then Anna heard a soft buzzing begin very near her. He had switched on a vibrator. She tensed in anticipation and let out no more than a sigh as something touched her cunt – the vibrator – and began to slide up and down over it. What was he doing? Her cunt was responding, the lips began to smile, to unfurl and moisten, and now he began to slide the vibrator home, its thick, buzzing length sliding into her in time with an increasing sensation of hollowness in her stomach (her bowels, contrarily, felt more bloated than ever, and she farted, detecting a faint briny undertone of cunt-juice in the burnt musk and roses carried to her by the expanding cloud of heat).

'Good,' Bärengelt's voices rumbled. 'Very good. Is that comfortable, little Anna?'

'Yes, master,' she said, feeling the blood-thickened tissues of her face and neck fill a little more in the darkness at the way the insertion of the vibrator and its continued, insistent, buzzing presence in the slickening chamber of her cunt had roughened her voice with pleasure. Then she grunted loudly, for the vibrator had suddenly jerked deeper inside her, as though sucking itself into her, sealing itself inside her.

'And snug-fitting?'

Anna blinked. Her head was too full of sensations – the pressure of blood, the sound of the vibrator, the burnt scents of the perfume and briny undertone of her arousal, the pleasurable stretching and vibratory stimulation of her cunt, the bloating of her bowels – for her to find words easily, even the simplest.

'Yes, master.'

Her voice had deepened even in the couple of seconds since she had last spoken, and she knew she was beginning the slide to orgasm, even though she feared the effect it might have: if the blood-pressure increased in her face and head, would she start to bleed from the nostrils, from the corners of her eyes, from her gums?

'Good. This is how you will see to shoot down the butterflies. It is a CMC – a cunt-mounted camera. It will give you almost an arse's-eye view of the butterflies flying past you. Of course, I could have given you a truly arse's-eye view by inserting a camera into your arsehole, but then how would you fart, hmm?'

'We c – could not, ma – ah! – master.'

'It was a rhetorical question, little Anna. Please do not try to speak again. Enjoy the sensations of the vibrator as it sucks its way deeper and tighter into you. But do not enjoy it too much, or you will not be able to shoot straight.'

She sensed that he had left her to cross to Beth and insert her CMC. She unpacked the acronym, trying hard

227

to keep her mind focused on the task ahead of her as the vibrator trembled again and moved even deeper inside her (he had said it was *sucking*, but how?). CMC. Cunt-mounted camera. Cunt-mounted. Camera. When would he switch it on?

'Good,' Bärengelt's voices were rumbling. 'Good. And is it snug-fitting?'

As though in answer Anna shook her head and farted, hoping that the puff of heat on her buttocks would hurt a little, drag her out of the pit of·lascivious indifference into which she was sliding. Orgasm awaited her at the bottom of the pit, a pool, a lake, a sea of waving phosphorescent *phalloi*, each of which, all of which, would find an orifice and fill it, feasting on the erotic energy waiting to burst inside her.

'G-o-o-o-d,' she groaned. She bit her lip, hoping pain would hold her back. No use: her greedy cunt, sucking in the sensations of the sucking, buzzing vibrator, seized on this new sensation like a glutton at a feast seizing on a spice, a sprinkling of salt, to season the food he was guzzling, to underline the pleasure, heighten it by contrast, incorporate the pain into it. She groaned again and tried to fart, to relieve the pressure in her bowels, which was on the verge of becoming painful and would doubtless be seized by her cunt too: she felt now like the owner of a sleek, voracious, carnivorous pet (*vagina dentata*) that she was trying to control in a larder piled high with cuts of fresh, oozing meat about to be cooked for the glutton in the overheated feasting hall. How could she distract it from the iron tang of the blood? If she tried to pick it up and remove it from the kitchen by force it would bite her, even take a morsel from her own flesh: turn on her, sink its teeth into her breasts.

But she couldn't even fart now: her arsehole was tightening as orgasm approached. Bärengelt's voices rumbled through the thump of blood in her ears.

'Are your helmet-screens now showing an almost arse's-eye view of the room and the butterflies?'

Anna blinked again, realising that she had not even noticed when the view on the helmet-screen had changed:

it was now showing a view of the room taken from somewhere very near her arse. The CMC. The cunt-mounted camera. An electronic ringsight suddenly glowed across the centre of the screen. To help her shoot down the butterflies.

Beth had spoken.

'Yes, master.'

And Gwen.

'Yes, master.'

Anna shook her head. Bärengelt had asked a question. He would expect an answer. Perhaps he would punish her for being slow. Disqualify her from the competition. Slide his thick cock into her bloated bowels (she suddenly imagining the gas whistling around the length of it) and begin buggering her. Ouch. Ouch. She licked her lips, opened her mouth, tried to find the words, couldn't, began speaking in the hope that they would find themselves.

'Yes, master.'

Her stomach dissolved in relief, glowing with the pleasure of her escape, and that was sufficient: she began to orgasm, squeaking, groaning, swearing to herself, as Bärengelt's voices rumbled in her uncomprehending ears.

'Good. Excellent. Then good luck: begin. Fart at will. I shall watch the outcome with a great deal of interest.'

Anna became aware that her orgasm was over but building again as the vibrator buzzed mercilessly inside her, rocking as it vainly tried to suck itself further into her. Her hands were sweating as she gripped the handles Bärengelt had promised would be within in her reach, and she was trying hard to suppress the waves of nausea that began to sweep over her as she experimented with them – the left handle controlled elevation, the right tracking – and the chair swung violently to and fro (she swore again as her cunt responded to the new sensations, uncaring that they were pleasant or unpleasant, caring only that they were sensations).

She jerked: a blue shaft of flame had shot ceilingwards and a butterfly was spiralling floorward trailing green sparks. Gwen had downed her first butterfly. Or was it her first? And was *that* – another blue shaft of flame, another spiralling butterfly trailing green sparks – her second? Or was it her third? Her fourth, fifth? How long had she, Anna, been gripped by orgasm while Gwen found targets, aimed, farted? Gwen was out to win this, spurred on by the thought that Bärengelt would possess her arse if she lost.

Anna jerked out of her reverie: a butterfly had shot across the ringsight and she tugged hard at the left handle to follow it. Too hard: the chair overshot and the violence of the movement made her fart involuntarily, a shaft of yellow flame harmlessly stabbing out, metres from any possible target. She bit her lip and tracked back, waiting for another butterfly to cross the ringsight.

Yes! One did almost at once, and she risked a quick fart, hoping that the previous one had not drained her bowels too much. But it had: her aim was nearly perfect and the shaft of yellow flame would have licked right around the butterfly – would have, if it had not been half the usual length. But it was, or even shorter, fading out centimetres short. Her chagrin was deepened as a shaft of red flame shot out and Beth had claimed her first butterfly (or was it?), which dropped trailing purple sparks as Gwen farted and claimed her third (or sixth or seventh). Every one of Gwen's shots seemed to have been successful so far, and she, Anna, having farted twice, had nothing to show for it.

She told herself not to worry about it, to focus her mind, clear her thoughts, and set about catching up. She only had to beat one of the others to avoid the penalty Bärengelt had gloatingly promised he would inflict. Just one. Not both. But her hands were still sweating, slipping on the handles as she swung the chair to and fro, hoping for an easy shot to float into the ringsight. Beth farted again . . . and the butterfly she had aimed at jerked aside at the last moment! The spark of relief that lit Anna's gloom was snuffed out almost at once, for the shaft of red flame somehow ignited the wings of another butterfly that had seemed out of range: the heat, she supposed. But why had that not happened to her? Were Beth's farts more potent, burning more fiercely? Was Bärengelt rigging the competition after all, despite his promise that he would be neutral?

Shut up, she told herself; *concentrate. Get your finger out* – and now she was laughing. She felt drunk, sick, nauseous all at the same time, and the vibrator was buzzing away in her hungry cunt, dragging her towards a second orgasm rather than sweeping her – how she longed to have a hand free for her clitoris – distracting her, making it impossible for her to concentrate, increasing her anxiety as Gwen farted again, and missed, and farted again, and hit, and Beth farted again and hit two in one. Green sparks, purple sparks, but no orange sparks.

And now she was worried the butterflies would run out before she even hit one. Already there seemed to be fewer of them circling the room. One of them brushed the fringes of her ringsight and she swung on it eagerly, holding down the sensations in her body and head by force of will, feeling that here, at last, was her chance. She could get this one, see orange sparks, drag herself back into the competition, overtake Beth, maybe even Gwen, be the spectator of the penalty, not an unwilling participant in it.

She tensed the muscles of her stomach and farted, remembering the instant after she started what – Christ! – Bärengelt had said about suck-back. She groaned in frustration, realising that she must have sealed her sphincter prematurely, for the butterfly she had aimed at passed serenely on – even as Beth and Gwen both farted again and both claimed new successes.

'Oh, fuck,' said Anna, as fear triggered her second orgasm. She started to cry as it rocked her body, tightening her sphincter again as two butterflies fluttered at what seemed like stalling speed across the ringsight, sitting targets, but she couldn't fart, and didn't even dare to taste the salt trickling down her face for fear of the new sensation being seized upon by her cunt, that Charybdis whose hungry maw was eternally famished for all things floating within reach.

She concentrated this time on the progress of the orgasm and was able to tell when it had left her sufficiently for her to start farting again. A butterfly brushed the ringsight and she swung after it, lining it up carefully, taking its speed

231

carefully into account, and then farting as hard as she could, ruthlessly suppressing her fear of suck-back in her desire to claim her first success. But for the fourth time she had failed: the butterfly fluttered aside at the last moment and the shaft of yellow flame passed through nothing but air. Beth farted again and another butterfly fluttered floorwards, trailing purple sparks. Gwen had always been impossible to catch; now she felt sure that Beth was too, and despair overwhelmed her.

She was going to be buggered by Bärengelt, but worst of all was the thought that she was going to enjoy it. Her hungry cunt would feast on the sensations of his cock in her arsehole and she would orgasm before he did, perhaps more than once, twice, three times, and if she clenched her teeth and remained silent he would know from the way her arsehole tightened on his cock what was happening to her: that she was taking pleasure in her humiliation, in the way he had forced himself unnaturally into her. Careless now of the consequences, she licked at the tears still trickling down her face and almost laughed at the way the bitter taste on her tongue was seized by her cunt and incorporated into the web of sensation it was spinning for incubation of her third orgasm. She felt the muscles and sinews of her thighs begin to stiffen, her buttocks begin to tense, her nipples begin to harden to the point of pain and beyond. Oh, Christ. Oh, Christ. And it was upon her.

'Stop.'

She realised that Bärengelt had been saying the word for some time. She blinked, passing her swollen, aching tongue over her lips, then over the gums and inner cheeks of her mouth. It was coated with thick, half-dried saliva in which she could taste the burnt musk and roses of her own farts: she had been gasping for what now seemed like minutes, an exiled queen in the kingdom of a body usurped by orgasm. The muscles and sinews in her thighs and buttocks were aching, the tendons feeling slack and weak, as though they had been overtightened strings on a musical instrument abused by rough fingers strumming at random and now flung aside as useless.

She tightened her left hand on the handle that controlled the elevation of the chair and swung herself upwards, head a few degrees above the perpendicular, arse a few degrees below, trying to ignore the vibrator still buzzing in her cunt. Bärengelt would be claiming her soon enough – no, Bärengelt was *already* claiming her. His leather-gloved hand closed over her arse, squeezed it, and then the CMC was pulled smoothly out (the scent of cunt-juice filled her nostrils again, competing with the perfumed fart-scent that lay thick on the surfaces of her mouth); its buzzing suddenly sharpened as it left the chamber of her cunt.

'Good. Good.'

The vibrator thudded to the floor. She imagined it glistening there in the darkness, coated with her juices. Or could anything be said to glisten in darkness? Or was the question whether anything could be said to glisten ever, without an eye upon it? Like the sound of a tree falling in a forest without anyone nearby? Was there a sound without anyone to hear it? Was there a glistening of cunt-juices on a vibrator in a brilliantly lit room when there was no one there to see it?

She shook her head. She was getting lightheaded as the blood drained from her head, and she was excited, she knew, at the prospect of paying the penalty Bärengelt had promised to the loser. Paying the promised penalty. P-p-p. Like the bubbling coda to a fart. Like balls slapping against buttocks as Bärengelt buggered her. B-b-b. P-p-p. B-b-b.

Bärengelt, who must have left her to withdraw Beth's and Gwen's vibrators (she had half-heard the thud of each falling to the floor, to lie glistening-or-unglistening in the darkness), returned to her and gripped her buttocks again. His voices began to rumble on the speakers, his hands tightening on her buttocks.

'List and learn, ye dainty roses. White roses. With your pink arseholes. One of which is mine to invade, soon. I want you to learn what it is I will invade, and occupy. The anus. The arsehole. The most ancient of the lower orifices, predating by many millions of years the evolution of the

233

urethra and that late-comer the cunt. The geometry of the anus is still the most perfect of all the orifices: not the slash of the mouth, the slot of the cunt, the slit of the cock, but a mystic circle set between, in the human female, two hemispheres of firm flesh, twin mounds guarding a secret entrance to the velvet-lined chamber of the bowels.'

Anna writhed silently, for his gloved hands were stroking and kneading at the flesh of her buttocks and the hot disk of her anus as he spoke.

'And more: the anus is set at the base of the spine –' a leather-encased finger ran between the cleft of her buttocks and up the knobbles of her spine, sending a flutter of arousal through her treacherous cunt and a prickle of incipient tumescence through her nipples '– the spine, the very centre of our being, that legacy of our worm-like ancestors whose nerve-rich heart we have ringed and enclosed in protective bone. Penetration of the anus –' the finger left her spine and returned to tease and prod at her anus '– sends echoes down millions of years of our history, and skilful sodomy can awake the nerves of the spine in ways inaccessible from the thick-walled chamber of the cunt –' his other hand dropped between her legs to pluck and squeeze dismissively at the lips of her cunt '– which dwindles to the impassable narrows of the cervix and is anyway sequestered from the interior of the body, terminating in the uterus and ovaries. Not so the anus: through it one can speak to the whole of the guts, to the mouth and sinuses, the throat and lungs, and through the throat and lungs the blood vessels and heart. To penetrate the anus is to penetrate the whole body, to *possess* the whole body.

'Examine the formal lexicon there is for this act: to sodomise; to bugger; to pedicate. All far more ancient and distinguished words than the dull colloquial "fuck" of cunt-penetration. Fuck. Fuck. What a feeble, anaemic, effete, starveling word. Fuck. Compare bugger. Bugger. Roll it round the tongue. Buuuggerrr. It is rich, resonant, virile, stern, martial, vigorous, rigorous. Bugger. Bugger. To say it is to evoke it. Bugger. To penetrate *per vas nefandum*. Through the unspeakable vessel. "Unspeakable" because holy, sacred, *trisagios*, like the Tetragrammaton of the ancient Hebrews. But, named in English, the *arse*. The arse. Savour that, too. What a rich, rolling, Germanic thunderclap of a word. Arse. From Anglo-Saxon *ærs*. Related to *Arsch*, in my own mother-tongue. To *ars*, in Swedish. To *aars*, in Dutch.

'But, strangely, it has the synonym *kont* in Dutch. Cognate, of course, with "cunt". How can one explain this but by that secret, primordial desire lying deep in the brain – and balls – of the human male? Lust for the cunt – the vagina – is a late development in vertebrate psychosexuality. Like the cunt itself, it is a late-comer in the history of life. Deep down, we males all desire the female arse. The way *kont* has drifted in Dutch from its original meaning proves this: the arse comes first, in all ways. Buggery is best, offers the finest pleasures, the greatest rewards. The arse is the hottest, tightest orifice, the surest way to the paradise of possessing the whole female body. It is an act of erotic cannibalism that leaves unconsumed what it feasts upon, a banquet of sensuality that eternally renews itself.

'And eternally desires to do so. Eternally desires to be consumed, to be feasted upon. For you females too have this dark, ancient desire lurking in the electro-chemical swamp of your lower brain centres – in the glistening nerves of your spine. The desire to be buggered. To be sodomised. To be pedicated. Penetrated anally. Penetrated *per vas nefandum*. For to you too the act offers the finest pleasures, the richest rewards. Deep-down, dark-down, you cannot deny this to yourself. Feel how well the arsehole reports the faintest touch upon its delicate puckering, the faintest tweak of the silky hairs that rim it.' Anna's body rocked as his fingers probed and stroked again at her anus before shifting, dropping between her legs to explore the lips and antechamber of her cunt. 'Compare its exquisite sensitivity with the sensitivity of its so-called rival, so-called mistress, the cunt. The walls of this leathery pouch are too thick, too dull, too coarsely equipped with too few and too late developing nerves to supply the rich and primal sensations of buggery.

'Pah! There is no contest, no competition. The cunt too knows it. You will see how she leaks when her dark sister is invaded. How freely she pours a libation of her scented juices to the dark goddess of the arse. Fools will tell you that her juices are for herself, to moisten and slicken her walls, to ease the passage of the cock to the cervix and the seeding of the womb. Nonsense. The juices of the cunt are a tribute to pleasure, and never flow more copiously or more freely than in the cunt of her who accepts and rejoices in her submission to buggery. The cunt knows this, knows the truth, knows that she is eternally the lesser, eternally overshadowed by the arse. The cunt is a usurper, a regicide, a heresiarch who has overthrown the true queen to whom the male should offer his worship, the Queen who lies enthroned in darkness beyond the gateway of the arsehole. *Vale vagina – ave regina!* Farewell the cunt, and hail the Arse, the Holy Arse, and the Holey Arse! *Regina Mysteriorum!* Queen of Mysteries! All hail the Arse! All hail! *Heil dir Arschloch!* And lay siege to the Arsehole! Prepare thyself, for I am armed and ready to batter down the gate, to enter the throne-room and wed the Queen!'

Anna groaned without realising that she groaned. Her traitoress cunt had begun to leak and she knew that Bärengelt's words were true: she lusted to be taken up the arse, lusted for the nerves of her buttocks and spine to be set afire by the ramming and rising of Bärengelt's cock, lusted for the dark Queen of her bowels to be seized and wed by force.

Bärengelt had stopped speaking, seemingly overcome by emotion, breathing heavily and menacingly over the speakers. Now he cleared his throat and began to speak again. His hands had returned to knead and pluck at the flesh of Anna's buttocks, stretching them apart, pressing them together, revealing and concealing her glowing, lusting arsehole to the blind, darkened air.

'And are you ready, my handmaiden? Surely you lost this contest deliberately, knowing that I lusted for you as strongly as you lusted for me? Is your arsehole ready to be thrust aside as I lower myself into you? Is the dark Queen of your bowels ready for me? Has she painted her face and attired her head, and does she now look out the window for me to enter in at the gate?'

His hands suddenly left Anna's buttocks, and she heard his boots rap on the marble floor as he turned violently away from her.

'Answer me! Are you ready? To be buggered? To be sodomised? To be pedicated? To be taken *per vas nefandum*? Yes or no? Yea or nay? *Ja oder nein*? ANSWER ME, GWEN! ANSWER ME, YOU SABLE-CUNTED BITCH!'

Fourteen

For a second Anna lay very still in her chair, the meaning
of his words in her head but not yet assimilated. He had
addressed Gwen. Not her, not Anna. Gwen had lost the
competition, not her. Gwen was the one who was about to
be buggered. Not her. Gwen was the one about to have
Bärengelt's cock inserted in her anus, about to have her
bowels invaded, battered, flooded with Bärengelt's warm
seed. Not her. She had not lost. Gwen had. But how?
How? She had scored nothing, shot down *no* butterflies.
Gwen had scored she didn't know how much, shot down
maybe a dozen butterflies, or more. How could Gwen have
lost? How could she, Anna, *not* have lost? How?

But Bärengelt was already explaining.

'Is it a surprise for you, Gwen? That you are the one
who lost? Are you seething with resentment and rebellion,
thinking that I have tricked you, deceived you? No, not at
all. Not in the slightest. The terms of the contest were
perfectly clear. Remember my words. I will replay them for
you. Listen.'

The bass in the speakers deepened even further and Anna
heard Bärengelt's words repeating from half-an-hour or more
before, lightly sprinkled with static as though to establish
their verisimilitude: 'The one with the least satisfactory score
– from her point of view – will lose, and I shall bugger her.'

Bärengelt's hands clapped together.

'What could be clearer? The least satisfactory score –
from her point of view. And of course, from her point of

239

view, the least satisfactory score is the score that loses her the competition. Anna scored nothing. Pathetic, Anna, but completely predictable. Beth scored eight. Highly commendable, Beth. Very highly commendable, but completely overshadowed by Gwen. For Gwen scored seventeen. Miraculous, Gwen. A triumph of willpower. How hard you were trying to ensure that it would not be you to lose the competition! And how surprised – and horrified – you must be now that you have learned you *had* lost it. By your own efforts. By your own foolishness.

'For consider: what was the penalty that awaited the loser? To be buggered. To be penetrated *per vas nefandum*. That same *vas nefandum* through which she had just been shooting down butterflies. But think of the muscular control required to shoot down butterflies with farts. Think of the skill, the resolution, the *effort*. With a tiny, pink, girly arsehole. Was it not obvious – is it not screamingly obvious *now* – that the loser would be the one who deployed the resources of her arsehole with the greatest skill and efficiency? I wanted to bugger the loser, not to be sucked off by her. Not to cunt-fuck her. I wanted a powerful arsehole, a skilful arsehole, a strong, energetic, victorious arsehole. An *anus mirabilis*. An arsehole of arseholes.

'Which Anna has demonstrated by her miserable failure that she does not possess. Which Beth has demonstrated that she does possess, to some extent. Which you have demonstrated that you possess in *spades*, Gwen. Seventeen butterflies. If you can fart so hard, so freely, so frequently, how could I do other than decide to extract the penalty from you? Though extraction will have nothing to do with it. Nothing at all. I will insert myself and ride your arsehole for as long as I can. Regard this as another contest, just between me and you. Squeeze yourself hard around me as I shuttle in and out. The sooner I come, the sooner I stop. But I will do my best not to come for as long as possible. I promise. Do you promise to do your best to make me come?'

Gwen did not answer. Anna listened and, as she expected, a sharp slap rang out after a couple of seconds. Bärengelt's leather-gloved hand had warmed itself fractionally

240

on Gwen's arse. It would probably be kneading and stroking the cheek it had slapped now. Anna shivered and farted again, lighting the room for a second with yellow light. As though reminded that her bowels too were still filling with gas Beth followed her after a moment, lighting the room for a second with red light, revealing that Bärengelt had turned away from Gwen. He sniffed loudly, then turned back to Gwen.

'Foolish, Gwen. Very foolish. In any contest of wills between us there can be only one winner: me. Are you planning to seal yourself against me when I advance to storm the gate to your dark Queen's throne-room? Are you? Let me see. Ah, yes, I was right. Foolish girl. Painfully foolish. You will not be able to resist me for ever. How can you? Look at my advantages. You are helpless. I can position you any way I like. Anoint your arsehole with all manner of aids to my pleasure. Make it sting or burn with herbal preparations that will have you begging for mercy. Begging me to wipe them away and enter you. Begging me to ride you hard and deep. Deep enough to entwine my pubic hair with your swiff. Though I might deswiff you before I begin, I think. Toy a while with that divine arsehole of yours. Swiffhulf you first. Yes. Would you like that? Would you like me to make Anna and Beth join in? Assist me in the slow, painful stripping of your glossy swiff, lying like black silk against the smooth pink disc of your arsehole? Would you like them to do that? Still not answering, eh? You have three seconds to do so. One. Two. Three.'

Another slap rang out.

'Anna, Beth. Come here.'

Anna tried to answer but Beth was there before her.

'Master? We cann –'

'You cannot what? Cannot move? Try, you foolish little bitches. The chairs will no longer hold you back. Come over here. Quick.'

Anna tested the straps that held her into the chair, realising that they had become loose. She pulled at them and two, three, fell away at once, leaving her left arm free. She tugged and twisted and the other straps came free.

'Quick!' Bärengelt's voices rumbled. 'When I command I expect instant obedience. Anything less than that makes me angry, and anger makes me cruel. Cruelty, of course, makes me stiff. And makes you suffer. Delightfully.'

Anna tripped as she scrambled out of the chair, a hanging strap catching one foot. She landed heavily on one knee and cried out, clutching the knee as she struggled to loosen and pull off her helmet. She pulled too hard and the helmet seemed to trap her for a moment. The screen flared and went dark, then returned. But not as before. She stared wide-eyed at the scene presented to her, motionless for a moment before she remembered that Bärengelt was waiting for her.

She pulled at the helmet again, got it loose, pulled it off, dropped it to the floor, and ran, limping, to the dull red glow of the fart-igniter that marked Gwen's chair, hearing Beth's feet patter on the floor ahead of her.

'Who was that who cried out?' Bärengelt's voices rumbled.

'It was me, master,' Anna said.

'You, little Anna? Are you hurt?'

'A little, master.'

'Where?'

'My knee, master.'

'Which knee, you silly little bitch? You have two. Two legs, two knees, two arms, two tits. And one arse. As you will learn very quickly if you answer inadequately like that again. Which knee?'

'My left knee, master.'

'Good. That is, good that you have hurt it. It will increase my pleasure to know that I am serviced by an injured maid as I service Gwen. Beth, there is a hulver in an alcove behind one of the tapestries. Find it. Quickly. Anna, come here. Show me your injured knee. Your injured left knee.'

Beth pattered into the darkness and Anna limped towards the darker outline of Bärengelt. His cock was out, glimmering faint white, jutting upwards sharply, betraying his excitement at the thought he was about to maltreat her.

'Here, master,' she said, reaching out to guide his hand towards the spot. Her voice had gone husky, betraying her excitement at the thought that he was about to hurt her. Squeeze her knee hard. Her left knee.

She cried out. His gloved hand had slapped hers away. He must be able to see perfectly well in the darkness. Using infra-red. Her white body must be naked in front of him, shimmering with colour-coded greens and blues and reds.

'I can find my own way, you little bitch. Never presume to help me in that way again. Do you understand?'

'Yes, master. I apologise, master.'

'Good. Very good. I have you well trained now. Very well trained. Stand still and do not make any sound as I examine you.'

He stepped closer, enfolding her in the smell of leather. And semen. He must have been masturbating as he watched them fart. The leather bodysuit was cool but she could detect the heat pouring off his cock. His hands closed on her head and began to move down over her body, stroking, gently pinching. She trembled, waiting for them to close suddenly and cruelly over some delicate spot: her throat; the cluster of nerves and tendons at her shoulder-joints; her tits (the hands lingered here, circling the base of each, climbing them, stroking and gently pulling at and squeezing the nipples). She trembled as she held back a fart straining in her bowels to be released. Perhaps she could release it slowly, silently. But he would smell it.

His hands stopped moving on her nipples, holding them lightly.

'What are you doing? Are you holding a fart back?'

'Yes, master.'

'Why?'

'Because I am near you, master. It would be disrespectful.'

His voices laughed harshly.

'*Too* well trained. Fart, you little slut. You will soon learn if I find it disrespectful.'

She farted, her body stiffening as she awaited the punishment for it. Wait for his fingers to tighten viciously on her nipples. Twisting and pulling them. But his fingers remained gentle, teasing her nipples, stroking them, tracing the areolae, then leaving them, leaving her breasts to travel down her body. When was he going to hurt her? When he reached her aching knee? Or would he dig his leather-encased fingers into her buttocks, kneading and wrenching at their soft flesh as though it were dough, reawakening the pain in her three-day-old bruise? No. They were on her buttocks now. Stroking. Gently. His helmeted head was resting on her shoulder. But carefully. Not with his full weight.

And now his hands were slipping down her buttocks, over the rear of her thighs, down to lightly grip and stroke each knee. Her body stiffened again. It was coming. His cruelty. Both hands were on her left knee now. They would grip and wrench at it now. Make her cry out. Her breath was coming shorter and faster. Anticipating the pain. She farted again. One of his hands instantly left her knee and rose to her buttocks again, tracing the cleft to her arsehole, where it rested, tapping at it slowly.

'Again. Do it again. I want to feel your arsehole open as you fart through it.'

She tightened the muscles of her stomach and strained to oblige him.

'I can't, master. It's stopped coming.'

Now he would hurt her. Dig his finger into her arsehole. Tighten the grip of his other hand on her knee. Slap her. Seize her and lay her over his knee for a spanking. The thought of the smooth leather under her belly, the strong, leather-encased left hand clamped across the back of her neck, the strong, leather-encased right hand rising and falling *thwack-thwack* across her reddening, birzing buttocks sent tendrils of delicious fright into her belly.

But nothing happened. He did not hurt her. She suddenly trembled, cramp tightening her thighs and buttocks, harsh tears stabbing at her eyes. There were words in her throat and mouth but she did not need to speak them: he had read the signs in her body. His hand had left her buttocks and anticipated her, exploring the surfaces of her cunt, sliding on the freshly slickened crust of cunt-slime on the inner surface of her thighs. His voices rumbled from the speakers, speaking to her intimately, privately, but her face burned at the thought that Beth and Gwen were hearing his words too.

'You want me to hurt you, don't you, little Anna? And it frustrates you that I decline to do so. Which makes you quimpf. Slowly. Painfully. Delightfully. So am I hurting you by not hurting you? Can you crack this paradox as I crack –' his fingers prised apart the swollen lips of her cunt '– the lips of your cunt? Can you find the truth inside the paradox as I find heat inside it? Can you? And can you feel me gathering its slime on my fingertips? Lifting it to the lips of her whose cunt it is and saying: "Take, eat, this is your body"?'

Anna licked at his cunt-slimed fingertips, tasting herself with a faint undertone of leather, trembling again, knowing that if he hurt her now the pain would bring her to orgasm in the spike of a single second, as though her body were very dry, very old paper touched for an instant by flame. But he suddenly rose against her, the leather of his bodysuit brushing against her nipples as it came with him, momentarily on the verge of being painful, but too brief, too indifferent, to be the spark. He pushed her away from him and she sprawled backwards, her bad knee twisting as she fell, but it was her own pain, not his, and it too was no spark. Why had he pushed her away? Ah, Beth was pattering in from the darkness, returning with the hulver he had ordered her to find.

'Here, master.'

'Thank you, Beth. Your efficiency and speed have been noted. Please assist Anna to her feet. She wanted pain before: I am still going to deny it to her. Deny her it. I will give her only pleasure. Good. Now make her bend over. Legs apart. This hulver needs warming.'

'Master? It is very thick. Perhaps it will be painful after all.'

A slap rang out and Beth sobbed once.

'When I need advice I will ask for it. Prepare her. But be gentle. She wants pain and she must not have it.'

Anna was climbing to her feet, dazedly piecing together the meaning of Bärengelt's words, and barely resisted as Beth took hold of her, guiding her to her feet, making her bend over, nudging her feet apart. What was a hulver? Yes, a candle. Large candle. Large thick candle.

'Good. Good. Can you feel it, little Anna?'

He was sliding one end of the hulver up and down the cleft of her buttocks, prodding it *en passant* at her anus.

'I . . . yes, master. Yes. I can feel it.'

Beth was gently gripping the nape of her neck, holding her face towards the floor. The position and the darkness and the heavy scents of musk/roses//musk/oranges//musk/frangipani were making her feel dizzy again. The blunt, smooth end of the hulver slid up and down the cleft of her buttocks, up and down, up and down, and stopped. Down. Resting on her gluft.

'Push her down on the floor, Betchen. On all fours, that's what you say, *nicht wahr*? Yes, good. But make her lift her arse a little higher. Raise her buttocks. Good. Good.'

And the blunt, smooth end of the hulver slid forwards over her gluft to reach her cunt. Bärengelt's leather-encased fingers joined it, teasing at her cunt-lips, smoothing them out like the lapels of a dress, sliding up and down, then veeing them open as he began to push the hulver into her. Thick, cool wax. She groaned. Bärengelt rocked it, rotated it as he pushed it in, and she could feel the swollen tissues of her cunt and labia respond, swelling further, filling further with blood, beginning to ooze and reek afresh (she felt the hulver suddenly roll and slip a fraction before Bärengelt was able to recover and take a firmer grip on it: her cunt had gushed thickly as it entered her, dribbling cunt-juice down it as far as Bärengelt's fingers).

Now he began to fuck her with it. Very slowly. In and out. Thick, cool wax. Though not so cool now. She could sense that it was beginning to soften. A stiff wax cock growing not so stiff. The muscles of her thighs and stomach were beginning to tighten, and she lifted a hand from the floor to finger her tits and their swollen, aching nipples.

'Stop her,' Bärengelt's voices rumbled.

Anna felt Beth's grip tighten fractionally on her neck.

'Stop her, master?'

'She's trying to finger her tits. Stop her. She's not allowed to come. I forbid it.'

Beth's hand intercepted hers and tugged it away from her tits (the ache in her nipples sharpened, hardened), pushed it back to the floor, rested a foot atop it to keep it in place. Bärengelt rotated the candle again, withdrew it, slowly pushed it back to its full length, withdrew it, slowly pushed it back, withdrew it. Then stopped. She longed to scream at him: *Keep going! Keep fucking me with it, please. Keep fucking me. Please keep fucking me.*

Bärengelt rotated the candle again, pushed it fractionally further inside her. His gloved fingers returned to the lips of her cunt, probing them, probing her left culk, her right, smearing and rubbing her yelm out over her skin. He was judging the state of her arousal.

'Feel her tits,' he said.

'Master?'

'Feel her tits, you silly little bitch. How turgid are they? But do not make her come. You'll regret it if you do, I promise you.'

Beth lifted a hand from Anna's neck and reached down beneath Anna's body. The fingers delicately traced the areola of the left tit, brushed the nipple, gently took hold of and hefted the mass of the whole mound. Anna trembled, wanting Beth's touch to be much firmer. Much harsher. Much crueller. Her cunt and tits and arse were longing for cruelty. Desire for it was burning inside her guts and cunt and she felt dizzier than ever. She bit her lip, hoping for a moment when she could hurt herself enough to come, but self-inflicted pain was no good: it had to be other-inflicted. Her lungs swelled and she exhaled slowly, trying to conjure herself by sheer force of will and imagination into a fantasy of oppression and humiliation where pain was inflicted on her at another's will.

She imagined she was a woman staked out face down on midnight, midwinter snow, waiting to be pissed on by dozens of men in ones and twos and threes and fives and sevens, to feel the hot liquid of their contempt splashing over her shivering skin, quickly melting the snow around her but not beneath her, so that her tits, crushed into hard packed snow, were tortured with cold even as her back and buttocks steamed and luxuriated in warmth, puddles of piss collecting on her skin and trickling down her flanks, down the cleft of her buttocks, over her shoulders.

No good. The impressions of reality – the darkened room; the musk and roses and oranges and frangipani of her own and her sisters' farts; her posture, crouched on the floor with a softening candle inserted in her aching cunt; Bärengelt's cruel refusal to be cruel – were too strong, too immediate. She inhaled and exhaled, pulling her mind away from the messages of her sense organs, trying to sink beyond the room, deep, wholly, into another fantasy of other-inflicted pain.

She imagined she was a woman – a novice nun – captured on one of the first raids by horn-helmeted Norsemen, riding in dragon-prowed longboats out of a Northumbrian mist. She and the stern Mother Superior [for a moment she was almost tugged away into another fantasy] *had been discovered, crouched and trembling, behind the altar of the chapel. The Mother Superior, gabbling prayers, raising a crucifix whose silver chain snapped like a thread as it was slapped aside by a bearded, chuckling giant, had been stripped and raped on the spot (her screams, strangely, had turned to gasps and moans halfway through) but she, after the initial stripping and examination, had been unmolested, merely forced to kneel and watch a succession of scarred, brawny buttocks pumping between the splayed legs of Mother Superior, until, as other giants lifting flaring torches aloft entered the chapel, her guard swung her over his oak-solid shoulders and carried her down to the beach, the thick, hairy fingers of one hand carelessly hooked in her virgin cunt as though he were used to handling naked young women, the harsh,*

fibrous hair of his beard rasping her soft thigh as he swung
his head to look back, bawling some joke in his barbarous
northern tongue as the crackle of flames began behind th –

But there was the scent of real fire in her nostrils. She came out of the fantasy, plucking at her memory for impressions of the last few seconds of reality. Something had cracked and flared and her nostrils had prickled for a moment with a sharp, chemical odour. Bärengelt had struck a match. Something was still burning somewhere behind and beneath her with a powerful but faintly flickering light.

'I should rechristen you Lucifera, little Anna. Or Phosphera. Shall I get Beth to piss on your head for the baptism? Or would you like to fellate me so that I can come on you?'

He laughed, obviously not expecting an answer, and he had lit the hulver inserted in her cunt now. She could smell hot wax and the first tendrils of rising heat were striking her belly and thighs. She wished she could see it. See herself with the candle stuck up her, projecting from her cunt, angled towards the floor but burning steadily. It converted her into an object: a living candelabrum. Reduced her to a thing. A toy. With no will or choices of her own. Humiliated. Crushed. But not hurt. And she longed for pain.

Bärengelt withdrew the hulver from her completely, the tissues of her cunt surrendering it with faint pops and sucks, and the light of the burning wick expanded outwards into the room, not shaded now by her thighs and belly.

'Look, Beth: it's got a definite bend in it. From the heat of your dear little sister's cunt. She's softened the wax.'

Anna felt Beth's hands jerk a little on her neck, as though she had shrugged.

'She's a slut, master. Gwen and I have always said it. That cunt of hers would swallow anything and beg for more. We had a dil –'

Anna heard Bärengelt grunt.

'Beth?' his voices rumbled.

'Yes, master?'

'Shut up. That's more than enough. You are not here as a partner in my sadistic pleasures but as an assistant, for the time being. Perhaps later Anna will take your place and you will take hers. Do you understand?'

'Yes, master.'

Beth's voice had quietened and she sounded abashed, frightened.

'Good. Let go of Anna now. Get down beside her yourself. On all fours. With your arse raised in the air. No, little Anna, you stay where you are. Exactly where you are. Exactly as you are. Good. Now, please, each of you: hold the cheeks of your arse apart. Lean forwards. Rest your tits on the floor. Good. Now, Betchen, what is this I have in my hand?'

'A candle, master.'

'Do you agree, Anna?'

'Yes, master.'

'Then you are wrong too. It is not a candle – or not *simply* a candle – it is a hulver. A hulver, girls. And what is a hulver for, Beth?'

'Hulving, master.'

'Anna? Is that right?'

'Yes, master. A hulver is for hulving, master.'

'No, you silly little bitches, you are wrong. You have not been learning your vocabulary. A hulver is for hulfing. *Fffff.* Not *vvvvv.* Hulfing. And hulfing means what? Anna?'

'I – I can't remember, master.'

'It means dripping wax, Anna. That is, the dripping of wax, not wax that is dripping. But what is the wax dripped on?'

'On . . . on someone who has displeased you, master.'

'Yes. Or on someone whom I wish to hulf, regardless of displeasure. But where on that someone? Where is the wax dripped?'

'I don't know, master.'

'Guess. What are you holding apart?'

'My arse, master. The cheeks of my arse.'

'Exposing what, little Anna? What tender disc of pink, puckered skin?'

'My arsehole, master.'

'Can you answer my question now? In hulfing you with a hulver, where will I drip the wax?'

'On my arsehole, master.'

'What about Beth?'

'On Beth's arsehole too, master.'

'Good. And what do you think it will feel like? Hot wax dripping on your arsehole?'

'It will hurt, master.'

'Good. It will hurt. And how do you think the wax being pulled off will feel?'

'It will hurt, master. Hurt a lot.'

'Good. So are you ready for it?'

'No, master.'

'Good. And you, Beth?'

'No, master.'

'Good. Very good.'

There was a moment of silence and then Anna heard Beth hiss with surprise and pain.

'Keep the cheeks of your arse apart, Beth, or I will lower my hand and the wax will have less distance to drip before it reaches your little hole. The less time it spends in the air, the hotter it will be. The more pain. Yes, that's right. That's a good girl. Take your punishment like a –' laughter rumbled on the speakers '– well, like a good girl.'

Anna heard Beth hiss again and began to tremble, feeling her own arsehole tighten and move, as though trying to suck itself inside her body, away from the threat of the hot, dripping wax. Her turn next. Hot wax on the delicate skin of her arsehole. Making Bärengelt's cock stiff. Stiffer. Maybe he was wanking himself as he watched them kneel before him, holding apart the cheeks of their arses. Beth hissed again, but now Anna caught, just faintly beneath the scent of the hot wax and the heavy, clinging scent of the musk and roses/oranges/frangipani, the salty scent-whisper of an aroused cunt. The pain of the hulfing had excited Beth.

'Your turn, now, Anna. I am going to hurt you. Give you the pain you longed for just a few minutes ago. But I want you to anticipate it for a few moments. Anticipation makes the pain grow stronger. Haven't you found that?'

'I – yes, master. I think so.'

'You think s –'

But halfway through his reply there was a searing pain on her arsehole that seemed to flash through her whole body, biting at the lips of her cunt, her nipples: a drop of hot wax on her arsehole. She squealed and heard Beth (bitch!) laugh softly beside her.

'As does surprise, little Anna. You weren't expecting that, were you? To anticipate pain and then find it still surprising is most painful of all. I have studied the subject very carefully and believe I know the body of a young woman better than she knows it herself. After all, does the violin know how it is to be played? No. You ar –'

Anna squealed again. The second drop of wax had landed on her arsehole and pain flashed through her body again.

'*Brava*, little Anna. Beth, why do you laugh at her? Unlike you, she did not move an inch when the wax landed on her arsehole. Not with drop one, nor with drop two. What do you think of that?'

'I think the silly little bitch is too scared to move, master.'

'Ah. That is what you think, is it, Betchen? But it was foolish of you to tell me so. Do you not remember the warning I gave you? You are not a partner with me in these games, only – occasionally and at most – an assistant. Plainly you must be taught a lesson. Anna will teach you it. Teach it to you. As soon a –'

Anna squealed for the third and final time. Another drop of hot wax had landed atop her arsehole, reignited the pain that the other two (she could feel them hardening) had given her.

'As soon as she has been thoroughly hulfed. Which now she has. Three drops of hot wax on her delicate pink arsehole. But now comes the most painful part of all. The deswiffing itself. The removal of the wax and, with it, your swiff. Can you imagine the pain of it, Betchen? Hairs plucked slowly from one of the most sensitive parts of your body? Do not worry if you cannot, for you are about to experience it for yourself: Anna is about to deswiff you. Anna, are you ready?'

'Yes, master.'

'Then to it. Deswiff your sister.'

Anna lifted her tits from the floor and shuffled on her knees towards Beth. She could feel the wax clinging to her arsehole as she moved, hardened, sealing her arsehole shut. She would be unable to fart now, even if she wanted to. But the bloated feeling in her bowels had subsided, and she hadn't heard Beth fart for minutes either. Or Gwen. Why was Bärengelt ignoring Gwen like this? But she knew the answer even as she asked herself the question.

Why was Bärengelt ignoring Gwen like this? Because he wanted Gwen to anticipate the buggering. He was leaving her to lie in her chair and seethe with anger at her own helplessness and the humiliation that awaited her. When Bärengelt's cock opened her, slid into her, began to fuck her. But maybe Gwen was seething with anger at more than her helplessness and humiliation. Maybe she was seething with anger at her response to them. To the excitement they brought her. The pleasure.

Anna heard Bärengelt grunt as she reached Beth. She shook her head, putting the thoughts about Gwen aside, knowing she had to concentrate now. Concentrate on deswiffing Beth. Stripping the wax from her arsehole and with it her swiff. The hairs clinging to her arsehole. The silky hairs. Coppery hairs. The silky, coppery hairs around her arsehole.

'Get hold of her,' Bärengelt's voices rumbled. 'Come on. Get her arse up higher, get your fingers into her arsehole, and get deswiffing. But slowly. I want this to last a long time.'

Anna took hold of Beth's waist (the warmth of the skin was a shock to her fingertips). She knew from the way Beth neither assisted nor resisted her attempts to adjust her that she was angry, too, like Gwen. Angry at what Anna was about to do to her.

'Sorry, darling,' she whispered. 'I can't hel –'

She bit her lip and screwed her eyes shut to keep from crying out. Bärengelt's hand had landed hard on the upper edge of her left buttock, leaving a slab of pain that slowly melted into heat and trickled over her arse, starting a treacherous glow of arousal in her cunt.

'Shut up, little Anna. Keep quiet and do as you are told. Deswiff the bitch. Slowly. As slowly as you can. I want her crying at the end of this. Crying with the pain of having her arsehairs pulled out by the roots. That will teach the little bitch.'

Anna drew a breath and reached for her sister's arse. She felt Beth wince as she rested a hand on one cheek, rubbing, trying to signal to Beth that she was doing this unwillingly, that the pain was inflicted through her, not by her.

'Anna,' Bärengelt's voices rumbled menacingly. 'Get on with it. Deswiff the bitch. Any more delay and as soon as you've finished she will be deswiffing you. But much more slowly.'

Anna swallowed and put a fingertip on Beth's arsehole. She felt Beth's cheeks quiver, tighten with indignation, but it was no good. She had to do it. Her cheeks were burning and her head was buzzing with fear . . . and excitement. As her fingertip had touched the wax hardened on her sister's arsehole she was no longer able to deny it to herself. She was going to enjoy this. She lifted her fingertip and shuffled on her knees, moving round to kneel directly behind her sister's arse, feeling the rim of her own arsehole tug at the shield of wax sealing the pink, puckered disc of skin in place.

She swallowed again, feeling her left tit tremble with the force with which her heart was beating beneath it, and put her fingertip back on Beth's arsehole. This was it. The pulse in her throat was almost painful. She swallowed, trying to dislodge the pulse, and began to scrape minutely at one edge of the hardened wax on her sister's arsehole, feeling the delicate skin tense and move beneath her fingernail. Bärengelt's voices began rumbling at her again.

'*Langsam. Langsam.* Slowly. Slowly.'

254

Even through the bass distortion his excitement was obvious. He too had tensed, waiting for Beth's first moan of pain as her swiff was slowly pulled out by the roots. The wax had lifted a little and Anna pushed her fingernail further beneath it, took hold of it, paused. *Sorry, darling*, she mouthed silently, and began to pull. The first piece of wax came away in a broad flake with odd, almost inaudible little *pop*s and *twing*s that Anna took a second to realise were the sound of Beth's arsehairs coming up by the roots or breaking in two. Beth hissed with pain, swore to herself.

'Good,' Bärengelt's voices rumbled. 'Good. Savour it, Betchen. Savour the pain. I have never experienced it myself but I am told it is exquisite. Searing. Quite unlike any other form of pain that can be inflicted. Slowly, Annalein. Slowly.'

The first flake of wax came away completely. Anna rubbed it between her index finger and thumb and could feel the hairs trapped in it. She dropped the flake and put her fingertip back into Beth's arsehole.

'As slowly as you can, Annalein. Think of the pain you are inflicting and respect it. Think of all those delicate hairs being pulled slowly from one of the most sensitive spots of the female body.'

Another piece of wax lifted and Anna put her fingernail beneath it and slowly began to pull it away. Beth groaned. Her swiff was tougher here, or thicker. Taking longer to come up by the roots or to snap.

'Yet the most delightful thing of all is that this is a pain that can be endlessly renewed. Are you listening, Betchen? Your swiff will grow again. And be plucked. And grow again. So savour that thought, Betchen, as your little sister continues.'

Beth hissed, groaned. Anna stopped for a moment, shocked by the feeling of liquid beneath her fingertip. Had Beth started to bleed? No. No, it was sweat. Rising through the pores of her buttock cheeks, trickling down their curves, finding the cleft of her arse, dreckling to gather in the arsehole.

'Carry on, Annalein. She's sweating, isn't she? I told you the pain was exquisite. Beth doesn't need telling. She knows how exquisite it is. How powerful. But she must remember that she's going through all this for nothing, because it will happen again when she's ready. Remember that, Betchen. A week, two weeks – what is the term? – a fortnight, and your arsehole will be ringed by swiff again. I will be interested to see if it grows back more luxuriantly.'

The second flake of wax came away. Anna dropped it to the floor and put her fingertip back into Beth's arsehole. She rubbed at it: about a quarter of the wax was gone, leaving the rim hairless, the skin smoother to the touch, but microscopically trembling as Anna touched it. She stopped, her breath frozen in her nostrils, then breathed slowly out, held her breath for a moment, then breathed slowly in. Oh, God. God. She began to scrape at the remaining wax, trying to lift another edge to begin pulling another flake away. A tremor ran through Beth's body and Anna stopped. Beth was speaking. Pleading.

'Master. Please stop this. It hurts too much. Please.'

Bärengelt started to laugh.

'It is utterly harmless, Betchen. It not only does no lasting harm, it does no harm at all.'

'It hurts, master.'

'It hurts. Yes, it hurts. It hurts more than anything else I can safely inflict upon you. Almost. As you may discover. Or, should I say, *will* discover?'

'Master! Please!'

Anna had kept her fingertip in place, motionless atop Beth's trembling arsehole, but pulled it away now. Beth's voice had been cracked with hysteria. But Bärengelt would only laugh again. How he must be enjoying this! Proud, self-sufficient Beth pleading to keep the hair on her arsehole.

'No, Betchen. Do not plead with me. I am quite merciless and my cock only rises higher at pleas for mercy. Anna will continue until you have been completely de-swiffed. Till your arsehole is perfectly pink and shiny and bald. Perfectly swiffless.'

'Master, it hurts so much. Please stop. I will do anything else you want. Let me do it to Anna. She is much softer than me. She will scream and groan and plead for mercy much more entertainingly than I ever could, master. It is not see –'

She broke off. Bärengelt laughed.

'Not what? What were you going to say? Were you going to say that it is not *seemly*? That Anna be the inflictrix and you be the patient? Then good: you have realised it. That is precisely why I arranged things like this. That you should suffer and she should inflict suffering. What could be better for me, worse for you, than this extreme of suffering, hurting both your flesh and your mind? Your arsehole and your pride?'

'Master. Please. It is too much suffering. Too much.'

'You are protesting too much, Betchen. Far too much. The possible cause is so obvious that I almost disregard it. Surely little Anna would have informed me? But let me see.'

Anna, kneeling behind Beth's arse, sensed Bärengelt stoop towards her – towards Beth's arse. Or, rather, her cunt, for she could hear Bärengelt's sniff rumble on the speakers. Anna began to shake.

'Yes. Yes, I was right. The obvious possible cause was the actual cause. I was misled by my trust in Anna. I trusted that she would inform me of your ... reaction, shall we say? But how would you put it, Anna? How would you *have* put it, if my trust in you had not been misplaced?'

'Sh – she's enjoying it, master.'

'Enjoying what, little Anna?'

'The pain, master. The pain of being plucked.'

'Deswiffed. Deswiffed. She is enjoying the pain of being deswiffed. But how can you tell?'

'I can smell it, master.'

'Smell what, child?'

'Her cunt, master.'

'Yes? Her cunt? Is that all you can say? What can you smell about "her cunt", as you put it?'

'Her cunt is ... It's oozing, master.'

257

'Oozing? Oozing what?'

'Juice, master. Cunt-juice. Yelm, master.'

'Ah, *now* it's a little clearer. Her cunt is oozing yelm because she enjoys the pain of being deswiffed. But just the pain? What do you think? Just the pain? Or the pain and . . . something else?'

'Master, I th – I think it isn't just the pain. It's something else.'

'What? What else?'

'The humiliation, master. She's angry that it is me doing this to her. In the past I've been the w – she has always done this to me, master.'

'And now the tables are turned?'

'Yes, master. The tables are turned.'

'And the arses?'

'And the arses, master.'

'Good. Good. Then carry on, little Anna. Carry on inflicting pain on your sister. Carry on humiliating her. Angering her. And pleasuring her. The ones shall feed upon the other, for I think the pleasure is more painful to her than the pain. Don't you agree?'

'I – yes, master.'

'Good. Then carry on.'

Despite herself, Anna was unable to prevent herself sighing with relief. Bärengelt was not going to punish her for not telling him. She reached towards Beth's arse again, lifted her index finger to explore for her arsehole, found it, began t –

Bärengelt's voices froze her, seeming to scoop out her insides. She swallowed, feeling the pulse throb painfully in her throat again.

'But, Anna.'

'Yes, master?'

'Remember that when it is over Beth will be doing the same to you.'

Blood roared in her ears and she had to bite her lip to keep from fainting. Her hand fell away from Beth's arse, muscles turned strengthless with shock, brushing the satin skin of one buttock-cheek, but in the instant before it fell she had felt Beth's arsehole tighten beneath her fingertip. Tighten with emotion. Strong emotion. The strong emotion of delight. Beth would be far crueller than she. Far slower. Far more lingering. And would Bärengelt object if she took the opportunity to improvise on the deswiffing of her little sister's arsehole? Anna feared he wouldn't. No, was *certain* he wouldn't. Beth would pinch and squeeze the sensitive flesh rimming the rim of her arsehole. She would take the rim itself between her fingernails and pull at it. Play her arsehole like an instrument. Christ. Oh, Christ.

'Anna, is there something wrong?'

'No, master. Nothing.'

'Then carry on. Beth would rather you got it over with, I'm sure, if she were not waiting to do it herself. Don't you agree?'

'Yes, master.'

She moved her hand towards Beth's arse again, then stopped, clenching her fingers to try and stop her hand shaking. She took a deep breath, released it, unclenched her fingers. Her hand was still shaking, but not so badly. Beth would notice, and Anna knew that she would smile cruelly in the darkness, knowing what it meant. Knowing how scared Anna was of her own forthcoming punishment.

She put her fingertip back into Beth's arse. The hot disc tensed as she touched it, but with a different kind of emotion now. Not anger. Beth would indeed savour the sensations of deswiffing now. Note every refinement of the pain Anna involuntarily inflicted upon her, in order that, when her turn came to inflict it on Anna, she could refine it still further. Paint the lily. Gild refinèd gold. Oh, Christ. Christ.

'Anna. I will not tell you again. Carry on. Strip that arsehole clean. I want it completely bald.'

She lessened the shaking in her hand by sheer force of will, reached out for Beth's arse, touched it, ran her fingers over its curves to orientate herself, lifted clear all her fingers but one, and ran it down, across, into the sculpted little pit of Beth's arsehole. She began to scrape at the wax again, feeling her head clear and the hollowness in her guts slowly fill and disappear. *It's not fair*, she told herself. *I don't want to hurt Beth, but Beth is still going to punish me for it. So . . . I might as well want to hurt Beth. I might as well try to hurt Beth. Try as hard as I can.*

Her heart was slowing now too, and her fear had lessened. Definitely lessened. Because she had rebelled. Yes, because she had rebelled. She hadn't asked Bärengelt to force her into this. She had tried to shield Beth from the humiliation of Bärengelt's discovery of her arousal. What good had it done her? None. None at bloody all. None at fucking all. So while she had the chance to act for herself, she was going to act. She was going to hurt Beth as much as she could. And enjoy it. Enjoy it as much as she could.

She realised that her free hand was lying in her lap, palm up, the way it had lain all the time she had been working on Beth. Bärengelt was standing behind her, watching avidly in infra-red (she didn't doubt) as her fingertip worked at Beth's arsehole. He couldn't see her free hand at all. Couldn't see what it was doing. Which had been nothing. Nothing at fucking all. And he couldn't see what it *would* be doing. Which would be a lot.

The edge of wax she was working on came up and she leaned forwards a little as though to concentrate, disguising the movement she made as she turned her free hand over in her lap. It was palm down now. She lowered the middle finger between her thighs. It couldn't quite reach. In another couple of moments she would shuffle from knee to knee as though to ease a twinge of cramp. She had done it before, innocently. This time it would be to disguise the movement she made as she eased her free hand lower, allowing the middle finger to reach what she wanted it to reach. Her clitoris. Her clitoris, sitting atop a cunt that was already moistening, opening in a long, vertical smile of anticipated pleasure.

She shuffled and the tip of her finger reached her clitoris. Just barely. Just brushing it. But less was more. Like the tip of a peacock's feather tickle . . . tickling at a tumescent nipple. Like drops of rose-flavoured semen drip . . . dripping from the slatch of an erect penis on to a tongue parched by lemon. Like a silver entomologist's needle pricking at the soft skin of a young woman's inner thighs. The minuteness of the sensation heightened it. She began to rub delicately at herself, rub at her clitoris, feeling her cunt widen and smile wetly, leaking threads of cunt-juice down the backs of her thighs, over her buttocks.

She paused ... rubbed ... paused ... rubbed ... still pulling at the flake of wax in her sister's arsehole. Pulling very, very slowly, pausing irregularly, out of time with the pauses of her masturbation, wanting Beth to be hurt exceedingly. Beth hissed and Anna sensed the arsehole in front of her tremble, then the iris open and give vent to a long sigh of gas, still heavy with the musk and oranges of Bärengelt's enema, heated by Beth's bowels so that Anna felt her face almost scorched by it and wondered whether the wax would be softened, come away too easily, leaving Beth's coppery swiff still rooted on the rim of her arsehole.

'Did she fart again, Anna?'

'Yes, master.'

'Why?'

'I think she is close to coming, master.'

'She is?'

'Yes, master. Listen.'

'To what?'

'Her juice, master. It is dripping to the floor. She is very close to coming.'

She was still rubbing at her clitoris ... pausing ... rubbing ... She wondered if Bärengelt would order her to lick Beth's cunt. The tang of Beth's cunt-juice was very strong now and she knew Beth's inner thighs would be wet, streaming with the stuff, and that a pool of it would be gathering on the floor beneath her oozing cunt. Would Bärengelt tell her to lick it up? Run her tongue along the gaping slit of Beth's cunt, down her thighs, over the pool on the floor, lapping, sucking, swallowing?

'And what about you, Anna?'

'Me, master?'

'How close to coming are you?'

'I – master? I don't understand.'

261

'Anna. Oh, Anna. I despair. How many times do I have to demonstrate to the three of you that you cannot trick or outsmart me? Stop deswiffing her.'

Anna lifted her hand away from Beth's arse. Her heart was pounding again and fear was beginning to buzz again in her ears.

'Good. Now, Anna, you have not answered my question. How close to coming are *you*? Because you have been working away quietly at yourself, haven't you? Thinking I would not notice. Thinking that the pleasure you took in the pain you inflicted on your sister would not be entirely . . . spiritual, shall we say? I hope you are listening carefully to this, Beth. Your little sister has grown horns. Or horn-buds, at least, but she hopes for them to grow into true horns very shortly. She has turned sadist, Beth.

'Well, Anna? Nothing to say for yourself?'

'No, master.'

'I despair. Truly, I despair. Beth!'

'Yes, master?'

Bitch, Anna thought, feeling her fear dissolve in anger. *Fucking bitch. Answering him as though butter wouldn't melt in your fucking mouth. You know exactly what he's going to say next.*

'Beth, your little sister has finished. You can pick the remaining wax out of your arsehole at your leisure, but now please prepare to deswiff Anna. And Anna?'

'Yes, master?'

Yes, cunt? she thought to herself. *You were always going to do this. Always going to find an excuse to have Beth deswiff me. That's why you hulfed my arse, too. You cunt.*

'Prepare yourself for Beth. She is going to deswiff you.'

'Yes, master.'

She turned away from Beth's arse and got down on all fours. Her arsehole was already beginning to tighten.

'Begin when ready, Beth.'

'Yes, master.'

Anna flinched as Beth's hand touched her arse, stroked at her skin. The fingers were hot, sweat – no, not sweaty. Slimy. With cunt-juice. Beth had found a chance to have a

262

quick frot at herself. The bitch! Had she been doing it while she, Anna, had been deswiffing her? She couldn't have been! Couldn't! Could she? Wouldn't Bärengelt ha . . . She bit her lip, suddenly knowing the truth. Bärengelt had known. Bärengelt had always known.

She flinched again. Beth's fingers had reached her arsehole. She closed her eyes and waited. The pain was going to be bad, but she could master it. She *would* master it. What had Beth said, trying to persuade Bärengelt to let them swap roles? *She will scream and groan and plead for mercy much more entertainingly than I ever could, master.* Well, she wouldn't. She wouldn't scream. Or groan. Or squ –

She squealed, and heard Beth, delighted with the success of her first gambit, chuckle throatily to herself. To herself, but quite loud enough for Bärengelt to hear. Quite loud enough for Bärengelt to hear and make her stop, order her to adopt the position again for Anna to finish deswiffing her. But he wouldn't. Beth was going to be allowed to do exactly what she wanted. Wring every last drop of pain out of every last nerve-fibril of Anna's cringing arsehole. Christ, oh, Christ.

Tears began to trickle freely down Anna's face as, a little less freely but almost as copiously, yelm began to trickle from the lips of her treacherous cunt. Beth would smell it soon and Anna knew she would tell Bärengelt. Between her chuckles. Christ, oh, Christ. She flinched again as Beth's fingers began to move slowly in her arsehole again, ignoring the wax shield as yet. Deswiffing could wait. There would be plenty of time for that in the hour or more of anal torture that stretched ahead of the pair of sisters, one kneeling at the arse of the crouching other.

Fifteen

Two hours had passed and Anna was still crying with anger and frustration. She sat at the far side of the bath from Beth and Gwen, who were making love, locked mouth to mouth, probing and stroking each other's bodies, their moving hands raising occasional little flurries of water. Anna watched them bitterly through a sheen of tears, feeling her cunt respond as treacherously as ever but nursing a curdling in her stomach as a physical sigil of her rage and desire for revenge. Revenge on them and on Bärengelt. Two bitches and a cunt. She licked at the tears that traced the curve of her lips and suddenly heard the splash of another brief flurry of water as the crack of a whip. Upon the white arses of her sisters. Upon the arse of Bärengelt.

She blinked and suddenly found herself able to smile, her eyes widening on the couple that strained together on the opposite side of the bath. Her smile grew wider, crueller. How she would love to beat them. Beat all three of them. Conduct a lingering session of tit torture on Beth. How proud Beth had always been of her tits. How delicately she had always self-excited them, slowly teasing the nipples, rolling them between gentle fingertips. So how exciting it would be to treat them roughly. Squeeze them. Pinch them. Scrape the nipples with her fingernails. Make Beth squeak with pain – and despairing, self-loathing pleasure (Anna's heart was beating faster and she was unaware that her legs had spread beneath the water until she found her hand slipping between them to rub and pull at the lips of her cunt).

She would make Gwen participate, then conduct a lingering session of torture on her too. A lingering session of pussy punishment. Drip molten wax on the mound of her pussy and slowly pull the congealed droplets of wax off, bringing a dozen or more pussy-hairs with them at a time. How proud Gwen had always been of her pubic hair: the glossiness of it, the thickness of it, the *colour* of it. Sable-cunted, Bärengelt had called her. How delightful it would be to strip her of her glossy fur. Denude her. *Depilate* her. That was the word. How delightful it would be to depilate her. Not by shaving, but by plucking. By dripping molten wax on to the furry mound of her cunt, then slowly – very slowly – pulling the congealed droplets off. Molten red wax. How Gwen would swear and threaten, biting her lip to hold back cries of pain and humiliation.

Perhaps she would go on to do the same with Gwen's armpits, those smooth white hollows silked with more delicate hairs, even more exquisitely sensitive to the pain of slow plucking. But no, she would leave that to another day, for Bärengelt would be waiting. She would have many things to do with him, but first she would torture his balls. He would be strapped to a steel grille, legs wide apart, cock strapped up against his belly, invisible beneath a tight black leather cumberband, balls dangling exposed and completely at her mercy. First she would be oh-so-gentle with them. Rub them. Tickle them. Hold them in the palm of her hand and slowly, slowly, gently, gently squeeze them and release them. Hold a finger to one side of them and swing them from side to side.

Then begin to mock them. Tell him how ludicrous they were. How laughable. Tell him how coarse and tasteless it was to wear one's sex-glands outside one's body. Typically ostentatious. Typically boastful. Typically male. Not that *he* had anything to boast about with these two peanuts in that ridiculous wrinkled sac. Balls? Ball-bearings, more like. And her hands would still be moving on them, rubbing them, tickling them. But more harshly now. More cruelly. Beginning to yank on them. Squeezing them harder, releasing them less quickly. Anching them. Interspersing this cruelty with frecks and nips at his scrotum. She would tell him how vulnerable his balls were. How they were completely at her mercy. How she could do anything she liked with them. Anything at all.

She came, pushing her fingers deep inside her cunt as it spasmed around them, lifting her other hand to her stiff nipples, teasing them, tweaking them, using them to ride the wave of her orgasm as it flooded across her and died, hissing on the sands. Beth and Gwen unsealed faces, gasping, and Anna submerged, not wanting either of them to see her flushed, shining face. She rose with her face wiped carefully clean of expression and discovered Beth and Gwen sealed mouth-to-mouth again, fucking as merrily as ever. Bitches. Revenge would be so sweet. And she would have it. And be ready to have it. Be merciless when the time came. When Beth and Gwen and Bärengelt were lying self-bound before her, chuckling silently to themselves as they thought they were fooling her once again. Manipulating her once again. As they had during the whole of her stay.

Her flush deepened as, for the fifth or sixth time, she reviewed her memories of what had followed Bärengelt's shouted demand for Gwen to 'ANSWER ME, YOU SABLE-CUNTED BITCH!'. Her memories of the hulfing and deswiffing. Her on Beth. Beth on her. And then, finally, Gwen's buggery. The swish and crack of the cane as Bärengelt forced Gwen to open her arsehole to him. Gwen's whimpers and moans as he slid beyond her arsehole, occupied her bowels, and slowly began to buttfuck her. His order to Beth that she come and lick his balls while he rose and fell against Gwen's cane-branded buttocks.

While she, Anna, crept away to the video-helmet she had discarded after getting off the chair. For she had seen something as she tried to pull it off. Something odd. And exciting. Very exciting. For it seemed to offer her a prospect of revenge. On Beth. On Gwen. Most of all, on Bärengelt. She took two or three minutes to find the helmet again, crawling to and fro on the cold marble, the sounds of Gwen being slowly and cruelly buggered a constant background to her search. Her cunt was wide and hotly oozing when her fingers brushed against the helmet and she knelt to put it on again.

The screen was still on, showing the room in infra-red: Gwen was glowing gold and orange beneath the purple and violet bulk of Bärengelt, his body-heat shielded by his leather bodysuit, with Beth glimmering red between his legs, her saliva cooling the glowing fruits of Bärengelt's balls almost to the purple of his pumping, leather-shielded buttocks.

But in the bottom left-hand corner of the screen there was also a menu. Like the menu on a computer screen. It read:

SCHLOSS.
ANNA.
BETH.
GWEN.

The words were in blue but as she read each it lit yellow, then faded back to blue as she read the next. Where had the menu come from? She didn't know for certain, but she thought that something had gone wrong with the helmet and that her helmet was receiving the image that only Bärengelt's should have received. With a menu. Allowing him to reach more screens, more images. More information. But how did she 'click' an option?

She looked at SCHLOSS. It lit yellow. What now? But suddenly the infra-red view of the room dissolved, replaced by a three-dimensional plan of the Schloss. What had she done? The menu in the bottom left-hand corner was the same, only SCHLOSS was red now. She looked at ANNA. It lit yellow. Suddenly the screen dissolved again – how? – and she was looking at text and pictures. Text in German. Pictures of her. Little videos of her being beaten and fucked. As she looked at each the border glowed yellow. Suddenly one of the videos expanded to fill the screen, with a back arrow in blue in the left-hand corner.

She realised how the navigation worked now. You looked at a word and blinked. Like clicking with a mouse. She looked at the back arrow. It lit yellow. She blinked. The video shrank and she was back on the page of text and pictures. The ANNA page. She couldn't understand the text but when she looked at the menu on the left-hand corner it read:

ZURÜCK ZUM HAUPTMENU.
ENGLISCH.

She wasn't quite sure what ZURÜCK ZUM HAUPT-MENU meant, but ENGLISCH definitely meant ENG-LISH. It glowed yellow as she looked at it. She blinked. The German on the screen was replaced by English. Simple as that.

Sixteen

'Simple as that?' Bärengelt's voices rumbled.

  'Yes, master.'

  'But didn't you think it was too simple?'

  'I do now, master.'

  'Too late, Annalein. Too late.'

  'Yes, master.'

The speakers began to rumble again, but without words. He was laughing. Laughing at her. At her foolishness. Words came into the laughter.

  'OK, that is enough. On your feet.'

She rose from the marble, each knee carrying a thin skin of cold, and the small room was as suddenly full of light as it had been full of the echoes of Bärengelt's voices. It was white marble, everywhere: floor, walls, ceiling. There was a couch in one corner, next to what looked like a painting-stand. Next to what *was* a painting-stand, for there was a canvas on it. Waiting. But for what? Bärengelt knew. He was standing ahead of her, very black against the white marble, light gleaming off the horns of his helmet.

  'Turn round.'

She turned. On the wall behind her there was a row of hooks with clothing hanging from them. Underwear, mostly. A brassière, stockings, a cut-away bodice. And a beret. Next to them was a shelf of books, some very old, some very modern.

  'Put the clothes on,' Bärengelt's voices rumbled.

  'Master?'

'Put them on.'

'But, master . . . clothing?'

'It is time for you to wear some. But not to wear some. Regard it as your birthday suit. Because that is what it is. The suit you were born in.'

'Master, I don't understand.'

'Feel them. What are they made of?'

She reached out and touched them. The material was white, smooth-looking, not quite like anything she had ever seen before, but as her fingers touched it she drew in her breath with surprise.

'It's leather, master.'

'Yes. Leather.'

'I'm a vegetarian, master.'

'I know. It is a leather suitable for vegetarians.'

'Did the animal die naturally, master?'

'No. The animal has not died at all.'

'That is cruel, master! I can't w –'

'Shut up. You can wear them and you will wear them. The animal has not died and the animal has not been hurt. Much.'

'What animal was it, master?'

'A young bitch.'

'Dog-leather, master?'

'No. The leather of a featherless biped. A primate.'

'But you said it was a bitch, master. That means it's dog-leather.'

'A primate can be a bitch, Annalein.'

'Which primate, master?'

'A hominid. *Homo sapiens var insipiens.* A human being, Anna.'

'Master! I hope you are joking. There is too much l –'

'No, Anna, I am not joking. This is human leather. Feel it again. Look closely at it. You know I am telling the truth.'

She reached out again, slowly this time, and touched the leather, her stomach crawling with nausea. But a dark fascination kept her fingers to their task. Feeling. Stroking. Human leather.

272

She choked a little, withdrew her hand, and turned back to Bärengelt.

'Master . . . you said the animal this had come from had not died and had not been hurt.'

'Not hurt much. Only a little. And only very briefly. Don't you remember?'

'Me, master? I don't understand.'

'Look at the books. Find a paperback called *Disciplined Skin*.'

She walked to the shelf of books next to the hanging garments and ran her eye along them. *De Vita Nostra*, Marcus Antoninus Varius. Τῶν τῆς Σαπφοῦς Μελῶν Βιβλιον. *Les Journées à Florbelle*, D.-A.-F. de Sade. *The Book of the Wars of the Lord. Disciplined Skin.*

'Here it is, master.'

'Take it off the shelf. Open it.'

She took it off the shelf and opened it. She read:

Anna relaxed her sphincter and what seemed like a gale of wind poured through it, slightly moist, still slightly chilled, but warming even as the flow continued. The scent of it filled her nostrils, dizzying her truly this time. Musk and roses.

She frowned, flicked back through the book, stopped, read again:

When she reached the edge of the bed she stared down at the carpet. A gold fleur-de-lys sat directly below her. The pile of the carpet was very thick. She sat on the edge of the bed and put her bare feet down on to the carpet. Into the carpet. Soft and warm.

She stopped reading and turned around.

'Master, what is this?'

'*Disciplined Skin*. The story of your stay in the Schloss. Look at the first page.'

She turned to the front of the book, found the first page, and read:

Sunlight. A thin golden bar of it had found its way somehow through the heavy curtains and lay in a small, elliptical pool on the carpet. Anna stared at it, wondering whether Madame Oursor had deliberately arranged for this to happen, so that she could observe what they did.

'See? It is the story of your stay in the Schloss, and of how you got here. It opens with the interview you had with Madame Oursor. Exactly what she said to you, and exactly what you – the three of you – said to her. Word for word. It then describes exactly what has happened to you since you came to the Schloss. If you can remember it, it is in the book. Some things you can't remember now are also in the book. When you read about them, you will remember them. Turn to page 36. Read the first long paragraph.'

She leafed through the book, looking for page 36. She found it, found the first long paragraph, and read:

She walked where he was pointing, not seeing the black apparatus clearly until she was almost upon it: a piece of surreal furniture with no easily apparent purpose, stooped over by the huge sculpture of a flower in black iron, its petals tightly closed. She turned back towards him as he followed her from the table, light gleaming off the tips of his horns.

'Do you remember that?'

She looked up.

'Yes, master.'

'Read the last paragraph.'

She looked back at the book, found the last paragraph, read it:

He tapped left and right with a long black cane that she had not noticed him pick up. She pushed her feet into the stirrups, wincing as her thighs opened again, then biting her lip as he tightened a strap savagely on her left ankle, then on her right. Something stung momentarily at her left buttock, as though he had flicked at her with the cane, catching her just with its tip.

274

'Do you remember that? How does it go? "Something stung momentarily at her left buttock." '

She frowned, trying to remember. Yes, now she could. She could remember a momentary pain, out of mind almost as soon as it had happened, in the fear of what Bärengelt had been about to do to her on the whipping-horse.

'Yes, master. I remember it now.'

'You thought it was the cane, didn't you? "As though he had flicked at her with the cane, catching her just with its tip." '

'Yes. That's what I thought. But I don't understand this. How is it all in this book?'

'It has all been choreographed, Anna. Everything. Everything you did, everything you said, everything you thought, everything you felt. All of it. Every moment since you saw that pool of sunlight in Madame Oursor's office. It is all in the book. Including that momentary sting on your left buttock, as you lay on the whipping-horse waiting for me to cane you. It was not the cane. It was me taking a sliver of your buttock-skin with a very sharp scalpel. I placed it immediately in a saline solution and later, after I had finished the first session with you on the whipping-horse, I prepared it for cloning. That is where the leather comes from. It is the cloned skin of your buttocks, grown in tanks in a room beneath the Schloss. That is why the leather is suitable for vegetarians: it involved the death of no animal and only a brief pain. It is your buttock-skin. Your birthday suit, as I said. So put it on. Now.'

She pushed the book back into place on the shelf and walked back to the hooks and the hanging leather. Bra. Stockings. Basque. Beret. Her birthday suit. She lifted one of the stockings down and fingered it. Oddly heavy, but oddly light too, for leather. Because it was human leather. Buttock leather. *Her* leather. Leather from her and leather belonging to her.

She felt a slow tickling begin between the lips of her cunt as she opened the top of the stocking and lifted her foot, tightening the toes, to slip into it. This was arousing her.

To put on leather. Human leather. It slid smoothly over her skin – it *was* her skin. How strange. And warm. Fitting her like, well, like a second skin. She stifled a giggle and tugged at the top of the stocking, adjusting it around the swell of her upper thigh, straightening the seam.

The lips of her cunt were open now and she was beginning to ooze. Yelm would run down her inner thighs, over her skin, and over her skin. Over her stockings. Her second skin. She lifted the other stocking down, opened the top, slipped her foot into it, drew the leather up her leg, more slowly this time, wanting to savour the feeling of the warm, smooth leather sliding over her skin. Skin over skin. Her skin over her skin. She could smell her arousal now. Thick and musky. Bärengelt would be able to smell it too. Her fingers froze on the leather of the stocking as a thought struck her. Was all this in the book, back on the shelf? Was what she was thinking already written down? What she had done? What her cunt was doing? Opening, oozing, olfing?

She shook her head, clearing the thought, and drew the stocking fully up her leg, tugging the seam around the swell of her upper thigh, straightening it, lining it up with the seam of the first stocking. She was wearing two stockings now. Two stockings of human leather. She looked down at them, wanting to slip a finger between the lips of her cunt and feel the swelling heat and moisture there. The thickening yelm.

The stockings were white against the white of her skin. White leather. Why did men like to see stockings against female skin like this? Something in her was aroused by it now too, adding to the tickle between the lips of her cunt. But it was more than a tickle now. A trickle. A thrickle.

'It is the three-dimensionality of it,' Bärengelt's voices rumbled from behind her. 'Stocking-tops emphasise the swell of the thigh. The thickness of it. The firmness of it. The ellipticality of it.'

The words had meshed so naturally with her thoughts that they didn't surprise her. Yes, that seemed right. Stocking-tops emphasised the swell of the thigh. The thickness of it. The firmness of it. The ellipticality – she reached down and adjusted a seam fractionally – of it.

'Perhaps there is an arithmo-erotic equation bubbling away somewhere in the swamp of the male mind. For the perfect thigh. $x^2/a^2 + y^2/b^2 = 1$. And the stocking-top allows one to recognise it more easily. Do you agree?'

'Yes, master.'

She let go of the stocking-seam and turned back to the hooks, reaching for the basque.

'No. Stop for a moment. Turn your back fully to me and bend over, legs apart. I want to see your cunt between your legs, framed by your stocking-tops. It is a classic pornographic image. Almost an icon. Or should I say it in French? *Icône*. Yes, nearly. *Une image iconique.*'

She turned her back fully to him and bent over, seeing between her thighs his legs and the heavy bulge of his prick straining against the black leather of his bodysuit. Was that human leather, too? Was it *his* leather? Dyed black? She tried to recall the feel of it. Was it smooth enough? Smooth enough to be human but too rough to be female? She couldn't decide.

'Feet a little further apart. A little more. Good. And a little more. My prick will tell me the perfect distance. Perhaps it's the golden ratio.'

She didn't understand what he was talking about but didn't care. The bass of his voices was enough, trembling in the soles of her feet. Her head was full of blood now and her cunt was fully open, oozing freely, olfing strongly. The thought of him watching it through the vee of her upper thighs filled her with a thick exhibitionist pleasure, heightening the dizziness of the blood in her head. Her nipples were hardening and a tremor ran through her at the thought of fitting the bra over them. She hoped it was tight. A tight leather bra. Rubbing against her nipples. Constraining her breasts. Disciplining them.

'Stop. Feet a little closer together again. Good. A little more. Stop. That's it. My prick salutes you. Yes. An icon. *Icône*. But that's enough. Continue. Put the rest of the leather on.'

She straightened, feeling the blood drain from her head, leaving her dizzy again. A hand dropped between her legs and she slipped a finger between the lips of her cunt, slowly rubbing the tip through the thick yelm as she reached again for the basque.

'Leave your cunt alone, Anna. I need it untouched for later. I said, leave it alone.'

She pulled the finger reluctantly out, feeling a thread of yelm stretch between the tip of her finger and her cunt, stretching, narrowing, stretching, snapping. She wanted to lick it. Taste herself. But he would punish her. She lifted the basque down with both hands, pressing the smeared fingertip hard into it. Again it was an odd weight. Heavy. But light. Light for leather. The tips of the drawstrings – there were dozens of them, it seemed – trembled against her skin like dry little tongues. She ran a fingertip along them.

'Put it on. Quickly.'

'Yes, master. But please, I need help. To tighten it.'

'No. You do everything yourself. I only watch. Put it on. Now.'

She bit her lip and fitted the basque around herself, stiffening as the warm, smooth leather brushed against the sensitive skin of her flanks and belly, the lower swell of her breasts. She wouldn't be able to tighten it. She couldn't even see to tighten it. And he would punish her. The cane would come out again and he would thrash her, planting red strokes across the fully ripened bruise he had planted on her arse all those days before. Make her bend over again, cunt gaping between the vee of her upper thighs, and thrash her. Swish, and crack. Again and again.

Both hands behind her back, one holding the basque in place around her as the other struggled to tighten the first drawstring, she felt her cunt respond to the thought of the thrashing. The pain of the cane slashing against her defenceless buttocks. The drawstring slipped from her fingers and she gasped with frustration. Her shoulders were starting to ache with strain and she could smell herself starting to sweat. She couldn't do it.

'Try harder, Anna. It is not impossible, merely almost impossible. It will hurt you to do it, but pain is good for you. It will make you sweat. And I want you to sweat.'

She gasped again. She had nearly done it that time, nearly threaded the first drawstring, nearly been able to tug at it, tighten it.

'Try again. Quickly. Get it done. I'm growing impatient.'

The ache in her shoulders was solid now and her armpits were moist with sweat. It smelt hot, fresh, musky, rising to her nostrils through the aroma of her cunt. The drawstring slipped into place and she sighed with relief as she tugged at it, tightening it, drawing the basque hard against the lower swell of her breasts. But there was another drawstring to tighten. And another. Quickly. While he watched. And her fingers were slippery with sweat now, the ache in her shoulders getting worse, answered by a deepening pleasure in her cunt. He was kind to her in being cruel. Making her hurt herself for her own pleasure.

Another drawstring slipped into place and tightened smoothly. She had to knot them too. Blind. With her hands behind her back. Fingers slippery with sweat. Shoulders screaming. Sweat beginning to trickle from her armpits down her flanks, over her skin, and over her skin. A third drawstring slipped into place and tightened, knotted, drew more of the basque against her skin. The pain in her shoulders had hardened and deepened, numbing the flesh around the joints, but it was getting a little easier now. To slip the drawstrings into place, tighten them, tie them.

'Tighter, you lazy bitch. Pull them tighter. Untie them and pull them tighter.'

Her mouth came open silently. No. It was too difficult. Numbness was starting to flow down her upper arms from her shoulders. She had been reaching blind behind her back for minutes now. He had waited till now to make the task harder. Bastard. But she loved him for it. She wanted him to impose more pain on her, so that the pleasure in her cunt would grow, the yelm flowing down her inner thighs thicken. She gasped, her knees beginning to buckle beneath her as she struggled to untie the first drawstring and pull it tighter. The knot was too small. She had pulled it too hard. She couldn't do it.

She vaguely heard his boots thud towards her. She was on her knees now, the numbness in her arms beyond her elbows now, her fingers almost useless, struggling vainly at the knots she had tied.

'Useless girl. Take your arms away and stand up.'

Breath hissed from her mouth and she let go of the drawstrings, sensation returning to her numbed arms as she brought them from behind her back and stood up. Bärengelt's gloved fingers were working at the drawstrings, pressing and brushing against the skin of her back. She could feel the leather of his gloves now. It was rough. Rough leather. Male leather. Or leather from a cane-toughened female arse. Like – she grunted as the first knot came loose and Bärengelt jerked roughly at the drawstring, sealing the leather of the basque hard against the hot skin of the lower swell of her breasts – the arse of Dalville's slave in *Les infortunes*. Poor bitch.

'Wrong,' Bärengelt's voices told her, rumbling from metres away as his gloved fingers worked against her skin. 'If it's arse-leather there was either a crime or Lamarckianism. Think about it, you silly bitch.'

She didn't understand again, didn't care as he tightened another drawstring viciously and she gasped, feeling it cut into her skin, sealing another section of the basque against her skin. He knotted it quickly and grabbed at another.

'Useless little bitch. Why do I have to do this for you?'

She gasped again.

'Master, you're hurting me.'

'Good. Do you like it?'

'Yes, master.'

'Then ask me for it.'

'Hurt me, master.'

'Delighted, little Anna. How is this?'

He wrenched at another drawstring.

'Good, master.'

'It hurts good?'

'Yes, master.'

'Right, then you can finish the rest. It will be easy enough now even for someone as useless as you.'

He shoved at her, sending her back down on to her knees, and his boots rapped away from her.

'And tight, remember. Tight.'

Shaking her head slowly, she reached behind her back again for the remaining drawstrings, feeling the pain flash back into her shoulders again. But it was easy this time, as Bärengelt had promised, though it hurt to pull the drawstrings tight and knot them. And it was a little hard to breathe now, the basque was gripping her so tightly. She hoped the bra would be just as tight. Or tighter.

She finished tying the last knot and got back to her feet, reaching up for the bra. She took it in her hands, running her fingers over the rim of the cups, then down into them. Smooth, warm, human leather. Crushed against her swollen tits and aching nipples. Rubbing against the delicate skin. But her fingers paused. There was something inside the cups. Right where her nipples would lie. Criss-crossing lines of something silky, half-smooth, half-soft-bristly. She looked more carefully at it. It was hair. Blonde hair. The leather of the bra was embroidered with hair.

'It's yours,' Bärengelt's voices rumbled.

Another tremor ran through her. The embroidery would lie right against her nipples. Silkily irritating them every time she moved. Human leather against her tits and human hair against her nipples. She fitted her tits into the cups, palming them straight, and put her arms through the straps, left and right, lifting them over her shoulders, left and right, reaching behind herself to pull the catch together and snap it into place. Her tits strained in the cups, the hair-embroidery pressed tight to her nipples. The catch was ready to snap into place but she held back for a moment longer, straining harder than she needed to, allowing her tits to tremble inside the bra-cups, her eyes closed as her nipples rubbed up and down against the lines of embroidery. Silkily irritated.

She allowed the catch to snap into place, opening her eyes at the sound, and her tits were imprisoned in the cups, held tight, firmed and dominated. Disciplined. Disciplined tits. She turned to Bärengelt, feeling the straps twist against her back, moving the cups of the bra slightly up and down, rubbing the embroidery against her nipples. A tendon tightened in her thighs and her knees trembled momentarily. Orgasm was stirring inside her like a giant cat stirring as it slept in its lair, its spittle running freely from its mouth as it dreamed of the hunt and hot blood, feline spittle leaking from the cave-mouth of her cunt, the musk of its pelt saturating the air.

'The beret,' Bärengelt's voices rumbled.

'Sorry, master. I forgot.'

She turned back to the hook and lifted the beret down, slipped it over her head, tugged it down, smoothed it with both hands. It was too tight, which was good. Her scalp was constrained too, clasped by the leather, starting to sweat.

She turned back to Bärengelt.

'Good. We are nearly ready. Come over here. Kneel in front of me.'

She walked across the floor to him, feeling the bra jerk against her. The straps were arranged to catch the movements of her body, to transmit them to the cups of the bra, to rub the embroidery against her nipples. She bent and knelt in front of him.

'Suck me.'

The zip of his trousers rasped and his cock came out, erect and ticking to his heart-beat, white against the black leather, the crystal eye of the fibre-optic camera staring unblinking into her face. She took the cock in one hand and moved it towards her mouth, closing her eyes as her lips closed over the head and she started to lick and suck. He slowly pushed it further into her mouth, the head like a hot fruit, waiting to split and spurt as her tongue moved against it.

'Take hold of my balls.'

She lifted her hands into the trousers of his bodysuit and took hold of his balls, grunting as his hands closed over her tits, grasping them, squeezing.

'Do to my balls what I do to your tits.'

He jiggled her tits, squeezed them, joggled them, loosened his grip, and she mirrored what he did, one of his balls in each hand, a hairy fruit, ready to split inside him and pump juice down the tubes that led to his urethra, down his urethra to the head of his cock, to spurt inside her warm, sucking, licking mouth.

'Stop.'

He let go of her tits.

'Stop sucking me.'

He was pulling his cock out of her mouth. She let go of his balls and opened her eyes. He was holding a triangular piece of dark wood – a palette – in front of his cock, holding the head down over the centre, his grunts rumbling on the speakers as he began to come and semen spurted from the head of his cock, splattering down on the palette, pooling in the centre of it. There were patches of colour at each apex of the triangle: blue, red, yellow. Powdered paint. He lifted his cock and she only had time to close her eyes as the final two spurts of semen shot at her, hitting her face, warm and heavy.

'Stand up. Lie over there. Head at the foot of it, with your arse in the air.'

He had a paintbrush in his hand now, gesturing with it at the couch near the wall. Near the canvas on a stand. He was going to do a painting of her. Using his own semen to mix the paints. A kind of water-colour. A come-colour. She walked to the couch and slipped on to it, lying out flat, her arse in the air. His boots came after her, rapping on the floor.

'Good. But swing your arse further up and flatter. Here, like this.'

A gloved hand closed over her buttocks, tugging and pushing them, positioning her the way he wanted her.

'OK, good. But open your legs. I need access to your cunt.'

She shuffled herself better into position and opened her legs.

'Good.'

She heard a soft sound and took a second or two to work out what it was. He was twirling the brush in the pool of semen on the palette, ready to put it into one of the patches of powdered paint, create the first colour.

'I am going to make a painting of your arse. The bruise is fully ripened now and I want to make a permanent record of it.'

She heard another soft sound. Brush on canvas this time. He was making the first strokes. What colour? Was he creating an outline of her arse first, ready to fill with colour and the broad stroke of the bruise? Or was he starting the line of the bruise first? The soft sound stopped and she heard the brush dab against the palette again, being reloaded with colour, being lifted back to the canvas. She tried to tell from the sound of the strokes what he was painting. Curves? A line?

Something touched her cunt. It was the paintbrush. She could feel the soft bristles lifting her cunt-lips apart, moving along them, slowly twisting. He was using her cunt to clean his brush, ready for the next load of paint.

'Talk to me. We are nearly at the end of the book. There are things to explain. So ask me your questions.'

The brush lifted from her cunt and she heard it dab against the palette again. What traces of colour had it left on her cunt?

'Master, I don't understand.'

'Ask me your questions. You have questions. Ask them.'

She was silent for a few seconds, hearing the brush slide over the canvas again. Then she licked her lips and said, 'Who are you, master?'

'I am your master. I am Abraham Bärengelt. Ask me another question.'

'When do we eat, master?'

'When I want you to eat. Another.'

'But why do we not remember eating, master?'

'Because I do not want you to remember. Another.'

She paused.

'Who wrote the book, master?'

'Which book? *Disciplined Skin*?'

'No, master. *222 Ways of Sodom*, master.'

He didn't answer for a few moments, filling the silence with the sound of the brush on the canvas, as though giving her time to savour the way her cunt tingled at the thought of the book.

'The author of *222 Ways of Sodom* must remain veiled for the time being.'

The brush returned to her cunt, lifting up a fold of her cunt-lips, sliding along it, being cleaned again.

'But when did I learn to read it, master? The alphabet, I mean. I've never seen it before and I don't even know what it is, but I can read it.'

'You learned to read it a long time ago. I have been preparing you all for your stay here for a long time.'

'How long, master?'

'If I said since you were born, would you believe me?'

'No, master. That's impossible.'

'Then I will not say it. Ask me another question.'

'Why don't I remember learning to read the writing in the book, master?'

'Some things that have happened to you, you don't remember, and some things that you remember never happened to you.'

'Do you mean hypnosis, master?'

'Yes. Hypnosis.'

'Why have you hypnotised us, master?'

'To teach you that you have no free will.'

'But I do, master. I know I do.'

'No, you think you do. In a little while you will see again how your thoughts are mistaken, but for now ask another question.'

She was silent, thinking.

'Master, what is underneath the patch of hair on the back of my head?'

'Alice.'

'I don't understand, master.'

'Alice. That is what is underneath the patch of hair on the back of your head.'

The brush returned to her cunt, was twirled and cleaned.

285

'OK, that is enough for the present. We are nearly out of time and you still have to prove to me that you possess free will.'

Something rustled. Cloth. He was covering the painting.

'Get off the couch. And prove that you have free will. Prove that the book does not foretell what you are about to do.'

She rolled over on the couch and put her feet to the floor. He had put a black cloth over the canvas and was standing watching her, still holding the brush and palette.

'Come on. I have told you we are nearly out of time. Do something. Prove that you possess free will.'

She stood up, wondering what to do.

'Can I do anything, master?'

'Anything. Without fear of punishment. Anything at all. Exercise your free will. For a minute. Then you do what I will again. Or rather, you continue to do what I will. For you do not possess free will.'

She walked over to the painting-stand and drew the black cloth away. He had painted the outlines of her arse first, ready for filling in with the white curves of her buttocks and the broad line of the purpling bruise that bisected them. She lifted the canvas off the stand, put it flat on the floor, and crushed one foot down on top of it. Her foot went through it easily.

She stood on it with both feet, working them as though she were treading grapes. Her soles were tickled and smeared with the half-dried fluids with which he had painted. She stepped off the smashed canvas and walked over to the bookcase. *Disciplined Skin*. She pulled it out and started to tear it up, having to wrench and pull at first to overcome the toughness of the spine. But the pages ripped easily, satisfyingly, falling to the floor to be stepped on and patterned by her smeared feet.

'Enough. The minute is up.'

He walked towards her and she dropped what was left of the book, backing away, brought up short by the cold marble of the wall on her arse. He had lied. He was going to punish her. For exercising her free will.

But he stopped when he reached the fragments of paper on the floor and bent to sort through them, stirring them apart with his fingers, searching through them. He straightened, holding a handful of fragments out to her.

'This is the last page of the story. Put it together again and read the final sentence.'

She pushed away from the wall and took the handful of fragments from him, and knelt on the floor to obey his orders. When she had pieced the fragments together she read:

When she had pieced the fragments together she read:

Glossary

Abbreviations: vb. verb tr. transitive itr. intransitive n. noun adj. adjective pr. pronounced

anch: tr. vb. to crush or squeeze the balls painfully.

birze: itr. vb. (of the buttocks) to grow hot during spanking or whipping.

crinny: n. one of the narrow patches of skin exposed by the lifting of the breasts or folding to one or another side of one of cunt-lips.

culk: n. the hollow in the inner surface of a female thigh.

deswiff: tr. vb. to shave or pluck the swiff (qv).

dreckle: itr. vb. (of sweat) to flow down the cleavage or the buttock-cleft.

freck: tr. vb. to pluck at the skin of the scrotum.

gluft: n. the female perineum

golm: tr. vb. to lick the sweat or other fluids collected in a crinny (qv).

hulf: tr. vb. to drop molten wax on to a sexual part.

hulver: n. a large candle used for dropping molten wax on to a sexual part.

naxter: n. the hollow behind the knee.

olf: (of the cunt) to give off the scent of arousal.

pre-swiff: n. the hair found on the perineum of a young woman.

quervil: n. combed and/or trimmed pubic hair.

quimpf: itr. vb. (of the cunt) to ooze under sexual frustration.

slatch: n. the semen-and-piss slot in the head of penis.

sprong: itr. vb. (of an erect nipple) to return elastically to the horizontal when pressed out of alignment.

sprongle: itr. vb. frequentative form of *sprong*.

swiff: n. the (silky) hair found around the arsehole of a young woman.

swiffhulf: itr. vb. to drop molten wax on to the swiff, as before deswiffing (qv).

swiflet: n. one of the (silky) hairs around the arsehole of a young woman.

tenge: adj. the pink of a young woman's sphincter.

thrickle: n. a strong trickle of arousal in the cunt.

tithulf (pr. tit-hulf): tr. vb. to drop molten wax on to the nipples.

tweng: tr. vb. to squeeze a nipple between the second joints of the index and middle fingers.

twengle: tr. vb. to squeeze and pluck a nipple between the second joints of the index and middle fingers, as though playing a musical instrument.

waftage: n. the distance over which an aroused cunt can be smelled.

yamble: tr. vb. to tongue the balls.

yelm: n. sexual secretions from the cunt.

NEW BOOKS

Coming up from Nexus

Nexus

Lessons in Obedience by Lucy Golden
5 December 2000   £5.99   ISBN 0 352 33550 5
What would you do if a young woman arrived unannounced on your doorstep one day to atone for someone else's sins? And what if you detected, beneath her sweetly naïve outward diffidence, a talent, an aptitude and a willingness you'd be a fool not to nurture? Faced with that challenge, Alex Mortensen starts carefully to introduce his pupil to the wealth of sensual pleasures that have always featured in his own life. But what should he do when she learns so fast, catches him up and threatens to overtake? When teacher becomes pupil?

Slave Exodus by Jennifer Jane Pope
3 December 2000   £5.99   ISBN 0 352 33551 3
When Detective Sergeant Alex Gregory has a nasty parachuting accident, it should be the end of the line for her. But when she wakes up in a new body she realises she's been given a new lease of life. Unfortunately her captors have very unusual tastes, including one for human pony racing. Alex's home is now a spartan stable, her only clothing an elaborate harness, with a bit that ensures her silence. Will her colleagues ever be able to rescue her?

Underworld by Maria del Rey
1 December 2000   £5.99   ISBN 0 352 33552 1
Behind a façade of professional respectability, a certain group of wealthy individuals is playing some very adult games. Games of master and servant where willing submissives suffer degradation and punishment in the most refined surroundings. Called on to find Anita Duncan, by a man who says he's her boyfriend, private investigator Pamela goes undercover to find out why Anita has disappeared. Drawn into an underworld of dark desire, she cannot believe what she's witnessing – and enjoying.

Captive by Aishling Moran
4 January 2001   £5.99   ISBN 0 352 33585 8

Set in the same world of nubile girls, cruel men and rampant goblins as its prequel, *Maiden*, *Captive* follows the tribulations of the maid, Aisla, as she endeavours to free her mistress Sulitea from a life of drudgery and punishment, only to find her less than grateful. As she struggles to return home with Sulitea, they must overcome numerous men, trolls and yet worse beasts, and when Aisla is taken prisoner in foreign lands, it is her turn to escape, or else face a humiliating public execution.

Soldier Girls by Yolanda Celbridge
4 January 2001   £5.99   ISBN 0 352 33586 6

Stripped of her uniform for 'sexual outrage', soldier-nurse Lise Gallard is forced to endure corporal punishment in the Foreign legion women's prison. But she is spotted there by dominatrix Dr Crevasse, who engineers Lise's release from her own flagellant purposes. Can Lise hope to escape her cruel mistress? Or will she in turn learn to wield the can?

Eroticon 1 ed. J-P Spencer
4 January 2001   £5.99   ISBN 0 352 33593 9

A Nexus Classic unavailable for some time; a selection of a dozen of the most exhilerating excerpts from rare and once-forbidden works of erotic literature. They range from the work of the French poet Guillaume Apollinaire to the most explicit sexual confession of the Edwardian era – Walter's *My Secret Life*.

Nexus

NEXUS BACKLIST

All books are priced £5.99 unless another price is given. If a date is supplied, the book in question will not be available until that month in 2000.

CONTEMPORARY EROTICA

THE BLACK MASQUE	Lisette Ashton	
THE BLACK WIDOW	Lisette Ashton	
THE BOND	Lindsay Gordon	
BRAT	Penny Birch	
BROUGHT TO HEEL	Arabella Knight	July
DANCE OF SUBMISSION	Lisette Ashton	
DISCIPLES OF SHAME	Stephanie Calvin	
DISCIPLINE OF THE PRIVATE HOUSE	Esme Ombreux	
DISCIPLINED SKIN	Wendy Swanscombe	Nov
DISPLAYS OF EXPERIENCE	Lucy Golden	
AN EDUCATION IN THE PRIVATE HOUSE	Esme Ombreux	Aug
EMMA'S SECRET DOMINATION	Hilary James	
GISELLE	Jean Aveline	
GROOMING LUCY	Yvonne Marshall	Sept
HEART OF DESIRE	Maria del Rey	
HOUSE RULES	G.C. Scott	
IN FOR A PENNY	Penny Birch	
LESSONS OF OBEDIENCE	Lucy Golden	Dec
ONE WEEK IN THE PRIVATE HOUSE	Esme Ombreux	
THE ORDER	Nadine Somers	
THE PALACE OF EROS	Delver Maddingley	
PEEPING AT PAMELA	Yolanda Celbridge	Oct
PLAYTHING	Penny Birch	

SAMPLERS & COLLECTIONS

NEXUS CLASSICS

A new imprint dedicated to putting the finest works of erotic fiction back in print

Please send me the books I have ticked above.

Name ....

Address ....

....

....

.... Post code........................

Send to: **Cash Sales, Nexus Books, Thames Wharf Studios, Rainville Road, London W6 9HA**

US customers: for prices and details of how to order books for delivery by mail, call 1-800-805-1083.

Please enclose a cheque or postal order, made payable to **Nexus Books**, to the value of the books you have ordered plus postage and packing costs as follows:

UK and BFPO – £1.00 for the first book, 50p for the second book and 30p for each subsequent book to a maximum of £3.00;

Overseas (including Republic of Ireland) – £2.00 for the first book, £1.00 for the second book and 50p for each subsequent book.

We accept all major credit cards, including VISA, ACCESS/MASTERCARD, AMEX, DINERS CLUB, SWITCH, SOLO, and DELTA. Please write your card number and expiry date here:

....

Please allow up to 28 days for delivery.

Signature ....